Jeanne Whitmee began her career as an actress. After her marriage she became a speech and drama teacher and began writing in her spare time. She has written numerous short stories and several romantic novels under different pseudonyms.

She has two daughters and four grandchildren and lives with her husband in Cambridgeshire.

Oranges and Lemons

Jeanne Whitmee

WARNER BOOKS

For Muriel

A *Warner* Book

First published in Great Britain
in 1993 by Judy Piatkus

This edition published by Warner in 1994

A CIP catalogue for this book
is available from the British Library.

ISBN 0 7515 0930 2

Printed and bound in Great Britain by
Clays Ltd, St Ives plc

Warner Books
A Division of
Little, Brown and Company (UK)
Brettenham House
Lancaster Place
London WC2E 7EN

Chapter One

Shirley was tired, hungry and, although it was only hours since she had left London, she was homesick already.

Standing there along with all the other children in the crowded reception centre, she felt oddly isolated. Many of them were crying for a variety of reasons – insecurity, hunger, fear. But although there was a huge lump in Shirley's throat and a queer sinking feeling in her tummy, she refused to give in to her own despair. Instead her small dimpled chin jutted out defiantly and her mouth set in an almost belligerent pout, determined not to make what her grandmother called an 'exhibition of herself'.

Hitching the string of the cardboard box containing the hated gas mask a little higher on her shoulder, she brushed fussily at the creases in the skirt of her best pink coat. The train had been crowded and hot and she'd been obliged to share a seat with some of the kids from the 'Buildings' – the very children her grandmother always warned her to avoid. 'Play with them and you'll come home with ringworm – nits too, more than likely,' she would warn, adding darkly: 'All them curls'll have to come orf if you do, my gel. Shaved to the bone your 'ead'll be if you bring them filthy things 'ome 'ere.' Itching at the very thought, Shirley scratched surreptitiously at her auburn curls and hopped from one foot to the other. She'd been wanting to go to the lav for hours, but she'd made herself wait. Not like Tilly Marks, who had already wet herself twice and stank to high heaven.

In the little corrugated-iron village hall at Houlton, the villagers came and went throughout the long hot afternoon, patriotically doing as the posters and leaflets had urged them, offering to share their homes with those less fortunate than themselves as part of the war effort. Outwardly, they were motivated by sacrifice and patriotism, but many had other motives of their own; like the childless Tom and Jenny Baker, who willingly took two children, seeking to fill their empty hearts as well as their home. They chose the ones who looked most in need of the abundance of love they had to give, bearing the two little girls off, all smiles, to the high tea Jenny had been preparing all morning. Farmers Bill and Ted Bates, on the other hand, chose four of the biggest and strongest-looking lads. With the village boys being called up almost straight out of school, they would need all the help they could get to provide the extra crops the government would soon be urging them to produce. If they played their cards right this war could be the making of them, provided they could get enough help. There were those who took the children out of what they saw as their Christian duty, like the two Miss's Pimm from Ivy Cottage. Whoever shared their spartan home would need to get used to kneeling for prayers twice a day in the sanctified front parlour, not to mention attending chapel three times every Sunday. So, as the late summer afternoon gently dissolved into evening the villagers came and went; making their choices, pledging their sacrifices, happily bearing home their prizes, or simply making the best of a bad job.

Finally only Shirley Rayner and Tilly Marks were left. Miss Grace, the vicar's sister, appointed as billeting officer, glanced anxiously down the hall at the two little girls and then at her Women's Voluntary Service helper in the sturdy shape of Edith Phipps, the postmaster's wife.

'Oh, dear. It looks as though we're left with those two on our hands,' she said. 'I confess I can understand why no one wanted to take the one in the mackintosh.' She wrinkled her nose. 'She really does smell quite dreadfully.

But the other one – she looks different, quite a cut above the others.'

Edith Phipps folded her fleshy mouth into a disapproving line. 'Different all right. Looks a proper little madam to me; a handful if ever I saw one.' Folding her arms over her vast bosom, she glanced patronisingly at Ellen Grace's stringy, unfulfilled body. 'If you'll pardon me saying so, Miss Grace, those of us who've had children of our own will have seen it in her right away. That's why she's been passed over.'

Ellen glanced at the children again. Shirley's pink coat with its velvet collar and her red-gold curls topped by a large pink butterfly bow were in sharp contrast to the waiflike Tilly's blatant poverty. Wearing an overlong, shabby brown mackintosh passed down by an elder brother, grubby plimsolls and no socks, Tilly Marks looked the very picture of dejection. Her mousy hair hung like chewed string around her pinched little face and the traces of something hurriedly eaten still ringed her mouth stickily. Edith Phipps followed Ellen's gaze.

'That little thing now – a hot bath and a good meal and she'll be good as new,' she said. '*Better*, in fact.' She looked at the child speculatively, her head on one side. 'Head lice, I shouldn't wonder, but some green soft soap and a sharp haircut'll make short work of them. I'll take her if you like,' she offered decisively. 'Just for a few days, mind, till we find a permanent home for her. I've still got some of my Sylvia's little frocks packed away upstairs. I'll soon fix her up respectable.'

Ellen cheered up. 'Oh, would you? That *is* kind. But what am I to do about the other one?'

'Holly Jarvis'll just have to take her,' Edith said, her lips tightening.

'Oh, do you think so?' Ellen looked doubtful. 'We can't force people, you know. I did ask, of course, but with her only being caretaker at Longueville Hall it was hardly up to her.'

Edith sucked in her cheeks again. She deeply resented the Jarvises, envious of their cushy job up there at the

Hall, living on the fat of the land with their employers hardly ever there. 'Well, just as you see fit, of course, Miss Grace,' she said, making it clear that she felt the Jarvises were getting off scot-free. 'But we are going to be at war after all, and even people like the Darrents will have to make sacrifices. There must be at least eight bedrooms in that rambling great place, and them Darrents and their stage friends are only there once in a blue moon. They could very easily take six kiddies, let alone one.' She fixed Ellen with her beady brown eyes. 'If you want my opinion, I think it's a crying shame for folk like them to have two homes when there are some poor souls with no roof over their heads.'

'Well, of course I do take your point,' Ellen said guardedly. 'But the Darrents are rather special and they have been *very* generous. You know they've done a tremendous lot for this village.'

Edith said nothing, indicating her disapproval by drawing her breath in sharply and folding her arms. It was easy enough to curry favour by chucking money about when you had more than enough of it. 'I believe the Jarvises are caring for the Darrents' child for the duration,' Ellen went on hopefully. 'She's at a boarding school on the east coast, but it's closing down in case of an invasion.'

Edith sniffed. 'All the more reason for them to take another, then. One child will rattle around that great house like a pea in a bottle.'

'Well, I suppose I've no choice but to ask,' Ellen said. 'Even if they take her on a temporary basis it would help. I'd willingly take her back to the Rectory, only now that the new curate has the spare room there's no room.'

''Course there isn't. Besides, you've done your share.' Edith looked pityingly at Ellen. The poor thing wasn't used to work, apart from parish visiting. And try as she would she couldn't imagine her coping with any child, let alone *that* one. 'Just you take her to the Hall,' she advised. 'We're all putting ourselves out, so why not them Jarvises?'

Ellen walked down the length of the hall to where the children waited, stretching her austere features into her

4

version of a kindly smile. To the children who watched her bearing down on them she looked like a tall skinny angel of doom with her long teeth bared and her colourless hair escaping from its bun in cobweblike wisps. Ellen addressed Tilly first, holding a lace-edged hanky to her nose and trying hard to summon up Christian compassion for the odoriferous child.

'Mrs Phipps is going to take you home with her, er . . .' She peered at the label tied to the child's collar, while still keeping her distance. 'Tilly, is it?'

'Yes, miss.' Tilly wiped her nose on the sleeve of her raincoat.

'Oh, dear. Haven't you got a handkerchief, child?' Ellen asked.

Tilly shook her head. 'No, miss.'

'Oh, well, it can't be helped then, I suppose. Run along then.'

Tilly picked up the brown-paper carrier bag that contained her few pathetic possessions and made her way resignedly towards the waiting Mrs Phipps.

Watching Tilly go, Shirley felt her throat constrict. Was she going to be left here alone all night? Fighting down panic, she bit down hard on her lower lip to stop it from quivering. Ellen turned to her.

'You come along with me, dear. We're going for a little walk. I'm sure we'll find a nice new home for you.'

Shirley watched as the fat lady with the WVS armband round the sleeve of her cardigan propelled Tilly Marks through the door, pushing her ahead of her with the tip of her umbrella. Shirley's fermenting resentment exploded into anger. Tilly might niff a bit but the old cow needn't treat her like something the cat had sicked up. It wasn't fair.

'I wanna go 'ome,' she said in a loud clear voice.

Ellen looked startled. 'I'm afraid that's out of the question, dear,' she said, 'Now, if you'll just come along with me.'

'I ain't goin' nowhere wiv no one.' Shirley's rosebud lips set in a determined pout and the cornflower-blue eyes flashed. 'I ain't gonna to be pushed about like *that*.' She pointed at Mrs Phipps's retreating broad back. 'I wanna go 'ome.'

Ellen sighed. It seemed that Mrs Phipps had been right and the child's angelic appearance was deceptive. 'Come now, dear,' she said soothingly 'We must all exercise self-denial. Our country is about to be at war and we're all going to have to do things we don't wish to do. Once Mrs Phipps has given – er – Tilly a bath and a change of clothes she'll be kindness itself to her, I promise you. Now, the place I have in mind for you is very nice indeed. I'm quite sure you're going to like it. And there'll be another little girl there who is just about your age.'

Shirley could see that she was fighting a losing battle. She'd have to give in – at least for the time being. After a long thoughtful pause, she picked the shiny red cardboard suitcase that Gloria had bought from Woolworth's for her just yesterday. If she didn't do as the woman said, she might get left behind. But if she didn't like the place they found for her she'd soon let them know.

The round blue eyes that looked up at Ellen glittered determinedly. 'All right then – but if I don't like it I'll bleedin' run away.'

Trying hard not to show how profoundly shocked she was, Ellen led the way. Her brother Bertram had worked in an East End parish in his younger days. He had warned her that these children would probably be coarsely spo-ken. It was difficult to know how to deal with it. If she admonished the child there might be more trouble. On the other hand, putting a child who used language like that into the home of people like the Darrents seemed, well, almost sacrilegious, especially when their own only daughter was to be there for the duration. The Darrents had made a more than generous donation to the organ fund only last month – *and* given the use of their garden for the church fête. If this girl proved to be a bad influence on little Imogen it would look so appallingly *ungrateful*.

As they set off down the lane towards Longueville Hall she glanced down anxiously at the small neat figure trotting beside her. She was clean enough, allowing for the rigours of the train journey; a sweetly pretty child – until she opened her mouth. But there was something about the way she was dressed – flashy was the word that sprang to mind. Indeed, if it wasn't for her charitable upbringing Ellen might almost have called the pink coat and patent-leather sandals *common*. She sighed. When she had taken on the job of billeting officer for the village she hadn't foreseen so many difficulties. 'Oh, dear, I do hope I'm doing the right thing,' she muttered anxiously under her breath.

To Shirley the walk seemed endless. In fact it was a little under half a mile. At the end of a lane they came to a pair of tall wrought-iron gates set in stout brick pillars, each topped by a stone eagle. Shirley perked up. It was just like something out of the film Gloria had taken her to see the previous week, *Wuthering Heights*. That posh family called Linton had lived in a place like this. Her interest aroused, she quickened her pace to keep up with Ellen's long strides and together they walked up a tree-lined drive. Eventually it opened onto a circular carriage sweep with a majestic copper beech in the centre. And Shirley stopped in her tracks to gasp. The house was magnificent. It was built of mellow red brick, square, with two rows of long, white-painted windows, topped by a roof that swept down over them and had little dormer windows jutting out from it. The front entrance had shallow steps leading up to it, flanked by white pillars, topped by a little pointed roof. She had seen nothing like it outside of the cinema.

'Ooo-er . . .' She looked up at Ellen. ''Ere – this ain't *it*, is it?'

'It certainly is,' Ellen assured her. 'The house is called Longueville Hall and it belongs to two very famous people.'

'Cor, go on – *who*?' Shirley's blue eyes were round with interest.

'Their name is Darrent. Mr Tony Darrent, who is an actor, and his wife, Leonie Swann, who sings on the stage in, er, musical comedies.' Would the child know what she was talking about? It seemed she did.

'Get *orf*! You're 'avin' me on,' she said disbelievingly. 'You don't mean the Tony Darrent what's on the pictures? I seen 'im in *The Prince of Hearts*.'

'I believe he has made some moving pictures, yes,' Ellen said disapprovingly. Did Londoners really take children as young as this to the cinema?

Suitably impressed, Shirley fell silent. Just wait till she told Gloria about this. Tony Darrent was Gloria's favourite star. She had photos of him, cut out of film magazines, pinned up on the walls of the bedroom they shared.

Walking up the wide steps, Ellen pulled the shiny brass bell beside the front door. It echoed through the house grandly. Shirley glanced up at Ellen.

'P'raps they're out,' she said hopefully, suddenly overawed by the dignified splendour of Longueville Hall. But almost immediately the door was opened by a man wearing a green baize apron, his shirt sleeves rolled up above his elbows.

Ellen treated him to a smile that reminded Shirley of the coalman's horse when you gave it a carrot. 'Oh, good evening, Mr Jarvis. I'm so sorry to trouble you, but, er, is your wife in?'

The man held the door open for them. 'Come in, Miss Grace. Molly's in the kitchen.'

They followed him through a hall with a black-and-white marble floor and Shirley gazed in amazement at the beautiful pictures on the walls and the wonderful staircase that curved up from it in a rising sweep. At the top a tall window cast shafts of golden evening sunshine down into the hall, turning the gilded wrought-iron baluster to gleaming gold. Jim Jarvis talked as he led the way.

'We were expecting the Darrents for the weekend and Molly has been getting ready for them all day but Mr Darrent has just telephoned to say they might not be able to get down with things being all at sixes and sevens. There's some talk of all the theatres being closed down.'

He shrugged resignedly. 'Can't be helped. I suppose our problems are nothing when you think of what those poor souls in Warsaw are going through. The war coming is bound to upset everything. I dare say they'll be making us dig up the tennis court to grow potatoes before long.' He opened a door and stood aside for them to pass, shaking his head at Ellen. 'It'll be a sight worse than the last lot, Miss Grace, you mark my words. We're all in for it this time and no mistake; at home as well as at the front.'

Ellen nodded her agreement. 'They do say we'll be safe here in Northamptonshire, though,' she said, 'with our only industry being footwear.'

Jim shook his head. 'No knowing what they'll have to turn their hands to, though,' he said darkly. 'Once they've made enough army boots they'll likely have to go over to munitions, I shouldn't wonder. And once the Hun gets wind of that . . .'

Ellen looked round for Shirley, who was still standing at the foot of the staircase, staring goggle-eyed around her.

'Come *along*, child,' she said sharply. 'Don't dawdle when Mr Jarvis is waiting for you.' She didn't want the Jarvises to think she was soft – or that she was personally responsible for bringing them this particular child.

Shirley followed the two adults through a short corridor to another hallway, much smaller and less opulent than the main hall. It had linoleum and a red carpet runner on the floor. Through an open door Shirley saw a small room equipped with a sink and shelves. In the centre was a table on which stood more silverware than she had ever seen before. As well as cutlery there were candelabra, fancy dishes, tea and coffee pots. Her eyes as round as saucers, she asked:

'Ooo-er. Are all those things made of real silver, mister?'

Jim looked down at her, seeming to notice the child for the first time. A smile tugged at the corners of his mouth. 'They certainly are, missie. Take a lot of looking after, too, I can tell you.' He smiled at Ellen, who returned his smile nervously. 'Come on in, Miss Grace. Molly'll be pleased to see you. You look fagged out. I dare say you could do with a cup of tea.'

'C'n I 'ave one too, mister?' Shirley piped up. Then, to Ellen's chagrin: 'Me stummick finks me froat's cut.'

The kitchen was huge, nothing like Ma's kitchen behind the little greengrocer's shop in Angel Row, which was a tight squeeze when the four of them sat down to eat in it. Shirley's eyes were round as she looked around her. A massive dresser filled one wall. On its shelves were an impressive array of blue and white dishes, everything from the tiniest cream jug to an enormous meat dish that would hold a whole suckling pig. The floor was made of polished red tiles and in the centre stood a large scrubbed-top table, covered now by a red chenille cloth edged with a bobble fringe. But best of all was the smell. The mingled aromas of apple pie and steak-and-kidney, fruitcake and scones filled the air. It made Shirley's mouth water and her tummy rumbled audibly.

Molly Jarvis stood by the big black cooking range that was set in a deep recess lined with tiles. She wore a bright print overall and her round pink face shone with good humour and the exertion of her afternoon's cooking.

'Well, what a nice surprise! Come in, Miss Grace. I've got the kettle on.' She wiped her plump freckled hands on a snowy tea towel and pulled out a chair. 'Sit down and – oh . . .' She caught sight of Shirley. 'Now then, who might this little lady be?'

'This is Shirley Rayner. I do hope you won't mind.' Ellen smiled apologetically. 'I've really come to ask a favour. All the other evacuee children have been placed. There's just this one left and I wondered – I know it's an imposition – if you, er . . .' She trailed off at the look on Molly Jarvis's face. She was looking down at Shirley, shaking her head and tutting under her breath. Ellen winced. She might have known it was out of the question to bring the child here.

'Poor little scrap, did no one want you then, lovie?' Molly sank to her knees, undoing the buttons of Shirley's pink coat. 'Don't you worry. Nanny Jarvis'll find you a comfy bed. Now – when did you last eat, my pretty?'

The lump came back to Shirley's throat and her eyes began to sting. It had been all right till now. Back at the

10

reception centre she could have taken on the lot of them and given as good as she got. But this woman's kind voice and gentle brown eyes completely disarmed her. Suddenly her lower lip began to tremble and she felt very small and very sad. 'B-breakfast-time,' she mumbled.

'*Breakfast?*' Molly Jarvis looked up accusingly at Ellen. 'You mean these little mites haven't had a bite since they left London?'

Ellen's sallow cheeks flushed a deep brick red. 'I was given to understand that the WVS gave them all tea and buns at the railway station,' she mumbled guiltily.

'*I* never got none,' Shirley complained. 'The big boys pushed us little 'uns out and got back in the line. There weren't none left when it was my turn.'

'Weren't *any* left,' Ellen corrected under her breath, wincing at the appalling grammar and horrible cockney accent. If only the child would keep *quiet*. 'You're, er, sure the Darrents won't mind?' she ventured, looking hopefully at Molly. 'I mean, I know it isn't quite what one would wish, but under the circumstances . . .' She lowered her voice. 'At least this one is *clean*. Some of them were quite revoltingly dirty.'

'Mind? Of course they won't.' Molly stood up, folding Shirley's coat over her arm. 'I told Madam on the telephone that you'd been round enquiring and she said she would leave it to my discretion. She'll be company for Imogen. The child would have been lonely, leaving all her school friends behind.' She smiled down at Shirley. 'There'll be someone for you to play with after tomorrow, lovie. And I've cooked enough for an army so we'll get you fed directly.' She smiled reassuringly at Ellen. 'Now, don't you fret, Miss Grace. I'll take good care of her.'

Jim watched his wife affectionately. She'd be in her element with children to care for again. She had missed young Imogen sadly when the child had been sent away to school. Hardly surprising since she had cared for her since the day she was born.

Taking in an evacuee was the least of their worries. They'd been anxious for a while in case the Hall might be requisitioned for a hospital or taken over by the military. If that happened they'd lose their position as caretakers. On the other hand, if the war went on long enough even old stagers like Jim would be called up and Molly would never manage this place on her own. But so far he had kept these worries to himself. Molly was worried enough as it was about the uncertainty of the future. Looking across at her as she fussed with the child he felt his heart lift. There was happy anticipation written in every line of her face. It was an ill wind, he told himself. At least having children to care for again would taken her mind off the war.

In the flat over the Rayners' greengrocer's shop in Angel Row, Gloria was getting ready to go to work. They were showing *Stage Door* at the Adelphi this week. It was all about a group of girls starting out in show business and Gloria loved it. Standing each night in her place behind the back row of the circle, she identified with the budding young actresses in the story, sharing their hopes and aspirations. And she never tired of the beautiful tragic bit where Andrea Leeds climbed to the top floor to throw herself to her death. It was so sad and so lovely. It had made her cry at every performance. As she slipped into the plum-coloured uniform with its gilt frogging, she glanced round the little bedroom. It seemed so quiet and empty without Shirley. Gloria swallowed the lump in her throat. Where was she now, she wondered? Would somebody kind take her in? Would Shirley be missing her too? How long before she could go and see her? She hated to think what was going to happen to them all once this war got under way. It was almost too frightening to think of. She'd been a small child when the last war ended so she couldn't remember what it had been like, but everyone said it was terrible, and that this one would be worse.

There was talk of all theatres and cinemas closing. If that happened she would lose the job she loved so much. Thank God there was always the shop to fall back on. Ma and Pa were always glad of extra help. The little shop which sold fruit and flowers as well as vegetables had always done well. 'Slap bang between the 'orspital and the cemetery. If we don't catch 'em goin' one way, we gets 'em going the other.' It was Pa's favourite joke. He said that folks would be turning vegetarian if the war went on long enough, and they'd make their fortunes. 'Just s' long as we don't all get gassed or blown to kingdom come first, that is,' he'd chuckle. It was just Pa's lugubrious sense of humour, his way of keeping himself cheerful. 'Whistling in the dark,' Ma called it. She would give him a shove and tell him not to be barmy, but it scared Gloria half to death.

It was only a matter of hours since Shirley left but already she was missing her unbearably. Ever since her daughter had been born nine years ago the little girl had been her whole life. She had named her after the multi-talented child star Shirley Temple, confident that she'd grow up to be just as engaging and cute; pinning all her own relinquished dreams and ambitions on her. Every week as soon as she was paid she'd go down to the market and buy remnants of pretty material to make little dresses just like the ones Shirley Temple wore in her films; glad of the apprenticeship she had served with a court dress-maker in the West End, which had furnished her with the know-how and skill.

Gloria had always been mad about films, which was why she hadn't minded too much when she was not allowed to resume her dressmaking apprenticeship after Shirley had been born. She had already seen the adver-tisement for usherettes needed at the nearby Adelphi cinema and, although Ma said it was a waste of her training, she applied.

She took Shirley along to the pictures as soon as she was old enough to sit still, and enrolled her little daughter on her fifth birthday for the sixpenny Saturday-morning dancing classes in the Mile End Road, where she soon learned to tap, pirouette and pose as engagingly as her famous namesake.

Gloria had been barely seventeen when Shirley was born. Ma and Pa had been shocked and horrified when

13

they first learned that their only daughter was 'in trouble'. But once the initial shock had subsided they made the courageous decision to live down the shame and the gossip and to stand by her. Although they had asked Gloria repeatedly to tell them who the father was, she steadfastly refused to reveal his identity. There was little point in telling them anyway. When she broke the news to him that she was expecting he had dropped a bombshell of his own, admitting that he was already married. He had made it clear that she was on her own and that he wanted nothing more to do with her. He had even tried to argue that the child could not be his. Deeply hurt and disillusioned, Gloria hadn't set eyes on him since, and after the initial pain of his betrayal she told herself she was better off without him. She had steered clear of men since Shirley was born, too. Her only heroes were the ones she admired from afar on the silver screen; Clark Gable and Robert Taylor were her favourites. Recently a British actor had appeared who promised to be just as famous, Tony Darrent, who looked like a blond version of the handsome Errol Flynn. At least it was safe to love them, she told herself. They wouldn't let her down.

Shirley grew up calling her grandparents Ma and Pa just as Gloria did. It had come naturally and somehow none of them had ever got round to telling the child that Sid and Ada Rayner were really her grandparents. It wasn't until the rumours of war began to look like a frightening reality that Gloria decided that the time had come to make the truth about their relationship known to her. If they were going to be parted she wanted to have things straight. Besides, it was surely only a matter of time before some busybody outside told her, and she didn't want it to come as a shock. Sitting in front of the dressing table now, Gloria remembered the day just two weeks ago when she had told her.

It was Sunday and she had taken Shirley Up West to Hyde Park for the afternoon. It had been a lovely warm day and Ma had packed sandwiches and a flask of tea for them. Sitting on the grass by the Serpentine, eating their picnic, Gloria had said suddenly:

14

'What would you say if I told you Ma wasn't your real mum, Shirl?'

The child looked round, only half listening as she threw a handful of crumbs to the waiting sparrows. 'Dunno – why?'

'Because she *isn't*, Shirley.' Gloria caught at the child's arm and looked into her eyes, demanding her attention. 'I mean it, Shirl. Ma *isn't* your real mum.'

Sobered by Gloria's serious expression, Shirley asked suspiciously: 'Who *is* my mum then?'

'Me. I am, love.'

For a second the child stared at her, open-mouthed, then she laughed and said: 'Oh, that's all right then.' Taking another sandwich from the basket, she began to munch happily. 'I thought you were gonna tell me I was an awful, like in *Heidi*.'

Gloria had laughed, weak with relief. Grasping the child, she hugged her till she had begged for mercy. 'Well, you're not an *awful*. You're my little girl and I love you very much.' Tears in her eyes, she looked down at Shirley. 'Do you love me too?'

Embarrassed by Gloria's display of emotion, the child had struggled out of her arms, pushing her away, embarrassed. 'Get orf, Glor, don't be soppy.'

But later that night, when they were both in bed and Gloria thought she was asleep, Shirley's plump little arms crept round her neck.

'Is it true, what you said this afternoon?' she whispered in her ear. 'Are you really my mum?'

Gloria hugged her close. 'Yes, it's true all right.'

'Why didn't you never tell me before?'

'I don't know really,' Gloria said truthfully, tucking the covers around them both. 'I just didn't, that's all.'

'I'm glad you're my mum, Glor.' Shirley snuggled close. 'An' I do love you.' She stopped, frowning as a thought occurred to her. ''Ere – do I have to call you Ma now?'

Gloria smiled and buried her face in the soft red curls. 'Don't you dare,' she said. 'Just as long as we both know, it don't matter, does it?'

'No.' Shirley frowned into the darkness with the effort of working it all out. 'But – if you're my mum, who's my dad then?'

Gloria bit her lip. 'You ain't got one, love.'

'Why not? Everyone else has. I thought you had to have a dad.'

'Well, you *don't*,' Gloria said firmly. 'There's some as do have one, and some as don't. And don't you let no one tell you no different. You an' me, we've both got Pa. We'll share him, eh?'

The explanation seemed to satisfy Shirley as she slipped a thumb into her mouth and cuddled closer.

Gloria held her little daughter. Lying awake long after the child slept, she reflected that there might not be many more chances to share moments of closeness like this. When they first started talking about war and the possibility of evacuating the children, she had been adamant that she wouldn't let Shirley go, but Pa had talked her round, making her see the sense of it. Pa was too old to join up, but he had volunteered for the Air Raid Precautions. He had fought in France in the last war and he knew a thing or two about what might happen. He warned that they'd probably close all the schools in the East End anyway and that clinched it as far as Gloria was concerned. She wanted Shirley to have a better education that she'd had herself. She wanted her daughter to be someone when she grew up. Not for her the wasted life, watching the world go by on celluloid from behind the back row of the Adelphi. Since making up her mind, she had tried not to think about it too much. Maybe it wouldn't happen after all. Maybe there wouldn't be a war. Old Mr Chamberlain was doing his best, wasn't he? He'd talk that Herr Hitler round, no danger. But after Hitler's troops goose-stepped into Poland things began to look black. It seemed to Gloria that all her worst fears were being realised. There was little doubt that she and Shirley were going to be parted.

After she and the other mothers had seen the children off on a packed train bound for an undisclosed destination that morning, Gloria had come home and sobbed inconsolably, sitting at the kitchen table behind the shop. Ma, with characteristic blunt stoicism, told her to pull herself together and dry her tears.

'You think your Pa and I wanted to see 'er go?' she asked. 'That little kid's all the world to us, but it's for the best, gel. Think yourself lucky that you've no man to lose, too,' she added. 'A lot of them women'll be sayin' goodbye to their 'usbands any day now. An' a lot of 'em won't be comin' back. Our Shirl'll land on her feet, you just see if she don't. Born lucky, she was.'

Gloria ran a comb through her hair and stood up. Better get off to work while there was still work to go to. She sighed and pushed the little pillbox hat that completed her uniform into her bag. It was such a lovely evening; hard to imagine the horrors that were taking place across the sea in Europe. It was a shame to be shut in when the sun was still shining. She'd walk to the Adelphi and make the most of it.

As she walked down Angel Row she looked at the newly erected blast walls that shielded each house, and the hastily constructed air-raid shelters that had been built in the street months ago. Fire buckets and sandbags stood in readiness beside street doors in case of incendiary bombs, and in every outhouse a stirrup pump and long-handled shovel stood in readiness. What unimagined evils were in store for them all? she asked herself despairingly. What with bombs, poisoned gas and everything else they were threatened with, they'd be lucky to be here this time next year. Pa had been right. Shirley was better out of it.

In the little room under the eaves, Shirley lay in the spotless white bed, bathed, fed and comforted by the woman who insisted on being called 'Nanny Jarvis'. It was a nice room, all painted white with a funny sloping ceiling and a little window that looked out over the treetops. It had white curtains with a pattern of pink roses and a frilled bedspread to match. There was a soft rug on the floor and a washstand with a big bowl and jug. They were patterned with roses too, to match the big chamber pot under the bed.

'This will be your room while you're here,' Nanny Jarvis had told her.

'Won't I have to share it with no one?' Shirley asked, her heart sinking a little. Ever since she could remember she had shared a bed with Gloria. She had never in her whole life slept alone and the bed felt so big and empty.

As though reading her thoughts, Nanny Jarvis said: 'Don't worry. Tomorrow you won't be lonely any more. Imogen will be home in the afternoon.'

'Who's Imo-gen?' Shirley found the name difficult to say. She'd never heard the name before and privately she thought it rather ugly.

'Imogen is Mr and Mrs Darrent's daughter. She's just your age,' Nanny said. 'You and she will get along like a house on fire. Such fun you'll have. Won't that be nice?'

Tucking in the blankets, she kissed Shirley's forehead and said good night, leaving her alone to think over all the bewildering events of the day. She had never been in a house as big as this. You could get lost among all the passages. She couldn't imagine ever knowing her way around it. There were even two lots of stairs and she'd had a bath in a real bathroom with black and white tiles and soft white fluffy towels. It had two big mirrors you could see yourself all over in and you didn't have to go outside to the lav. At home they washed in the kitchen and had a bath once a week in the big tin tub that hung on a nail in the yard next to the outdoor 'khazi' as Pa called it.

Now that it was almost dark outside she could hear all the strange sounds of the country. An owl hooted eerily and she discovered that the strange rustling sound she could hear, like hundreds of people whispering, was the wind shaking the leaves on the trees. She missed the sound of the traffic rumbling by in the Whitechapel Road, the rumble of cartwheels and the heavy clop-clop of the drayman's big grey horses. At home in Angel Row the Prince of Wales would be chucking out about now. If she was at home she'd hear Joey Harris, the cobbler from up

18

the street, making his unsteady way home. 'Red Sails in the Sunset', he always sang, or sometimes, if he was feeling sad, 'The Miner's Dream of Home'. She liked to hear him: it made her feel safe. Tears stung her eyes. Soon it would be time for Gloria to come home from the Adelphi. Sometimes she brought her sweets on a Saturday night, or maybe a bag of crisps. And if she was still awake she'd let her sit up in bed and eat them – because it was Saturday and no school tomorrow.

This final thought was too much and Shirley stuffed one small fist into her mouth, tears squeezing out from under her tightly closed eyelids. All her toughness and determination to stand firm dissolved like the candyfloss she had eaten on Hampstead Heath on Bank Holiday Monday. She felt bleak and lost and alone.

'I – I want – Glor,' she hiccupped. 'I want M-ma – and Pa and *Glor*.'

At breakfast next morning she sat silently at the kitchen table, eating little. Molly thought she looked peaky and said as much to Jim when he came into the scullery to change his boots. He smiled and shook his head.

'She's bound to be feeling strange, love, and a bit homesick,' he said. 'Tell you what, I'll take her to the village with me to pick up your groceries, then she can help me finish cleaning the silver. She seemed really taken with it yesterday. We'll need to find out what's going to happen about schooling for the kiddies, too. I don't know how the village school is going to fit them all in.'

Fortified by the cornflakes and boiled egg that Nanny Jarvis insisted on feeding her, standing over her while she ate, Shirley seemed to cheer up and went off happily enough with Jim Jarvis, sitting proudly beside him in the elderly Austin Seven. She was wearing her favourite yellow-and-brown dress with a jaunty bow to match in her red-gold curls.

'I ain't never been in a motorcar before, mister,' she said as they drove out through the gates and set off along the road into the village, ''Ere, 'as Tony got one like this 'n' all?'

Jim chuckled. 'Mr Darrent has a car but not like this. His is a Rolls-Royce. And by the way, young lady, better not let him catch you calling him Tony. It's Mr Darrent to the likes of us.'

Shirley coloured. She was so used to Gloria referring to her idol by his Christian name that it came naturally to her. 'What's a Rolls-Royce?' she asked.

'You'll see,' Jim told her. 'You'll see, missie. All in good time.'

As they drove, Shirley noticed things that had escaped her yesterday. She pointed to a herd of black and white cows grazing peacefully in a field.

'What are them things, mister?'

Jim smiled. 'Those are cows. That's where our milk comes from.'

Shirley stared at them in surprise. 'Go on. You're pullin' me leg,' she said, searching his face. 'Milk comes from the milkman.'

Shirley waited outside the village store while Jim went in with the order Molly had made out for him. Across the road was the post office – not at all like the one back home in Whitechapel. This one had a thatched roof and a garden in front with brightly coloured flowers growing in it. A huge tabby cat sat in the window, sunning himself among the dummy packets of Nestlé's chocolate and adverts for Mazawatte tea and Reckitt's Blue. Shirley walked across to press her nose against the window, making faces at the cat, who stared unblinkingly back at her with an expression of disdain. After a moment or two a girl came out of the shop. Shirley looked at her – then looked again, staring in amazement. It was Tilly, but a very different Tilly from the one she had seen on the end of Mrs Phipps's umbrella yesterday afternoon. This Tilly wore a clean blue cotton-print dress. Her hair had been cut very short, which seemed to alter the shape of her face, and her skin shone with cleanliness.

'Wotcher, Tilly,' she said amiably.

Tilly looked back at her. 'Wotcher. I gotta new frock.'

'Yeah. Looks nice. What's your lady like?' Shirley asked.

'Orl right.' Tilly sniffed. 'She cut me hair and made me 'ave a barf, but she give me a lotta new clo's. 'S all right 'ere,' she concluded. 'Grub's a bit funny, though. There ain't even a fish 'n' chip shop.'

'I had a ride in a motor car,' Shirley boasted. 'I'm livin' in a house just like on the pictures. It's got '*undreds* of rooms.'

Tilly wrinkled her nose disbelievingly. 'You ain't. You tells lies, Shirley Rayner. My mum says you and your Gloria's always been too big for yer boots.'

'It's *true*, I tell you.' Shirley pointed. 'That's the car over there, see? An' this house where I'm stoppin' belongs to two film stars.'

'Dirty *liar*.' Tilly stuck her tongue out as far as it would go. 'You'll be struck dumb if you're not careful, tellin' whoppers like that. Always thinks yerself better than the rest of us, don't you – you 'n' your poncy dancin' an' yer Shirley Temple frocks.'

'At least they're *my* frocks – not someone else's,' Shirley jibed.

The dart found its mark. Tilly's pasty cheeks reddened. 'My mum says you're a bastard, so *there*.'

Shirley's jaw dropped. She'd heard the word before, but she didn't know what it meant, only that it had to be something really bad by the venomous way people always said it. Her quick redhead's temper roused, she took a step towards the other child, her blue eyes blazing and her hand raised. But she stopped in her tracks as burly Mrs Phipps came out of the shop.

'Now then. What's going on here?' she challenged.

'She was gonna clout me,' Tilly wailed, pointing accusingly at Shirley. 'She's been tellin' 'orrible lies and now she's tryin' to '*it* me.'

Shirley burned with the injustice of it. 'She called me a bastard,' she protested.

Mrs Phipps gasped and flushed a deep crimson. 'Wash your mouth out with soap, you wicked girl,' she said, outraged. She put a protective arm round Tilly and drew her into the shop doorway. 'Go away, you dreadful child.

I know your sort, you little demon. Don't you dare come here making trouble, or I'll be onto Miss Grace about you.' She flapped at Shirley with both hands. 'Go on – shoo. Get off with you now.'

When Jim Jarvis came out of the village store ten minutes later, he found Shirley waiting for him in the car. She looked subdued and thoughtful. 'All right, love?' he asked.

She nodded uncertainly. 'Mr Jarvis . . .' She looked up at him with large round cornflower-blue eyes. 'Mr Jarvis, what's a bastard?'

Chapter Two

Leonie sat in her dressing room and stared moodily at her reflection in the mirror.

'It's so bloody unfair,' she wailed as Tony poured them another whisky each. 'What's the point anyway?'

'With the bombardment they're expecting, it would be mad to encourage people to assemble in large numbers,' Tony explained patiently. 'Think of the casualties.'

His wife shrugged her beautiful shoulders, totally unable to visualise this bombardment everyone was talking about. Things like that only happened in other, uncivilised countries. They didn't happen in England, surely? 'But what's going to become of *us*?' she wailed. 'Is this to be the end of my career? Just when I was getting such divine notices, too. I suppose the new show will have to be shelved now and as for the film Peter was talking about . . .'

Peter Jason was the couple's agent and he'd had them both in the office only a week ago with an exciting proposition: a new high-budget musical film with Leonie and Tony starring.

Unlike Leonie, Tony was guiltily grateful for this respite. He had yet to tell her that he didn't want to do it. Sitting down beside her, he took both her hands in his. 'Darling, listen. This shut-down thing is only temporary. It has to be. One of the most vital things in wartime is to keep morale high. And how can they do that without entertainment? They'll have to find some way to start up again, you'll see.'

'People won't want to go out to the theatre if they insist on keeping up this ridiculous blackout idea,' Leonie said pouting. 'Especially when they still have the wireless to listen to in their own homes.'

Tony laughed. 'They'll soon get tired of that, darling. You have to admit it's pretty dreary stuff.' He patted her shoulder. 'Cheer up. You'll see, everything will sort itself out. Maybe we'll join Basil Dean's ENSA and entertain the troops.'

Leonie threw back her head and snorted derisively. '*ENSA*? By all accounts they're taking anyone – raw amateurs. You know the joke they're already making about it: Every Night Something Awful. Being involved with that is hardly likely to enhance my career, is it?'

Tony looked at Leonie's lovely reflection in the dressing room mirror with iits border of light bulbs. She really was incredibly self-centred, but even when she was being shrewish and petulant she was still devastatingly beautifull.

They'd been married now for almost eleven years. Tony had been playing juvenile leads with Birmingham rep when they first met. The year was 1928 and he was twenty-seven, and just recovering from the break-up of his disastrous early marriage to Gillian Fane, who had since made her name in Hollywood. Leonie had been plain little Eileen Smith then, the pretty, stage-struck daughter of a local butcher. She never missed a performance and every night there she'd be, waiting for him outside the stage door, just to smile shyly and exchange a few words. He'd been flattered by her open admiration. In spite of his talent and good looks, the break-up of his marriage and the loss of his baby son had dealt him a devastating blow, undermining his confidence badly.

When the theatre had run a talent competition, Eileen had entered. He'd been amused to see her name on the list, thinking it was just another ploy to attract his attention, but it turned out that she really did have talent. When her turn came to perform, she stood in the middle of the stage, looking tiny and fragile in a scarlet dress, and sang 'After the Ball', incorporating a floaty little dance she had choreographed herself. Her voice was surprisingly strong and melodious for someone so young and she moved with a natural grace and charm. Watching her that evening he suddenly saw, too, that she was more than just the pretty teenage girl he had taken her for. Her dark hair was cut in a fashionable bob, and her deep violet eyes were large and lustrous, fringed with silky black lashes. Tony was utterly captivated.

She had won the competition, of course. Tony and two other members of the company had made up the panel of judges. He had talked them into it, but they hadn't taken much persuasion. The Darrent family had been well known and respected in the theatre for five generations. Tony instinctively knew star quality when he saw it, however raw and unpolished it might be. He was easily able to convince his fellow judges that little Eileen Smith had been blessed with a very special gift. With his contacts he could help her build a remarkable career if she would let him, and when over dinner later that evening he outlined his plans to Eileen, her eyes had sparkled up at him with undisguised delight.

In spite of Eileen's parents' horror and disapproval at the idea of her throwing in her lot with a 'strolling player', she had left home and joined Tony in London and with his help and enthusiasm she had climbed effortlessly from one success to another. Tony worked hard with her to iron out the flat Midlands vowels and improve her diction. He took her to dancing classes and persuaded his agent to take her on. Together he and Peter had dreamed up a new and more glamorous name for her – Leonie Swann, soon to be displayed in lights outside one of London's leading theatres. Since then they had starred together in three long-running West End musicals and their highly successful film, *The Prince of Hearts*. Two years ago Leonie had signed a recording contract with Parlophone, making records of all the hit songs from her shows.

On the first night of their current West End hit, *Sunshine Sally*, she had received the accolade all young actresses dreamed of. After the show she had had an unexpected visit in her dressing room from none other than the master himself, Noël Coward. He had pushed in among all the other well-wishers, a bottle of champagne in his hand with which to toast her, hinting that he intended to write a musical play especially for her. In view of all this it was hardly surprising that Leonie had become obsessed with her career, Tony reminded himself. Or that she resented the approaching war, which to her was simply a tiresome obstacle to her ascendant star.

Tony knew of old that Leonie could be formidable when thwarted. He recalled the last time her career had been temporarily halted – when she had discovered that she was pregnant a year after their marriage. For himself, Tony had been overjoyed at the prospect of a child. He had never quite recovered from the loss of contact with his small son, Marcus, now living with his mother in far-off America. But Leonie did not share his enthusiasm. In fact, she made herself quite ill with dismay.

Her pregnancy had been difficult and fraught with sickness, which hadn't helped. She was moody: tearful and petulant by turns, fretting constantly about the frustrating interruption of her career, the ugly thickening of her petite figure and what she saw as her ruined looks.

When she went into labour and suffered three long days of excruciating agony, Tony had begun to fear for her sanity. When the newborn baby girl was finally put into her arms, she had screamed at the nurses hysterically to take it away and turned her face to the wall.

But the moment when Tony first took his little daughter in his arms and looked down at her was a memorable one. He would name her Imogen after his mother, he decided. He hoped fervently that Leonie would come to love the child in time, but if she could not, then it would be up to him to be mother and father to her.

Once the hell of childbirth was over, Leonie had recovered remarkably quickly from her ordeal. When her looks and figure returned without any effort and she found that her voice, far from being ruined, had gained a new mature depth and richness, she put the past months behind her. But she made no real attempt to be a mother to the child. The couple bought their first permanent home, Longueville Hall, a beautiful Georgian manor house deep in the leafy countryside of Northamptonshire, and engaged the homely Jarvises: Molly as housekeeper and nanny to Imogen, and her husband, Jim, as gardener and handyman.

It was only when Tony tried to resume the passionate relationship they had enjoyed before Leonie's pregnancy that he began to realise that things between them would never be the same again. Imogen was three months old and they were spending their first weekend at their new country home. Leonie had slept alone since the birth, protesting that she was not yet fit to allow his lovemaking. But Tony himself had spoken to the doctor, who had seemed surprised, assuring him that there was no reason for them not to resume a normal married life together. So when Leonie had fought him off and dissolved in floods of tears, making him feel a brute, Tony had been upset and perplexed. Over the following weeks and months he had been patient, but the situation had not improved. Finally Leonie had told him that she could not risk another pregnancy and for that reason she refused to allow him back into her bed except on very rare occasions. Even then she was tense and rigid with apprehension, despite all his loving reassurances.

His first affair had been little more than a desperate attempt to bring her to her senses. He made sure that she found out and when she did she was furious. But his triumph was short-lived when he realised that it was bruised pride and not a broken heart that angered her. She told him coolly that if he must have affairs he must insist on his discretion. She would not tolerate being made to look a fool. She would also prefer to remain in ignorance about his extramarital activities. Finally Tony was forced to acknowledge that Leonie's beautiful head housed a hard and calculating brain, and her exquisite body, a heart as cold as ice. At times he even questioned whether she had married him simply to fulfil her ambitions as an actress.

As the years passed they learned to come to terms with the sad charade that was their marriage. In public they were the well-known romantic theatrical couple beloved of the popular press. Their successful marriage was a show-business legend. In private, although they continued to support each other professionally, Leonie reserved all her emotion for her career, while Tony went from mistress to mistress, searching in vain for the loving closeness so sadly lacking in his marriage. He was a handsome man with a passionate nature, a popular romantic actor whom women fantasised over and queued to see. In the course of his work he came into close contact with many beautiful actresses. There was never any shortage of women both in and out of the business who were eager to minister to his physical needs; indeed, an affair with Tony Darrent was something of an achievement to many of the young aspiring starlets who vied for his attention at first-night parties.

If Leonie resented his brief and frequent flings, she gave no hint of it, choosing to turn a blind eye as long as she was left alone. As for Tony, none of his affairs meant more to him than mere physical gratification – until the day almost a year ago when he had walked into his agent's office and met Claire DeLisle, Peter Jason's new secretary. From that moment his whole life had changed.

'Have another drink. It'll make you feel better.' Tony refilled his wife's glass. 'Tell you what, we'll drive up to Houlton tomorrow afternoon. Imogen will have arrived by then and we can all be together for a few days.'

Leonie pulled a face. 'Do you think it's wise to leave London? Suppose Peter wants to get in touch – or Noël?'

'I doubt if either of them will be making firm plans over the next few weeks,' he said. 'But if they do, they both know how to use a telephone.' Standing behind her, he laid a hand on her shoulder, looking at her reflection in the mirror. 'Chamberlain is making a broadcast to the nation on Sunday morning. I'd like us all to be together when we hear what he has to say.'

As Leonie looked up and met the gravity of his expression, her mouth began to tremble with apprehension. 'Tony, you don't think that ghastly little man Hitler will *really* drop bombs on us, do you?' Her lovely eyes widened with sudden panic. 'Tell me the truth: are we all going to be killed?'

'Of course we're not,' Tony said, squeezing her shoulder reassuringly. 'I'm sure it's just the frenzied raving of a madman. All the same, there's no sense in taking chances. The government has been far too complacent as it is. I think that the countryside will be safer for the time being. Maybe you should stay there with Imogen for a while. At least until we see the way the land lies.' He stood up and moved towards the door. 'I'll ring Nanny and Jim now, shall I? Say we're joining them tomorrow.'

Leonie sighed, her shoulders slumping disconsolately. 'Oh, if you must. What an absolutely *bloody* choice – buried dead in London or buried alive in the country?'

'While I'm gone perhaps you could start packing up here,' he suggested, looking round at the litter of clothes strewn around the dressing room. Leonie was notoriously and incurably untidy. 'Then we can make an early start tomorrow morning.'

But when he returned ten minutes later, Leonie still sat where he had left her, staring gloomily into the mirror, her eyes blank.

'Nanny tells me she's taken an evacuee,' he told her. 'A little girl of Imogen's age.'

'Really?' Leonie said abstractedly, leaning forward to pluck out a stray eyebrow hair.

He looked round with irritation. 'Leonie, you haven't even started to get your things together. We may not be coming back here, you know. It's possible the run may have to be suspended indefinitely.'

She shrugged. 'Letty can do it. What else is a dresser for?'

He sighed. 'Darling, I've *told* you. Letty has joined up.'

She turned to stare at him. 'What on earth do you mean, joined up?'

'She's going into the ATS. She rang to say so this morning. We're on our own now.'

'Oh, really! It's *too* tiresome. Everyone seems to have gone quite mad.' She stood up and switched off the dressing-table lights. 'Be an angel and pack for me, will you, darling? Shove as much as you can into a bag and leave the rest where it is. It's all too boring for words, this absurd war thing.' She swung her silver fox furs around her shoulders, picked up her gloves and bag and walked to the door. 'I've got the most fearful headache coming on. I'm going home to lie down.' She blew him a kiss. 'See you later.'

Tony waited until her footsteps had died away, then went into the corridor and lifted the receiver of the pay-telephone. He slipped two pennies into the slot, dialled the number and waited, breathing in the dusty stuffiness that all backstage corridors have and listening to the unnatural silence all around him. Normally at this time of day the theatre was a hive of activity, ringing with the sound of excited voices, alive with the buzz of anticipation and the tension generated in the hour before curtain-up. Now the dressing rooms were dark and empty, and no good-natured banter came from the stage hands in the prop room as the stage manager coaxed and chivvied them. Listening to the telephone ringing, he visualised the great stage on the floor above: the red plush curtain raised on the sightless, gloom-filled cavern of the auditorium; the ropes and pulleys hanging from the flies above, swaying slightly in the draught – like a forest of hangman's nooses. Tony shuddered. Empty theatres always gave him the creeps. So full of ghosts, so redolent of heightened emotions and shattered dreams. Suddenly he felt desperately lonely, as though he were the only person left alive in a doomed world.

At the other end of the line there was a click as the receiver was lifted and he heard Claire's cool tones say: 'Good afternoon. Peter Jason Theatrical Agency.'

The utter normality of her voice was as comforting as a light switched on in a dark room. Tony hastily pushed button A. 'Darling, it's me. I was praying you wouldn't have gone home yet.'

'*Tony* . . .' Her voice was breathless with relief. 'Thank God! I was terribly worried. I rang the theatre earlier but there was no reply. No one seems to know what's going on except that all places of entertainment are closing down indefinitely.' There was a pause, then she said: 'I suppose there's absolutely no chance of the weekend we were planning?'

'I'm sorry, darling. It's out of the question now, I'm afraid. I can't tell you how disappointed I am.'

'Me too.' There was a pause, then she said quietly: 'This wretched war scare is messing up everything, isn't it?'

'I'm afraid it's more than just a scare now, darling. It looks pretty certain that we're in for it. But I had to ring you. Nothing will change between us, Claire. I want you to know that whatever happens I love you. I always will.'

'I love you too. Oh, darling, what are we going to do?'

'I'm driving up to Houlton first thing in the morning. Imogen's arriving there today. Her school has closed. I'm trying to persuade Leonie to stay there with her for a while. After that, God only knows what will happen.'

'And you? I've been wondering all day. Will you be called up?'

He sighed. 'It'll be a while before they get round to calling up my age group, but with my flying experience I really feel I should volunteer.' He heard her stifled gasp at the other end of the line and said quickly: 'Darling, can we meet now – before I leave? Even if it's just for an hour?'

'I wish we could. I can't bear the thought of you going away without seeing me. We might . . . we could all be dead this time next week.'

'Don't say things like that.' There was a pause, then he said: 'Look, I'm at the theatre. There's no one else here. I'm packing up Leonie's things. Can you come round here now?'

'Of course I can.' He heard her catch her breath in what sounded almost like a sob. 'If I can get a taxi I'll be there in ten minutes.'

' "I love my ceiling more
Since it was a dancin' floor for-*or* my love." '

Wearing her best pink dress with the frilly skirt and lace collar, Shirley pirouetted daintily for Molly and took a bow. Molly clapped enthusiastically.

'Bravo! Every bit as good as the real Shirley.'

'Aren't you a clever little girl then? Where did you learn to sing and dance like that?'

'At the dancing classes down the Mile End Road,' Shirley told her proudly. 'I've been going every Sat'day morning since I was five.'

'And who made you this pretty dress?' Molly fingered the rose-pink crêpe de Chine, examining the hand-finished seams and hems with approval.

'Gloria. She makes all my things for me.'

'Is Gloria your big sister?'

'No. She's my mum.' Shirley wriggled into the chair more comfortably and took a deep swig of the glass of home-made lemonade Molly had poured her. After lunch Jim had driven into Northampton in the Austin to meet Imogen's train at the Castle Station. Knowing that train timetables were erratic owing to the evacuation programme, he had started out early, right after lunch, leaving his wife and her new small charge to get to know one another better. Nanny Jarvis had taken Shirley on a tour of the grounds. Wide-eyed she had viewed the kitchen garden, immaculately kept by Jim, and the steamy hothouse with its pungent mingled odours of tomatoes and exotic fruits. Discreetly hidden behind a mellowed red-brick wall, against which espaliered pear and nectarine trees grew, was the swimming pool the Darrents had had installed the previous year, its turquoise water sparkling in the sunshine. Last of all Shirley had been introduced to Toffee, Imogen's piebald pony, who grazed happily in a paddock all his own that was at least ten times bigger than the Rayners' back yard.

After gazing in awe at these hitherto undreamed-of delights, Shirley said half to herself: 'I wish Tilly Marks could see all this.'

Misunderstanding, Nanny Jarvis said: 'Then you must ask your little friend Tilly along to tea one day soon.'

In return for the guided tour, Shirley had changed into the pink flounced dress and entertained Nanny with a song and dance from her extensive repertoire. Now they were having a companionable break together, with lemonade and home-made biscuits.

'Y'see,' Shirley went on conversationally as she bit into a biscuit, 'Ma and Pa are Glor's mum and dad really. I ain't got a dad of me own. But it don't matter. Glor *said* so.'

'I see.' Molly was silent, her head bent over her knitting. Jim had told her about the embarrassing question Shirley had asked him on the way back from the village this morning. Obviously Gloria Rayner was an unmarried mother. But it was clear that Shirley was a very much loved and wanted child for all that.

'Why's Imo-gen gone back to school?' Shirley asked suddenly. 'The 'olidays ain't over yet.'

'She went back two weeks ago,' Molly explained. 'St Margaret's broke up at the end of June this year because a lot of the parents had booked holidays abroad. They were afraid that if they didn't go in early summer the war might prevent them going at all.'

'I ain't never been on 'oliday,' Shirley said thoughtfully. 'Only to Southend on August Monday – oh, an' once Glor an' me went to Kent for the 'op pickin'.' She smiled reminiscently. 'That was *lovely*.' She looked at Molly, her head on one side. 'Where's abroad?'

'Abroad? Oh, France and so on. Across the water.'

'Cor – would they go in a boat? Pa went in a boat when he was a soldier in the Great War. He told me about it.'

'They must all be missing you very much,' Molly said. 'Tell you what, shall we send them a postcard to let them know you're safe and happy?'

Shirley gasped and clapped a hand over her mouth. Gloria had given her a stamped addressed postcard, tucking it into her luggage when she packed. She should really have posted it that morning but she had forgotten. There had been so many new things to see and do. She told Molly about the card and ran off to her room to get it. Together they composed a message for it and Nanny wrote it out for her, then Shirley sat at the kitchen table and copied it onto the postcard in her best writing, the tip of her tongue protruding from the corner of her mouth. At last it was done and she handed it to Molly for her approval.

'You've done that very nicely,' Molly said smiling. 'Now, shall we walk down the lane to the postbox with it?'

As they walked, Molly looked down at the little girl trotting beside her. Shirley was a lovely child: bright, clever and pretty. Very different from her poor, plain, inhibited Imogen. It would do Imogen good to have a companion as outgoing as Shirley – provided they got along together. For all her privileged background, Imogen had never known the security of a loving family as this child had. Sadly, Leonie had never taken to her for some reason and the fact that the child had grown up to be plain and gauche hadn't helped the situation.

Imogen was painfully thin. No amount of feeding ever seemed to fill out the child's spare frame. Her mousy hair was straight and lifeless and she had worn spectacles from the age of four to correct a pronounced squint. Although Molly loved the child dearly she sometimes despaired of her. How could the offspring of such glamorous and attractive parents turn out so plain? She seemed to have inherited all the wrong attributes of each. Her father's strong nose sat incongruously on her mother's delicate facial bone structure; her father's long arms and legs looked somehow all wrong on the fragile body she had inherited from her mother. When her permanent teeth appeared they were large and strong, like Tony's, not small and pearly like Leonie's. They threatened to overcrowd her mouth and were already being corrected by the use of an ugly brace, adding to the catalogue of disadvantages cruel fate had already dealt her.

As they were walking back from the pillar box Jim passed them in the car and waved cheerily. Shirley peered into the car's rear window as it passed, curious to catch a glimpse of her new playmate. The face that looked back at her from under the straw school hat was not encouraging. Sharp grey eyes stared coldly at her through a pair of ugly steel-rimmed spectacles. Shirley lifted her hand in a tentative greeting, but Imogen turned her head away, pretending not to notice. Shirley looked up at Molly.

'She's a bit stuck-up, ain't she?'

Molly smiled. 'She'll be all right once you get to know her, my duckie, never you fear.'

When they reached the house, Imogen was standing in the drive, surrounded by her school trunk and all her other belongings, waiting for Jim to put the car away. Shirley looked with interest at the tennis racquet and the hockey stick leaning against the expensive suitcases. She saw now that the other girl wore a long school-uniform dress made of green-and-white checked gingham, topped by a green blazer, its pocket embroidered with a badge worked in gold thread. On her head was the regulation summer boater, sitting straight on the lank hair and secured by elastic under the chin. On the girl's feet was the ugliest pair of shoes that Shirley had ever seen; black and heavy, with laced-up fronts. Shirley was infinitely grateful that she didn't have to wear such monstrosities. But the critical way Imogen's eyes took in her own pink flounced dress and patent dancing pumps made Shirley blush indignantly. The unspoken criticism in the candid grey eyes was plain to see.

Molly ran forward to embrace the child warmly. 'There you are, then, my duckie. Was the train journey horrid and tiring? Are you hungry?' She turned to Shirley, standing apart, her eyes wary. 'Look, this is your new little playmate, Shirley Rayner. Shirley is from London. She's an evacuee and she's going to stay with us. Say how-do-you-do nicely, pet.'

Imogen, who had returned Molly's hug warmly, turned cold, resentful eyes on Shirley. Reluctantly she extended her hand. 'How do you do,' she said in what to Shirley was an excessively posh voice. Her eyes did not meet Shirley's and her long pointed nose averted itself as though to avoid an unpleasant smell.

'Please ter meecher,' Shirley returned carefully in the proper polite way that Gloria had taught her. She reached out to shake Imogen's hand but the other girl's arm was hastily snatched back before their fingers could meet. As Imogen turned and walked ahead of her with Molly, Shirley quite plainly heard her say:

'How long will *she* be staying here, Nanny? She's *frightfully* common, isn't she?'

Shirley stared at the tall, straight back of the girl in front. Disappointment engulfed her. She had never met anyone quite like Imogen Darrent before and she was filled with dismay at the odd feeling the other girl gave her. 'She ain't a bit pretty. She looks just like Key'old Kate in the *Beano*,' she whispered to herself. 'And she don't like me.'

Shirley was used to the petty spite and occasional jealousy of her schoolmates in the East End. But they spoke their minds. They voiced their grievances to her face in no uncertain terms, and that she understood and could cope with. Shirley was well able to stand up for herself and could give as good as she got, both verbally and physically. But Imogen didn't challenge, she merely condemned without words, dismissing with a single scathing glance. Her cold, silent disdain precluded all retaliation, and her attitude of superiority stirred up a bewildering mixture of unfamiliar emotions inside Shirley which made her feel very uneasy indeed.

Claire had obviously been lucky enough to find a taxi at once since it was less than ten minutes later that Tony heard her footsteps descending the stairs and echoing down the empty corridor outside the dressing room. He opened the door and looked out eagerly, his heart quickening as it always did at the sight of her.

Claire was the opposite to Leonie in every way including her looks. She was tall, almost as tall as Tony. She wore very little make-up and with her taste for plain, classic styles some people might almost have called her ordinary – until they looked more closely. Then they saw that with her naturally blonde hair and straight, slender figure she was attractive in a quiet, subtle way that was all her own. For Tony her eyes were her best feature. They were a deep turquoise blue, the colour of the sea on a summer's day, and they shone with a transparent honesty and candour, rare in the other women he had known. Her taste in clothes was conservative; not for her the furs and luxurious fabrics that Leonie loved. Her style, like her personality, was quieter, but no less attractive. This afternoon she wore a grey suit and a white silk blouse – the ordinary clothes worn by a thousand secretaries every day in London. Yet Claire wore them with a flair and an easy elegance that was all her own. Tony felt his heart contract with love as he held out his arms to her. She quickened her pace, running into them, and for a moment they clung to each other wordlessly.

'Thank you for coming, darling,' he said at last, drawing her into the dressing room and closing the door. 'Damn this war! All our plans . . .'

She took his hand urgently. 'Listen. I can't stay long. I told Peter I was slipping out to the post office. I've got to clear my desk before I can leave. Peter's closing the office tonight for a couple of weeks, so I've got some time off.' She looked into his eyes. 'How long do you intend to stay at Houlton?'

His heart quickening, he said: 'I haven't thought. A couple of days perhaps. Why?'

'Friends of my family have a little holiday cottage on the east coast. I've got a key. I can always go there if they aren't using it. I thought I might go for a few days. You could join me.' The blue-green eyes gazed into his, pleading silently, and he felt his heart melt with longing for her. She wound her arms around his neck. 'A few days to ourselves – just the two of us. It may be the last chance we get to be together. Please say yes, darling.' Her body pressed close to his was irresistible and he crushed her to him, kissing her deeply.

37

'When will you be going?' he asked, his lips against hers.

'First thing tomorrow morning. I'm taking the car. I expect I'll have to sell it when I get back. There won't be any petrol for private motorists, so they say. We must make the very best of the next couple of weeks. It might be the only chance we'll ever get.'

He released her and took out his diary. 'Give me the address. I'll join you the moment I can.' He scribbled down the address, then drew her down onto the couch. 'Don't let's talk any more. Just hold me for a few minutes, then I'll put you into a taxi and send you back to the office.' He kissed her. 'I promise I'll be there, darling. I'll manage it somehow, come hell or high water.'

The four of them sat at high tea in the kitchen. Molly had prepared all Imogen's favourites: home-cooked ham with a crisp salad from the garden, strawberry blancmange and cream and a big chocolate cake with a rich fudge frosting. But the atmosphere was, as Jim said later to his wife, 'that thick you could have cut it with a knife'.

'I had a phone call from your daddy while I was getting tea,' Molly said. 'He and Madam are coming up tomorrow. Won't that be nice?'

Imogen nodded. 'It seems ages since they were here last.' All through the meal she had ignored Shirley, pointedly talking to Jim and Molly about subjects in which she was unable to join. She spoke of her school friends and her teachers, her achievements on the sports field, and how lovely it would be to be home with the Jarvises indefinitely.

'I went along to see Mr Hawkins at the village school this morning,' Jim told her. 'The children are to have an extra week's holiday while he and his staff sort out how all the newcomers are to be fitted in.' He smiled. 'That'll give you two girls a chance to get to know one another, won't it?'

Molly picked up his lead, trying to draw Shirley into the conversation. 'Shirley thinks Toffee is lovely, don't you duckie? And I'm sure she'd like you to teach her to ride, Imogen – and to swim in the pool. Looks like the weather's really settled. You two are going to have a grand old time together, I know.'

Shirley, who had been feeling sad and left out, looked hopefully at Imogen, but the other girl just shrugged her shoulders noncommittally and changed the subject. Later, Molly pressed them into taking a walk together. Walking along the lane in the evening sunshine, Shirley looked at Imogen and said:

'Will you really teach me to ride and swim? If you do, I'll teach you to tap-dance if you like.'

Imogen turned and looked her in the eyes for the first time. Her grey-eyed gaze was icy cold. '*Tap-dance*? Why on earth would I want to do that? And you might as well know now that no one is allowed to ride Toffee but me. You'd probably ruin his mouth.' She pulled at a blade of grass and walked on ahead of Shirley, easily outstripping her on her long legs.

Burning with indignation, Shirley hurriedly caught up with her, 'I wouldn't *touch* his mouth,' she protested. 'I like 'orses. I give the milkman's 'orse a carrot every mornin' and it ain't ruined '*is* mouth yet. An' plenty of people wants to tap-dance. I go to the classes down the Mile End Road. The teacher says I'm a dead ringer for Shirley Temple.'

Imogen stopped walking to stare at Shirley. 'I'm sorry, but I don't understand a *word* you're saying,' she said.

Shirley stopped in her tracks as the other girl walked on. She was cut to the quick. There it was again: no argument, nothing she could come back at; just that dismissive put-down – as effective as a smack in the mouth. Shirley ran after the other girl and trotted beside her lanky form.

'Don't s'pose you could do it anyway on them skinny legs,' she said breathlessly, trying hard to goad Imogen into retaliation. When there was still no response she added: 'You're a stuck-up cat, Imo-gen Darrent. I don't like you an' I don't like your name – so there.'

Imogen turned abruptly, almost causing Shirley to bump into her. 'Go *away*,' she hissed. 'When my mother and father come tomorrow I'm going to ask them to send you away. We don't want nasty little London children who can't speak properly here.' She took a step forward, towering over Shirley. 'And another thing. Don't you dare call Mrs Jarvis Nanny. She's not your nanny and never will be.' And without another word she walked back to the house, leaving Shirley gazing open-mouthed after her.

Once again that night Shirley cried herself to sleep. If only Gloria were here! She wrapped her arms around herself, pretending it was Gloria cuddling her, but it wasn't the same. She thought of them all, Ma, Pa and Gloria, sitting round the kitchen table having their dinner without her. When would she see them all again? Maybe *never*. The thought made her panic badly. She'd write tomorrow and ask to be taken home again. It was horrible here now that snotty Imo-gen had arrived. She spoiled everything. What did *she* have to complain about? Her mum and dad were coming tomorrow, then Shirley would really feel out of it and alone. She snuffled unhappily into her pillow, trying to gain solace from the forbidden thumb in her mouth, till at last a restless, dream-filled sleep claimed her.

After breakfast next morning Imogen went off, wearing jodhpurs and a yellow polo-necked sweater, to see her pony. Shirley stayed behind in the kitchen, hanging around and begging to be given a job with which to fill her time. Molly glanced at Jim anxiously.

'Didn't you want to go with Imogen to see Toffee?' she asked.

The one thing Shirley had never done was tell tales. Among her contemporaries in the East End it was an unwritten law that you didn't tell of people, however rotten they were to you. 'No,' she said. 'Didn't feel like it this mornin'. I'd rather help you wash up, Nan – er, Mrs Jarvis.'

When the washing-up was done, Jim provided her with a soft duster and set her on the task of polishing the brass door plates in the hall. Alone with Molly in the kitchen he said:

'Those two don't seem to be hitting it off, do they? I suppose it's only to be expected. Chalk and cheese they are if ever I saw it. Chalk and cheese.'

'They'll shake down,' Molly said hopefully. 'They'll find something in common eventually. The trouble with Imogen is that she's never been asked to share. She asked me this morning if we couldn't send Shirley away. I was quite shocked.'

'The poor kid may have a lot to share materially,' Jim said perceptively. 'But I don't think it's that that worries her. She's afraid of sharing you, my love.'

'*Me?*' Molly turned to look at him.

Jim nodded. 'You're the most important person in that child's life. You're her rock – her security; the one person she can rely on to be always there and always loving. And she could see you were taken with pretty little Shirley. She feels threatened.'

Molly frowned. 'Oh, dear. I never thought. I was just trying to get them to be friends. What can we do about it?'

'Nothing, love,' Jim said resignedly. 'This war is going to change a lot of things. A lot of people are going to have to learn to compromise. And if you ask me, most of them'll be a lot better for it.'

When the silver-grey Rolls drew up outside the front door of Longueville Hall that afternoon, there was great excitement. Tony and Leonie had been too busy working to see anything of their daughter during the holidays, so this visit was a bonus. Imogen had been waiting ever since lunch, not moving from her place at the landing window from where she would get the first glimpse of the car as it drove in through the gates. The moment she saw it she gave a shout and ran down into the hall.

'Nanny, Jim, they're here!' Pulling open the heavy oak door she ran down the steps into the drive and hurled

41

herself into her father's arms, almost knocking him off his feet as he got out of the car. Shirley watched in silence from inside the door where she stood concealed in the shadows.

'For heaven's sake, Imogen,' Leonie said irritatedly as she watched the display of excited emotion. 'Give your father time to draw his breath.'

Tony hugged his daughter and whispered in her ear: 'Go and give Mummy a kiss.'

Imogen obediently walked round to the other side of the car and held out her arms to her mother. Leonie bent and offered her cheek for the child to kiss, delicately fending off her hands for fear of sticky marks on her eau-de-Nil linen suit.

Shirley watched with eyes like saucers. She had never seen two such glamorous people before. She could hardly believe that she was about to meet the stars she had seen on film at the Adelphi; Leonie Swann herself, and the man whose handsome face had looked down at her from the bedroom walls for the past year. Seeing him in the flesh gave her a funny feeling. She was astonished to see that apart from his expensive clothes and posh car, he looked just like anyone else as he laughed and hugged his daughter. Leonie, on the other hand, was quite different. Standing in the drive, tapping her foot impatiently, she was the very picture of glamour and sophistication – everyone's idea of a film star, in fact. In her pale-green suit and white shoes, she looked very elegant; her face was like some exquisite flower and her mass of dark hair was piled on top of her head in a glorious profusion of curls.

Jim, who had followed Imogen down the front steps, began to unload suitcases from the car's boot.

'Come along now, duckie,' Nanny Jarvis laid a gentle hand on Shirley's shoulder. 'Come and be introduced. No one's going to bite you.' She noted with approval that the child had changed – without being told to – into a pretty pink-and-white-checked gingham dress with a white collar and tiny puffed sleeves. Shirley looked up at her and

42

took the hand that was offered, allowing herself to be led down the front steps. For all the world – as Molly said later – like a lamb to the slaughter.

'Good afternoon, Mr Darrent – Madam,' Molly said respectfully. 'I hope you had a good journey. This is little Shirley Rayner, the evacuee I told you about.' She gave Shirley a little push towards Tony. 'Say how-do-you-do,' she prompted under her breath.

Shirley held out her hand. 'Please ter meetcher,' she said with a shy smile.

Tony shook her hand solemnly. 'Hello, Shirley. I'm pleased to meet you too. I hope you'll be happy here at Longueville Hall.'

Leonie brushed past Imogen and walked round the car. 'My God, I expected some little ragamuffin. What a beautiful child!' she said loudly. 'Where on earth did you find her, Nanny?'

Molly tried not to wince as she registered the crestfallen expression on Imogen's face. 'The, er, billeting officer, Madam. I didn't go down to the hall. Miss Grace brought her up here herself.' She turned towards the house. 'If you'd like to come in, I've laid tea in the drawing room. I'm sure you must be dying for a cup of tea.' But to her dismay Leonie remained where she was, her eyes fixed on Shirley.

'What did you say your name was, darling?'

'Shirley, Mrs – er, miss. Shirley Rayner.' Shirley blushed to the roots of her auburn hair and Leonie's silvery laugh rang out delightedly.

'Tony, listen to the way she speaks. She's the perfect cockney answer to Shirley Temple. Isn't she pure heaven?'

Tony slipped an arm round Imogen and walked up the steps with her. He sensed the child's humiliation, felt the tension in her shoulders and silently cursed Leonie's brash insensitivity. Couldn't she see what she was doing to the girl? Why couldn't she at least pretend to be interested in her own daughter for once?

In the drawing room Leonie inisisted that both children should be allowed to have tea with them. Tony could hardly argue. It would look bad to leave the evacuee child out, yet he knew perfectly well that Leonie was only amusing herself. All through the meal she asked questions, gaining the child's confidence and flattering her outrageously. With careful coaxing she got her to reveal that her clothes had been made by her mother and copied from her namesake's film costumes, that she attended dancing classes every Saturday morning and that her mother was a cinema usherette. Even more embarrassing, she also persuaded the child to part with the information that her mother was unmarried and that they lived with the grandparents above their greengrocer's shop in Whitechapel. At last, unable to stand any more, Tony turned to Imogen who sat silent and white-faced on the settee beside him.

'And how is Toffee?' he asked. 'Have you ridden him yet? And tell us about your swimming and tennis. Did you do well this summer?'

Imogen's face brightened. 'I was chosen to play in the school tournament,' she said. 'I was the youngest ever to be chosen.'

'And did you win?' Leonie asked coolly, one eyebrow arched enquiringly.

Imogen coloured. 'No,' she admitted. 'But I almost won the junior swimming cup.'

'Almost isn't winning, is it, darling?' Leonie said, helping herself to another scone. 'Still, I'm sure you'll try harder next year.'

'Let's all go and see Toffee,' Tony said brightly. 'We'll go and see if Nanny can let us have some carrots and sugar lumps, shall we?'

That night Shirley went to bed happy. Mrs Darrent, or Leonie, as she insisted on being called, really liked her. She had said she wanted to see her dance. That'd shown that snotty, stuck-up Imo-gen where she got off. She closed her eyes and popped her thumb into her mouth. If only Gloria could see her! If she could only tell her that she was going to dance in front of Tony Darrent tomorrow. Maybe it wouldn't be too bad here after all.

In their bedroom on the first floor overlooking the garden, Leonie faced her husband angrily.

'You're only staying till tomorrow afternoon? But why? You never told me before. What's going on, Tony?'

'Nothing's *going on* as you put it.' Tony sighed and began to pull off his tie. 'If you want me to see Peter for you, if you don't want everything to grind to a halt, then I've got to go back to town and keep a finger on the pulse.'

Leonie gave a derisive snort. '*Finger on the pulse?* Don't make me laugh. Who is she this time?' Her eyes glittered challengingly.

'What do you care?' Tony picked up his dressing case and moved towards the door. 'I'll sleep in the dressing room. I'm sure you'll be happier alone.'

'For Christ's sake, Tony. What will the Jarvises think? It was your idea to share a room when we're here, so as to keep up appearances.'

'Don't worry. I'll remove all traces in the morning,' he said over his shoulder. 'And I'll be gone tomorrow night.'

'If you think I'm going to be buried alive by myself here while you go off whoring yourself stupid . . .' Her voice trailed off as the door closed firmly behind him. She swore loudly and hurled her hairbrush at the wall. This time it was serious. All her feminine intuition told her so. This time he was actually in love. And she wasn't bloody well having it.

'. . . I have to tell you now that no such undertaking has been received and that therefore this country is at war with Germany.'

Tony and Leonie, the Jarvises and both children sat silently in the library listening to Mr Chamberlain's announcement on the wireless. When it was over they stared at each other in stunned silence for a moment, then Tony stood up and switched off the set.

'Well, that's it, I'm afraid. Official confirmation of what we all knew anyway.'

For a moment they looked at each other, then Jim asked: 'Will you be joining up, sir?'

Tony shrugged. 'I don't know. Perhaps the RAF could use me. We'll all have to wait and see what happens.'

At that moment the air-raid siren began to wail its mournful warning and Leonie jumped to her feet, clapping her hand to her mouth. 'Oh, dear God, they're here already!'

The threats and fears of the past months were at last reality. The war had begun in earnest.

Chapter Three

It was late when Tony arrived at the cottage. He'd got hopelessly lost in the winding Suffolk lanes and eventually stopped at a pub to ask the way. The locals sitting outside in the evening sunshine with their mugs of ale had stared in amazement at both him and the car and he had begun to wish he'd left the Rolls behind and borrowed Jim Jarvis's baby Austin. But that would have aroused Leonie's suspicions even more. He couldn't understand why she was so angry about his leaving. She certainly didn't want his company. He had felt mean leaving Imogen so soon, but he'd promised to make it up to her later. He might even have time on his hands if the shut-down lasted long.

Holly Cottage was at the end of a lane that was little more than a cart track. It was thatched, with whitewashed walls and a garden that was a profusion of late-summer colour. Through the car's open window he caught the scent of roses and saw that they were climbing over the tiny front porch, fat and pink and evocatively fragrant. Hearing the car bumping along the track, Claire came out to meet him. She wore a blue cotton dress and sandals, her legs were bare and brown and her fair hair was streaked with sunlight. He felt the familiar rush of love for her.

They went inside with arms round each other and he found himself in a room with a beamed ceiling, so low that it only just cleared his head. Claire had drawn a low table up in front of the stone fireplace between twin settees. It was laid for two with a single lighted candle in a brass candlestick in the centre. He smiled at her.

'You've been busy.'

'Busy counting the hours,' she said. 'So – it's happened. We're at war.'

'We are indeed.'

She went to him and wound her arms around his neck in the way that he loved. 'Do you think it's possible to pretend it isn't happening – just for a while?'

He kissed her. 'We can try.'

She had cooked chicken and fresh green vegetables and potatoes, all of which she'd bought from the farmer at the top of the lane. Tony had brought a couple of bottles of his best Chablis, smuggled out of the cellar at Longueville Hall. He chilled them in a bucket of ice-cold water from the wall in the back garden. Finally, replete and relaxed, they sat together close to each other, finishing the last of the wine and gazing dreamily into the dying embers of the apple-wood fire.

Tony sighed deeply. 'This is wonderful – idyllic.'

'You don't regret coming then?'

He frowned as he looked down at her. 'Regret it? Of course not. Why do you say that?'

She shook her head. 'After I'd asked you I felt guilty. This is a time when families should be together. I was only thinking of myself.'

He drew her head down onto his shoulder. 'What Leonie and I share could hardly be called family life. You know that as well as I do.'

'But there's Imogen.'

Tony sighed. 'Yes, there's Imogen. But I'll make it up to her. Now that she's going to be at Houlton for the duration there'll be plenty of opportunities. This time is just for us, my darling. For a little while we'll be thoroughly selfish. We won't think of the past of the future or of anyone but ourselves. Will you promise me that now?'

He didn't say 'It may be our last chance', but she read it in his eyes as she took his face between her hands and kissed him. 'I promise. Whatever else happens, this time – these few days – belongs only to us . . . for ever.'

On the floor above, reached by a tiny twisting staircase, was one large bedroom. Tiny dormer windows peered out from under the thick thatch both front and back. The room was cool, dim and cosy. Under the sloping ceiling the large double bed with its brass bedstead was covered by a patchwork quilt. Claire had made it up with lavender-scented sheets from the airing cupboard in the tiny bathroom next door. On the dressing table was a small glass vase with three pink cabbage roses she had picked from the garden; their scent filled the room. For the rest of his life Tony was never able to smell roses without thinking of Claire, that room and those few precious stolen days. Slightly tipsy with wine and the scent of roses, they undressed slowly, pausing to kiss and caress, and finally they tumbled into the big feather bed together to make love in an atmosphere of peace and tranquillity they had never known before.

Long after Claire slept in the crook of his arm, Tony lay awake. He was reluctant to waste this precious time in sleep, wanting to store every moment of it, filing it away in his memory to feed on in the dark days to come. God only knew when they would find another opportunity to be alone together like this – if ever. If only he and Claire could have met years ago! His life would have taken a totally different direction; he would doubtless have developed into another kind of person; even his career would have expanded and grown. All his acting life so far had been spent playing lightweight parts. He had drifted from juvenile leads into light romantic heroes and now that he was approaching his middle years he could see the dreaded path that lay before all so-called matinee idols looming ahead, unless he could make the necessary departure soon. He had seen it so many times in the past: the toupee to cover the thinning hair, the specially made corset to whittle the bulging waistline, the carefully applied make-up and lighting on stage and the dark glasses worn in public to conceal the puffy eye-bags and incipient wrinkles. Finally, the ultimate humiliation; the incognito trip to a Swiss clinic for plastic surgery in a last desperate attempt to maintain the illusion of youth. It was all so sad and pathetic and Tony was determined not to let it happen to him.

The worst of it was that he had never intended his career to take that direction. It had always been his ambition to be a classical actor in his family's tradition. Shakespeare had provided wonderful parts for great actors of all ages, beginning with Romeo and ending with Lear. His father, the respected and well-loved Richard Darrent, had played them all to great acclaim. Tony longed to play them too. But somehow Leonie's career had come between him and his aspirations. Starring with her, the first of her successful plays had labelled him as a romantic lead and the outstanding success of their film, *The Prince of Hearts*, seemed to have set the seal, typecasting him for ever.

It had been ten months ago, on his thirty-eighth birthday, that he had made the momentous decision to change course. He'd gone to his agent's office that morning determined to achieve his aim, even if he and Peter Jason, who had been his agent for the past twelve years, had to part company.

Walking up the stairs in a positive mood, he had thrown open the door, determined that this time he would have his way. At the desk in the outer office sat a girl, her fair head bent over her work. Tony paused. Miss Harrison, the elderly secretary who had worked for Peter as long as Tony could remember, was nowhere to be seen. When the girl looked up at him he saw that her eyes were startlingly blue. He was reminded of the Mediterranean and for a moment his reason for coming was completely forgotten.

'Yes – can I help you?' She smiled disarmingly, obviously completely unaware of who he was.

'I'd like to see Peter, please. I have an appointment.'

The girl drew the appointment book towards her. 'What name?'

Tony was faintly amused. He was used to being recognised everywhere he went and had certainly always received VIP treatment in this office. Little Miss Harrison would have been on her feet by now, fussily offering him a chair, a cup of coffee and one of the home-made fairy cakes she always brought for her elevenses. He cleared his throat.

'Tony Darrent.' He was slightly abashed to hear himself using his 'actor's voice'.

The girl simply nodded and stood up. 'Oh yes, that's right. I'll just slip in and see if Mr Jason is ready for you.'

When she got up and moved out from behind the desk Tony saw that she was tall and slim with an extremely good figure, accentuated by the plain skirt and blouse she wore. She had classic looks; a flawless complexion, straight nose and wide mouth. When she spoke he saw that her teeth were white and even; but it was her eyes that mesmerised him. Their astonishing blue gaze quite took his breath away with their candid directness and her smile lit them brilliantly. It was as though the sun suddenly shone, warming him through and through with its glow.

When she came out of the office a few moments later she was smiling apologetically. 'You can go in now, Mr Darrent,' she said. Then, a little shyly: 'I think I owe you an apology. I should have recognised you – at least known your name. It was unforgivable to keep you waiting. I come from the Channel Islands, you see, and we haven't had any of your films over there.'

'Please don't apologise.' Tony held out his hand. 'How do you do, Miss – er?'

'DeLisle.' She put her cool hand into his. 'Claire DeLisle.'

Sitting opposite Peter in the office, Tony asked: 'Where's Miss Harrison?'

'Retired last week. She was long past the age. We all miss the old dear. She'd been with us for years.'

'And the new girl?'

'Daughter of a distant cousin of mine. She was born and bred in Jersey – wanted to come over and sample life in the great metropolis. She just happened to write to me at the right time.' He nodded and offered Tony his silver cigarette box. 'Very efficient. I couldn't have chosen better if I'd advertised the job.' He raised an eyebrow at Tony as he lit his cigarette. 'What can I do for you?'

Tony leaned back in his chair and blew out a cloud of smoke. 'I know I've mentioned this before, Peter, but I want to go legit.'

Peter sighed. 'Oh, dear. I thought you'd forgotten all that nonsense.'

'Well, I haven't. I want you to let it be known that I'm available for classical roles.'

Peter rubbed his chin. 'Aren't you forgetting something? You've got a contract to finish. Three more films to make, including this extravaganza with Leonie.'

'I'll buy out of it – anything.' Tony leaned forward and stubbed out his barely smoked cigarette. 'If I don't do it now, Peter, I'll never do it at all.'

'Christ, you're really serious, aren't you?' Peter Jason got up and went to a filing cabinet in the corner. From the top drawer he took out a bottle of whisky and two glasses. Pouring two generous measures, he passed one to Tony. 'Come on,' he said. 'Whatever it is, you'd better get it off your chest.'

Tony took a deep draught of his whisky and looked at his agent over the rim of the glass. 'It's nothing new. You know that I've always wanted to be a classical actor. After all, it's what I was brought up on. I just drifted into popular light stuff along with Leonie. I'll be forty before you know it and if I don't do something about it now it'll be too damned late.'

'Have you talked this over with Leonie?'

Tony shook his head impatiently and reached for another cigarette. 'What kind of question is that? You know we never talk. I'm in deadly earnest about this, Peter. I'm sick of dancing to Leonie's tune, playing the adoring husband *and* leading man. Any ham with good teeth and a modicum of talent could do what I do. Look, I made Leonie what she is, but somehow along the way I messed up my own career doing it.'

Peter shook his head. 'You could lose a hell of a lot of money, you know.'

Tony glared at him. '*You* could, you mean.'

Carefully containing his patience, Peter ignored the barbed remark. 'Look, supposing – just *supposing* I could get you a season at Stratford, there's no guarantee you'd be right for it. It could be a disaster. You could make a laughing stock of yourself.'

'Thanks for the vote of confidence,' Tony said wryly.

'I'm just being realistic. I've every confidence in you, Tony, but you're the matinee-idol type. And the British public – and that includes critics – tends to like actors doing what they've seen them do successfully time and again.'

'Bugger the British public,' Tony said explosively. 'And *that* includes critics.'

'They put you where you are, Tony, and don't you forget it,' Peter admonished with a frown. 'Look, you're going through a bit of a midlife crisis. Don't tear up your contract. I'll see if I can wangle you a guest appearance at Stratford next season. You can work it in between shooting. How's that?'

'Hold a bloody spear, you mean. Don't patronise me, Peter. This isn't the old cliché of the clown who wants to play Hamlet. I'm deadly serious. I won't consider anything less than a lead.'

A spark of annoyance flickered in Peter's eyes as his patience began to wear thin. 'Look, Tony, to be frank, companies like Stratford expect classical training, RADA at the very least. I'm not at all sure that I could convince them that –'

'RADA?' Tony sprang to his feet and glowered angrily down at his agent. 'My family have been in the theatre for the past five generations. My grandfather played Horatio to Irving's Hamlet. My grandmother understudied Ellen Terry. And everyone remembers my father, Richard Darrent. His name is a bloody *legend*, for Christ's sake. Don't you talk to me about RADA! I learned my craft where it should be learned, in the theatre – from real pros. And I started learning it the minute I was born.' He walked towards the door. 'If you don't believe in me, Peter, then you only have to say so and I'll find an agent who does.'

When he'd gone, slamming the door behind him, Peter Jason threw up his hands in exasperation. '*Actors!*' he muttered, flapping his hands towards the door. 'Egotistical bloody hotheads, the lot of them. Sometimes I wonder what I'm doing in this business.'

As Tony stormed through the outer office, he was halted by a cool voice.

'Is anything wrong, Mr Darrent? You look upset.'

He turned to see Claire looking at him, her blue eyes genuinely concerned. Suddenly his temper evaporated and he smiled shamefacedly. 'Oh, not really. I got a little overheated in there. Look – tell Peter I said I'm sorry, will you?'

'Of course I will. Do you want to go back and tell him yourself?'

Tony shook his head. 'No. Just tell him for me.'

'Is there anything I can do? I mean – I don't want to intrude, but if you want to talk about it? Sometimes it helps.'

'You're right.' He smiled at her. 'Let me buy you lunch.'

Claire blushed. 'Oh, I didn't mean . . . I wasn't . . .'

'I know you weren't. But you're right, I do need to talk to someone impartial. Please have lunch with me.' He looked at his watch. 'I'll pick you up at one. Do you like the Savoy Grill?'

'I'd prefer somewhere less – er . . . There's a little restaurant round the corner from here. They do a very good plaice and chips.'

He laughed and was about to ask if she was shy about being seen with him in public, then he remembered that she really had no idea just how well known he was. Unlike most of the women he met, she was genuinely friendly and utterly guileless. It was as soothing and refreshing as summer rain. 'All right,' he said. 'I'll pick you up at one and you can take me there. I'll look forward to it.'

Peter hadn't managed to get him a leading part with a Shakespearean company, but Tony hadn't minded too much. After that first lunch with Claire his obsession had lessened. She was so sweet and sincere. She understood how he felt, almost without his telling her. It was uncanny.

He popped into the office several times a week after that first meeting, but Peter was relieved to find that his failure to get his best client the part he wanted was received with a surprising tolerance. Tony's visits were merely an excuse for seeing Claire. Eventually he gave up pretending and began to invite her out regularly. Her quiet calm was becoming addictive to him. Being with her was becoming a necessity. They kept to quiet places, mainly because Claire preferred them. Sometimes she would cook him a meal in her tiny flat in Earls Court, where he found the kind of relaxation he had almost forgotten existed.

He hadn't bargained for falling in love. When he first realised what was happening to him he was alarmed and dismayed. It was a complication he hadn't encountered before. Their relations had so far remained chaste. Claire was reluctant to sully their relationship by making it physical too soon, but Tony had to face that what he felt for her was deeper than anything he had ever known before – even for Leonie in their early days together. He tried not seeing Claire, but it hadn't worked. When they were apart he couldn't concentrate, couldn't work, couldn't think of anything but her, and when he had turned up at her flat two weeks later he found her in tears because she felt the same. They had fallen into bed together there and then. After that he knew there would never be anyone else for him but Claire. As soon as he could he would tell Leonie and ask her for a divorce. Then came the serious possibility of war with all its attendant complications and insecurities. They had decided to wait and see. Perhaps – vain hope – it wouldn't happen after all. But now it had.

He wakened to the scent of fresh coffee and someone shaking his shoulder. Opening his eyes he stared disbelievingly up at her, his eyes slightly unfocused. She laughed down at him.

'Wake up, dozy. Drink this coffee and get dressed. We're going for a walk.'

He sat up, brushing his dishevelled hair out of his eyes. 'What time is it?'

She held the bedside clock up for him to see and he stared at it. '*Half-past seven?* There's no such time. Come back to bed.' He reached out for her but she jumped back out of his reach.

'Not on your life. The sky's blue and the sun is shining. The sea is just across that field. I want to walk beside it with you; making footprints on the sand; breathing the air before anyone else has. Just the two of us with no one else about.' She pulled the bedclothes off him and threw him a sweater and slacks from the bag he had brought. 'Here, put these on.'

The air was salty and fresh with the tang of early autumn. They walked with their arms around each other's waists across the field to the dunes and down onto the hard sand at the water's edge, then suddenly Claire was pulling her sweater over her head, stepping out of her cotton skirt and kicking off her sandals.

'Come on, let's go for a swim.'

'In *there*? Now? It must be freezing.' But she was gone, running into the surf to plunge under the first wave that rolled in. Tony hopped on one foot, taking off his shoes, undoing his slacks. A moment later he joined her, gasping as the icy water splashed remorselessly over his warm skin. Claire laughed, bobbing on the water like a seal yards away from him. Droplets of sea water sparkled on her eyelashes and flew around her in a glittering shower as she shook her head. She dived and came up in front of him. Grasping his shoulders she pushed him under.

'There. Now you're in. Race you to the breakwater.'

Gasping and laughing he struck out and followed her powerful crawl, but he couldn't catch her up.

Later, as they lay drying in the shelter of a deep sandy dune on Claire's outspread skirt, he asked her where she had learned to swim like that.

'When you grow up surrounded by sea you have to learn to swim well,' she told him.

She talked affectionately about her home in Grève de Lecq, in Jersey, and the loving family she had left there running their boatbuilding and chandlery business. In return he told her about his early childhood, touring theatres and living in digs with his mother and father; the heartbreaking parting when he was sent away to boarding school and, later, his first small parts in rep where he began his career as student assistant stage manager. Claire knew about his consuming ambition to be a classical actor. Her quiet confidence and steadfast faith in him buoyed him up as nothing else could.

'It was a happy childhood,' he told her, gazing up into the dissolving morning haze. 'But I missed having a stable family home. Till I met you I didn't know what a real home was – or how wonderful and special it felt to have the love of a real woman.'

He dried her with his sweater, brushing the fine sand from her smooth skin, following his caressing fingers with his lips until he had kissed every inch of her. Finally they made love there on the sand and vowed their love for each other for the thousandth time. As they lay watching the sun slowly climbing the sky, Claire said suddenly:

'Tony, I've been thinking. Now that we're actually at war, maybe I should join up – the ATS or the WAAF.'

He raised himself on one elbow to look down at her. 'But if you do that I'll hardly ever see you.'

She reached up to pull him down to her, holding him close, her lips against his cheek so that he wouldn't see the pain in her eyes. 'Let's face it, darling. It could be almost impossible to us to meet again once things begin to hot up. Anyway, I dare say you'll do the same yourself. With your flying experience you'd be of immense value to the RAF.'

'I know,' Tony said thoughtfully. Flying had been his hobby and relaxation for years. When they bought Longueville Hall he had joined the flying club at nearby Sywell aerodrome, from where he flew regularly. For the past two years he had been a voluntary instructor, working with beginners as often as his professional commitments allowed. The thought of Claire joining up and putting herself in danger turned his blood to ice. 'What about your folks, though?' he asked. 'Shouldn't you just go home? If I can't see you I'd like to think of you safe among your family.' The sunlit morning seemed suddenly dark with storm clouds, but he pushed the shadows from his mind determined not to be depressed. Getting to his feet, he took her hands and pulled her up with him.

'What did we promise? No war, no problems, just here and now and *us*.'

She smiled into his eyes. 'You're right. I'm sorry, darling.'

They walked back across the field in their crumpled clothes to eat an enormous breakfast outside in the tangled garden and plan what they would do with the rest of the day.

Leonie was bored. She was also furious with Tony. How could he just go off like that and leave her here alone with Imogen? Especially after it had been announced that they were actually at war. They'd even had their first air raid, too – almost as soon as the announcement was made. Well, if not an actual raid, a *warning* of one. It had been dreadful. That ghastly Mrs Phipps from the post office had come trundling up the drive on her bicycle wearing a World War I tin helmet to ask if they'd filled the bath and every other receptacle with water. Being in the WVS seemed to have gone to the woman's head. Leonie had sent her off with a flea in her ear. Bossy old bag! And now Jim Jarvis had started talking about digging up the tennis court to grow potatoes. She had told him what she thought of that idea, too.

'If there has to be a war, Jim, there also has to be some place where we can get away from it,' she told him firmly. 'And as far as I'm concerned, it's here at Longueville Hall.'

There was only one thing to break the terrible monotony and that was the evacuee child, Shirley. She was absolutely fascinating. The way she spoke and some of the expressions she used were straight out of Dickens, yet she looked like an angel with her red-gold curls and cornflower-blue eyes. Why couldn't she – Leonie – have managed to produce a child who looked like that instead of Imogen? Really, the girl seemed to grow plainer and duller by the minute.

On Monday morning she had telephoned Peter Jason at his office in Charing Cross Road. When there was no reply she rang his home number.

'I've closed the office for a couple of weeks, Leonie,' he told her. 'Till we see how the land lies.'

'But Tony said he was going back up to town especially to see you,' Leonie said plaintively. 'Here I am at Houlton, all alone, waiting for him to bring me some news. Our whole *future* is at stake, Peter. I think it's rather selfish of you to take a holiday at a time like this.'

Peter swallowed his irritation and thought quickly. He had guessed months ago that there was something going on between Tony Darrent and Claire. Privately he thought Tony must be mad to play around so close to home, but it wasn't his place to tell him what to do with his life. Claire had told him she was going to Suffolk and hearing about Tony's disappearance he didn't have to be a genius to guess that he was probably with her.

'I'm not on holiday, Leonie,' he said. 'I've only closed the office. I'm available here at home to all my special clients and Tony knows that.'

'So you'll be seeing him there at Richmond?'

'Undoubtedly,' Peter said warily.

'So – have you any news? What about the new film, Peter? And has Noël been in touch?' Leonie bit her lip in anguish. 'God! I don't think I can *bear* much more of this uncertainty. What a time for a war to start!'

'Don't worry, darling,' Peter said soothingly. 'It's my guess that things will soon be back to normal. Entertainment will be the order of the day. It's just a question of when and where to put it on.'

'Oh, well, I suppose I'll have to leave it all in your capable hands,' she said resignedly.

'That's right. Just you enjoy relaxing with little Imogen,' Peter advised. 'Let Tony and me do the worrying for you.'

She replaced the receiver with a trembling hand. Her arrogance and impatience were a protective shell that was becoming more fragile with each passing day. It concealed her innermost secret feelings of fear and insecurity. Fear of his new situation – the war and its unknown evils – and insecurity about her crumbling marriage.

Tony had had plenty of affairs. She was so used to them now that she could read the signs as easily as ABC. She always knew when they were about to begin and she could follow their progress through from climax to conclusion by Tony's moods. She even welcomed them. When there was a new woman in his life he was always in a good mood, at his most handsome and charming. With the adrenaline flowing copiously he did his best work and when he was engaged in chasing some dumb blonde or dizzy brunette he was a tolerant working partner and amusing companion, seeming to see the world through rose-coloured glasses. But this time it was different. He was never in the same mood twice; preoccupied and pensive one minute, elated the next. And she was sure he hardly heard a word she or anyone else said to him.

It had all begun with his obsession to play a classical role. That frightened her more than anything. She would never have admitted to anyone, not even Tony himself – least of all to Tony – but she was terrified of being left to carry a show alone. His abandonment of their marriage, she could stand. In truth there had been no marriage for years, and she was willing to admit that it was largely her fault. But if Tony stopped acting with her, if their celebrated partnership on stage were to end, she was terribly afraid that it could be the end of her career.

But what to do about it? Who *was* she, this very special woman who had finally won Tony away from her in mind as well as body? Not knowing tore her nerves to shreds. It was like fighting an enemy blindfold with one hand tied behind her back. It was Leonie's guess that she was a classical actress – well known, beautiful, young? *Younger than she?* Leonie would be thirty next birthday and she was having trouble coming to terms with the fact.

Sitting there, staring unseeingly out of the window, she visualised them playing opposite each other at Stratford or in London – Hamlet and Ophelia; Romeo and Juliet even. Tony was still youthful and athletic enough to get away with Romeo. Consumed with jealousy, she got up and paced the room, racking her brain for something to do to take her mind off the demons that gnawed mercilessly at her.

In the paddock Imogen, dressed in jodhpurs and a white shirt, was putting Toffee through his paces; trotting him round and putting him over the small jumps placed at intervals around the field. Shirley watched enviously from the fence. Imogen had hardly spoken to her since their first meeting. She behaved as though Shirley didn't exist, doing all the things she always did when she was at home and making no attempt to share anything with her unwelcome 'playmate'.

The weather was fine – what Jim Jarvis called an Indian summer – and Shirley had worn her selection of cotton dresses in rotation. Today, in a desperate attempt to attract someone's attention, she had chosen the buttercup yellow with panels piped in white. She wore her white ankle socks and sandals with it and got Nanny Jarvis to tie a big white bow in her hair. Even Imo-gen's *unschool* clothes were dowdy to Shirley's eyes, but she had the uncomfortable feeling that they had what Gloria would have called 'class' and she found this slightly intimidating.

Apart from Imo-gen's obvious dislike of her, Shirley liked it here. It was very different from the little shop in Angel Row. Never in her life had she had so much open space in which to play, so much green grass to run on or such fresh air to breathe. Instead of the weekly bath in the tin tub in the kitchen, in water shared with Gloria, she had one all to herself every night before bed in the big white bath that was almost big enough to swim in. And she had never tasted such delicious food. Home-made bread, fresh farm butter and eggs, and milk that came up every morning from the farm in a gleaming churn, still warm from the cow. At first she had been sceptical about drinking it. It didn't seem right somehow – having milk that came out of an animal instead of a bottle. But once she had tasted its delicious creaminess she soon changed her mind. Porridge and cornflakes would never be the same again.

In spite of Imo-gen's mum's interest in her, Shirley hadn't been asked to dance for the Darrents and now Mr Darrent had left for London again. Everyone seemed so preoccupied now. The only exciting thing that had happened was when the siren had sounded soon after the old man on the wireless had said there was a war on. That horrible fat lady from the post office had come up to the house that morning in a funny tin hat slipping over her eyes. She'd tried to boss everyone about, telling them what to do. Mrs Darrent had told *her* where to get off and no mistake. She'd called her a rude word that Shirley wasn't allowed to say. She had enjoyed that.

'Go on – give us a go,' she called out as Imogen trotted past on the pony. Imogen ignored her as usual, but just at that moment Nanny Jarvis appeared with two glasses of milk and a plate of biscuits on a tray.

'I thought you girls would like your elevenses out here as it's such a lovely morning,' she said. Putting the tray down on a bench, she called to Imogen, 'Come and have your milk and then you can let Shirley have a ride.'

'She can't ride,' Imogen returned with a toss of her head.

'Never mind. You had to learn once too, didn't you? You can hold the reins and lead her round the paddock.' She smiled down at Shirley. 'You'd like a ride on the pony, wouldn't you, duckie?'

'Yes please.' Shirley took her glass of milk and drank thirstily, looking at Imogen over the rim of her glass and trying to assess her reaction. The other girl took her own glass and drank with dainty sips.

'You've got milk all round your mouth,' she told Shirley scathingly. 'It looks disgusting.'

'That's all right.' Nanny handed Shirley a hand-kerchief. 'You were thirsty, weren't you?'

Shirley wiped her mouth and handed back the hanky, staring back at Imogen. 'Can I get on now then?' she asked with a sidelong look at Nanny Jarvis.

Looking furious, Imogen walked silently with her to the waiting pony and stood holding the reins, resentment in every gesture. 'Well, what are you waiting for? Aren't you going to get on?' she asked coldly.

Nanny stepped forward and lifted Shirley into the saddle. 'You're supposed to show her how to mount and give her a leg up,' she admonished Imogen. 'You're not a very good teacher, are you?'

Shirley smiled. 'Thank you, Nanny,' she said.

When Nanny was out of earshot Imogen mimicked Shirley's cockney accent: '*Fank you, Nanny,*' she jibed. 'Little angel, aren't you? Little goody-goody. I thought I told you not to call her Nanny.'

'Shall if I want,' Shirley said defiantly. 'Anyway, she told me to.'

'I see. You always do what people tell you, do you? Well, so does this pony.' She threw the reins across Toffee's neck and gave his rump a sudden slap. The startled pony began to canter round the field, taking the small jumps with glee, delighted at his sudden freedom. Shirley held onto his mane determinedly, trying not to let Imogen see how scared she was. When they came round to where Imogen stood the girl gave the pony another slap, harder this time, making him increase his pace and set off on a second circuit.

'P-please – m-make 'im s-stop!' Shirley could feel herself gradually slipping sideways out of the saddle and her heart was bumping with fear, but Imogen only laughed mercilessly.

Suddenly there was a shout. 'Imogen! Catch those reins at once. Stop that pony this minute before there's an accident.'

Shirley saw Imogen's gaze freeze with dismay as she saw her mother running across the grass. Leonie climbed the paddock fence quickly and ran forward to catch the pony's bridle, bringing him to a halt. 'Are you all right?'

she asked a quivering Shirley who hung half in and half out of the saddle. Lifting her gently to the ground, she turned to a sheepish-looking Imogen. 'Here, take him back to his stable and give him a rubdown,' she said sternly. 'And don't you *ever* let me catch you doing anything so spiteful again, you horrid child.' As her daughter walked away, leading the pony, Leonie looked down at Shirley.

'Are you hurt, darling?'

The kind words brought a lump to Shirley's throat. 'N-no,' she said. *She* wasn't hurt, but her pride and her feelings were. It wasn't fair. She'd done nothing to Imogen. Why should she want to hurt her?

Leonie seemed to understand. Bending to wipe a smudge from the child's face with her own handkerchief, she said: 'Poor sweetie, you're trembling. Tell you what, you shall have lunch with me today. And we'll make horrid Imogen have hers in her room. How's that?'

Shirley shook her head vigorously. 'I'm not very 'ungry.'

'But you will be by then. I'm having fresh salmon. You can have some too if you like. And afterwards I'll play the piano and you can dance for me as you promised. How's that?'

It sounded lovely and Shirley longed to agree, but how could she make Mrs Darrent see that if she did, it would only make matters worse between herself and Imogen. 'Can – Imo-gen come too?' she asked. 'She never meant to make the 'orse go too fast. She was just tryin' to learn me to ride.'

Leonie looked taken aback for a moment, then she laughed. 'Well, well. What a generous little girl you are! Very well, if that's what you want. I've got some news for you both anyway.'

Shirley changed out of the dirtied buttercup-yellow dress into her pink and white polka-dot. Imogen, however, appeared in the dining room still wearing her jodhpurs and shirt. Leonie looked at her disapprovingly.

'I hope you've at least washed your hands. You look a perfect disgrace, child.'

Molly, who heard the remark as she came in with the first course, said: 'I tried to get her to put on something more suitable when you said the children were to lunch with you, Madam, but she insisted on staying in those things.'

'It's quite all right, Nanny. I'm sure it's not your fault. We both know that Imogen is incurably stubborn, don't we? She gets more like a donkey every day.' Leonie smiled at Shirley. 'You look perfectly *sweet*, darling.' She winced slightly as Shirley began to slurp her soup. 'But, er, when you eat soup you hold your spoon *so* – do you see?'

Imogen picked up her own spoon and bent her head over her plate. Under her breath, and just loud enough for Shirley to hear, she said: 'Common little pig.'

Shirley turned to look at her. She took in the lank mousy hair, the large front teeth with their ugly brace, and the resentment that gleamed at her from behind the steel-rimmed spectacles. And for the first time in her short life she knew the meaning of the word hate.

Imogen blushed bright red. 'Don't you know that it's rude to stare?' she demanded.

'Children, *please*.' Leonie glared at them both. 'Any more and you'll have to finish your lunch in the kitchen.' She helped herself to salad and passed the bowl across the table. 'Now listen. I've had a telephone call this morning from Mr Hawkins, the headmaster of the village school. He's beginning the new term next week. Just to begin with and because there are so many evacuees, it is to be divided into two groups. Half will go in the mornings and half in the afternoons. The under tens – that's you – are to go in the mornings and as you're the same age you'll be in the same class. Won't that be nice?'

Imogen put down her knife and fork and looked at her mother. 'Why do I have to go to the village school?' she asked. 'I don't like the village children. They're dirty.'

'Don't be difficult, Imogen,' Leonie said coldly. 'There's a war on. You're lucky to be getting into a school at all. And you'll be able to sit next to Shirley here. She certainly isn't dirty. Which is more than I can say for you at this moment.'

Crushed and crimson-faced, Imogen lowered her eyes and the rest of the meal was eaten in silence. When the time came for Leonie to invite Shirley to dance, Imogen asked to be excused, but Leonie shook her head.

'No, Imogen. You are to come to the drawing room with Shirley and me.' She led the two girls across the hall into the drawing room and sat down at the piano.

'Shirley is going to entertain us,' she told a reluctant Imogen. 'It will do you good to see what some little girls can do when they try to please their parents.'

To the strains of 'Animal Crackers' Shirley did her favourite song-and-dance routine as taught by Miss Kent at the Saturday morning dancing classes, her feet in their white sandals tapping away on the parquet floor of the drawing room. When it came to an end, Leonie clapped delightedly.

'That was *sweet*, darling. You must dance and sing for us again soon. What a clever little girl you are.'

Stony-faced, Imogen asked: 'May I go now, please? It's time to feed Toffee.'

'Oh, go along then if you must,' Leonie said. 'But first say thank you to Shirley for entertaining us so nicely.'

Blushing furiously Imogen muttered a grudging 'thank you', but when Leonie turned her back she surreptitiously wrinkled her nose and thrust out the tip of her tongue. Shirley returned the gesture, withdrawing her tongue and adjusting her sunny smile quickly as Leonie turned back again.

Later that night, when she passed Imogen's bedroom door, she heard her crying and felt a stab of guilt. Was it because she'd got told off for making the pony run fast? No. It'd be because she didn't want to go to a school that wasn't posh. That was the sort of thing Imo-gen would cry about. Why should she feel sorry for her?

Tony and Claire crossed the field hand in hand. Every morning since they'd arrived the sun had wakened them.

66

Although it was September there was only the faintest nip of autumn in the air and the breeze from the sea was fresh and invigorating. Tony, who had spent most of his life in cities, inside theatres, knew he could soon get to like the open-air life, especially if it were shared with Claire. Each morning they had swum in the sea, then returned to the cottage to laze. In the afternoons they worked in the cottage garden. Claire said it was the least they could do for their hosts in return for their rent-free stay. After an early supper they climbed the stairs and lay together in the big brass bed, talking, making love and talking again, until sleep overtook them.

This morning, as they reached the far side of the field and climbed the stile that gave onto the dunes, Claire said: 'Isn't it funny, you can't even see the sea from here. Until you climb to the top of that ridge of sand you wouldn't know it was there.'

'You would. You can hear it,' Tony said. 'Stop and listen.'

They stood quite still together hand in hand, listening to the sounds of the morning. High above, almost hidden by the haze, a skylark sang, its pure, silvery notes mingling with the roar of the waves as they washed the pebbly shore. Then Claire's hand tensed in his as another, more intrusive sound cut rudely into the peace of the morning. She looked apprehensively at Tony, who frowned.

'What? What is it?'

But Claire didn't have to look. She already knew. It was the sound of a tractor. And as they climbed the soft, slippery sand of the dunes the mechanical rumble was joined by the clang of metal and the voices of men, talking and laughing together as they worked. Standing at the top of the ridge they watched them filling sandbags and throwing them onto a trailer. Further along the beach another team was hammering steel posts into the sand and nearby they saw huge coils of barbed wire. Without voicing their thoughts, both knew that this was the end of their stolen time together. The end of love and happiness, the end of peace. A cloud momentarily crossed the sun and Claire shivered.

'It's going to rain,' she said, turning away. 'Let's go back.' In her heart she knew that the time had come to pack and leave.

On the day that term began at St Luke's village school, Shirley was up early. She was looking forward to it. She was lonely for the company of other children and she hadn't seen any of her old schoolmates since she arrived at Houlton – apart from Tilly Marks, and you couldn't count her. Tilly was a year younger and in a different class anyway.

Shirley and Imogen ate breakfast together in the kitchen and while they ate Nanny Jarvis packed each of them some biscuits for their mid-morning 'lunch'. Imogen was pale and silent. She wore her school skirt and a dark-green jumper with a white blouse underneath. Shirley privately thought it was a bit silly to wear thick clothes when it was still quite warm. She had chosen her blue and white gingham for her first day at the new school and she knew she looked nice in it. Gloria always liked her in that. On the other hand Imo-gen did look quite smart, she told herself, giving the other girl a sidelong look.

Nanny kissed them both goodbye and wished them a happy day and Jim walked down to the lane with them. He showed them the armband he would soon be wearing.

Shirley examined it carefully. 'What's LDV stand for?' she asked.

'Local Defence Volunteers,' Jim told her proudly. 'All the men who haven't joined up are getting together to protect our own village from danger, like a little army. We'll have proper uniforms when they're ready but till then we're wearing these armbands.'

When they got to the ornate gates that had so impressed Shirley on the day she arrived, he told them that all the iron railings and gates throughout the country would soon be taken down and collected for something called salvage. 'To help make aeroplanes,' he explained.

Shirley said she thought that was a shame and that an aeroplane with wrought-iron gates would surely be too draughty, which made Jim laugh.

Imogen did not join in their good-humoured chatter. Walking on Jim's other side, she was silent and tense.

He left them at the top of the lane and as soon as he was out of sight, Shirley said: 'Come on, Imo-gen, let's be friends.' She reached out and tried to take the other girl's hand, but Imogen rejected it with a shrug of her shoulder, quickening her pace to walk on ahead.

'I don't make friends with girls who show off,' she said. 'You think you're really clever, don't you? Sucking up to Nanny and Jim and my mother and getting them all to make a fuss of you. Well, I *hate* you and I always will, so there. I'm going to get my daddy to send you away when he comes home again.'

'You can't. You've gotta do everythin' you can to help the war,' Shirley said, her chin thrust out and her lower lip trembling. 'There's gonna be bombs in London. That's why all the kids've gotta come 'ere. You don't know nuthin', Imogen Darrent.'

'I know you're a nasty little show-off. You're common and you've got no manners. You're a – a *slum* child.'

Shirley's throat ached with the pain of the other girl's insults but she refused to give Imogen the satisfaction of seeing her cry. Blinking hard at the threatening tears, she burst out: 'How'd you like ter leave yer 'ome and yer mum and dad and go where people don't want you? You're ugly and mean an' 'orrible, Imo-gen Darrent, an' I don't *want* to be friends with you now. Not *ever*.'

She ran on ahead, her gas mask in its cardboard box bumping uncomfortably against her back. In the High Street she was comforted by the sight of a group of children from Whitechapel. Running up with a shout of greeting, she joined them as they converged on the school building next to the church. She'd find her own way and make her own friends just like she always had. Under her breath she said one of the forbidden words with immense satisfaction.

'*Bugger* you, Imogen Darrent. *Be* rotten then. See if I care.'

Chapter Four

Anticlimax was the word everyone was using. Weeks had gone by now since war was declared and so far nothing had happened. When the first siren had sounded that Sunday morning they had all feared the worst. Everyone in Angel Row was convinced that the bombs and poison gas were about to be showered on them, but so far there had been nothing.

In spite of the unexpected lull, Pa had made the most of his newfound authority as an ARP warden, making himself thoroughly unpopular with all the neighbours with his shout of 'Put that light out!', and Ma had set to work clearing out the large cupboard under the stairs and making it comfy, because right from the start she had announced her veto against the street shelters.

'The kids've already started peein' in 'em,' she said, wrinkling her nose. 'What with them an' the courtin' couples they ain't fit for decent folk to sleep in. If I'm gonna be buried alive I'll be buried in me own 'ome in comfort and that's flat.' And both Gloria and Pa knew by the set of her mouth that nothing on this earth – Hitler's Luftwaffe included – would shift her.

To Gloria's delight the Adelphi had opened its doors again within the first fortnight, as did most of the other cinemas and theatres. Working hours were not quite the same as before, though. Because of the blackout the theatres put on only one performance each night instead of two, with two matinees a week. And the cinemas opened at two and closed at ten.

As the nights began to draw in, the blackout made things difficult. There were no street lights. Shop as well as house windows were dark. Even the cars and buses had their headlights muffled, which made crossing the road after dark hazardous. But people were gradually getting used to finding their way around with the help of dimmed torchlight and the difficulties were met, for the most part, good-humouredly. Every day there were hilarious new stories of adventures – and misadventures the previous night on the way home.

Gloria still missed Shirley sorely. There were letters, of course. They wrote to each other every week without fail, but the laboriously penned letters in Shirley's rounded handwriting told Gloria very little about the things she really wanted to know. When her first postcard had arrived Gloria hadn't known whether to believe what the child had written or not. She knew her daughter was no liar, but, an avid cinema-goer from an early age, Shirley was given to daydreams and romancing. Perhaps, in her own way, she was just making the most of the traumatic break. But on making some enquiries about the address Gloria soon discovered that her daughter really *was* living in the country home of Tony Darrent and his wife Leonie Swann. Shirley had written that Mrs Darrent – or Miss Swann – had even asked her to dance for her and told her she was clever. Gloria was ecstatic with pride. She told all her friends at work about it, though most of them received the story with scepticism, exchanging disbelieving looks when her back was turned. They all knew of Gloria's high-flown ambitions for her daughter.

In the bedroom they had shared, the magazine pictures of Tony Darrent still adorned the walls and sometimes when she lay looking up at them, Gloria tried to imagine what it would be like actually sharing a home with her idol. Not that he was there much. According to Shirley's letters he had left his wife and daughter in the country and gone back to London the moment war was declared and he hadn't been back since. Gloria wondered if he and the glamorous Leonie were as happy together as the magazines would have their readers believe.

71

In the corner by the wardrobe the wind-up gramophone stood on its table, the pile of well-played records they both loved standing idle beside it. Listening to them without Shirl made Gloria cry so she didn't put them on very often now. There were all the songs from the Shirley Temple films, 'The Good Ship Lollipop', 'Animal Crackers' and the others, bought for Shirley to practise her dancing to. Then there were Gloria's favourites, 'Dancing in the Dark', 'The Way You Look Tonight', 'They Can't Take That Away From Me' and all the other lovely romantic numbers from Fred and Ginger's films. The hit from last year that Shirley and she had played till it almost wore out was the jolly 'Beer Barrel Polka', but Gloria's latest favourite was the hit from the new film *The Wizard of Oz*, 'Somewhere Over the Rainbow'. She had bought that one just last week after hearing it on the wireless. Listening to its wistful lyrics, she knew Shirl would love it and she longed to be able to play it to her.

Already she was saving up to make the trip up to Northamptonshire to see her. That would be a real treat. As well as looking forward to seeing Shirley she was dying to get a glimpse of her favourite stars – or at least to see the place where they lived. She'd begun to hope that maybe if things stayed as they were, she could even bring Shirley home again, though when she had suggested it to Pa he had shaken his head pessimistically.

'I don't trust this quiet,' he told her, sucking his breath in noisily and gazing up suspiciously at the sky. 'Them Gerries know 'ow to lull you into a false sense of security. Look at what they done already, over there in Poland and Czechoslovakia. Mark my words, one o' these nights they'll be over here – *then* we'll cop it. You leave the kiddie where she's safe, gel.'

His words struck a deathly chill through Gloria's bones and she prayed he was wrong. But all the same – better to be on the safe side.

Among the girls she worked with there were often tears these days. Ma had been right; the husbands and 'young men' of most of Gloria's workmates were being called up

72

or volunteering for service. In one way Gloria was glad she didn't have to go through the heartbreak, though in another she longed to be part of it all. Since Shirley's birth she had kept out of the way of fellers. The decent ones steered clear of her once they knew she had a kiddie anyway, and the ones who were interested were mainly after one thing. And anyway, most of the blokes her own age or older were either married or spoken for – not that *that* stopped some of them. A long time ago Gloria had made up her mind that, sadly, marriage wasn't for her. Not now. And after what had happened to her she wasn't prepared to risk her trust again. But the atmosphere of war, of sacrifice and emotional partings, of the longed-for letters and the prospect of ecstatic reunions stirred her to a new restlessness, making her wonder wistfully at times what her life might have been like, if things had been different.

The shortages that everyone had warned about hadn't occurred yet, though there was talk of rationing and price controls to come into effect soon. It was rumoured that ration books had already been printed and lay in big stacks somewhere up at Whitehall, waiting to be distributed. Here again, Pa was sceptical.

'It'll be a case of business as usual for them as can afford it, you see if I'm not right,' he predicted. 'Black market, just like it was in the last lot. Folks like us, tryin' to earn a decent livin' 'll be expected to keep prices low and to 'and most of our profits over to the bloody government. The workin' classes don't never win.'

When Shirley came out into the playground with her small group of friends, she saw that they were at it again. Over in the corner behind the lavs, well out of view of the school windows, a group of six or seven girls – some evacuees and the rest village kids – were gathered round a lonely figure in a green jumper. It had been going on ever since the first day of term. Even where Shirley stood on the steps she could hear their taunts floating across the playground:

'Polly Longfrock. She talks with a plum in her gob. Too posh for the likes of us. Go on, let's hear you speak then. Stuck-up cat. Teacher's pet. Rotten little snob.'

Shirley could see Imogen from where she stood. She was taller than the other kids. Her face white, she stood with her back pressed against the wall, red-eyed from crying. At first they hadn't been able to get to her. She'd remained aloof, ignoring them just as she had Shirley. But the constant jeers and taunts had chipped away her natural reserve until at last her persecutors found to their delight that they could make her cry whenever they wanted to. To begin with Shirley thought she would probably tell the teacher, or her mum, who would come down to the school and have it stopped. But to her surprise Imogen said nothing. Although each day must have been sheer misery, she never breathed a word about it to anyone, not even Shirley, who was obviously aware of her predicament.

'Come on, Shirl. Come and play skipping with us.' One of the group tugged at her arm. But Shirley shook her head.

'In a minute.'

Imogen had been nasty to her and when the teasing first began Shirley had felt triumphant. That'd show her what it felt like to be on the outside – disliked and unwanted. But as it went on getting worse day by day, it began to make her feel uncomfortable, then guilty and finally angry. It was unfair, so many against one – and for so long. She admired Imogen for not splitting, too. If she wanted to she could have had them all caned for what they were doing.

Making up her mind suddenly, Shirley strode determinedly across the playground and shoved her way through to the front of the gang of jeering kids.

'Wanna play skippin' with us, Imo-gen?'

The gang stopped their jeering and stared at her in surprise. Imogen stopped weeping and looked up. The ringleader, an older girl with sharp, spiteful features, was the first to break the shocked silence.

'Whatcher wanna play with a four-eyed snob like 'er for? She's ugly. Look at 'er teeth, they got iron bands on 'em.'

Shirley turned to face the girl, looking her up and down critically. 'Look oo's talkin'. *You* ain't got much room to shout, 'ave yer?' she said. 'Yer frock's all mucky and yer nose needs wipin'. Ain't you got an' 'anky? Uses yer sleeve, do yer?'

The rest of the gang began to snigger and their leader turned away, unwilling to provoke any more of Shirley's blunt criticisms.

'Aw, come on,' she said. 'Let's leave 'em to it. They ain't worth botherin' with.' From a safe distance she called: 'You wait, Shirley Rayner. I'll get you for this.'

'Smack yer silly face for you if you try,' Shirley returned shrilly.

The hubbub of playtime, momentarily stilled by the heated exchange, soon resumed and Shirley turned to Imogen. 'You all right?'

'Yes.' Imogen nodded, dabbing her eyes and putting her spectacles back on again. She sniffed and looked at Shirley. 'Thank you for making them stop.'

Shirley shrugged. ''S orl right. 'T ain't fair, six onto one. Do you wanna play skippin' then?'

Imogen smiled gratefully. 'Can I really? Yes please.'

Shirley's group, who had watched the whole encounter with fascination, accepted Imogen without questions. Seeing Shirley in action, they knew better than to object. For the rest of playtime they took turns at the rope and Imogen proved herself adept at the skill, executing 'bumps' and even 'double bumps' with an expertise that earned her the respect of every one of the group.

As Shirley was walking out through the school gates at lunchtime, Imogen caught up with her. 'Shall we walk home together?' she asked.

Shirley looked round. ''S orl right. Them kids won't touch you again.'

'I know,' Imogen said. 'I'd like to walk with you anyway.' She gave Shirley a sidelong glance. 'May I?'

'If you want.' Suddenly Shirley smiled at her. 'Come on. I've got a penny in me knickers pocket. We'll get some gobstoppers at the shop. Race you – last one there's a soppy 'aporth.'

'Why didn't you never split on 'em?' Shirley asked with her mouth half full of bread and jam.

The girls were sitting under the hedge in the field next to Toffee's paddock. Nanny Jarvis had packed up raspberry jam sandwiches and a bottle of lemonade so that they could have a picnic. She'd been relieved and delighted to see the two of them getting along at last.

Imogen pulled at the long grasses. 'I didn't think anyone would be on my side,' she said.

'The teacher would've,' Shirley said. 'She'd've given 'em the cane.'

Imogen lifted her shoulders helplessly. 'They'd have been worse than ever to me if I'd sneaked, though, wouldn't they?'

Shirley had to agree that they probably would. 'What about your mum then? She'd've gone down there and given 'em what for, wouldn't she?'

'I don't think so.' Imogen sighed. 'Mummy doesn't like me, you see. She'd probably have been pleased.'

Shirley was shocked. 'She must *like* you. You're 'er little girl.'

Imogen shrugged. 'I heard her telling Nanny once that she never wanted a baby at all. She thinks I'm ugly just as those girls at school do. She wishes I'd never been born.'

Shirley stared at her incredulously. At home in London she knew a few mums who didn't seem to care all that much. She knew some kids who didn't have proper clothes or even enough to eat. But if anything went wrong, or someone did something to hurt their kids, they sprang fiercely to their defence like enraged tigresses defending their cubs. The attitude Imogen described was totally alien to her. She had always thought that posh kids had more of everything – including love.

'I thought ladies always wanted babies,' she said thoughtfully. 'If they don't, why do they keep 'avin 'em?

P'raps it's 'cause she don't see you much. What with you bein' away at boardin' school an' everythin'. Glor and me ain't never been away from each other. We even sleep together at 'ome.'

'Who's Glor?'

'Gloria. She's my mum. I ain't got no dad so me an' Glor, we share everythin'.'

Imogen looked at her with envy. 'I bet you wish she was here.'

Shirley nodded. 'Yes. But she's savin' up to come an' see me. That's if your mum'll let 'er.'

'Of course she will. Mummy'd do anything for you. I expect it's because you're pretty.'

'Is that why you hated me?' Shirley asked. 'Were you jealous?'

'*No*.' Imogen looked away. 'Well – a bit.' She selected a juicy grass and began to chew it. 'I can't help being ugly. It's not my fault.'

'You're not *really* ugly,' Shirley said, studying Imogen closely. 'If you didn't wear them specs, an' that – that wotsname thing on your teeth . . .'

'I won't always have to wear them,' Imogen told her quickly. 'The dentist says that by the time I'm twelve or thirteen I'll be able to do without the brace. And if I keep wearing my glasses my squint will come right too – eventually.' She looked at Shirley's hair with envy. 'I wish my hair curled like yours, though.'

'You could do it up in rags,' Shirley said helpfully. 'I'll 'elp you if you like. Ain't you got any nice frocks?'

Imogen shook her head. 'Mummy says there isn't any point. Apart from school I only come here to Houlton and most of the time I just play in the garden or ride Toffee.'

Shirley was silent, assessing her new friend. 'I bet Glor'd make you some frocks,' she said. 'She gets lovely stuff down the Brick Lane market. It's ever so cheap. When she comes we'll ask her, shall we?'

Imogen smiled. 'Do you really think she would?' She paused, licking her lips nervously. 'Shirley, I've been thinking. There's something I want to ask you.'

'Yeah? Go on,' Shirley encouraged.

'Well, you said once that you'd teach me to tap-dance.'

Shirley grinned delightedly. 'I will if you want.'

Imogen blushed. 'I thought if I could do something like that Mummy might like me better.' She bit her lip anxiously. 'I'm terribly clumsy, though, I'll probably be no good at it.'

''Course you will,' Shirley said cheerfully. 'You should'a seen some o' them in our class. Like cart 'orses they was when they first come. Now they can dance as good as Ginger Rogers.' She stopped, her face suddenly serious. 'Tell yer what, Imo-gen. If I learn you to dance, will you learn me to talk proper?'

Imogen looked surprised. 'Do you *want* to? I thought everyone hated the way I speak.'

'Nah – they're all jealous really. That's why they tease you. Didn't you know that? They used to do it to me – cause of me frocks an' that. That's how I know.' She paused to frown thoughtfully. 'I wouldn't talk like it at school – not at first. But I'd like to know how to so's you 'n' me could talk the same – when we're here at 'ome.'

'At *h*ome,' Imogen corrected with a smile.

'At *h*-ome. That be''er?'

Imogen shook her head. 'Be*tt*er, you mean.'

'Right, be*tt*er.' Shirley's face broke into a delighted grin. 'See? I'm learnin' real quick.'

'You can ride Toffee whenever you want,' Imogen offered. 'I'll show you how to ride him properly. Maybe Daddy will even get you a pony of your own.'

'Cor!' Shirley's hand flew to her mouth as she gasped with delight. The two girls laughed delightedly. Suddenly the future looked much brighter – for both of them.

Claire had decided to go home. She would remain in London for a while, however. There seemed to be no immediate danger. Her family in Jersey didn't seem unduly troubled about the war in Europe. Surely it wouldn't affect them? The War Office had said that the Channel Islands would be of no strategic value to either side. The tourist office was still advertising holidays as usual and there really seemed no cause for concern. They urged their daughter to return home again as soon as possible. She would surely be safer there than in London and, like Tony, they were horrified at her notion of joining one of the women's services. So Claire had decided she would stay with Peter Jason till he had managed to find a suitable replacement and then leave for Jersey. The longer she remained, the harder the parting with Tony would be for her.

When they left Suffolk they had returned to London separately; she to her flat in Earls Court; he to the Mayfair apartment he and Leonie occupied when they were working in town. Apart from the taped windows and heaps of unsightly sandbags, precautions they were already used to, London looked the same. So normal that it was hard to believe that the country was at war. There had been no onslaught of menacing bombers as prophesied and people were beginning to tell each other that all Hitler's dark threats were just so much sabre-rattling. Places of entertainment reopened and the city's night life slowly began to return to normal. In spite of the blackout it was a case of business as usual, and the public let out its collective long-held breath.

One of Tony's first priorities was a visit to Peter Jason's home in Richmond. He found him and his wife, Eve, having tea in the pleasant garden that ran down to the river. They looked happy and relaxed, sitting on the lawn in the autumn sunshine. Eve welcomed Tony warmly and went off into the house to get another cup.

'I've been hoping you'd come. I've got good news, old boy,' Peter said brightly. 'Theatres are to open again the week after next; at least, that's the latest tip that going round.'

'I was hoping you'd have something a bit more positive to tell me,' Tony said tetchily. The sight of Peter sitting there dressed in flannels and an open-necked shirt, puffing away on his pipe as though all was right with the world, caught him on the raw. 'Have you been lazing about here like this ever since I last saw you? Haven't you done anything at *all* on our behalf?'

Peter frowned. 'As it happens, I reopened the office unofficially last Monday,' he said. 'I've been going up to town every morning – and working my backside off at home the rest of the day, if you really want to know. What's the matter with you? It's the same for all of us, you know. I stand to lose by the war, too. I'm losing my secretary for a start.'

'I know.' Tony sank into a deckchair and pushed his fingers through his hair. 'I'm sorry, Peter. It's just the uncertainty. Good news about the theatres, of course. Am I to take it that *Sunshine Sally* is to open again, then?'

Peter shook his head, puffing thoughtfully at his pipe. 'Well, no. There was a meeting of management and backers yesterday. As you know, the run was to have ended at the beginning of December anyway and the bookings were all cancelled with the shutdown. At the meeting the general consensus was that *Sunshine Sally* was too frivolous a subject for the present climate, so it was decided unanimously to call it a day as from now.'

'What about the new film?'

Peter shrugged. 'As that's a light-hearted subject, the same probably goes for that too. For the time being, anyway.'

'I see.' Tony could hardly conceal his relief. 'Were you there – at the meeting, I mean?' he asked.

'Yes – on your behalf. I tried to get hold of you as soon as I heard about the meeting, but I couldn't locate you anywhere. By the way, Leonie has been onto me several times. I let her think we'd been in touch.'

Tony gave him a sheepish sidelong glance. 'I see. Thanks, Peter. So – not such good news after all. Seems we're in for a long rest.'

A smile twitched at the corners of Peter's mouth and he paused to refill his pipe. 'As a matter of fact, no. At least, not in your case. The backers were talking about putting on something patriotic to stir up the right spirit and lift morale. It seemed likely that they were prepared to put their money where their mouths were, so I suggested Shakespeare – *Henry V*.'

Tony sat upright in his chair, his attention suddenly riveted. 'Go on. Did they buy it?'

'They were very enthusiastic and so was the management. Striking while the iron was hot, I went on to suggest you for the name part.'

Tony held his breath. 'And . . .?'

'They weren't too sure at first, then I reminded them about your long family tradition of classical acting.'

What Peter had actually said was that people who wouldn't normally touch anything by William Shakespeare with a barge pole would flock to see it if Tony Darrent were starring.

'I see. That did the trick, did it?'

Peter smiled. 'Certainly did. They want to see you as soon as possible. Graeme Hamilton will be directing. I know you and he get along well together. And I insisted that you're to have your choice of supporting cast. If you're agreeable I'll start drawing up the contract at once, then you and Graeme can get together and talk about auditioning.'

Tony was elated. All he could think about was getting to a telephone to tell Claire. Then a sobering thought struck him. 'What about Leonie? Have you told her about *Sunshine Sally* closing and the film being postponed?'

Peter took his pipe out of his mouth and studied the bowl. 'No, old son, I rather thought that was your province.'

Tony sighed. 'She's not going to like it one little bit. And you *are* her agent.' He brightened. 'Tell you what. Why don't you and Eve come up to Houlton for the weekend?'

'Sorry, can't be done. Too much on at the moment.'

'You mean you don't want to face up to your responsibilities.'

'Not mine – yours. You could always find her a part in *Henry*, I suppose.'

Tony shook his head. 'Come off it, Peter. Leonie's a musical-comedy actress. She couldn't handle a Shakespeare role and you know it. It might be different if it were some other play, but *Henry V*? Not a chance. The only female part is Princess Katherine and she doesn't speak French for a start. Apart from that there's only the serving girl, and I can't see her taking kindly to that.'

'Mmm.' Peter thought for a moment. 'ENSA would be ideal for her, of course. They'll be looking for glamorous singers to entertain the troops.'

Tony winced. 'I wouldn't suggest it if I were you. Not if you want to walk away with your teeth intact.'

They both laughed, then Peter said casually: 'Everything all right between you two, is it?'

Tony looked up. 'Of course. Why do you ask?'

Peter leaned out of his chair to tap out his pipe against the table leg. 'I've noticed that your latest, er, *diversion* seems to be touching you a little more deeply than usual, if you don't mind my saying so, old boy. I just wondered if Leonie might have noticed too. Women have an uncanny instinct for that kind of thing.'

'None of your business, actually, Peter,' Tony said bluntly. 'But as it happens it's over anyway.'

'Really? Maybe that's just as well – for all concerned.'

Pretending he hadn't heard, Tony got to his feet. 'I'd better be off,' he said. 'I've one or two other calls to make. Tell Eve I'm sorry to rush off, will you. And if you change your mind about that weekend at Houlton . . .'

Peter returned his wave and watched him stride away across the lawn towards the house. 'Handsome sod,' he muttered to himself. How many hearts had he carelessly and unfeelingly broken over the years? Claire had told him of her intention of returning home as soon as she returned from Suffolk and he'd guessed that her decision had more than a little to do with Tony. Would she be going home to Grève de Lecq as heartwhole as she had left it? Shrugging, he told himself that Tony was right. It was none of his business and anyway, there was nothing he could do about it. Perhaps now that Tony was getting the role he wanted, he would settle down and stop womanising. This time it had done neither his work nor his temper any damned good at all.

Leonie had agreed enthusiastically to Shirley's request to have her mother at Houlton for the weekend. Anything to lift the sheer boredom of being buried alive in this hole while Tony had the satisfaction of getting a new show off the ground. At the time she agreed to Gloria's visit she hadn't known that Tony would also be home that weekend.

He arrived quite unexpectedly on the Friday evening and after dinner he told her about his visit with Peter down at Richmond. He had already told her over the telephone a week ago that the show would not reopen but after dinner that evening he broke the news to her that there was no part for her in the new production that was to take its place. Leonie was incredulous. She had been prepared for *Sunshine Sally* to close. The run had been almost at an end anyway. But she'd thought then that she had the new film to look forward to, not to mention Noël's half-promised play. Now it looked horribly likely that she was doomed to stick out the duration of the war on her own at Longueville Hall while Tony cavorted around the West End stage brandishing a sword and making a complete twerp of himself in hose and doublet. If she wasn't so angry she could have laughed.

'How convenient! Just what you wanted. Congratulations, darling.' Her eyes flashed dangerously. 'It won't run, of course. Who do you think will want to come and see you in that dreary old drivel? And may one ask why isn't there a part for me in it?'

'There's only one female part of any importance,' he explained. 'That of Princess Katherine. And most of her lines are delivered in French.'

'I could learn.'

Tony shook his head irritably. 'You're not right for it, Leonie. Katherine is shy – timid almost.'

'I *am* an actress, just in case you've forgotten.'

'A musical actress. It's just not *you*, Leonie.'

'Oh, come on, Tony.' She tossed back her hair. 'Surely we could get someone to write in some numbers for me.'

He snorted irritably. 'Don't talk such utter rubbish.'

'Why is it rubbish? They do it all the time in Shakespeare plays. What about *Midsummer-Night's Dream* and *Twelfth Night*?'

'They are musical plays. This is a drama.' Tony strode across the room to take a cigarette from the box on the coffee table and light it. 'Anyway, it's already cast.'

There was a long silence as Leonie watched him walk to the window and blow out a cloud of smoke. 'I see,' she said. 'So there's really no more to be said, is there?'

'Not really, no.'

Leonie took a cigarette herself and lit it with deliberate calm. 'May one ask who she is – this Sarah Bernhardt you've chosen to play opposite you?'

'Her name is Juliet Fabergé. She's a relative newcomer.'

Leonie laughed. 'The stage name is a little pretentious, don't you feel?'

'As it happens it's her own. She's half French.'

'How convenient. Aren't you lucky?' Leonie drew hard on her cigarette and narrowed her eyes at him through the smoke. 'She's young, of course. Attractive?'

'Naturally. You don't imagine I'd pick an ugly old crone to play the part of a beautiful young French princess, do you?'

Leonie stubbed out her half-smoked cigarette viciously. 'No, darling. That wouldn't be your style at all. Clever of you to pick an unknown, too. She won't take any of the limelight from you, will she? You'll be able to bag top billing – *and* get the best of the notices.' She threw him a challenging look. 'What did she have to do to get the part? Or shouldn't I ask?'

'Don't be so bloody childish.' Tony turned angrily and took a step towards her, then checked himself and took a deep breath. 'Look, Leonie, I'm really sorry there isn't anything on offer for you at the moment, but there will be.

Peter's working hard on it. I'm pretty sure he'll be able to get you some radio work and maybe some concerts too – personal appearances. There's some talk of entertainment for the factory workers.'

'Factory workers, eh?' Leonie laughed. 'What *fun*! It's a wonder to me that you haven't suggested sending *me* into a factory – or down a coal mine, perhaps. I'm sure you'd love to see me packed off to help the war effort.'

When Molly Jarvis returned to the kitchen with the coffee tray, she shook her head. 'Going at it hammer and tongs up there, they are,' she told Jim. 'Seems Mr Tony is going to do a Shakespeare play in London and there isn't a part for Madam in it.'

Jim grinned wryly. 'Oh dear, oh dear. That'll have set the cat among the pigeons and no mistake. Is she mad with him?'

'Mad isn't the word,' Molly told him, unloading the tray and beginning to wash up. 'She's in one of those sharp-as-a-dagger moods of hers. Claws out, ready to fly. I wouldn't be in his shoes.'

Tony and Leonie passed the evening in tense silence, speaking to each other only when they were obliged to. In their room later Tony collected up his things. 'I'll sleep in the dressing room.'

'No!' Leonie turned to him suddenly. 'Darling, don't go. I'm sorry if I was bitchy. It's just so dreary here all by myself with nothing to do and nothing to look forward to. I was disappointed, that's all.'

Tony sighed. 'Of course. I understand.'

She held out her arms to him. 'Stay with me tonight, darling. I've missed you.'

She wore a peach chiffon negligee trimmed with cream lace, and with her dark hair tumbling over her shoulders she looked quite breathtakingly beautiful. At one time Tony would have been delighted at her gesture, but now he had to force himself to put his arms around her and hold her close. He felt sorry for her. She was having a rough time and she was desperately worried about her future career. He knew and understood that. In the past, if she had looked at him like this, clearly inviting him to make love to her, he'd have taken up the offer gladly, whether or not there was someone else in the offing. But ever since the arrival of Claire in his life he had found himself wanting to be completely faithful to her.

Leonie looked up at him, her lips soft and inviting. 'We are friends again, aren't we, darling?'

'Of course.'

'Then . . . shall we go to bed?' There was a flicker of uncertainty in the eyes that held his. She was losing him; she could feel it – sense it in every nerve. And she knew that if she lost him, she would lose everything. She would never act again without his guidance and support. Her first reaction had been to make him suffer for indulging his own ambitions without a thought for hers. But common sense stepped in, telling her that if she were to win him back she must play the right cards. Tony was a sensual man, and he had loved her devotedly and passionately – before Imogen. However much she feared another pregnancy, she must allow him back into her bed. Not only that, but she must prove to him that she could give him more than any of the other women in his life; that she was the only woman who could truly satisfy him.

Slipping her arms out of the peignoir she let it slip to the floor with a soft whisper. Tony stared at her, transfixed. It was so long since he had seen her naked that he had forgotten the exquisite beauty of her body, her perfect proportions, the high, firm breasts and smooth creamy skin. Her eyes were dark and luminous as she stood motionless, barely breathing as she looked up at him. Her lips, devoid of make-up, were petal-soft and full. He felt his heart beginning to quicken and took an involuntary step backwards, physically resisting the magnetic pull of her.

'What is it, darling?' She took a step towards him. 'You're not still cross with me?' She loosened his robe and slipped her arms around his waist, running her fingers lightly up and down the bare skin of his back. 'Please, darling – please love me. It's been so long.'

Almost without being aware that he did it, his arms pulled her against him. 'I – thought you didn't . . . that you were afraid that . . .'

'You'll be careful.' Her lips were warm against the corner of his mouth. 'You know how to be careful. It'll be all right, won't it, darling? I do love you so. I always have – always will. I need you – now.'

His control snapped. After all, she was his wife, he told himself as he bent to scoop her up into his arms. If he wanted to make love to his wife, surely to God there was nothing wrong in that? Putting her down on the bed, he threw off his robe and joined her there. Leonie enfolded him in her arms and gave herself with all the passion she possessed, carefully closing her mind to the risk she was taking – the possibility that so repelled her. Closing her eyes, she concentrated on the art of lovemaking, employing all the little tricks she had learned to please him in the old days; teasing, holding back a little and then throwing aside all inhibitions to let the searing fire of her unleashed passion devour them both.

Driven by the powerful urge she created in him, Tony was momentarily oblivious. He was aware of nothing but two bodies sharing one all-consuming sensation. Time hung suspended. No one and nothing else existed for him. But at the moment of climax it was Claire's face he saw and not Leonie's. Throwing back his head, he cried out her name.

As he collapsed on top of her, his body trembling convulsively, Leonie felt numb with shock and fear. *Claire*, so that was her name? Who was she? Leonie knew no one of that name, but there was no denying that Tony had thought only of her while they made love. She turned her face into the pillow. In that moment she knew the bitterness of defeat.

Gloria felt as though she'd been travelling for weeks. The train from Euston had been late and from the start the platform had been full of impatient, bad-tempered passengers, nerves frayed by the delay. Gloria climbed aboard, fending off the thrusting elbows of her fellow travellers with her suitcase. She found a seat, only to give it up fifteen minutes out of London to a frail old gentleman who looked perilously close to collapse.

The journey to Northampton had taken more than twice as long as it should, and then she had discovered that Houlton was a six-mile bus ride out of town – and that the railway and bus stations were inconveniently situated on either side of the town. Finally she had alighted from the green single-decker bus outside Houlton post office, lugging her heavy suitcase wearily after her. It wasn't that she had brought that many clothes, but at the last minute she had decided to bring the gramophone and records. Shirley might as well have the benefit of them. Gloria never got time to play her records nowadays anyway, what with her civil-defence classes and fire-watching duty at the Adelphi.

'Can you tell me the way to Longueville Hall?' she asked a man coming out of the Post Office.

'Yes. Walk up to the crossroads.' He pointed. 'Then take the left fork. There's a lane about half a mile along. Turn down there and you'll come to it. Big gates with the name carved in the pillars.'

It sounded quite a walk. Gloria picked up her case resignedly, fervently wishing she'd left the gramophone at home. 'How far down the lane is it?' she asked.

'Oh, not far,' the man said cheerfully. 'About three-quarters of a mile, I'd say.'

She felt as though she'd been walking for hours when a car drew up beside her and a voice said: 'Hello there. You wouldn't be Mrs Rayner, would you – Shirley's mother?'

Gloria blushed bright red as she turned and found herself looking straight into the eyes of the man she had adored from afar. 'Oh – er, yes. I am.'

He smiled the famous smile and reached across to open the passenger door for her. 'Wonderful. Jump in. Just throw your suitcase into the back.'

Gloria sank gratefully into the leather upholstery of the Rolls and breathed in the perfume of wealth and success. If only all the others at the Adelphi could see her now! If only she had a camera with her.

'Jim, our handyman, has been up to the village to meet the last two buses,' Tony Darrent was saying to her. 'He brought the children with him. They were so disappointed when you weren't on either bus.'

Gloria wanted to tell him she was sorry she was late but that she was glad it was in his car she would arrive. But when she opened her mouth to speak, something seemed to have happened to her throat and no sound came out. She thought of all the cool, smart, sophisticated things she would have said if she was like Joan Crawford or Bette Davis. Instead she sat with her eyes on the road and her cheeks pink, mumbling her thanks and making a stumbling apologetic remark about the trains and the weather. She was glad she'd worn the blue coat she had made herself, though, and the little frothy black hat perched on top of her blonde Veronica Lake hairstyle. Everyone had said she looked nice when she was ready to leave this morning.

They drove in through the gateway. Tony explained to her that the gates had been taken for salvage and that new wooden ones were being made. When she saw the house she caught her breath in wonderment. Fancy her Shirl living in a place like this! It was just like something off the pictures. Tony pulled up outside the front door. It opened and out tumbled Shirley with another, taller child. Shirley hurled herself down the steps and into Gloria's arms. Laughing and crying both at the same time, they clung to each other, hugging and kissing, while Imogen stood to one side, looking awkward.

'Glor, this is my friend Imogen.' Shirley pulled Gloria across to where the other girl stood.

'Hello, Imogen.' Gloria held out her hand. 'Pleased to meet you. Shirl has told me such a lot about you in her letters.'

The girl shook hands solemnly. 'Good afternoon, Mrs Rayner. We've been looking forward to your visit.'

'Gloria, please. Everyone calls me that.'

'Nanny Jarvis has had tea ready for ages,' Shirley said, pulling her mother up the steps. 'Come in and meet everyone else.'

But a smiling Molly Jarvis, who was waiting in the doorway, insisted that Gloria be allowed to go to her room to freshen up after her journey. Tea could wait another few minutes, she told the excited girls.

Gloria was totally stunned by everything she saw. She had expected to be sharing Shirley's room and when Mrs Jarvis had shown her to a room of her own on the first floor she had been slightly disappointed at first, but when she saw inside she changed her mind. The room was enormous and airy. You could have dropped the whole of the flat in Angel Row into it and still had room to spare. The furnishings were luxurious and it had the most breathtaking view of the garden. Standing at the window looking out she saw acres of green lawns and flowerbeds. She was surprised to see that there were still flowers blooming, too, even though it was well into autumn. She could see the sparkle of glass in the distant kitchen garden, and she even fancied she could glimpse the blue water of the swimming pool Shirl had written about. The whole house was like something out of a fairy tale.

But the thing that had shaken her even more than the house was Shirl. She had grown so much, for a start. Her skin and eyes glowed with health and the sun had sprinkled freckles across her nose and cheeks. Her limbs had rounded out, too. Now she looked more like the real Shirley than ever before. But it was the way she *spoke* that really shook Gloria. The natural cockney tones had faded almost to nothing. She spoke with what Pa would have called a 'plum in her mouth'. Gloria couldn't make up her mind whether she liked it or not. It was a little worrying – almost as though Shirley were growing away from her and turning into someone entirely different. On the other hand, this might just be the chance to get one foot on the ladder to success that Gloria had always dreamed of for her.

Unaware of the ordeal she was putting her guest through, Leonie had insisted that they all took tea together in the drawing room. Gloria changed into her best black skirt and new little blouse-jacket she had made out of a remnant of scarlet crêpe-de-Chine. Leonie admired it at once.

'I saw one just like it in *Vogue* last week,' she observed. 'By Molyneux.'

Gloria, who was trying hard to drink her tea with one finger daintily crooked, said: 'That's right, Molyneux. I got the idea from *Vogue*. Ma's friend at the newsagent's lets me have it if she's got a copy left over. I copy the fashions out of it.'

'How *clever*! It must save you an absolute fortune in dressmaker's fees.'

Gloria laughed. 'It's a case of 'avin' to. If I didn't make my own things I'd have to buy cheap 'n' cheerful.' She glanced across at Shirley sitting there so politely, eating her little cucumber sandwiches as to the manner born. 'I brought the old grammy, Shirl,' she said. 'And all the records you like. You'll be able to practise your dancin' now.'

'Oh, how *kind*,' Leonie said. 'They must have been so heavy for you to carry. But there was no need. I've been playing the piano for Shirley to dance to.'

Gloria felt slightly crestfallen. 'Oh, I see. That's very good of you.'

'Not at all. I've nothing else to do at the moment and Shirley is so talented. It's a joy to watch her.'

Gloria looked across the room at her daughter and wondered if it was her imagination that the child avoided her eyes. She cleared her throat and turned her attention to Imogen, who seemed almost as ill at ease as she was. 'Do you dance, lovie?' she asked.

Imogen looked at Shirley, who nudged her and whispered, 'Go on. Tell them.'

'Shirley's been teaching me, actually.'

'And she's doing ever so well,' Shirley put in. 'Soon as we've got a routine worked out for her she's going to do it for you, Mrs Darrent.'

Leonie's delicately arched eyebrows rose slightly. 'Well, *well*.' She smiled at Gloria. 'These two are terribly good for each other, you know. They surprise me more each day. At first I thought they'd never hit it off, but now they're just like sisters.'

The door opened to admit Tony. Oblivious to the impact this entrance had on Gloria, he glanced round the room, slightly surprised to find a tea party taking place. 'Ah, there you are, then. Any tea?'

'Of course, darling. I was beginning to wonder where you'd got to.' Leonie said, reaching for the teapot. 'Our guest must think you dreadfully rude, coming in so late.' She treated Gloria to one of her blinding smiles. 'I think you'd better ask Gloria to forgive you, don't you?'

Gloria blushed as Tony turned his attention upon her. Sitting beside him in the car she had hardly dared to look at him. Now that they were face to face she saw that he was far better-looking than any of his pictures.

'Please, Gloria, forgive me,' he said theatrically, bending towards her. He added in an undertone: 'If you don't, my wife will never speak to me again.'

Gloria giggled, acutely embarrassed. Did people like them always talk like this – in riddles and put-on voices so that you'd no idea what they meant and what they didn't? Tony had seemed so ordinary and friendly in the car earlier. Now it was almost as though he and his wife were acting in a play. She wished she could escape and be alone with Shirl.

Leonie, the smile still firmly glued to her face, was shrewdly studying the pretty cockney girl who was Shirley's mother. She was younger than she'd imagined, and attractive in an obvious sort of way. Out of the corner of her eye she observed that Tony thought so too. But then Tony had always had an eye for this kind of girl – at least, he had before this present infatuation had taken hold of him. The girl was quite besotted with him, of course; speechless and practically paralysed with adoration. Leonie took in the flushed cheeks and shining eyes. It was quite pathetic really.

It was then that the idea hit her – hit her with such a force that she almost dropped her cup. It was so simple, and – she hoped – so effective. Very carefully, so as not to let her excitement show, she put down her cup and said evenly:

'When the girls have gone to bed, you *will* dine with us, won't you Gloria?'

Gloria bit her lip uncertainly. She'd never actually *dined* before. Suppose she disgraced herself – used the wrong knife and fork or something? 'Oh, well . . .' she began.

'There'll only be us,' Leonie went on hurriedly. 'We don't stand on ceremony. And we'd *love* to have your company, wouldn't we, Tony?'

'Sorry – what?' Tony, who hadn't been listening, looked at the expectant, upturned faces and realised that his agreement on something or other was required. 'Oh, *yes*,' he said enthusiastically. 'Of course.'

Leonie smiled. It would work, this plan of hers. It would be an absolute piece of cake.

'I'm planning a Christmas charity concert,' Leonie announced, smiling at Gloria across the lighted candles. 'I haven't found a suitable venue yet but I'm confident that I soon shall.' She helped herself to more cheese and biscuits. 'I'd like to have your permission for darling little Shirley to perform,' she went on, smiling at Gloria. 'I was going to ask you that anyway, but now that I've met you I've had the most *marvellous* brain wave.' Enjoying the suspense she was creating, she bit into a cracker and chewed thoughtfully. 'You're so clever with your needle, Gloria. What would you say to designing and making the costumes? We'd put your name on the programme, of course. Can't you just see it? *Costumes by Gloria Rayner*. It's such a pretty name.'

Gloria's mouth dropped open in surprise. '*Me*? Oh, but surely I live too far away to be of any help to you?'

Leonie smiled. 'Ah, yes, but you see I've thought of that.' She looked at Tony. 'My husband is to open soon a new play in the West End, but he'll be joining us here every weekend, won't you, darling? In fact, he'll be helping me with the production. He could pick you up at some given point and drive you up.'

Gloria looked doubtfully across at Tony. 'I have to work till half-ten on Saturdays.'

'And so will I once we open,' Tony put in. It was the first he'd heard of this concert idea and he was wondering just what Leonie was up to.

'Well, of course. I've thought of that,' Leonie said. 'Tony, you could collect Gloria from her cinema and drive her up here on Saturday nights after the show. We'd have all day Sunday and then you could drive back to town on Monday mornings.' She turned to Gloria. 'I don't suppose you have to go in till the afternoons, do you?'

'Well, no, but . . .'

'It would mean you'd see Shirley every weekend, too, of course,' she went on, playing her trump card. 'It would mean *so* much to her, I know.'

Gloria felt a tingle of excitement. The dining room with its gleaming table, flowers and candles had impressed her enough. But now this . . . 'Well, if you really think I could do it. It sounds ever so exciting.' Turning to Tony, she asked shyly: 'What do you think, Mr Darrent?'

He gave Gloria the smile his fans described as 'bone-melting'. 'I think it's a splendid idea, Gloria. I'm sure we'll all have the most tremendous fun. And please – you will call me Tony, won't you? After all, if we're all going to be working together we might as well be chums.'

Chapter Five

Leonie's Christmas charity concert promised to be an enormous success. The snap decision to organise it had surprised even her, but once it was made she had thrown herself into the project with the energy and enthusiasm usually reserved for her stage performances. She became so engrossed that she almost forgot her original reason for initiating it. Almost – but not quite. Tony certainly seemed more relaxed since he'd been seeing Gloria regularly. So far she had no evidence that his interest in the girl was more than friendly, but from the adoring, goggle-eyed way that Gloria looked at him she felt sure it was only a matter of time before an affair started. Tony never could resist flattery. Maybe she would help him forget the woman who had bewitched him and they could all get back to normal.

The venue she finally found was a disused cinema in Northampton. Just before the outbreak of war it had been scheduled for demolition, but the town council, who had purchased it in order to carry out a redevelopment scheme, now indefinitely postponed, had succumbed to Leonie's charm and lent it willingly and free of charge when told that the proceeds of the concert were to go to the war effort.

To Leonie's delight, she found that the interior was still intact, complete with seating and even a workable front drop. She set an army of voluntary helpers to work cleaning, repairing faulty equipment and making good where necessary.

Leonie occupied herself with compiling a variety programme of sketches and musical numbers taken from West End shows. She wheedled and cajoled permission from her various friends in the business, getting them to waive royalty fees by various means – some more devious than others. She decided to do a couple of numbers herself – songs that she would dedicate emotionally to all the wives and girlfriends left behind – and she had also persuaded one or two actor friends who were, like her, temporarily 'resting' to come and take part as celebrity guest artists. The supporting company she made up from members of local amateur dramatic and operatic societies, each one carefully auditioned and hand-picked.

At home Shirley rehearsed Imogen mercilessly. Using Gloria's wind-up gramophone, they rehearsed in secret in the swimming-pool changing room, well out of sight and sound of the house. Shirley was determined that the routine she had worked so hard to create must be perfect before Leonie was allowed to see them perform. She had chosen the music from Gloria's collection of records. It came from an Astaire–Rogers film and the song was 'Isn't This a Lovely Day?' Imogen, being taller, was to take the part of Fred and Shirley was Ginger. Gloria had been let in on the secret. She was to make white trousers and a striped blazer for Imogen and a long dress with romantically swirling skirt and puffed sleeves for Shirley. Jim Jarvis, who was building most of the scenery, had been persuaded to paint a bandstand backcloth to represent the one in the film.

When they performed their dance for Leonie she was almost speechless with amazement. She could hardly believe her gangling, awkward daughter could move so gracefully. In the sleek trousers and blazer Gloria had made her, she danced her part in the duo to perfection. There and then, to their delight, she allotted the girls the closing spot in the first half of the show.

Unaware of Leonie's plan for her, Gloria was enjoying her part in the preparation for the concert too. All her spare moments were taken working away on the sewing machine in the parlour in Angel Row. Leonie had provided most of the material, bought or begged from her various contacts in the theatrical-costumier trade. One hire firm had given her some costumes intended for disposal and Gloria had worked hard replacing beads and tarnished sequins, washing and starching collars and cuffs and generally transforming them until they looked as good as new.

But what she loved best was her weekends at Houlton. Every Saturday night after the last showing at the Adelphi she could change quickly and hurry to the corner of the street where Tony would pick her up in his car. Those drives through the frosty winter nights in Tony's Rolls were the highlight of her week, the most romantic thing that had ever happened to her.

At first Tony had chatted amiably to her during the drive about everyday things like her job and the films they had both enjoyed. Soon she forgot her awed shyness and learned to relax in his company. Then one night he suddenly said: 'Tell me about yourself, Gloria. You talk about Shirley and your job, but never about yourself.'

She felt herself blushing. 'There's nothing much to tell,' she told him. 'I was born and grew up in Whitechapel. I went to the council school till I was fourteen, then left to be apprenticed to Maison Juliette, a court dressmaker in the West End.'

'So that's where you learned to be such a wizard with the needle?'

'That's right.'

He glanced at her. 'Why did you give it up?'

Gloria shrugged. 'My Shirley came along. I thought her dad was going to marry me, but I was wrong. Turned out he already had a wife. Ma and Pa were good, letting me stay on and keep her. Well, when I was ready to work again they wouldn't have me back at Juliette's so I took the job at the Adelphi.'

'And you like it?'

'It's all right. The hours are a bit funny, but I love seeing all the films. I'd have liked to be an actress myself,' she admitted shyly, looking down at her hands. 'I don't suppose I'd ever have been clever enough, though, but maybe Shirl will some day.'

'And Shirley's father?' Tony glanced at her again and she felt herself going hot. Her kind of people didn't talk much about love and anyway most folk steered well clear of any mention of Shirley's dad.

'Oh, him. He hopped it,' she said. 'Scared stiff I'd make trouble for him, I expect. Never saw him again after I told him about the baby.'

'What rotten luck for you. Did you love him?' When she paused he added: 'I'm sorry, Gloria. I shouldn't have asked. Does it still hurt?'

'No,' she said truthfully. 'I was very young, not much more than a kid. Silly, too, I dare say. It seemed like the end of the world at the time, but now – well, I've got Shirl now, haven't I? She makes up for everything.'

'So there's never been anyone else?'

'No. Well, there wouldn't be, would there? No decent feller wants to take on some other bloke's kid.'

'That's rather a cynical way of looking at it.'

Gloria shrugged. 'Dunno about cynical. It's how it is. I don't mind. I've got used to it now.'

Tony was silent, his eyes on the dark road in front of him. Everyone had their problems. Not everyone could walk away from them. But Gloria's resigned acceptance was touching.

After that the horizons of their conversations during the drives widened and their acquaintance began to develop into a sincere friendship. Tony found her down-to-earth logic and candour refreshing. He felt she understood the human condition in a way that was unusual in women. Unlike most of the women he knew, she accepted people as they were and wasn't continually trying to change them to suit her. Perhaps best of all, they moved in entirely different circles and he knew that anything he said to her was unlikely to reach the ears of any of his own acquaintances.

When he asked her if she liked Shakespeare and she admitted that she didn't know, he brought her a ticket for the play. She went Up West on her evening off and sat enthralled in her front stall at the New Theatre, watching a new swashbuckling Tony Darrent playing Henry V with a vitality and panache that held her spellbound. Sitting there among the smart people in the posh seats, she was glad she had decided to wear the little black silk evening jacket she'd copied from a Hartnell design. Watching her painstakingly embroidering the shoulders with beads and sequins, Ma had admonished her for the waste of time and money. 'You'll never wear it. You know you won't,' she'd said. 'Where do you ever go to wear a thing like that?' But Gloria had hoped that some day an opportunity would come along.

Tony had invited her to come backstage afterwards and tell him what she thought of the show. She had never been backstage in a real theatre before and she wondered if she really dared go. At last her curiosity and the desire to see Tony and congratulate him got the better of her shyness. The stage doorkeeper had been told to expect her. He took her along to Tony's dressing room, where she found him sitting in front of the mirror, wearing a dressing gown and taking off his wig and make-up.

'Gloria!' He turned to beam at her, his eyes still smudged with black liner. 'How pretty you look! I was afraid you might not come. Just give me a minute and we'll go upstairs for a drink.' He turned back to the mirror and lavishly applied more cold cream. 'I want to hear your opinion of the play. Your honest opinion, mind – warts and all.'

She was so flattered that he actually wanted to know what she thought. *Her* – Gloria Doris Rayner from Angel Row who'd hardly known that William Shakespeare existed till tonight.

Seated in the cosy little bar that Tony called the green room, Gloria sipped her port and lemon, glancing hesitantly at him.

'I liked the play ever so much,' she said slowly. 'I'll be honest with you; I thought I wouldn't be able to understand it – written all them years ago – but I did. Well, most of it, anyway. It was a lovely story, specially the bit where he falls in love with the French princess.' She smiled at him shyly. 'I thought you were ever so romantic in that bit.'

'You haven't told me what you thought of the rest of my performance, though,' Tony said earnestly. 'Any fool can be romantic looking at a pretty girl like Juliet.'

'You're teasing me now,' Gloria said. 'You don't need people like *me* to tell you how good you are.'

'Ah, but that's where you're wrong. I do.' He put down his glass and leaned towards her. 'You see, I'll let you into a little secret. I've never actually played Shakespeare before. And this production was put on especially for people like you, Gloria. People who aren't familiar with Shakespeare, I mean. It's meant to bring him to the people – show that his plays are not just for the wealthy and privileged but for everyone to enjoy.'

Gloria looked at him with rounded eyes. 'No kiddin'? Are they really?'

'Of course. He wrote them for ordinary people back in the sixteenth century. They were performed right here in London, down by the Thames in open-air theatres. People would come in and walk about, eat, meet their friends. Theatregoing was a glorious, informal occasion in those days.'

'Didn't the actors mind? I mean – all that noise when they were trying to act.'

Tony laughed. 'I suppose they were used to it.' He covered her hand with his and looked into her eyes. 'So you enjoyed it? You're not just trying to please me?'

'Oh, no. I mean *yes*. It was lovely.'

'Marvellous.' He gave her hand a squeeze. 'I'd better get you home now or your mother will be worrying.' He tossed back the last of his drink and stood up, holding out his hand to her.

Long into the night Gloria lay thinking; about the brave, romantic King Henry; about Tony and the way he had held her hand. He was so wonderful, and she was so lucky to know him. Oddly enough she hadn't told her friends at work about the Saturday-night drives and their long talks. They wouldn't have believed her. And anyway, it was much too special to share.

Sundays were hard work in many ways: going to the theatre and fitting costumes; improvising; solving problems when someone dropped out of the cast and a person of an entirely different size and shape took over. Most weekends she came home with piles of more work to do – repairs, alterations – but she didn't mind. Watching the rehearsals and seeing the show slowly taking shape was so exciting. And being with Shirley, seeing how happy she was, was more than adequate reward.

Early on Sunday mornings Shirley, who was fast asleep when Gloria arrived late on Saturday night, would creep into her bedroom and wake her by snuggling up beside her. They would cuddle up together and tell each other all their news. It was most special hour in the week for both of them. One Monday morning at the beginning of December, as Shirley and Gloria were saying their goodbyes, Gloria whispered:

'Ma wanted me to tell you you're to come home for Christmas. And if things stay quiet like they are now you might be able to stay for good soon, Shirl. Won't that be lovely?' She was dismayed to see the child's face drop momentarily. *She'd rather stay here*, she told herself. This is getting to be more her home now than Angel Row is. The sad, unhappy feeling clouded her mind for the rest of the day.

At last the week of the concert arrived. By the time Tony and Gloria left London on the Saturday night, the first performance was already over. As she climbed into the passenger seat Gloria remarked wistfully that she wished they could have been there.

Tony shrugged. 'We saw the dress rehearsal last Sunday.'

'Yes, but with an audience it's so much more exciting. I'd love to have seen how the girls went down in their number.'

'The audience will have loved them,' Tony said with a smile. 'Imogen has surprised us all and it's all down to Shirley, you know.' He smiled at her. 'You have a very talented daughter.' After a pause he added: 'The only thing that worries me is what Leonie will do with herself once it's all over.'

'Won't she be in another play? I mean, doesn't she want to act any more?' Gloria asked.

'At the moment there isn't much call for her kind of work. There will be soon, of course. But try telling her that.'

Gloria was silent. Over the past weeks she had sensed the tension between them and guessed that their marriage wasn't as happy as the press and magazines would have the fans believe.

He turned to look at her as though he had read her thoughts. 'You must have noticed these past weeks that our marriage isn't all it should be.'

Gloria shifted uncomfortably in her seat. 'It's none of my business,' she muttered.

He went on as though he hadn't heard: 'Leonie and I haven't been . . . what you'd call close since Imogen was born.' He looked at her. 'In a way I'm rather like you, Gloria. I have a daughter whom I love, but because of her I have to face life without the kind of love all human beings have a right to.'

'I'm sorry.' It sounded so inadequate, but she didn't really understand what he meant and she couldn't think of what else to say.

He smiled at her. 'You don't make judgements, do you? You're a good friend, Gloria. May I tell you something? Completely in confidence, of course.'

'Well . . . yes, of course – if you want to.'

'I know I can trust you, you see. There aren't many people I can say that to, believe me.' He slowed down and pulled the car over to the side of the road, switching off the engine. Taking out his cigarette case he offered her one, then took one himself and lit them both. In the brief flare of the match she saw the pain in his eyes and wondered what she was about to hear.

'There's someone else in my life, Gloria.' He inhaled deeply and blew out the smoke. 'Not just an affair, but someone very special, whom I love very deeply. She and I were going away together. I was about to ask Leonie for a divorce. Then came this damned war.'

'Oh.' She swallowed the shock that quickened her heart and made herself look at him. He had wound down the window and was leaning his elbow on the frame. In the darkness his eyes shone luminously as though there were tears in them. 'Do you . . . do you still see each other?' she asked, sensing his need to talk about it.

'No.' He looked at her. 'Her home is in the Channel Islands. She came to London to work. She's gone back there to be with her family. It was I who urged her to go, because she'll be safe there. But, *Christ*, Gloria, I miss her.'

'I see.' She bit her lip, wishing she could think of something more intelligent to say. She was beginning to sound like a parrot, What did he really expect of her? Suddenly he threw away his cigarette and wound up the window.

'I'm sorry, Gloria. I'm embarrassing you with my confidences. I've no right to burden you with it. It's just that sometimes I feel I'll go stark, staring, bloody mad if I can't talk to someone about her. And you – well, you're always so sympathetic, because you've been through it too.'

Immediately she understood. He saw her as a friend, impartial and outside his class; someone he could trust and confide in. It was a tremendous compliment, yet here she was offering him no help or comfort at all. Reaching out she touched his hand.

'Tony, I'm really glad you feel you can talk to me. Of course I understand and if ever I can do anything to help, anything at all, I'll be glad to. I . . . I want you to know that.'

His fingers curled round hers warmly and he looked at her for a moment, a smile on his lips. Then he leaned forward, cupped her chin and kissed her very gently on the lips.

'Bless you, Gloria. You'll never know how much that means to me.' A moment later he had switched on the ignition bringing the car instantly to life. They were on their way once more to Houlton, just as though nothing had happened. But for Gloria, staring dazedly into the darkness, life would never be quite the same again.

When they arrived at Longueville Hall the atmosphere was electric.

'A man came from the paper and took photos of us all,' Shirley said, jumping up and down with excitement. 'He took *ever* so many of Imogen and me. They're going to be in the paper on Monday. Not just the little paper we get here, but the big London ones too. Imogen was nearly sick before we went on.' She giggled, grasping her friend's hand. 'But once we started off she never got one step wrong and we got *ever* such a lot of clapping when we was – *were* finished. The curtain had to go up again *twice* so's we could take another bow. It was *lovely*. Ooh, I nearly forgot.' She pulled a carefully folded programme out of her pocket. 'Look – here's your name. It says, Costumes by Gloria Rayner.'

Gloria looked proudly at her name printed in bold type on the programme. So Leonie had been true to her word. Gloria thought briefly of the secret Tony had told her and felt slightly guilty about knowing it. She turned to Imogen. 'Did you enjoy being in the concert then, lovie – once your nerves settled down?'

The girl nodded, smiling happily. 'Oh yes, thank you. It was marvellous.'

Gloria couldn't help noticing the child's glow of pride when her mother said:

'They both did very well indeed. I was proud of them.' Leonie clapped her hands. 'Now let Nanny take you off to bed. If you don't get your sleep you'll get no applause on Monday night at all.' She looked at Tony. 'And if I don't get a large gin and tonic soon I shall expire. Fix some drinks, darling, will you?'

Christmas at Angel Row was not the success Gloria had hoped for. Jim Jarvis put Shirley on the train at Northampton two days before Christmas Eve, and Pa was there waiting to meet her at Euston. All the way to Whitechapel on the Underground the child chattered away about the concert, her friend Imogen and her famous parents, and Jim and Molly Jarvis, none of whom Pa knew from Adam, as he pointed out later to his wife in the privacy of the kitchen.

'She's come 'ome a little stranger,' he complained.

'She's grown a lot,' Ma observed with a sniff. 'Grown *up* too. A damn sight too fast if you asks me. All this actin' on the stage an' livin' with them bohemian theatricals 'as gone to 'er 'ead.'

Although Shirley had looked forward to being at home and seeing her grandparents again, she found it oddly disappointing. The shop and the flat in Angel Row seemed to have shrunk. She was sure everything wasn't this small when she was last here. The bedroom she shared with Gloria seemed so cramped and she missed having a bathroom and an indoor lav – or loo, as the Darrents called it. Going out into the yard on cold dark evenings was an inconvenience she had happily forgotten all about, and reacquainting herself with it was irksome, to say the least.

Ma had done her best with the Christmas dinner, but food shortages were already beginning to bite and the turkey they normally had was replaced this year by a rabbit; stuffed and roasted, but sadly lacking in festive appeal. Gloria had made Shirley a new party dress, of white organdie, spotted with blue. She had made one for Imogen too, at Shirley's request, making a note of the measurements used for her concert costume and choosing some taffeta in a deep gold shade that she found in the market. Ma and Pa's present to Shirley was a little gold bracelet with her name engraved on a heart-shaped locket.

After the crackers had been pulled, the mottoes read and the hats tried on, there was nothing to do except play Ludo with Gloria or listen to the wireless, and Shirley found it hard to conceal her boredom. What made things worse was that Gloria had to work on every day except Christmas and Pa was on duty at the ARP post most evenings. Once the holiday was over things were slightly better. Shirley helped Ma in the shop, putting potatoes and vegetables into bags for the customers, but, although she didn't say so, she found it poor substitute for her daily rides on Toffee or the country walks she and Imogen enjoyed, making up stories for each other as they walked and daydreaming about the exciting things they would like to see happen in their grown-up future lives.

The day after Boxing Day Gloria had the afternoon off and she took Shirley Up West to see *Gone With the Wind*. Gloria enjoyed it enormously, weeping copiously into her handkerchief in all the sad bits. But the three and a half hours running time proved too much for Shirley, who shifted uncomfortably in her seat for much of the last hour. At home over tea, when Ma asked her if she had enjoyed the film Shirley shook her head.

'It was boring,' she announced.

Gloria looked stunned. 'How can you say that, Shirl? Vivien Leigh was lovely in it. It got an Academy Award nomination too.'

'I don't care. It was boring.' Shirley began to get down from the table, but Ma frowned at her and tapped the table sharply with her knife.

'Just a minute, milady. What d'you say 'fore you get down?'

Shirley pulled down the corners of her mouth. 'Nanny Jarvis doesn't make us say it,' she mumbled sulkily.

'Well, more's the pity,' Ma retorted. 'When you're in this 'ouse, my gel, you does as *I* says, never mind this Nanny Jarvis o' yours we keep hearin' so much about.'

'Thank-you-for-my-tea-may-I-get-down?' Shirley chanted.

Ma folded her arms and nodded. 'You may.' When Shirley had gone upstairs she turned to Gloria. 'That child is gettin' too big for 'er boots if you asks me,' she said. 'If you're not careful you'll 'ave trouble with 'er.'

'It's the war,' Gloria said unhappily. 'She don't know where she belongs any more. She'll be gone the day after tomorrow. Don't let's make her miserable, Ma.'

Tight-lipped, Ma began to clear the table. She said nothing but the look on her face and the clatter of the dishes said it all for her. It wasn't only Shirley who was changing. There had been a change in Gloria too since she'd been making those weekend visits to the country. Ma had watched it taking place as the weeks went by. Ideas above her station were what she'd be getting next.

The new year came in quietly enough, but soon changes began to creep into the everyday lives of people in city and countryside alike. The ration books everyone had been talking about were issued early in the New Year, much to Nanny Jarvis's dismay.

'How shall we ever manage on *this* much food a week?' she wailed, staring at the books. 'We'll all starve.'

But Jim protested that they certainly would not starve — not while he could still hold a spade. In spite of Leonie's objections he had finally managed to get her to agree to his 'digging for victory', as all the posters urged. He had already begun to plant potatoes on what was once the tennis court and now he was wondering how hard he'd have to fight for permission to keep some chickens and maybe even a pig. With his Home Guard duties, he was busy almost round the clock, and if it hadn't been for worrying about Hitler's invasion he would have been enjoying every minute.

In the next village an aircraft factory had been built. It had been assembled hurriedly, appearing to sprout from the ground almost overnight like a gigantic mushroom to turn out the urgently needed planes. Engineers and fitters were already being recruited and there was even talk of women being employed there.

Leonie was working again at last and only came up to Houlton at weekends. This week after the charity concert Peter Jason had telephoned to say that, following the publicity the show had attracted, he'd had several offers for her. The best of these was to make a series of radio shows for the BBC's Forces Programme. She was to sing special songs dedicated to the wives and families of servicemen in a programme which would be called *With Love from Leonie*.

'It seems you put such feeling into the songs you sang at that concert of yours that they can't wait to sign you up,' he told her.

It hadn't taken her long to decide to accept. She longed to get back her status as a popular artist once again and she was confident that she could manage a radio show without Tony's support – though she let Peter believe she had accepted the offer out of patriotism. She insisted that she must be allowed to choose her own music and write her own material, presenting it in her own style, and left Peter to negotiate the contract for her.

Tony was still playing to packed houses in *Henry V* at the New Theatre. His notices had been encouraging and he was happy to have achieved his ambition to play a classical role successfully. Claire wrote regularly and lovingly from her home in Jersey. When the run of *Henry* came to an end he planned to go over and visit her before joining the RAF. It would be so wonderful to see her and share a summer break. During the week he and Leonie occupied the Mayfair flat together fairly amicably, mainly because their paths rarely crossed; she was working in the daytime, he in the evenings.

Shirley and Imogen found school easier as the spring term progressed. Many of the first evacuees had gone home again, leaving more space in the overcrowded classrooms and playground. Shirley enjoyed her first game of snowballs and built her first snowman that winter. She and Imogen tried sliding on the village pond and got a good scolding from Nanny Jarvis when they fell in and came home shivering and covered in green slime.

With the spring came more changes. In May the prime minister, Mr Chamberlain, died and the flag on the school was lowered in respect. Some weeks later the girls came home from school one afternoon to find Nanny and Jim huddled over the wireless in the kitchen, shushing them as they tumbled noisily through the door.

'My God, we're done,' Jim muttered, his face ashen. 'The lads have been beaten back into the sea. We're done for. Gerry'll be coming now and no mistake.'

Nanny burst into frightened tears and Imogen ran to her and began to cry in sympathy.

'What's happened, Jim?' Shirley whispered, frightened by his solemn face. 'Is Hitler coming?'

'The soldiers we sent over to fight are coming home, lass,' he said. 'But England's tougher than to let one setback make her roll over and die. We'll see them off, don't you fret.'

After that everyone was talking about the little boats that went to Dunkirk in France to help bring the soldiers back. There were stories of trains full of them seen in the town, dirty and battered, their uniforms in rags. The news bulletins were full of what was called the Battle of Britain. No one was allowed to speak while the wireless was on in case some vital scrap of information was missed. When they weren't listening to the news they were listening to *With Love from Leonie*, which was on every week and proving to be one of the most popular programmes on the Forces Programme. It was earning Leonie Swann more fans than she had yet had in all her career. Shirley and Imogen didn't know what to make of it, but they were encouraged by Jim's assurance that the new prime minister, Mr Churchill would certainly win the war for them and make everything come right. Jim always knew best. After all, he was in the Home Guard. He had a proper soldier's uniform and a real gun now, so he must know what he was talking about.

As the year progressed, Gloria's visits to Houlton grew fewer. Ma hadn't been well, and with Pa down at the ARP post so much she had to help in the shop and flat when she wasn't at work; besides, she really couldn't afford the train fare very often. One evening in July she finished her shift in a light-hearted mood. It was warm and still quite light as she came out of the staff entrance of the cinema and waved a cheery goodbye to her friends. Life wasn't so bad. They were all getting used to the changes, and she was lucky. Apart from parting her from Shirley, the war didn't seem to have made all that much difference to her life. Pa was always shaking his head and foretelling gloom and doom. He'd come home from the ARP post with stories about things being worse than they were led to believe and news of German planes seen flying over the southeast coast. He used words like 'reconnaissance' and spoke of German spies parachuted in secretly to infiltrate and undermine them all. She and Ma took these rumours with a pinch of salt. She was smiling to herself about his bizarre stories as she reached the corner of the street – then suddenly she stopped in her tracks, her heart leaping into her throat, as a man stepped out of the shadows in front of her.

'Gloria – don't be frightened. It's only me.' He reached out a hand to steady her.

She let out her breath in a sigh of relief. '*Tony*! You did give me a turn.' She looked up at him. He wore a raincoat and a trilby hat pulled down well over his face. Under it his face looked pale and haggard. 'Is anything wrong?' she asked, concerned. 'Shirley . . . ?

He took her arm. 'No, Shirley's fine. Look, I've got to talk to you, Gloria. The car's along here – please . . .' Without waiting for her answer, he hurried her along the street.

As they got in, he didn't start to speak but drove, his eyes concentrating on the road and his lips set in a grim line. Gloria became anxious when ten minutes later he was still driving.

'Tony – look, Ma will be expecting me. She'll wonder where I am. Where are we going?'

'Maple Court – to the flat,' Tony said. 'Leonie's gone home for the weekend and I . . .' His voice faltered and he said no more. Gloria looked at him, concerned for him now. Her own problems were forgotten. There was obviously something seriously wrong. He needed a friend – needed *her*. This was no time to be thinking of herself.

The flat took her breath away. Unlike Longueville Hall it was ultramodern and more glamorous than anything she had ever seen. If it hadn't been for Tony's obvious desperation she would have liked to look round. In the hall he pulled off his coat and hat and threw them both carelessly into a cupboard. Gloria looked at him helplessly.

'What's wrong? Please tell me.'

He took a crumpled letter out of his pocket and thrust it into her hand, then walked through into the kitchen to stand with his back towards her, staring out of the window. Slowly and uncertainly she smoothed out the single sheet of notepaper and began to read.

Dear Tony Darrent,

I am Claire's elder brother. I know about your secret relationship as she and I have always been very close and she confided in me. I knew she would want me to write to you at this time. One week ago, on 28 June, the Germans bombed our island. Here at Grève de Lecq we were safe, but my sister was shopping that day in St Helier. Tragically she was in a building which caught a direct hit and was killed along with many others. The funeral was yesterday. I am so sorry to bring you this news.

Yours in deep sorrow,
Gerald DeLisle.

Gloria caught her breath. 'Oh, God, Poor Tony!' She ran to him and took his shoulders, turning him towards her. Tears were streaming down his cheeks and he shook his head at her wordlessly. Throwing her arms around him, she held him close, drawing his head down onto her shoulder and rocking him as she would have rocked Shirley. 'Don't cry,' she whispered into his hair. 'She can't have suffered, poor girl. Oh, Tony, *please* don't cry like that.'

His harsh sobs tore at her heart. She felt so helpless. Keeping one arm round him, she helped him into the hall and pushed open a door that turned out to be a bedroom. Pushing him down onto the bed, she pulled off his shoes and drew the counterpane up over him. Back in the living room she opened the cocktail cabinet and searched through the bottles till she found some brandy. Splashing a generous amount into a tumbler, she went back to the bedroom with it and sat on the side of the bed.

'Here, drink this. It'll help.' She slipped an arm round his shoulders and held the glass to his lips. As the warming liquid slipped down his throat, he gradually calmed.

'I loved her,' he whispered. 'She was the only woman I've ever truly loved. I was going over to see her next month – and now . . . I can't believe it. Oh, God, I can't believe it.' He looked at her. 'I keep thinking I'm dreaming and I must wake up in a minute.'

Her throat tight with tears, she stroked his face. 'I know, I know. It's terrible.'

'How will I bear it, Gloria? How will I go on – acting, both on stage and off? I can't even let Leonie know. It goes too deep for me to risk the look of triumph I know I'd see in her eyes. She knew there was someone special, you see. How will I . . . ?'

'You still have Imogen,' Gloria reassured him. 'You still have a daughter, Tony, and she needs you. She always will. That's what I told myself when Jack took off and left me to face it alone.' She pulled him close. 'At least you know she died loving you. You didn't get dumped like I did. You'll have that love to cherish for the rest of your life now. It can never die now and no one can take it away from you.'

He dropped his head onto her shoulder and his arms around her tightened. 'Thank you, Gloria. What would I have done without you?'

After a moment or two she gently freed herself from his clinging arms. 'Look, why don't you get undressed and into bed properly?' she said. 'I'll make you a hot drink. Have you had anything to eat?' He shook his head. 'Right. I'll make you some scrambled eggs. I know it won't make the hurt go away, but you'll feel better able to face it with some food inside you and a night's sleep.'

She got up and opened the glass door to the adjoining bathroom. It was cool, green and sweet-smelling. 'I'll run you a bath,' she said over her shoulder. 'You can have it while I do the eggs.' She turned to look at him lying there on the bed, staring numbly at the ceiling. 'Come on, love. Please try – for me.'

Sitting opposite him at the kitchen table half an hour later, she coaxed him mouthful by mouthful through the plate of eggs and toast, just as she had done with Shirley when she had the measles the year before. Gradually he began to look a little better. The colour came back into his ashen cheeks and the haunted look began to clear from his eyes. When he had finished, Gloria said: 'Go to bed now and try to get some rest. I'll wash up these dishes, then I'll be off home.'

He reached out a hand to grasp hers as she began to rise from the table. 'Please don't go.'

She stared at him. 'I *must*, Tony.'

'No. Please. I need you. I don't want to be alone tonight.'

She carried the dishes to the sink, her mind racing. What would she tell Ma? What would people say if they found out she'd stayed here all night? She turned to say something, but the look of mute appeal overrode her anxieties. 'All right,' she said. 'If you really want me to, I'll stay.'

She insisted that she would make herself comfortable on the settee in the living room where she could hear him if he called. She dozed a little on and off, her ears alert for the smallest sound. Eventually she must have fallen asleep and she had no idea how long she slept or what the time was when she was wakened by a hand on her shoulder. She sat up with a start. '*What* – who . . . ?'

'It's all right, it's only me.' Tony lowered himself onto the settee beside her. 'I can't sleep, Gloria. It's useless. I keep seeing her face . . . hearing the crash . . . the screams. Every time I close my eyes I can see her lovely body all broken and bloody. I keep wondering if she knew – if she thought of me. Christ, I can't bear it, Gloria.'

'Shh.' She sat up and slipped an arm around his shoulders as he sat there with his head in his hands. 'I think you should see a doctor tomorrow,' she told him, stroking the dishevelled hair back from his brow. 'You'll make yourself ill if you go on like this. Go back to bed, Tony, I'll get you some aspirin.'

But he held tightly on to her hand. 'Come with me – please.'

She couldn't bring herself to refuse, but went with him willingly. In the bedroom she slid fully dressed into the rumpled bed beside him and held him close in her arms. 'I'm here,' she whispered. 'Go to sleep. I'll still be here when you wake. I promise.'

He clung to her like a frightened child, his face buried in her neck. 'I insisted on her going home, Gloria,' he said. 'It was I who sent her to her death.'

'No, no. You mustn't think of it like that. You thought you were doing the right thing.' She held him till he calmed, then lay very still, hardly daring to breathe. Gradually she heard the pattern of his breathing change until, after a few minutes, she knew he had fallen at last into an exhausted sleep.

As the dawn crept in, reaching fingers of thin light into the corners of the unfamiliar room, she marvelled at the strangeness of life. Who would have ever thought that she would be here, in bed with the man whose unattainable image she had loved for so long – bringing him comfort of the most innocent kind? If it hadn't been for the war . . . life was full of surprises . . . Her eyelids drooped, heavy as lead. They closed and finally she slept too.

'Where the bloody 'ell have you been?' As Gloria crept in through the back door, Ma faced her with arms folded challengingly over her heaving bosom. 'Pa an' me've been up half the night, worried out of our wits about you. Sat 'ere till nearly two o'clock this mornin', we did.'

'I went home with a friend,' Gloria muttered, avoiding her mother's steely eyes.

'You lyin' little bitch. Now tell me the truth or I'll take me 'and to you. You're not too old for it, y'know.'

'Oh, don't go on so Ma.' Gloria sank wearily into a chair. 'Is there any tea going?'

'Tea?' Ma had worked herself up into a state and she wasn't going to be cheated out of a showdown by Gloria's apathy. 'You stop out all night. like some alley cat, then you come waltzin' in 'ere calmly askin' for *tea*?' She stood demandingly over Gloria. 'Come on then, let's 'ave it. What friend is this? One of the girls at the Adelphi treated 'erself to a posh car now, 'as she?'

'I don't know what you mean.'

'Oh, no? Well, I'll tell you, shall I? Your father was on his way 'ome last night when he sees you gettin' into this big car. So whose car was it? That's what I want to know. And what were you up to? As if I didn't know.'

'I *was* with a friend,' Gloria said. 'A friend who's just lost someone very close. I offered to stay the night. That's all there is to it.'

'So why couldn't you come and let us know first? And why didn't you tell me that in the first place?'

'Because you kept *on*.' Gloria's voice trembled, close to tears. Lack of sleep and the emotionally fraught hours behind her had left her completely drained. 'For heaven's sake, Ma, where did you think I was? I'm not a giddy schoolgirl. I never go out with men. I haven't since before Shirley. You ought to know that by now.'

'And you better not, my girl.' Ma took a step towards her. 'It's 'im, isn't it? That Tony Darrent? You're soft on 'im. I've seen it comin'.' She shook her head exasperatedly. 'Wake up, gel. He'll 'ave 'is fun and then drop you just like the other one did. A gel like you don't stand a chance with 'is sort. Wake up and use yer loaf 'fore it's too late.'

Gloria didn't wait to hear any more. Getting up, she flung out of the kitchen and up the stairs to the privacy of her own room. There she threw herself down on the bed and buried her face in the pillow. How could she have fooled herself into thinking just a few hours ago that her life could be untouched by the war? It would lay its evil hands on them all before it was over. No one would escape. All the pent-up emotion she had generated last night erupted. The tears flowed and she sobbed till her whole body ached; for Tony; for poor dead Claire, whom she had never met; and for Shirley, who was slowly slipping away from her. But most of all for the love that had been steadily growing in her heart since last Christmas. The love that she knew could never be returned.

For Shirley and Imogen the long hot summer holiday was a delight. Tony did not buy Shirley the pony Imogen had promised, but he did buy the girls a bicycle each and they rode out on most days with packed lunches or teas to explore the countryside.

Gloria managed to get up for the occasional weekend visit, but Shirley hardly seemed to notice whether she was there or not. She never saw Tony again once all that summer. Molly Jarvis told her that as soon as the run of his play finished in September he was going to join up. Gloria reluctantly accepted that Ma's remarks had been unacceptably close to the truth. He had needed her that night when he was so upset, but she meant no more to him than a shoulder to cry on. Maybe the memory of it even embarrassed him. Sadly, she took his pictures down from her bedroom walls. He was still the most beautiful man and the best actor she had ever seen, but somehow she no longer saw him in quite the same way. He was a *man* to her now with all a man's faults and frailties; a man – not a star. She went to work, helped Ma in the shop in her spare time and looked forward to the time when the war would be over and she could have Shirley back. Surely once it was over she would want to come back and carry on just as they used to – wouldn't she?

At Longueville Hall Imogen taught Shirley to swim and in return Shirley taught Imogen how to sing 'Over the Rainbow' like Judy Garland and how to curl her hair. Both girls helped Jim Jarvis with his digging for victory. But their favourite pastime was playing at 'shows'. Shirley would choose the music and teach Imogen the words.

Together they would choreograph dance routines and stage their performances in the garden with all Imogen's dolls and teddies for an audience. While the Battle of Britain raged, while the Germans invaded the Channel Islands and England tensely defended its shores and awaited the same fate, the children played, made up stories and confidently planned a golden future.

On Saturday 2nd September Sid Rayner left Ma and Gloria to the Saturday afternoon shoppers' rush and, with his ARP satchel and steel helmet slung over his shoulder, set off to put in his shift at the ARP post. At the top of Angel Row he stopped to wait for the traffic to thin before crossing the road.

'Lovely afternoon, Sid,' called a fellow shopkeeper. 'Just the weather for goin' down to Southend for the day, eh?'

'Chance'd be a fine thing,' Sid pointed to his satchel and steel helmet. 'On duty, me.'

'Best o'luck then, mate.'

On the next corner Pa looked up, his attention suddenly caught by a low rumbling sound. The next moment he stood riveted to the spot, staring dumbly into the clear blue summer sky, High above him rode a great V-shaped flotilla of black planes – hundreds of them, the sound of their engines gathering to a roaring crescendo. As he stood staring up at them, Pa could see smaller fighter planes sparkling in the sunlight as they darted in and out, like pilot fish among a herd of whales. Along with others he stood on the pavement and watched, almost mesmerised by the sight. Then, in the distance, he heard a long whining scream followed by an explosion that shook the ground. Immediately there were cries of alarm as people began to scatter, running for the shelters. Quickly donning his helmet, Pa ran the rest of the way to the post. As he ran along the street, head lowered as though running into a storm, he thought of Ma and Gloria and hoped they were taking cover, but once he arrived there was little time for worrying. The bombs were falling thick and fast all around by now. Word came in that the target was the docks. One bomb hit an electricity main and all the lights went out. Pa set about putting the emergency supply – candles in jam jars – into operation.

Long after the sun had done down that night, the eastern sky was brighter than day. Great plumes of smoke, blood-red flames and showers of dancing sparks provided a macabre firework display as building after building succumbed to the onslaught. To those who gazed helplessly up at the sky that night it was as though the city had become a living hell. The long-threatened, long-dreaded Blitz had begun.

Chapter Six

The success of the radio programme *With Love from Leonie* was greater than anyone could possibly have foreseen. Articles about Leonie and her life and career appeared in the *Radio Times* and several of the popular women's magazines. But when Leonie agreed to give an interview to a journalist from *Home and Beauty*, she found the woman inquisitive to the point of impertinence.

'Our readers are always fascinated by a star's education and family life,' she gushed, pencil poised over her notebook. 'We all know, of course, that you are married to Tony Darrent and have a little daughter, but could you tell me something about your own childhood, Miss Swann?'

Somewhat dismayed, Leonie cleared her throat. 'Oh, it was really very ordinary,' she said, playing for time. 'I'm sure your readers would be dreadfully bored.'

'Not at all. We find that our readers like to identify with their favourite stars,' the woman said. 'And if your background is as mundane as theirs it makes them feel closer to you.'

As mundane as theirs. What a cheek! As if she was going to admit to a mundane background. Clearly she was going to have to invent something. Leonie shuddered inwardly as she recalled the poky little flat above the little butcher's shop in Snow Hill, Birmingham, where the pungent odour of raw meat seemed to permeate everything and where the sawdust from her father's boots crept into every corner. She pictured her mother standing over the copper in the washhouse at the rear of the shop, boiling her father's bloodstained overalls. She had hated it all then and she hated it now. 'I grew up in the country,' she heard herself saying in a clear, positive tone, 'I was always surrounded by animals.' Well, at least that was true, even though she didn't add that they were dead ones, dissected ready for the table. 'We had a beautiful old house,' she went on. 'Standing in its own parkland, looking back I suppose it was quite a privileged childhood, really.'

The woman looked suitably impressed. 'You were an only child?'

'Oh, yes,' Leonie said firmly. She had always *felt* like an only child. Her brother, Norman, was six when she was born. He had resented her as a baby and they had never got along. He had left school at fourteen, a gangling, pimply youth, to help their father in the shop. Her only vivid memory of him was when she was in her early teens and he'd begun to hang around her bedroom door, a lecherous leer on his face, trying to catch a glimpse of her undressing. She had caught him once looking through her bedroom keyhole and threatened to tell Dad. They hadn't spoken to each other much after that.

'I see.' The woman was scribbling rapidly. 'And you said your background was ordinary. You're too modest.' She looked up. 'So you grew up in the country? That must be why you choose to live there yourself.'

'Yes, Longueville Hall is very similar to my own childhood home, which is what attracted me from the moment I first saw it.'

'Your father – was he in, er, farming?' The journalist looked up enquiringly.

'In a way.' Leonie searched her mind for a suitable title. 'I suppose you could call him an, er, a landowner.'

'You're being modest again, aren't you, Miss Swann?' The woman wagged her finger and smiled archly. 'What you really mean is that he was the local squire; lord of the manor. How fascinating! So with that kind of family background I suppose you must have been presented at court?'

God! Had she gone too far? To hide the flush that was slowly creeping up her neck, Leonie got up and crossed the room to take a cigarette from the box on the mantelpiece. 'Actually no,' she said, making a flamboyant show of lighting it and blowing smoke at the ceiling. 'Mummy wanted me to have a coming-out ball like all my debutante friends, of course, but I wasn't in the least interested in that kind of thing. A career in music and singing was my ambition. I wasn't interested in snaring a rich husband.'

'I see. So you intended to go into the theatre from quite an early age?'

'Oh, yes.'

'Did you meet opposition from your parents?'

'Not really. They were always very keen on the theatre themselves,' Leonie said. 'There were always lots of house parties at home. The house was always full of famous people. It was the most tremendous fun.'

'How exciting! Tell me about your first job. I did hear that it was your husband who discovered you.'

Leonie smiled. 'That's right. As I was saying, our house was always full of theatrical celebrities. I was singing at one of our weekend house parties. Tony was there and he confessed to me later that he was quite captivated. Afterwards he begged me to go to London and meet his agent.'

'And he fell in love with you too. How romantic!' The interviewer looked around her. 'This is a beautiful flat, Miss Swann. You and Mr Darrent live here when you are working in London, I suppose?'

'That's right.'

'So brave of you to stay in London. You're not worried about the bombing at all?'

'So far we've been lucky; only the odd broken window, though the raids have been a strain, of course. But I'm leaving London shortly on a tour of army camps. I'm not allowed to tell you where – it's all terribly hush-hush.'

'I do hope that doesn't mean that *With Love from Leonie* is to come to an end. It's compulsive listening for so many people.'

'Oh no. We shall be broadcasting some more pro-grammes later.'

'All your fans will be reassured to know that. And what about your husband?'

'Now that the run of his play has ended, his plans are quite fluid,' Leonie said cagily.

'There has been a whisper that he may go into the RAF.'

Leonie smiled. 'We'll have to wait and see. He's very keen to do his bit for the war in whatever way he can.'

In fact, Tony had already spoken to his old friend Johnny Langdon from the flying club. Johnny was now a wing commander in the RAF and over lunch at the Garrick Club the previous week Tony had asked about his chances of getting a commission. Johnny had pursed his lips doubtfully.

'I'm afraid your age is pretty much against you, old chap. The job is pretty arduous, you know.'

'I think I'm fairly fit, and at thirty-nine I'm hardly over the hill,' Tony protested.

But Johnny drew in his breath and shook his head. 'Most of the fighter pilots are pretty well just out of the sixth form and even some of them crack up under the strain. Of course, with your flying experience there must be some way you could be useful. Look, why don't you go along and offer your services – see what happens? I'm sure they'll be able to find you something.'

Tony was disappointed and more than a little put out. He had expected to be snapped up and given a commis-sion right away. He wanted to fly a Spitfire, not a desk, but, all the same, he went along a couple of days later and volunteered his services.

After a rigorous medical, he was told that he was unfit for flying duty and advised off-the-record by a kindly and well-meaning medical officer who was secretly a fan of his that he could most certainly serve his country better by remaining in his own profession and entertaining the troops. Tony was shattered. His medical report, which he insisted on seeing, showed that he had raised blood pressure, poor muscle tone and – most depressing of all – fallen arches. He resolved to do something about all three as soon as possible.

The only person to whom he confided his ignominious rejection was Peter Jason. The block in Charing Cross Road where Peter previously had his office suite had been badly bomb-damaged in October and Peter had now set up a temporary office in his own house in Richmond. When Tony told him that his plans for joining the RAF had been shattered, Peter heaved a sigh of relief.

'Well, at least you've got it out of your system,' he said. 'As a matter of fact, something has just come up which I think might interest you. I'd made a note to ring you about it in the morning, so I'm particularly pleased you've dropped in today.' He looked up at Tony. 'Heard of the Crown Film Unit?'

Tony nodded. 'Aren't they the people who are doing the war documentaries?'

'That's right. Well, now another group is getting started. They're calling themselves Combat Films. A team of documentary filmmakers have got together to make some realistic, dramatised war documentaries. Churchill is behind it all the way. Apparently he's very keen. So as to get the realism they want, they'll be filming during actual battles wherever possible. And of course people with your kind of experience will be invaluable.'

Tony looked doubtful. 'But surely if the accent is to be on realism they won't want well-known actors taking part?'

'It wasn't just acting that I had in mind. Some of these chaps are from the world of commerce. The stuff they've been turning out – training films and such – is very different from what's planned, so they're going to need help with the direction. Then if – as they hope – they cast actual servicemen with no previous acting experience they'll need someone to coach them. Last but not least there's your flying experience, of course. There's no end to the ways you could help. It could be a rewarding and fascinating job and one that will last for the whole dura- tion of the war if you want it to.' He pushed his cigarette box across the desk. 'So what do you say? I can tell you now that they'd jump at the chance to have you on the team.'

Tony took a cigarette and lit it thoughtfully. 'Well, it sounds interesting, I grant you, but won't it be at the expense of my acting career? It could be hard to pick up the threads again when the war is over.'

'I've already thought of that,' Peter told him. 'You can always fit in the odd play or film. Leave it to me. I won't let your name fade out.'

Tony brightened. 'All right then. If they'll have me I'll give it a try.'

'*Have* you? They'll consider themselves bloody lucky to get you, believe me.' Peter pressed the button to the intercom and asked his new secretary to bring in some coffee. It was late November now, and he'd been concerned about Tony since the summer. He looked gaunt and ill. Peter wasn't surprised he had failed the RAF medical. He seemed to have lost all his enthusiasm and even some of his confidence, too. Shrewdly, he guessed that Claire's death had a lot to do with it.

After the girl had brought the coffee and withdrawn, he decided to bring the subject into the open. Maybe it would help Tony to talk about it. 'Are you feeling better now?' he asked. 'You've been pretty depressed over the past few months, haven't you?'

Tony picked up his cup, carefully avoiding Peter's eyes. 'I suppose I have. The war – one thing and another – you know . . .' He trailed off, knowing that he had no hope of fooling Peter. He had the sharp-eyed, shrewd perception that all good agents have, and a sixth sense where a client's state of mind was concerned.

'It was Claire's death, I dare say,' Peter went on softly. 'It hit me hard too. She was an exceptionally lovely girl. It was a terrible tragedy. The family is still badly shaken. The occupation of the Channel Islands is a stinking business, too. It must be hell for them, having to put up with all that the occupation entails after losing their only daughter because of the bastards. But life has to go on, old chap. A lot more have lost loved ones since this damnable bombing started. We aren't the only ones. Before we're finished the cost in human lives will be enormous.'

Tony gulped at the scalding coffee. 'We were in love, Peter,' he said bleakly. 'Really in love, I mean. It wasn't just some cheap affair.'

'I'd guessed as much.'

'The awful thing is that it was I who urged her to go home. I can't shake off the feeling that it's some hellish kind of retribution.'

'None of us could possibly have foreseen what would happen. Who could possibly have predicted the German occupation of the Channel Islands?' Peter reached across to touch Tony's sleeve. 'You and Leonie – is there any comfort to be had in that quarter?'

Tony shook his head. 'She didn't know – and she never must now. What Claire and I had was too precious to risk cheapening it – especially now that the memory of her is all I have left.'

Peter sighed. It was much worse than he had thought. 'Look, old boy, you've grieved enough,' he said at last. 'It's not good to bottle things up like this. Put some of that emotional energy into this job. You can make a huge success of it, I know you can. Go home and make plans; offer them your ideas and innovations.'

Tony looked at him. 'All right, I will. I suppose you're right, Peter. Tell them I'm on. I'm already beginning to look forward to it.'

The article about Leonie in *Home and Beauty* was published two weeks later. The magazine had given it a centre-page spread with glamorous colour photographs of both the Mayfair flat and Longueville Hall. Leonie sat in satin lounging pyjamas, draped decoratively over a Regency chaise longue; Leonie wearing jodhpurs and feeding sugar lumps to Toffee, with on either side of her, her daughter and the evacuee she had generously taken to her heart. The caption under the photograph made it appear that Shirley was her daughter and Imogen the evacuee. When Tony pointed this out, Leonie shrugged it off as immaterial. Reading on through the article, he laughed derisively.

'Where the hell did they get all this stuff about your family being the local gentry?'

Leonie blushed. 'You know what these people are,' she said defensively. 'They don't want the truth, they obviously wanted something glamorous. So I gave them the kind of thing I thought they'd enjoy.'

Tony put down the magazine and looked at her. 'Do you ever think about your parents, Leonie?'

She shrugged. 'Not often, why?'

'How do you think they'll feel when they read this?'

'How should I know? It's more than likely they won't even see it. The *Daily Herald* is more their style than *Home and Beauty*.'

'Have you listened to the news or read the papers lately?'

'Not specially – why?'

'Don't you know that Birmingham is being razed to the ground in much the same way that Coventry was? Doesn't it ever occur to you to wonder if they're all right?'

Leonie got up and walked to the fireplace, turning her back on him. 'Have *they* ever wondered if *I'm* all right? They could have got in touch at any time over the years. They haven't. They don't even know they have a granddaughter.'

'Maybe the time has come to put that right. That brother of yours is probably in the forces by now. Things might be hard for them.'

His soft tone angered her and she rounded on him. 'You've become boringly sanctimonious lately, Tony. Since when have you been worried about other people's feelings, especially my parents'? As for Norman, a dose of strong discipline is just what he needs. Why should I worry about him?'

He shrugged. 'War makes one think. It brings out latent qualities in all of us; the best in some, the worst in others.'

126

'I suppose you think this job you're taking qualifies you as some sort of hero,' she snapped. 'I'm off to entertain the troops, remember. All over Christmas I'm going to have to pig it in a series of dreadful barracks. I'm doing my bit, too.'

The words were hardly out of her mouth when the siren began its doleful wail. She broke off. '*Hell*, they're early tonight.'

Tony stood up and held out his hand to her. 'Shall we go to the shelter?'

She grasped his hand and stood looking up at him. 'I'd rather stay here. Tony, why are you so distant? You've been so far away these past months, there's just no reaching you. Is something worrying you? It's not the medical you had – you're not seriously ill, are you?'

Softening a little, he pressed her hand. 'No, of course I'm not – unless you count fallen arches as serious.'

They laughed together and the tension eased. Suddenly she looked up at him beseechingly. 'Tony, let's go to bed. It's been so long. You haven't made love to me since that night at Houlton . . .'

The first bomb of the raid fell somewhere down by the river, rattling the windows, and Tony's arm went round her in an instinctively protective gesture. 'We really should go to the shelter.'

She began to unbutton his shirt. 'But we won't – will we? Please, darling. I hate the shelter. Let's stay here.'

With the blackout curtains in Leonie's bedroom drawn back they could see the winter night sky lit up by searchlights and barrage. With each succeeding explosion Leonie's need seemed to grow. It was as though her urgent desire to survive manifested itself in frenetic love-making, and her passion built to a crescendo that was heightened by an explosion so near at hand that the whole building shook and trembled around them. Leonie clutched feverishly at Tony, her long fingernails painfully tearing at the skin on his back as she strained her body upwards beneath him. In a frenzy of elation her mouth sought his voraciously and he was suddenly struck by the unpleasant notion that she was trying to devour him, to join his body permanently to hers so that he would never again be free of her.

'Now – *now*,' she hissed into his ear. 'Make it happen. Oh, God, I want – I want . . .' Suddenly her body arched and convulsed, then she slowly relaxed, letting out her breath in a long low howl of animal pleasure.

Unfulfilled, Tony rolled away from her. He felt utterly repulsed. In that moment he loathed himself and knew that he never wanted to touch her again, but before he could escape she fastened her fingers round his arm, holding him captive.

'Darling, don't go. Don't leave me – not yet,' she said breathlessly. 'God, it was marvellous – wasn't it? I'll tell you a secret. I adore making love during an air raid. It's even more exciting than a thunderstorm – wild and primeval.' She leaned over to growl softly into his ear. 'It brings out the animal in me.' She pressed her lips to the pulse in his neck and ran her hand down the length of his thigh.

He lay quite still, wanting nothing more than to get away from her. He could never live through a raid without thinking of Claire; dying her death with her; feeling her pain; suffering again the devastating loss. The thought of the same situation causing Leonie's sexual excitement sickened him. He lay quite still, listening as her breathing steadied; praying that she wouldn't expect him to begin the whole nauseating charade again. Suddenly to his horror, she looked into his eyes and said softly: 'It's over, isn't it – between you and Claire?'

He froze. It was as though someone had kicked him hard in the solar plexus, taking his breath away. Sitting up, he stared down at her, his heart thudding raggedly. 'What – what do you know about Claire?'

She smiled languorously up at him. 'Nothing really. You called out her name once when we were making love. I knew then that it must be serious. It hurt, Tony. It made me realise how much I love you. But it's over now, isn't it? I always know when your affairs are over. I'm going to be the important one in your life from now on. I can make you happy again just like before. Haven't I just proved it?'

Nausea almost overwhelmed him as he shook off her hand and got out of bed. 'The raid – it's getting too hot for comfort.' He was pulling on a sweater and slacks. 'Get up, Leonie. We're going to the shelter.' He was already moving towards the door.

She slipped her long legs over the edge of the bed and stood up. Making no attempt to cover her nakedness, she stood between him and the door. Winding her arms around his neck, she pressed herself against him seductively.

He put her firmly from him. 'Get dressed, Leonie.' Reaching for her dressing gown, he draped it around her shoulders. 'We owe it to Imogen not to take stupid risks like this. She's the one we have to think of.'

'*Imogen*?' Her eyes glittered angrily. 'Is she all you can think of?' She shrugged the gown to the floor and he looked at her standing before him, nude and with that blatant, predatory gleam in her eyes. She laughed suddenly and held out her arms. 'Stop being so stuffy, Tony. Come back to bed. You know you want to. Let's make a night of it like we used to in the old days.'

To his horror he felt himself becoming aroused and his stomach lurched sickeningly. He thought of Claire and what he saw as his disloyalty to her memory. 'Put some clothes on, for Christ's sake,' he snarled, turning away in disgust.

She remained where she stood, her eyes glistening with angry tears. 'You go to the shelter if you're so bloody scared,' she snapped. '*I'm* not going.'

'Then stay here,' Tony threw over his shoulder as he flung out of the room.

The tears welled up and began to slip down her cheeks. 'That's right, *coward* – scuttle off to save your worthless bloody skin,' she shouted at his retreating back. 'I'm staying here and I don't care if I do get killed. *You* obviously don't give a damn.' But Tony was already out of hearing as he made his way to the shelter shared by the other residents of the flats.

Leonie was turning back towards the bed when there was a massive explosion as a bomb fell in nearby Green Park. It threw her so violently back against the wall that all the breath was dashed from her body and her teeth seemed to rattle in her head. Plaster showered down from the ceiling, coating her hair with white powder and clinging to her eyelashes. On the other side of the room splinters of glass from the bedroom window showered the carpet and dressing table. Still winded by the blast, Leonie slid down the wall to land in a crumpled heap on the floor. She watched numbly as ornaments toppled and smashed. The shredded brocade curtains fluttered like ribbons and the aroma of Joy mingled with the stench of destruction as the contents of a smashed perfume bottle made a widening stain on the carpet.

As the floor beneath her feet began to shudder and tremble, Leonie leaped to her feet and let out a terrified shriek. Sobbing with fear, she snatched up a dressing gown, pulled it round her, thrust her feet into slippers and wrenched open the door. As she made a frantic dash for the staircase she knew with fearful certainty that she wanted nothing more than to stay alive.

The train journey back to London from Northampton that Sunday evening took more than twice as long as it should. Perched uncomfortably on her case in the crowded corridor, Gloria was tired and dispirited. She should have been fire-watching at the Adelphi last night but she had changed with Freda Harris so that she could go and spend a weekend with Shirley, yet the child had barely seemed to notice that she was there half the time. There was a party on in the village hall the next week and she and Imogen were providing the entertainment. They were doing the Fred-and-Ginger routine they'd done last Christmas for the concert and they were much too busy rehearsing to be bothered with her. She had spent most of the weekend helping Molly Jarvis in the kitchen.

'You mustn't mind them,' Molly had told her good-naturedly, sensing her disappointment. 'Just be glad Shirley is so happy here and away from all that dreadful bombing.'

But Gloria wasn't happy. Each time she saw Shirley the child seemed more distant than the last. There was no hope of her coming home this Christmas and Gloria had a horrid suspicion that she wouldn't want to anyway.

'I wonder you don't move up here yourself,' Molly said one evening as they sat over bedtime cocoa. 'Several of the London mothers have, you know. With their husbands away at the war, there's no reason for them to stay in London any more. And this is a better place for the boys to come on leave to than poor Blitz-torn London.'

Gloria shook her head. 'My job is in London,' she said. 'Ma and Pa too. They're Londoners through and through. They'd never dream of leaving and I don't think they'd expect me to.'

Jim looked up from his Sunday paper. 'But if you were to be – if the worst happened, what would become of Shirley?' he asked. 'Have you ever thought about that?'

Molly shot him a warning frown, but he ignored it. 'These things have to be considered,' he said insistently. 'There are cinemas here, you know, Gloria. I dare say you'd get another job easy enough.'

Gloria shook her head doubtfully, but Jim's words gave her food for thought. He was right, of course. If anything happened to her, Shirley would have no one. The child was still only ten. It would be a terrible thing to be left at that age. There would still be Ma and Pa, but whole families were often wiped out in one raid. It happened all the time. Of course they were careful. They always went to the shelter when the siren went – even Ma, in spite of her misgivings. They spent most of the air raids down the Underground nowadays. Sometimes it could be quite good fun even if there wasn't much sleep to be had. There was a great feeling of comradeship and sometimes there was entertainment too. They sang to drown out the sound of the bombs and keep their spirits up.

Later, when she was in bed, she thought again about Jim Jarvis's remarks. Twice the shop in Angel Row had suffered bomb damage, though so far they hadn't actually been bombed out. On each occasion they'd had to manage without water and electricity for several days and the rear wall was still shored up and likely to stay that way now for the duration. The whole street was a far cry from what it had been. But they put up with it and managed the best they could. Ma and Pa prided themselves that they had carried on business without a break and they promised their customers that as long as they were still there and could get up to Covent Garden of a morning they would trade as usual. But Gloria could see the strain on her mother's face as night after night of bombing took its toll of her health, and Pa came back from the ARP post after his spells of duty looking gaunt and exhausted. Neither of them was getting any younger. Maybe if she could find a place to rent in Houlton she could persuade Ma to come too. Pa would never leave his beloved ARP but he could always come up for the occasional rest. Best of all, they could be with Shirley. They could be a family again. That was the important thing.

Over the breakfast washing-up next morning, she asked Molly about the Darrents. She hadn't seen either of them for months. She knew Leonie was busy with her broadcasts, but it was Tony she really wanted to hear news of.

'Madam is off to entertain the troops over Christmas,' Molly told her. 'And Mr Tony has joined this film unit. They're making war documentaries.' She shook her head ruefully. 'Between you and me, it sounds just as dangerous as going to war.'

'He didn't join the air force then?'

'Bless you, no. Unfit,' Molly said.

Gloria's heart plummeted. 'You mean he's ill? Something wrong with him?'

Molly shook her head, 'Just his age, I think. They only want the really young boys for the flying, apparently. It's full of strain, all that night flying and getting shot at. I

132

don't mind telling you, Jim and I were relieved when he didn't go. But this documentary thing sounds almost as bad. They're going to film in the battle zones, so I hear.'

'So he'll be flying anyway?' Gloria asked fearfully.

'I don't really know all the ins and outs of it, but it seems he's there to teach the young servicemen how to act,' Molly explained. 'And to direct too – something like that. All I do know is that we hardly see either of them these days.' She shook her head. 'That poor child won't see her parents at all this Christmas. I'm really glad she's got Shirley. Those two kiddies are real pals now, you know. Inseparable, as they say.' Her face suddenly brightened. 'Tell you what – why don't you come here for Christmas? Bring your mother and dad too if they'll come. I'm sure the Darrents wouldn't mind.' She raised her eyes to the ceiling. 'All those rooms up there empty. It seems a shame not to give a London family a rest from the bombing.'

On the interminable journey home Gloria thought about Molly's offer. She doubted whether she could persuade Ma and Pa to go to the country, even for the weekend, but she might go herself if the holiday was long enough to make it worth while. She'd get Shirley the best present she could find and make her some new dresses. She could hardly believe the rate at which the child was growing. Somehow or other she had to win her back again, she told herself desperately as she rocked backwards and forwards in the gloomy corridor as the train crawled onwards.

If she were truthful with herself she'd have to admit that she had hoped to see Tony this weekend. She hadn't seen him since that night last July when they spent the night together. She wondered if he was over the loss of his Claire yet. Time and again she relived that night, remembering his anguish and her own bewilderment. What would have happened, she wondered, if he had wanted to make love to her? What would her response have been? Deep down she knew that at the time she would have refused. But now, in retrospect, her view was very different. Perhaps she should have offered him the comfort of her body. It would have been an adult, womanly gesture, something she could have done for the man she loved and admired so much, to help him to bear his suffering. And now she had lost her chance to give the only thing she had to give; and perhaps to mean more to him than a mere passing confidante. She would never know now what the outcome might have been. And the worst of it was that Ma still didn't believe her when she insisted that nothing had happened.

As the train pulled in to Euston Station the siren was wailing. Wearily Gloria followed the crowd down onto the Underground platform and there she stayed till first light when the 'all clear' sounded, getting what rest she could, her head pillowed on her small weekend case.

As she walked out of the station at Whitechapel, devastation faced her. She picked her way through streets piled with the rubble and debris of last night's raid. The acrid stink of burning filled the air and water from the fire hoses glistened on the road and formed sooty puddles everywhere. The whole landscape had changed. Bombed houses stood with rooms exposed to view, torn wallpaper hanging in shreds. In one a picture still hung pathetically askew from its nail. Broken and charred timbers and joists hung precariously overhead, some with scraps of blackened linoleum still attached to them. And in the midst of all this hellish devastation, exhausted, dispirited people scrabbled among debris looking for any small possessions that might have survived intact.

Anxious about Angel Row, Gloria quickened her steps. But as she turned the corner into Grainger Street she stood still and gasped with shock. There was nothing. The whole street had gone; houses, shops and, most shocking of all, the Adelphi. Where the cinema had stood there was nothing but a heap of smoking rubble. Her hand to her mouth, Gloria began to run. On the corner a group of grey-faced men were standing. She recognised one of them as an ARP warden from Pa's post.

'Were there any casualties?' she asked breathlessly.

The man looked at her wryly. 'What do you think, luv? They all copped it.'

'*All*?'

'We dug two out of the rubble still breathing but I'd be surprised if they lived long enough to get to the hospital,' he said bluntly.

'There was a girl fire-watching at the cinema,' Gloria said, her heart in her mouth. 'Freda – Freda Harris. Please, can you . . .?' The man was shaking his head.

'Cinema copped it first. Direct hit.' The man looked at Gloria's white face. 'Friend o' yours, was she?' Gloria nodded numbly. 'Well, she couldn't've known anything, luv. Must've been instantaneous. Lucky it was a Sunday and no performance,' he added. 'Could've been much worse.'

Could have been much worse. The words echoed in Gloria's head all the way back to Angel Row. If she hadn't gone to Houlton for the weekend, if she hadn't got Freda to change places with her, she – or what was left of her – would be lying in the mortuary now. Instead she would have Freda's death on her conscience for the rest of her life. By the time she reached Angel Row, which, to her enormous relief, was mercifully still more or less intact, she had made up her mind what she must do.

When Gloria had first tentatively voiced her intention of going to Houlton for the duration, Ma had been tight-lipped.

'You must do as you think fit, o'course,' she said noncommittally.

But Pa had taken a more practical view. 'The girl's right, Ma,' he said. 'She's got young Shirl to think of. We wouldn't want the kiddie to be left motherless, now would we?'

'Don't you see, Ma?' Gloria urged her mother. 'If I hadn't gone to Houlton last weekend I'd have been dead now. Poor Freda got killed instead of me. I'll never forgive myself for that. But it made me see what might still happen if I stay here. I'm not just thinking of myself.' She paused to lick her lips, assessing her mother's reaction. 'In fact, you could come too if you'd a mind to.'

Ma's eyebrows shot up. '*Me*? Leave London? And who do you think'd look after your pa and run the shop if I upped and slung me 'ook?'

'I'd be all right –' Pa ventured bravely, but the look on Ma's face silenced him in mid-sentence.

'*No*,' she said, leaning back in her chair and folding her arms. 'I ain't movin' from my 'ome an' my shop. Not while it's still standin'. If that 'itler wants to make me give in 'e's gonna 'ave to kill me first.'

Gloria sighed. 'Mrs Jarvis asked me to invite you both for Christmas,' she said. 'Why don't you come? We could all be together again, even if it was only for a few days.'

At last Ma gave in and the three of them travelled to Houlton for the Christmas holiday. Ma was grudgingly impressed by the size of Molly Jarvis's kitchen, the big, shiny refrigerator and the massive range. And though she made no comment, her eyes widened at the freshness of the home-grown vegetables and farm produce that they took for granted in the country. But when Gloria asked if she had changed her mind about going to live there, she shook her head stubbornly.

'I was born and bred in the dear old Smoke and that's where I'll stop till me time's up,' she said with a sniff. 'You can 'ave too much fresh air, you know,' she added darkly. 'Catches me at the back o' the throat somethin' chronic sometimes, it does.' She wrinkled her nose. 'All them farmyard pongs can't be 'ealthy either if you asks me.'

Ma and Pa hadn't seen Shirley for almost a year and they were both astonished by the way she had grown. On Christmas night they all gathered in the drawing room to watch the girls dance for them and, though Ma pulled down the corners of her mouth in mock disapproval, she couldn't disguise her pride in her talented granddaughter. However, she couldn't resist warning Gloria later.

'Mark my words. All this performin' will go to the child's 'ead. 'Fore you know it she'll be wantin' to go on the stage proper.' She sucked in her breath and shook her head. 'An' we all know where *that* leads.'

Gloria stayed on for a week after the holiday and tried to get a job, but it wasn't as easy as Jim seemed to think.

None of the Northampton cinemas had any vacancies. Without work she couldn't even begin to make plans to settle and at last she was obliged to return to London with a promise from Jim and Molly that they would keep their eyes and ears open and get in touch the moment they heard of anything going.

It was several weeks later that the letter arrived from Jim. When Gloria opened it, a small newspaper cutting fluttered to the floor. Picking it up, she saw that it was an advertisement from a local paper. Women were needed to work in the new aircraft factory. Sitting back in her chair at the breakfast table, she read it thoughtfully, then passed it across to Pa, who studied it carefully, his lips moving as he read.

'Well, it's a job,' he said, looking up at her at last. 'And I heard tell that women are going to get called up if things go on the way they are. I dare say if you was in war work that wouldn't 'appen. It says 'ere they pay you while you train, too. It's worth thinkin' about.'

Gloria sighed. 'Factory work, though, Pa. That's something I never thought I'd come to.'

Pa looked again at the cutting. 'Where is this Boothley Bottom place anyway? Funny name.'

'It's about three miles from Houlton. The next village.'

'So you'd be close to Shirl.' He handed back the scrap of paper with a shrug. 'Well, it's up to you, gel. Make up your own mind. Don't ask your ma, though. You know what she'll say.'

Gloria took his advice. For the next few days she did a lot of thinking, not mentioning the letter to her mother at all. Ma was still waging her fierce, unbending one-to-one war with Hitler and she saw Gloria's plans to move away from London as 'giving in'. Then suddenly it seemed that everywhere Gloria looked there were articles about women going into war work. It stood to reason that there weren't going to be enough men to staff the factories with them all being called up, but so far there had been resistance to the idea of women taking over. Now, though, the newspapers and magazines were full of it.

Posters began to appear everywhere; an emotive image of a willowy feminine figure, arms outstretched in glorious triumph as a factory spewed out shoals of aeroplanes in the background. Mr Bevin appealed to the patriotism of all women to step into the breach to save their country. Gloria decided to apply.

On the day she received the letter, telling her she had been selected for an interview, she broke the news to her mother.

'The shop can't support all of us anyway, Ma,' she said. 'You know how hard up we've been since my money stopped coming in. I'd have had to get another job soon, and what is there here for me? There's hardly a cinema round here left standing.'

'Why beat about the bush? You've made up your mind anyway, ain't you?' Ma said, tight-lipped. 'I don't know why you're makin' out you're asking for *my* advice. You've known all along you were goin'. Admit it.'

'I've *got* to go, Ma. Can't you see, I miss Shirl and I want to be with her?' Gloria pleaded. 'She's growing up without me. Sometimes I feel as if she's not mine any more.' She reached across to take her mother's hand. 'If I can find a little place to rent, you and Pa could come too. Please, Ma.'

Ma snatched her hand away abruptly. 'Go on then, you go if you must. I ain't stoppin' you. But don't expect me to up and run.'

Resigned to her mother's stubbornness, Gloria stood up. 'All right, Ma. I really *would* like us all to be together somewhere safe for the rest of the war. But if you won't come, you won't. I've got to think of Shirl first. You've forced me to make the choice.'

Unblinking, Ma watched her walk out through the door. She made no attempt to stop her or to protest any further. But as the door closed behind her only daughter her hands clenched into fists at her sides and her eyes filled with rare tears.

'*Bugger* that there 'itler,' she muttered thickly, thumping one fist down on the table. ''E's gorn and done it now all right. If I could only get me 'ands on 'im I'd squeeze the life out of the little bleeder.'

The interview at the aircraft factory at Boothley Bottom went well, but Gloria could see right from the start that the work was very different from anything she had ever done before. And it was obvious that the hours were such that it would be impossible for her to have Shirley to live with her. It was made clear to her that, unfettered, she would be free to work the maximum hours, and the wages offered for shift work took her breath away. Never in her wildest dreams had she envisaged earning so much. There was a hostel for unmarried female workers too, which meant cheap living, and a hot meal could be had in the works canteen at the end of every shift. Gloria worked out that on that kind of money she might actually be able to buy a home of her own in a few years' time; if she saved up really hard and provided the war lasted that long. A little cottage perhaps, somewhere pretty and peaceful where she and Shirley could settle down together after the war. Maybe she could even find enough to pay for Shirley to go to a private school where she could learn the things Gloria yearned to know more about – how to speak French and appreciate great writers like Shakespeare. Talking to Tony and seeing him act in the theatre had made her regret all the gaping holes in her own education and wish for better for her daughter. A whole exciting new future seemed to open tantalisingly before her as she sat there waiting to hear if the job was hers.

All the way back to Longueville Hall on the bus Gloria kept thinking of the new job she'd been offered and wondering if she could really take it. It would all depend on Molly Jarvis – or rather the Darrents. She kept her fingers crossed, hoping her bright new dream wasn't about to crumble.

The moment Molly looked at her she knew. 'You've got it. I can tell by that sparkle in your eyes,' she said with a smile.

Gloria slipped off her coat and sat down at the kitchen table. 'There were ten of us interviewed. Eight of us were offered jobs,' she said. 'The two who didn't get chosen had young kids. It's too bad, you know. The pamphlets all said there'd be crèche facilities for women with kiddies, but there's no such thing at that factory.'

Molly nodded sympathetically as she poured boiling water into the teapot. 'Typical. They want the women to work but they don't make the proper provisions. If you ask me, it's a woman they want, organising things up there at Whitehall.'

Gloria cleared her throat. 'The thing is, Molly, I'd have to work shifts – all night sometimes – and live in the hostel, which means . . .'

'That you'd like Shirley to stay on here with us.' Molly finished the sentence with a smile. 'It's all right, I'd foreseen that. Don't worry, dear.'

But Gloria shook her head. 'It's good of you and I'm grateful, but it isn't really what I wanted. I was looking forward to Shirl and me being together again. The thing is, the money's so good I couldn't afford to turn it down. I'll pay you extra, of course.'

'For what that little one eats? I should think not. Anyway we all love having her here. You know that.'

When she came home from school, Shirley too was happy with the news. A little *too* happy for Gloria's peace of mind. The two little girls hugged each other and danced ecstatically round the kitchen at the news that Shirley would not be leaving Longueville Hall. Later, when they were alone, Gloria asked Shirley how she felt about having her close at hand.

Shirley looked at her mother's wistful face and knew she needed reassurance. 'It'll be lovely,' she said. 'I'll be able to see you much more often and you'll be able to come to all our concerts and everything – yet I'll still be able to stay here with Imogen and Nanny and Jim.'

'Don't you miss London at all?' Gloria asked.

Shirley bit her lip, trying to assess the reaction her mother wanted from her. 'Well, I do a bit,' she said. 'I miss Ma and Pa and you, of course. But everyone says it's horrible in London now. Miss Frost, our teacher, says it'll never be the same again.'

'I don't suppose it will,' Gloria said sadly. 'That's why I thought maybe we might stay here after the war, buy a little place, just me and you. And perhaps when Pa and Ma retire they'll come too. Would you like that?'

'Ye-es.' But for Shirley 'after the war' was another world. It was impossible to foresee the kind of life she might have after the war. She'd be grown-up then; a new, different, exciting person to whom anything might happen.

'Come and give us a cuddle,' Gloria invited, holding out her arms. Shirley came to her willingly enough, but in her arms the child already felt different. She was losing the comforting chubbiness of childhood and the old intimacy they had shared was fading. Her body was already beginning to develop adult characteristics, growing slender and firm. She was supple and strong from regular exercise and her dancing. So much about her was different; her speech, her manners . . . With a sudden stab of regret Gloria realised that she even smelled different. Shirley was almost eleven, she reminded herself. Before she knew it she'd be a young woman.

Chapter Seven

At first Gloria found the work at Boothley aircraft factory hard going. It was repetitive and boring, and during the training period and the few months following she often thought despairingly that she would never stick it. But whenever she was tempted to quit she made herself think of the money she could save. Closing her eyes she would visualise the pretty little cottage with roses and geraniums in the front garden and the idyllic life she and Shirley would live there. It never failed to spur her onwards.

The hostel was spartan, but the food in the canteen wasn't bad and the friendship of her workmates more than made up for the home comforts she missed. They were a mixed bunch of women of all ages and from varying backgrounds. On her bench there was a doctor's daughter who hadn't fancied the services but wanted to do her bit, a middle-aged woman who had worked all her life as a hotel manageress, a housewife who had never been out to work in her life before and an ex-parlourmaid who insisted that she had once worked for six months at Windsor Castle.

As the weeks became months Gloria gradually settled into the routine. The work became easier as she grew more adept and the off-duty hours were enhanced by the company of the other women. It wasn't long before they discovered her dressmaking skill, and she found that she could make herself some extra money doing alterations and adding innovative touches to tired, much worn dresses. Disappointingly, she didn't see Shirley nearly as often as she had hoped to because of the odd hours she worked, but in the school holidays she spent as much time as she could over at Houlton.

On Saturday evenings dances were run in Boothley Bottom village hall. Gloria had never been much for dancing. Her unsocial hours as a cinema usherette had precluded it and in the first few weeks at the factory she was so exhausted that all she wanted to do on her Saturday evening off was fall into bed and sleep. But her roommate, Jane, finally persuaded her to go with a crowd of the other young women and she found that after her first stumbling efforts she soon picked up the steps and began to enjoy herself. It was nice to have a reason to get dressed up again, to do her hair and put on make-up, and to talk to men other than the bossy middle-aged foremen at the factory. Soldiers from a nearby army camp often attended the dances. Most of them were awaiting embarkation orders so the faces were always changing. It wasn't possible to form any lasting friendships, but nevertheless the dances made a pleasant diversion to the week's hard work.

Monthly lunchtime concerts were something the workers looked forward to at the factory, and great excitement was generated when the news went round that Leonie Swann was to be the next star turn. There was standing room only that day, and Gloria's workmates were impressed when she told them that she actually knew the star and that her daughter had been evacuated to her country home. Some of them looked sceptical, so to prove that she wasn't shooting a line she volunteered to go up and speak to Leonie when she toured the factory after the concert. To her dismay and humiliation, the star received her friendly overture with a look of shocked surprise, staring through her as though she had never seen her before. As the little party moved on, the accompanying foreman turned to mouth a silent admonishment at Gloria, shaking his head at her behind Leonie's back. As she returned, red-faced, to her bench, the other girls lowered their eyes. Her friend Jane leaned close and said above the din of the machinery:

'Take no notice, love. Wouldn't have hurt the stuck-up cow to give you the time of day.' She nudged Gloria good-naturedly. 'Cheer up. It's nearly three. *Music While You Work*'ll be on in a minute and we can have a good old sing.'

1941 was a busy year for everybody. In September Tony's first film, *Blitz*, was released. It had been shot during some of the worst of London's air raids and highlighted the courage of the civil-defence workers, the ARP and the Auxiliary Fire Service in particular. *On Target* came out soon after. It was a half-hour documentary about a bombing raid, filmed during an actual raid over Germany with members of the RAF taking part. Both films were hailed as successful morale boosters and Tony's skills as a director were highly praised.

Leonie's career was climbing from strength to strength. Her tour of army camps had been so successful that another, more extensive tour was planned. Her records were selling as fast as they came out and her face was on the cover of one magazine or another almost every week.

At Longueville Hall Shirley and Imogen were busy with school work. Soon they would sit for the scholarship, hoping for a place at the high school. Imogen had the advantage, the curriculum at her private school having been much more extensive than anything the village school could offer. Shirley feared privately that her friend would sail through the exam, leaving her behind, so she resolved to work really hard in order to keep up. She couldn't bear the idea of Imogen moving on without her. The alternative, from what she could gather, was to remain at the village school till she was fourteen and then go into a job in a shop or one of the many shoe factories. She knew instinctively that if she were to let that happen, life and all its delights would travel on without her.

In the evenings, after the girls were in bed, Molly and Jim would sit in the kitchen with their cocoa, listening to the radio. As the months went by Jim's face grew grimmer each night as he listened to the nine-o'clock news.

Nothing seemed to be going right for poor old England. They had held Hitler at bay so far and the bombing raids didn't seem as bad as they had been, but overseas the news was critical. Jim reckoned that winter must surely be the worst England had ever known. In December came the shocking news that Pearl Harbour had been bombed, knocking out many American ships and taking a heavy toll of lives. On Christmas Day, as the Jarvises once again shared their festivities with Gloria and the other Rayners, Hong Kong fell. February saw the surrender of Singapore, quickly followed by Rangoon and Burma. Things looked very black indeed and Jim began to fear that the worst might happen, they could be losing the war.

He didn't communicate his fears to Molly. She had enough to cope with, running the house and making the rations go round. The one bright spot, as Jim saw it, was that America had joined the fight at last. It must be a sad day for many American homes, but it was a huge relief that Great Britain no longer stood alone.

In the early spring of 1942 Imogen and Shirley sat the scholarship examination. Rigid with nerves they sat in the big room that was the top class of the village school. The headmaster, Mr Hawkins, invigilated, looking up ferociously over the tops of his spectacles whenever anyone fidgeted or coughed. Halfway through, they were allowed out into the playground for a break. Shirley found Imogen and grasped her hand excitedly.

'How did you get on?'

Imogen pulled a face. 'Not bad. You?'

'Easy. The sums were cushy and the English comp was *fun*.' She jumped up and down gleefully. 'I bet we both pass. Just think – we'll be High School girls, Imo. Won't it be smashing?'

Imogen was more blasé about the prospect. 'It's got to be better than this hole anyway,' she said as they filed back into the building for the second half of the exam.

It was June when four of the pupils were called to Mr Hawkins's office and told that they had achieved a place at the high and grammar schools. The one boy was a local child. Two of the three girls were Shirley and Imogen, and the fourth, surprisingly, was Tilly Marks, now unrecognisable as the grubby waif taken in by Mrs Phipps at the post office. That evening Jim put through a telephone call to the hostel at Boothley Bottom to give Gloria the news. She walked back into the communal rest room with shining eyes.

'You'll never guess what. My Shirl's gone and got herself a place at the high school,' she said triumphantly. 'My kid's gonna *make* something of herself.'

Jane and the others crowded round her with congratulations, hugging her and patting her back. 'That's lovely, Glor. Wonderful news.'

The letter had travelled all round England by the time Leonie received it. She was up in Orkney, performing for the officers and men of HMS *Erebos*. From the envelope she saw that it had been sent first to the BBC, then on to the London flat; from there to Longueville Hall, where Jim had forwarded it to her in Orkney. She turned the tattered envelope over in her hand. In one corner the sender had printed in large black capitals: PRIVATE AND CONFIDENTIAL, which explained the forwarding. The BBC usually kept her fan mail until she was in London. She did not recognise the handwriting and the envelope was of a cheap quality, as was the flimsy sheet of notepaper it contained. It was headed with the name and address of a bank and read:

Dear Eileen,

I read the piece about you in an old copy of *Home and Beauty* in the doctor's last week and felt I had to write to you. It's funny but I don't remember our house in the country or all them stars we used to entertain at weekends. You must have a different sort of memory to me, our Eileen.

Mum and Dad have had a very hard time of it, what with the bombing and everything. Dad can't work no more. He relies on me to keep him and Mum. I didn't

146

get taken in the army because of an injury to my leg five years ago when a car knocked me off the delivery bike. It left me with a bad limp and it's a job for me to get about sometimes. All we've got is the shop and I have to manage it on my own now. It's a hard life, our Eileen. Not like yours.

We've been bombed twice. Last time Mum was in hospital for three weeks with shrapnel in her back.

We could do with a bit of that money you're earning, our Eileen, and I'm sure you'll want to send us some now that you know how bad things are. But don't let Mum and Dad know. They're too proud to ask for anything, as you know.

Maybe that magazine would like to know about your *real* family and upbringing. But I'm sure it won't come to that, will it, Eileen, you being so loyal and all?

Hoping this finds you as it leaves me, I remain, your affectionate brother,

Norman.

Speechless with fury, Leonie crushed the note in her hand and hurled it across the room. Of all the slimy little toads! How dare he imagine he could blackmail her? And in such crude, blatant terms too. *Our Eileen*, indeed. But after a moment's thought she got up and retrieved the letter, smoothing it out again and rereading it thoughtfully. He'd do it. There was no doubt about that. It was just the kind of thing he'd enjoy. He had always been jealous of her. Mum and Dad had been getting on when she was born. They had always wanted a girl and Norman's nose had been put well and truly out of joint by her arrival. Oh yes, he'd take great delight in seeing her exposed as a liar and a poseur, especially now that she had made a success of her life. She bit her lip hard. If *only* she hadn't made up that ridiculous story. But as she thought about it she could see that she could turn the situation to her advantage. She remembered the conversation she'd had with Tony and his remark about the war bringing out the best in some, the worst in others. It might be nice to be

147

able to write and tell him she had re-established contact with her family and was sending money to help them. Maybe it would help to improve their relationship. No need to mention Norman's letter, of course.

She and Tony saw each other rarely nowadays and when they did he was decidedly cool towards her. He'd shown absolutely no inclination to sleep with her since that night when the flat had been bombed. She had wondered lately if he'd found a new girl in that film company of his; or even if the mysterious Claire could have returned to claim his affections. How much would Norman settle for? she wondered. She pulled her chequebook out of her handbag and unscrewed her fountain pen. He might have the cheek of the devil and a certain ratlike cunning, but Norman had never been all that bright. She'd try him with fifty. That should keep him quiet.

Shirley and Imogen had just broken up for the summer holidays when Tony took his much needed break. He'd been working flat out for a year now and he had just come back from Tobruk in Libya, getting the film crew out just in time before the disastrous fall. He had found the work exciting and exhilarating at first, but lately the tension had begun to chip away at his nerves. He found himself running out of ideas, too. What he really needed, he told himself, was to get away from it all and recharge his batteries. He decided to take a couple of weeks off while the editing and cutting of the latest film was taking place. He'd go down to spend it with Imogen at Houlton. He had written to Leonie to tell her, asking if there was any chance of her joining him there. He pointed out how long it was since they spent any time with the child. But she'd replied rather tetchily that it was out of the question and that she'd have thought that if he had leave he might have made the effort to spend it with her up in Scapa Flow, where she was dying of boredom. To her annoyance Tony replied that he felt Imogen deserved a treat after passing her scholarship exam.

As it happened, his visit coincided with Gloria's holiday. As soon as she learned the dates, she made arrangements with Molly to stay at Longueville Hall so that she could be with Shirley. But when she heard that Tony was to be there too, she was filled with apprehension. He might think it a cheek for her to invite herself there for her holiday. He might not want to have her around; he might feel awkward about the night they had spent together at the Mayfair flat. It seemed so long ago now, but she hadn't forgotten it and she doubted very much that he had either.

She need not have worried. When she got off the bus at Houlton post office, Tony and the two girls were there to meet her. Tony was at the wheel of the camouflaged car provided by the film company. As she stepped down from the bus, he got out of the car to take her suitcase from her, a smile of welcome on his face.

'Gloria! How nice to see you. It's been simply *ages*.'

He looked thinner, but fit and handsome, tanned from his recent visit to the Libyan desert. Gloria was glad she had let Jane do her hair in the new upswept style that was becoming so popular, and that she had stayed up to finish the blue dress that she'd copied from the one Ingrid Bergman had worn in *Casablanca*. All the girls swore that she looked the image of Ingrid in it and that the blue was the very same colour as her eyes. She smiled shyly back at Tony.

'It's ever so good of you to come and meet me,' she said politely.

'Not a bit.' He hoisted her case into the boot and slammed it shut. 'These two would never have forgiven me if I hadn't.'

By now Shirley was out of the car too, hugging her mother and chattering excitedly. 'I've got to have a uniform,' she announced. 'For the high school. It's brown with a yellow hat band and a badge. It's hard to get some of the things but when the older girls grow out of theirs or leave, they sell their uniforms. There's a special sale on at the school tomorrow and Imo and I are going with Nanny to see if there's anything that will fit us.'

Gloria hugged her daughter. 'What a good idea! I'll come too and make sure you've got everything you need. Can't let my clever little girl go to her posh new school without the proper uniform, can I?'

Shirley glanced at Imogen and lowered her voice. '*Glor* – don't call me that,' she whispered.

The girls sat in the back of the car and Gloria sat in the front with Tony. All the way back to the Hall he kept the conversation flowing; asking about her job at the factory; talking about the girls, their success at winning scholarships and the way they had both grown since he last saw them. Gloria felt shy and awkward with him, and deflated at Shirley's obvious embarrassment. Tony was making polite small talk as though she were some casual acquaintance to whom he was trying extra hard to be nice – someone he had only just met. Clearly he wanted to pretend that his confidence and the intimate moments they had shared that night at the flat had never happened.

At Longueville Hall he took her case from the boot and carried it into the house for her. Molly stood in the hall, waiting to welcome her, her round face beaming with pleasure.

'Welcome home, my dear. We've all been looking forward to seeing you so much.' She took both Gloria's hands and looked her up and down, shaking her head and exclaiming at her thinness. 'My, but you've lost weight. You mustn't overdo it, you know.'

'Fat chance of doing anything else,' Gloria said with a laugh. 'I was quite glad to lose a few pounds. It doesn't bother me. Munitions work is the best slimming treatment I know.'

But Molly shook her head. 'I read where a lot of girls have gone down with TB from overdoing it in factories. These long shifts ruin your health. It's not natural, working all the hours God sends like that.' She smiled. 'Anyway, I'm going to make sure you get a good rest and plenty of wholesome food while you're here. At least I can send you back in good shape.'

Upstairs Gloria found Tony putting her case at the foot of the bed in the room she always occupied. The window

150

was open and the curtains fluttered in the breeze. The room was filled with the scent of summer: newly mown grass, roses and lavender. Gloria went to the window and leaned out, breathing deeply. 'Mmm. It's lovely to think I've got seven whole days to enjoy this,' she said.

Tony crossed the room to stand behind her, looking over her shoulder. 'Gloria,' he said softly. His tone made her turn to look at him and she saw that his eyes were serious. 'I want you to know that I haven't forgotten what you did for me that night. I'll appreciate it for the rest of my life.'

She shook her head, suddenly lost for words. 'It was nothing.'

He reached out and grasped her shoulders, turning her so that she was obliged to look at him. 'Oh, but it was. It meant a very great deal to me. I've realised since that it must have been difficult, explaining your absence that night, and yet you didn't even hesitate when I asked you to stay.'

'I told my parents I'd been with a friend. It was all right.'

'You're sure?'

'Of course.' She smiled wryly. 'Anyway, there's been more to worry them since then.'

'They're all right?'

'As well as can be expected, what with the bombs and everything.'

He smiled. 'That's good. Well, anyway, I wanted you to know that I'm grateful. And it's good to see you again, Gloria.'

'It's good to see you too, Mr Darrent.'

His eyebrows rose. 'Oh *dear*. I thought we'd agreed on Tony.'

She blushed and looked away. 'It was a long time ago. I didn't know if . . .'

He squeezed her shoulders, then let his hands drop to his sides. 'And if I can make your holiday happy and relaxed, please let me. I'm at your service, madame.' He laughed and tipped up her chin. 'Come on, relax and smile for me. We can be friends, can't we, just as we were before?'

'Of course. Thank you – Tony.'

'That's good. Now you'd better unpack and get downstairs. Nanny's got the biggest tea you've seen since before the war waiting in the kitchen and I don't know about you, but I'm ready to do it full justice.'

Gloria had looked forward to going with Molly and the girls to buy the school uniforms next morning, but at breakfast Molly insisted that there was no need.

'I know what they need, my dear. You just stay here and put your feet up.'

'Oh, but I'd like to come,' Gloria assured her. 'It's a special occasion, isn't it – buying her school uniform?'

Molly looked uncomfortable but Shirley was more direct. 'It's all right, Glor,' she said. 'See, if there's just the three of us we can get a lift there and back in Mr Morris's grocery van. He goes into Northampton on Mondays to pick up the magazines from the wholesaler's. We often go. Nanny sits in front with him and Imo and me squeeze in the back. He doesn't mind if there's only the two of us and we sit still.'

'Oh, I see,' Gloria said.

Molly's face was flushed with embarrassment. 'He helps us out because Jim lets him have our surplus vegetables,' she said. 'We all have to do what we can for each other with the shortages and everything. It's not that we don't want your company, dear, but queuing for the bus can take so long now that they've cut down the service.'

'Oh, that's all right,' Gloria said with a smile. 'I shall look forward to a mannequin parade when you get home.' She opened her handbag. 'Here, let me give you some money.'

But Molly waved a hand. 'Pay me when I get back,' she said. 'I've got no idea what we'll be able to get secondhand at the school, but at least we won't have to part with our precious coupons. We'll go to the Co-Op for the rest, if that's all right with you.' She bustled round, pulling on her coat and reaching for her handbag. 'Now, come along, you girls. No dawdling. We don't want to keep Mr Morris waiting. He said he'd be at the end of the lane at half nine.'

Trying hard to fight down the feeling of disappointment, Gloria wandered out into the garden. Of course Molly was right, it would have been tiring, waiting around for buses. Much better to accept a lift when it was offered. It was Shirley's dismissal that hurt. She was so proud that her daughter was going to get a real education, but wounded that she wasn't allowed to share in her achievement. 'It's only natural,' she told herself, trying to justify the child's attitude. 'Molly has done everything for her for almost three years now. And after all, it's only a few school clothes. Shirl still likes the dresses I make for her specially.'

'You're looking very pensive.' Tony had come round the end of a tall yew hedge and was facing her before she noticed him. 'What is it – lost something?'

'I'm beginning to wonder,' Gloria said, half to herself. 'Molly has taken the girls into town to buy the new school uniforms.'

'And left you behind?'

Gloria shrugged dismissively. 'Not on purpose. They had the chance of a lift in someone's van and there was only room for three.'

Tony frowned. 'But I would have driven you all in.'

'Molly wouldn't ask. I expect she thinks you need a rest – and to save your petrol allowance, too.'

'All the same . . .' He grinned at her ruefully. 'I do know what you mean. It's the girls, isn't it? Do you get the feeling sometimes that you're surplus to requirements?'

She sighed. 'I do.'

'Me too, but it's hardly surprising, is it?' he said. 'We've been off doing our bit for the war, you and me, but life has to go on. Let's just be grateful for the Mollies and Jims of this world.'

'Oh, I *am*,' Gloria said quickly. 'When I think of some of the people Shirley might have been billeted on. I wouldn't want you to think . . .'

153

'I *don't*.' He slipped an arm around her shoulders. 'It's just that sometimes we look at the children and wonder what we're missing, but sadly there's nothing we can do about it.' He smiled. 'I'll tell you what. Why don't we slip off for the day ourselves? We could have lunch at a little place I know where you can still get a good steak. When they come back they can just miss *us* for a change. What do you say?'

She bit her lip. 'Oh, I don't know – do you think we should?'

'Yes, I most definitely do.'

They looked into each other's eyes and laughed. Gloria felt herself beginning to relax as Tony took her hand and drew her along with him towards the garage. As they passed the hedge that separated the lawn from the kitchen garden, Jim could be seen hoeing between the rows of lettuces. Tony put a finger to his lips and they both ducked down, chuckling like a couple of children playing truant.

The car wasn't as comfortable as the Rolls, but to Gloria it was a treat to ride in any car. Tony explained that he'd had to lay the Rolls up for the duration.

'I used to get her out now and again, but now that the private petrol ration has been withdrawn I can't run her,' he explained. 'I'm lucky to have the use of this old bus, even though she is a bit of a rattle-trap.' He turned to look appreciatively at Gloria's crisp print dress with its white collar and cuffs. 'By the way, how do you manage to look so pretty on the clothing coupons we're allowed?'

She blushed. 'I make my own. I've found a stall in the market where I can pick up remnants. It's nothing new for me, I used to do it in London. Usually there's only enough for a blouse or a little dress for Shirley, but sometimes I find a piece big enough to make a frock for me if I cut carefully.'

'You're a clever little thing, aren't you?' He smiled, his eyes on the road ahead. 'You haven't found a young man yet, then?'

'No.'

'I'm surprised.'

'The other girls and I go to dances sometimes at the village hall. The soldiers from Boothley camp come, but you hardly ever see the same fellers twice. It's no time to be getting fond of anyone, is it?'

He was silent for a moment and his eyes clouded, then he said quietly: 'No Gloria. It certainly isn't.'

'*Oh!*' She looked at him anxiously. 'Oh, I'm sorry. I wasn't thinking.'

He smiled his sudden, quick smile. 'It's all right, Gloria. I'm all over it now. You don't have to be careful what you say.' He pressed his foot down on the brake and turned right into a lane. 'We're almost there. The Wheatsheaf is just down here. I know you're going to like it.'

It was a long time since Gloria had eaten food like the lunch Tony bought for them at the Wheatsheaf. Succulent steak, garnished with crisp brown onion rings; golden chips and homegrown carrots and peas. It was followed by apple pie with thick cream. And because Tony was a special customer, the landlord had unearthed a bottle of his best Beaujolais from deep in the bowels of his cellar.

'How do they do it?' Gloria whispered, leaning across the table.

Tony tapped the side of his nose. 'Their son is a farmer – that and what we'll call careful management.'

He snatched up the bill quickly when it came, but not before Gloria had seen what she thought an outrageous figure in the last column.

'Please, let me pay my share. I'm earning good money now and –'

He held up his hand and frowned at her. 'Shhh. Do you want to get me a bad name? It'll be a black day when I can't buy a pretty woman lunch.'

Gloria felt decidedly tipsy when they left the pub and Tony suggested a walk to settle their meal and blow away the cobwebs. He parked the car by a copse of trees that led down to a stream and they walked in the lazy afternoon sunshine. To Gloria there had never been a more perfect afternoon. The air was warm and mellow, heavy with the scent of clover and buzzing with the sound of a thousand insects. They sat down on the bank of the stream and Tony said suddenly:

'Are you happy, Gloria?'

She looked at him in surprise. 'I suppose so. I haven't really thought.'

He pulled a long blade of grass from its sheath and nibbled at the sweet green stem. 'That's about it nowadays, isn't it? We don't get time to ask ourselves the important questions any more. Life slips past and half the time we don't know whether it's a living death or a dying life we're living.' He paused, then said: 'Did I ever tell you I had a son?'

'No.' She was shocked, and unsure of whether he was serious or not.

'Well, I have. He lives in America with his mother, Gillian Fane. Ever heard of her?'

Gloria's mouth dropped open. '*The* Gillian Fane? The one who was in *Song of Granada*?'

'That's the lady. Our marriage was all over a long time ago, long before I met Leonie. Gill and I were a couple of silly stage-struck kids at the time. It was never right. Marcus was just two when we parted. A beautiful little boy, and now he's almost a man.' He sighed wistfully. 'I still miss him, but I'm glad he's not old enough to be drafted into the army now that America has joined the war.' He smiled at her. 'Do you know, that's the first time I've spoken about him to anyone for – oh, I don't know how long.'

'Will you see him again – after the war perhaps?'

He shrugged. 'Who knows? I'm a stranger to him even now, so heaven knows what he'll make of me then. No, I suppose I have to face the fact that I've lost him.'

Gloria was moved by the wistful smile that she knew concealed his sadness. It seemed he was destined to lose all the people he loved. Sudden tears blurred her vision, intensifying the stream's glitter and the trembling of the leaves. The wine, the food and the mellow summer afternoon had loosened her inhibitions and she reached out instinctively to take his hand. 'You said you were over it – Claire, I mean – but you're not really, are you?'

His fingers curled warmly round hers. 'Not really, if I'm honest. But maybe I never will be, not completely.' He turned to look into her eyes. 'Dearest, sweet little Gloria. You understand, don't you?'

'Yes.' She swallowed hard. 'I should have been killed by rights,' she told him. 'One weekend when I came up here to see Shirl, the cinema where I used to work had a direct hit. I'd swapped fire-watching with another girl. She was killed.'

He put his arms around her shoulders and pulled her close. 'Poor Gloria. How terrible for you.'

'It seems like fate, doesn't it?' she said. 'Makes us see that there's a pattern to things somehow – that God hasn't finished with us yet.'

For a long moment they were silent, then Tony said: 'It's so restful, being with you. I can be myself and not what people expect me to be. People like you are rare, you know.' He kissed her lightly on the lips. 'You should be patented, made into pills for peculiar people – like me.' He glanced at his watch and sighed with regret. 'I suppose it's time we were getting back or I'll get the wigging of a lifetime from Nanny for keeping you out so long.' He got up and pulled her to her feet. 'Thanks for today, Gloria.' He looked at her, his head on one side. 'What is it that Shirley calls you – Glow?'

'Glor,' she told him, grimacing. 'Horrible, isn't it?'

'I like Glow better. It suits you. You're like a little glow-worm, shining in the dark; sweet and bright and comforting.' He drew her close and kissed her again, his lips lingering on hers and making her head spin in a way that had nothing to do with the wine. Then suddenly he was laughing light-heartedly and pulling her along with him through the trees and back to the car, leaving the sadness, the joy and the dreams behind with the willows and the shining water.

In the kitchen at Longueville Hall Shirley and Imogen were parading in their new school clothes for Jim. Gloria and Tony arrived in time to see Shirley in her hockey shorts. Using the kitchen table as a stage, she was strutting up and down, singing a chorus of 'Run, Rabbit, Run' and using the hockey stick as though it was a gun. Imogen, Molly and Jim applauded loudly when she took a final bow.

In the doorway Tony said to Gloria: 'That little girl of yours is very talented, you know.'

She blushed with pride. 'I know. I've always encouraged her. I used to think that maybe she could make a career of her dancing, but now I've changed my mind. If she gets a proper education she might go to college and make a teacher or something.' She smiled. 'Isn't it funny? If she hadn't come to Houlton – if it hadn't been for the war – she might never have had the chance.'

Tony looked thoughtful, the seed of an idea beginning to germinate in his mind.

'Where have you been, Glor?' Shirley was saying. 'We were ever so lucky. Imo and I got almost everything we needed at the school sale. They showed us round, too, and you should just *see* it. There's a big art room and a science lab; oh, and the biggest, *best* gym you ever saw, with wall bars and ever so much apparatus. It's a *really* posh school. We're to have dancing lessons too – folk dancing and ballroom and –'

'Wait!' Gloria laughed. 'Let Imogen get a word in. I'd like to hear what Nanny has to say too, if you don't mind.'

But Shirley paused only for breath before going on: 'Hey, you'll never guess – Tilly Marks was there with Mrs Phipps. Her mum wrote and said she wasn't to go to the high school but Mrs Phipps is sending her anyway. She's paying for all the stuff herself. She told Nanny, didn't she?' She looked at Molly, who drew down the corners of her mouth.

'Now then, Shirley, you mustn't gossip, it's not nice. Off you go upstairs and change now, both of you, while I get the tea. You can show Gloria the rest of your uniform after.'

When the girls had gone, Gloria looked at her. 'Was it true about Tilly?'

Molly nodded. 'The child's mother wrote back in answer to the letter about Tilly's scholarship, saying that she didn't want her to go. She said she couldn't afford the expense and that girls weren't worth educating anyway.'

'And Mrs Phipps was annoyed?' Tony put in.

'She certainly was. That girl has come along in leaps and bounds since she's had her,' Molly said. 'Such a poor little scrap she was when she first came to Houlton; dirty and scruffy – barely housetrained. And her *language* . . .' Molly raised her eyes to the ceiling. 'Edith Phipps has worked miracles on her. Mind you. I don't know that I approve of what she's doing over this school thing. Overstepping the mark, if you ask me. I mean, what'll happen once the war's over and Tilly has to go back to London? It'll be a rude awakening for the child then, all right.'

Gloria looked at Tony and saw that his thoughtful expression had developed into a gleam of excitement in his eyes. She raised an enquiring eyebrow at him, but he nodded towards Molly's back and frowned. Maybe he'd tell her later what was on his mind.

When she saw Shirley to bed later that night, Gloria asked her if she was happy.

'Oh, *yes*,' Shirley said as she snuggled down. 'There's so much to look forward to – the holidays, then the new school.'

'You love it here with Nanny and Imogen, don't you?' Gloria asked wistfully. Molly's remark about the way Tilly Marks would feel when she went back to London had reinforced her plan to settle down near here when the war was over. She didn't want Shirley feeling resentful at being made to go back to London.

'Yes.' Shirley was looking at her mother's pensive expression. 'It doesn't mean I don't love you, though, Glor,' she said softly.

'But you don't like being called my little girl any more, though, do you? And you never come into bed with me for a cuddle either.'

Shirley frowned. 'That's because I'm older,' she said gravely.

'Is it? Or is it because Imogen thinks it's soppy?'

Shirley shook her head. 'Imo's never had a mum like you. She thinks you're smashing. I bet she wouldn't mind have someone to cuddle. It's just that with you being away such a lot I've got used to *not* having you with me. And I don't want people to think I'm a baby, specially now that I'm going to the high school.'

'What about when we're alone?'

Shirley reached up her arms to pull Gloria down to her. 'It's okay then, I s'pose,' she said.

Gloria hugged her tightly, her heart full of gratitude. She hadn't lost Shirl after all. She was still her little girl, thank God; even if she wasn't allowed to say it.

'I'm going to make a documentary film about the evacuation.'

Gloria stared at Tony. 'But I thought all your films were about the fighting?'

'They have been, so far. But this is a kind of fight too, isn't it? One that's closer to home – and to all our hearts. It was Nanny talking about the Marks child that made up my mind; that and you talking about Shirley and the chances she wouldn't have had at home. So many children's lives have been changed. They've seen a side of life they might never had known existed had it not been for this war – both better and worse. It's almost the biggest social upheaval since the industrial and agrarian revolutions in the last century. It's going to mean that the next generation will be very different from the present one. More understanding and tolerant but also more thrusting and ambitious.'

By now he'd lost Gloria but, nevertheless, she could see that the subject might make an interesting film. 'Well, it'll keep you out of the firing line for a change,' she remarked.

He laughed. 'I have to admit that you have a point there. Now, the thing is, will you give me your permission for Shirley to take part?' He took in the look of doubt on Gloria's face and added quickly: 'She'll get paid, of course.'

'It isn't that,' she said quickly. 'I don't want her school-work interrupted.'

'I've thought of that. It'll be shot during these holidays, with a bit of luck,' Tony said. 'We don't have to shoot in sequence and I can get all the scenes with the kids done before they go back to school if I get on to it right away.' Already he was making mental notes. 'I'll need a first-class writer, someone who's used to working with kids and can get the emotional slant right. Mmm . . . Ben Maycox would probably do it. I'll ring him –'

'It isn't *just* that, Tony,' Gloria interrupted his flow of thought sharply.

'Oh?' He looked at her. 'What then?'

'It's what I was saying to you yesterday. Now that Shirl has this chance of a good education I'd like to get her mind off the stage. Now that I know she's capable of it I want her to grow up to a good job with prospects and maybe a pension at the end of it. Security.'

He pulled a face at her. 'It sounds deadly dull, Gloria. I doubt if you'll get a girl like Shirley interested in that kind of future. She'll make up her own mind when the time comes.'

'I can steer her, though. From what I can see of it, the stage is very insecure. You either make a lot of money or nothing.'

'That's not quite true,' Tony said. 'A lot of people make a reasonable living, and Shirley does have a natural talent.'

'Would you let Imogen take it up?' she asked quietly.

'If she wanted to, yes. Shirley has done a lot for Imogen. She's brought her out – given her confidence. She doesn't have Shirley's sparkle and vivacity, but if I detect the slightest hint of talent in her I'll encourage it for all I'm worth.'

Gloria said nothing. She felt slightly ashamed. It wasn't that she wanted to squash Shirley's ambition – the ambition that she herself had fostered. Just that since she herself had been earning better money she could see brighter horizons opening up for them. And since this new chance to better herself had come Shirley's way it seemed positively criminal to throw it away. But with Tony's background and hers being poles apart, she could hardly expect him to see that.

'Of course she can be in it if she wants to,' she said. 'She'd never forgive me if I said she couldn't. But you won't want her to begin work this week, will you? I'll be back at work on Monday and this is the only time I have to spend with her.'

'Good heavens, no. It'll be at least ten days before I can even get a team together.'

Tony's plans for spending time with Imogen went by the board as he spent hours on the telephone in his study talking to the Ministry of Information and to scriptwriters and producers, as well as his own crew, who were scattered around the country enjoying their few days' leave. Gloria found herself taking Imogen with her when she took Shirley for picnics and jaunts. Not that she minded. Tony's daughter was now Shirley's closest companion. She had changed; the sharp-tongued plain-featured girl had become more relaxed. She smiled and chattered instead of scowling and it was suddenly possible to see that the thin little face with its expressive grey eyes could very possibly develop into something close to classical beauty in a few years' time.

The week flew by and Gloria found herself waking on the morning of her last day. She was on the landing going down to breakfast when Tony waylaid her.

'How about having dinner with me this evening?' he invited. 'I feel I've neglected you all week.'

'You mustn't feel that. You're not here to entertain me,' she said.

'Nevertheless, I feel I owe you a thank you for taking care of Imogen while I was busy.' He smiled his engaging smile. 'Besides, I've missed you. You will come, won't you?'

She relented. 'Thank you. I'd like to.'

As they drove into town that evening he told her that everything was arranged and that shooting would begin on Monday.

'I'm using archive material of the children leaving London,' he explained, his eyes alight with enthusiasm. 'And I'm planning to dramatise the story of two children, slanting it in a positive way to show the brighter side. Most of our films have been used to boost morale and this will be no exception.'

'Thank you for not mentioning the film to Shirley.'

He turned to smile at her. 'I didn't want to divert her attention. I knew you wanted to enjoy as much time with her as you could and I didn't want to do anything to spoil that. As it was, you had to have Imogen tagging along.'

'Imogen is part of Shirley's life now.' Gloria sighed a little wistfully. 'I'll be gone this time tomorrow. I almost wish I could stay and watch the filming myself. The girls are going to love it.'

'I hope so. I imagine Shirley will need something exciting to help her not to miss you too much.'

'Thanks. It's kind of you to say so, but I'm afraid she'll hardly miss me at all.'

He had booked a table at a hotel on the outskirts of the town. The meal was not as good as the one they had enjoyed at the Wheatsheaf and for Gloria it was tinged with sadness because she knew it might be some time before she came to Houlton again. Maybe the next time Tony would not be there. All through her meal her thoughts persistently returned to the night they had spent together at the London flat – and the way he had kissed her on the first day of her holiday. Sometimes when she caught him off guard there was a sad, lost look in his eyes. It seemed to her that in spite of all he had, and the fact that he was enjoying his new work, he was often lonely. She longed to be able to make him happy again.

'You're not eating. Is it all right?' Tony was looking at her with concern.

'Oh yes, it's lovely.' Gloria applied herself to her sweet with a relish she did not feel.

163

'You're very quiet. Is it something I said?'

She made herself laugh. 'No. It's just that it's my last night.'

'Is it grim at the factory?'

'Oh, no. Hard work, yes, and boring sometimes, but we have fun too. We have lunchtime concerts once a month. Leonie came once. She toured the shop floor afterwards. Did she tell you?'

'No, she didn't. So, did she come and see you – have a word?'

'No,' She looked at her plate. 'But I dare say we all look the same in our overalls and caps.'

His mouth hardened. 'You're saying that she ignored you.'

'Oh, *no*. At least, not on purpose. There was a lot for her to see; so many people and –'

'That's typical.' Tony signalled to the waiter for the bill. 'Let's go. It's getting hot in here and you can't hear yourself speak.'

In the car she looked at him. 'I've made you angry. I shouldn't have mentioned –'

'Why not?' He turned to look at her. 'Leonie came from a similar background to you, you know, only she was from Birmingham, not London. Her father was a back-street butcher and she's had no formal education at all. I first met her when she took part in a talent competition at the theatre where I was appearing.'

She looked at him in surprise. 'But – that's not what it said in that article in *Home and Beauty*.'

'No, it wasn't, and what I've said is strictly between you and me. I just thought you should know.'

Gloria was silent for a moment, digesting the fact that Leonie Swann had begun life just as she had. 'It just shows, doesn't it?' she said quietly. 'If you have talent you can go a long way.'

'With luck and a lot of help, you can,' Tony said with a hint of bitterness in his voice. 'Too far sometimes.'

'Maybe I shouldn't stop Shirley from going in for the stage, if that's what she really wants,' she said thoughtfully. 'But whatever she does I wouldn't like her to forget who she is or where she comes from. I think . . .' She glanced at him and bit her lip. Had the wine loosened her tongue too much? Would he think her presumptuous, voicing her own opinions just as though she was his equal? But he was looking at her. Waiting.

'Go on,' he invited. 'What do you think?'

'I think that . . .' She paused, searching for the right words to express what she felt – what she was just discovering that she felt. 'I think that what you are – where you start from is what makes you the kind of person you turn out to be. If you forget it and try to turn into someone different, you finish up . . .'

'One-dimensional,' Tony supplied, then substituted: 'A sort of cardboard cut-out of a person?'

A smile lit her face. 'That's right. That's *just* what I was trying to say.' The smile vanished from her face as she realised the gaffe she'd made. 'Oh – I didn't mean . . .'

'Don't apologise. You've hit the nail on the head.' He took her hand and pressed it warmly. 'But you're no cardboard cut-out, Gloria, thank God. You're real and human.' He drew her towards him. 'And very, *very* sweet.' He kissed her gently and drew her head down onto his shoulder. 'I'm going to miss you,' he said, his lips moving against her hair. She made no reply, unable to think of one, and after a moment he put his fingers under her chin and tipped her face so that he could look at her. 'That was your cue to say you'll miss me too,' he said softly. 'Or maybe you won't?'

'Of course I will,' she whispered.

'I'll be at Houlton for some time, shooting the scenes with the children,' he said. 'Is there any chance you might get over again – for a weekend, perhaps?'

She sighed, her heart heavy with regret. He wanted her. He actually *wanted* her. 'I wish I could, but the next weekend I get I'll have to go and see Ma and Pa. I haven't seen them for months.'

'Of course. I understand.'

She looked up at him, desperately anxious to let him know what being with him meant to her. 'Tony, what you were saying the other day – about the night I didn't go home. Ma still thinks I was up to no good. She never did believe my story about staying with a friend.'

'Oh, dear. That was my fault. I'm sorry I was so selfish.'

'You weren't. That part isn't important.' She bit her lip. 'It's just that it seems a shame – getting the blame for something that never happened.'

He searched her eyes for a long moment before he kissed the soft, eager mouth so invitingly uplifted for him. Then, very gently, he took both her hands in his and said: 'Darling little Gloria. I'm afraid I've given you too much wine to drink.'

'No.' She shook her head. 'I'm not tipsy, honest. If you want . . . I'd like to . . .' She trailed off as she saw him shaking his head.

'You might think you do now, darling, but tomorrow morning you'd hate me, and yourself too. I couldn't have that on my conscience.' He kissed her softly. 'But I do appreciate your sweet generosity.' He pressed the car's starter button. 'I'm taking you home now before we do something we'll both regret.' He glanced at her hurt face. 'While we're still friends, eh?' She nodded unhappily. 'Good. I value your friendship, Gloria. That's why I won't let anything spoil it.'

As he put the car into gear and moved forward, Gloria sank deep into her seat, misery and humiliation eating into her heart like acid. *I value your friendship.* He didn't want her after all. He never had. How could she have been such a fool?

Chapter Eight

Shirley and Imogen sat side by side in the darkened cinema with Molly and Jim on either side of them. As *Jenny and Joan*, the story of two evacuees, unfolded they held hands in delight at seeing themselves and some of their friends on the screen.

Tony's patient and skilful direction and an inspired script had brought about the most natural piece of amateur acting ever seen, so said the critics. And the story of the upheaval wrought on families by the outbreak of war, the emotive parting of parents and children and the triumphant emergence of two of the children in their new environment was both powerful and moving.

When the lights went up there were tears in Molly's eyes as she turned to Jim. 'Well! It was well worth all the weeks of having the film crew about the place, wasn't it?'

'I'll say it was.' Jim leaned across the look at the girls. 'What did you think then, seeing yourselves up there on the screen? Proper little film stars now, eh?'

It had been made clear from the outset that no fuss was to be made over the girls' appearance in the film. There was no cast list and no report in the newspapers. At the end of the film the only acting credit read: *Performed by the children of London, evacuated in September 1939*.

Shirley smiled with blissful satisfaction. 'It was smashing, wasn't it?'

All the way home on the bus she was silent. In her mind she was already an experienced actress. It was the only dream she had ever had, and now she knew for sure that it was within her grasp. When she was grown up she would ask Tony Darrent to give her a job. And of course he would. It was all out there, her glittering future – just waiting for her.

'Don't you want to act too, Imo?' she asked later when the girls were sitting on Imogen's bed drinking their bedtime cocoa.

Imogen frowned, her head on one side. 'I don't know. Probably not.'

Shirley stared at her in amazement. 'But you enjoyed being in the film with your dad, didn't you?'

'Ye-es, I suppose so. It was only a small part, though, and there was an awful lot of waiting about.' She smiled. 'I can think of something I'd like much better.'

Shirley, who couldn't imagine *anything* better than being a real actress, stared at her agape. 'What's that?'

Drawing her knees up and hugging them with both arms, Imogen said: 'I'd like to be married and have lots of children.' The grey eyes twinkled dreamily behind her spectacles. 'Just think. It'd be such *fun*.'

Gloria saw the film with her friend Jane and three of the other girls from the factory. She was intensely proud of Shirley, but apart from Jane, to whom she confided most things, no one knew that the child who played the leading part in the film was her daughter, Shirley. Leonie's snub and Tony's kindly meant but humiliating put-down had made her wary of such self-indulgence. Taking the respect and acceptance of others for granted was something she was rapidly learning not to do.

In the darkened cinema she watched, swelling with pride as Shirley acted out her part; appearing first as a sad and lost-looking little evacuee waif, progressing to the confident, healthy child who danced and sang in a Christmas concert. And finally the growing girl who emerged, radiant and triumphant in her high-school uniform, ready to begin the education that would prepare her for the opportunity-filled future awaiting her after the war. The character that Shirley played was based on Tilly

Marks, a fact which made Gloria vaguely uncomfortable. She knew that Ma would be less than pleased at her granddaughter's portraying a member of the feckless family she despised. She would just have to try to explain to her that it was only acting and what Tony called 'artistic licence'.

Since the summer holiday she had spent at Houlton, her dream of owning a cottage in the country had suddenly and unexpectedly become reality. Alf Martin, one of the foremen at the factory, told her casually one lunchtime in the canteen that an old aunt of his had died, leaving him her cottage and all its contents. He seemed to think it a bit of a liability and told her he intended to sell it.

Holding her breath, Gloria asked him what price he was asking.

He rubbed his chin thoughtfully. 'Well, it's only a little two-up, two-down job. There's no electricity or bathroom and all the water comes from a well in the back yard. Furniture's old-fashioned, too. My missus wouldn't give any of it houseroom.' He sucked in his breath noisily. 'Dare say I'd be lucky to get a couple of hundred for it – if that.'

Gloria's heart was beating fast. She had saved almost that much. Trying not to appear too excited, she asked: 'Would you let me have first refusal, Alf?'

He looked at her in surprise. 'Thought you were happy with your mates in the hostel?'

'I am. But it'd be nice to have a place of my own where I could have my little girl to live with me,' she told him. 'When can I see it?'

He scratched his head, looking at her doubtfully. 'Any time, duck, but I reckon you're in for a disappointment. It's not like London houses.'

She smiled. Alf had obviously never been to the East End. 'I'd like to see it just the same.'

'Right you are then. I'll take you round there soon's this shift's finished, if you like.'

Rook Cottage stood on the very edge of Boothley village, conveniently close to the one and only bus stop. It had a thatched roof, latticed windows and a stout front door almost hidden by a trellised porch covered in tangled clematis. Alf produced the key and opened the door. As they stepped inside Gloria found herself in a small, spotlessly clean front parlour. The floor was covered in oilcloth with a home-made rag rug spread before the fireplace. The high mantel shelf was draped with a red, bobble-fringed cloth and adorned with a pair of Staffordshire figures and a brass oil lamp. A horsehair sofa was flanked by two matching high-backed chairs and in the window stood a pedestal table holding a large aspidistra.

Alf studied her face. 'Told you it weren't no palace,' he said. He crossed the room and threw open a door. 'Kitchen's through here.'

Gloria saw a small living-room-cum-kitchen with a window overlooking the back garden. In the centre stood a deal table covered by a chenille cloth; four ladder-backed chairs were tucked under it. In a deep recess a range sat gleaming like ebony from years of black-leading. Under the window was a shallow stone sink and a wooden draining board with a blue-and-white-checked skirt enclosing shelves underneath. Her heart fluttering with excitement, Gloria preceded Alf through the door in the corner that opened immediately onto a narrow staircase. At the top were two bedrooms. The front one, complete with brass bed, looked out over the porch, while to the rear a smaller room had a view of the back garden.

Alf pointed down to the well with its little slated roof and winding gear. 'They used to reckon that was the purest water in the county,' he told her. 'When I were a lad I'd stop off here on my way home from school for a drink. Cold as ice, it were. My, but it tasted good on a hot summer's day.' He looked at her, his head cocked enquiringly. 'Well, what do you think of it? Told you it weren't nothing special, didn't I?'

'I think it's perfect,' Gloria said with a smile. 'I love it. Would you take a hundred and seventy-five, Alf?'

His eyebrows rose. 'You sure, duck? Don't you want to talk it over with anyone?'

'No. I've made up my mind,' she told him. Already she could picture herself and Shirley living here, enjoying the ice-cold well water in summer, snugging round the parlour fire in winter, all cosy. It was just what she'd always dreamed of.

She kept the cottage as a surprise, not telling Shirley until all the formalities were completed and the place was hers. But when she took her to see the place for the first time she was to be disappointed.

'You mean you want me to come and *live* here?' Shirley stood in the little front parlour and looked around her with obvious distaste. 'But how could we? There's no bathroom and no lights, and you have to pull all the water up from that well thing in the garden. Besides, I don't want to leave Houlton.'

'I thought it would be fun.' Gloria was so disappointed she could have wept. 'Just you and me, Shirl. We'd be together again.'

'How'd I get to school?'

'The bus stops at the end of the lane. Oh, Shirl, say you like it. I got it for you – for us.'

'But we wouldn't see much of each other anyway,' Shirley argued. 'You work such long hours. I'd be here on my own a lot of the time.'

Gloria had to concede that she was right. 'We could always get a wireless – one with an accumulator battery,' she suggested hopefully. But already she knew that she was losing the battle. She should have thought – should have realised that Shirley had grown used to being with her friends; with Imogen and Molly and Jim Jarvis. She was accustomed now to the kind of luxury Longueville Hall had to offer. Perhaps she hadn't been fair, expecting her to move at the moment. *Later*, she promised herself. In another year perhaps, when she'd had electricity laid on and saved up enough to modernise the place a bit. Maybe then Shirley would want to come here. For a moment they stared at each other, each dismayed over the disappointment they'd unwittingly caused each other, then Gloria smiled and slipped an arm round her daughter's shoulders.

'Never mind, love. It was only an idea. You and Imogen could always come and spend weekends here with me, though – if you'd like to.'

Shirley heaved a sigh of relief. She hadn't wanted to hurt her mother's feelings. 'Yes,' she said. 'Perhaps we could. That'd be fun.'

But the weeks went by and Shirley never came for the promised weekend visit. Somehow she was always too busy with homework or other school activities. When they did meet she was full of all the exciting new things she was learning. They were teaching her French and Latin, it seemed. Gloria was vastly impressed: just fancy a daughter of hers being able to speak French! But as the weeks grew into months, Gloria's feeling that they were growing ever further apart intensified. She was glad that her daughter was getting opportunities that she herself had never had, but there were times when she wondered just how high a price she was going to have to pay.

She put off moving into Rook Cottage. She had toyed with the idea of asking Jane to share it with her, but with them both working awkward shifts she knew it would be neither economical nor practical. Alf had been right, she should have taken advice before deciding to buy. In the meantime the cottage remained empty and Gloria tried not to worry too much about her unwise investment.

Whenever her shifts allowed, Gloria would make a flying Saturday visit to Northampton and take the girls to the pictures and out for tea afterwards. She hadn't seen Tony at all since the summer before, and though half of her longed to see him again, the other half was glad to avoid him. She shrank from facing him, quite sure she would make a fool of herself if she did. What she saw as his rejection of her still hurt, though she blamed herself. It must have been the wine she had drunk that night that had made her ruin everything and humiliate herself like that. She was so ashamed that she hadn't even told Jane about it.

The United States Air Force had begun to make its presence felt. A base had been set up six miles from

Boothley at Melthorpe, a tiny hamlet on the Cambridgeshire border, and it wasn't long before the loose-limbed servicemen in their smart, expensive-looking olive-green uniforms were to be seen around the village mingling freely with the locals. They nodded and spoke politely to the older folk, carried shopping baskets for weary housewives and plied the schoolchildren, to whom each one was a glamorous hero, with packets of chewing gum and sweets, but they whistled audaciously at every passing pretty girl, delighting some and putting up the indignant hackles of others.

The news soon circulated round the shops and factories that on Saturday nights dances were to be held at the base. A flyer appeared on the hostel notice board announcing that American service vehicles would tour the villages, providing free transport for any girls who wanted to go.

At first the girls were wary of the open invitation, then some of the bolder, more adventurous among them decided to try it. They went at first in twos and threes, maintaining that there was safety in numbers, all of them curious to discover for themselves what these exotic creatures who spoke like film stars were actually like. When the first girls returned, telling of the sumptuous buffet suppers with the kind of food no one had set eyes on since before the war – whole hams, whipped cream and fresh fruit, not to mention free drink of every conceivable kind – eyes widened and mouths gaped disbelievingly. All the same, when the girls next appeared, wearing stockings made of the delicate new fabric called 'nylon' and proudly displaying bottles of perfume and lipsticks that the other girls would have happily given up a month's sweet ration for, the numbers attending the weekly dances began to creep up.

But while the others dressed up and flocked to Melthorpe on their Saturday evenings off, Gloria remained where she was, sewing dresses for Shirley or reading the true-romance magazines she loved to relax with. Those girls with the gossamer-fine stockings and make-up; what did they have to do to get them? she asked herself suspiciously. No. She would have nothing to do with it. No more humiliations. All that was behind her.

Oddly enough it was on one of her Saturday trips to Northampton that she met Billy. It was a February evening with the first hint of spring in the air and she was on her way back to Boothley on the bus. She was deep in thought about *Mrs Miniver*, the moving film about a wartime family she and Shirley had just enjoyed, and she didn't hear the polite enquiry until it was repeated.

'Excuse me, ma'am, is this seat taken?'

Looking up, she saw a young man with soft brown eyes looking down at her. He wore the familiar olive uniform and immediately she was on her guard. She had heard all about the brash way these Americans had of picking a girl up. 'Er, no.' She edged carefully along the seat. 'No, it isn't taken.'

'Thank you.' He sat down beside her and she was pleased and relieved that he kept carefully to his half of the seat. After a moment he glanced at her.

'I'd be obliged if you'd be so kind as to tell me when we get to Melthorpe, ma'am,' he said with studied politeness. 'You see, I'm kinda new around here.'

Gloria smiled in spite of herself. As if she hadn't guessed. 'I get off before we get there,' she told him. 'But it's the next stop after mine so you can't miss it.'

He laughed and she saw that he had strong white teeth and that this dark eyes crinkled attractively at the corners. 'Why do you English always say that?'

'Say what?'

'*You can't miss it*. They say it most every time. But I still do. Do you know that your English towns are the most difficult places to figure out?'

'In peacetime we have signposts,' Gloria told him. 'But they've taken them all down in case of an invasion.'

'Is that so? I thought it was just to confuse us GIs.' His eyes twinkled at her. 'One thing's for sure. If the Germans ever came here they'd sure give up and go home pretty fast. Never did know a place with so many twists and turns.'

'It's a very old country,' Gloria said. 'I suppose that's why.'

'Do you come from around here? You don't sound like the local folks.'

'I'm from London,' she told him proudly.

'From London? The capital city. Gee, I'd sure like to see that. They tell me that even after the bombing, it's still a beautiful place.'

'Oh, it is. The most beautiful city in the world. Everyone says so.'

'I'm Billy Landis.' He held out his hand. 'Sergeant Billy Landis, United States Air Force. Glad to know you, ma'am.'

After a slight hesitation, she put her hand into his. 'Gloria Rayner. I work at the aircraft factory at Boothley Bottom.'

'Hi, Glory.' He chuckled. 'That's another thing – these place names. They slay me. Where 'n the world did they get a name like *Boothley Bottom*?'

His laugh was infectious and Gloria found herself joining in. Then she noticed that the bus was nearing her stop. 'I get off in a minute,' she said.

He looked disappointed. 'Gee, that's a shame. Hey, listen, I'd get off with you but I only have a four-hour pass. Look, do you come to the base dances?'

'What? Oh, no. Sorry, I don't.'

'But you *should*. We have a great time. Why not try and make it next week, Glory?'

She was already standing up and trying to edge past him. 'Excuse me,' she said agitatedly. 'If I don't get up the driver'll go right past my stop.'

'Only if you promise to come to the dance.' The brown eyes teased her. 'I'll look out for you. Aw, c'mon, Glory. Say you will.'

Gloria glanced around her. In the seat behind a fat woman with a bulging shopping bag was glowering disapprovingly at her and two youths across the aisle were sniggering behind their hands. She shot them a disdainful look.

'Oh – all *right*,' she said, acutely embarrassed. 'I'll come. But please let me out now, will you?'

He swung his long legs aside and she edged past into the aisle. The woman behind muttered something about 'Yanks and brazen hussies' as Gloria pushed her way down the bus to the door. It was with great relief that she jumped down as the bus came to a standstill. Hoisting the strap of her bag onto her shoulder, she set off along the lane at a brisk pace but a moment later she was alarmed to hear hurrying footsteps behind her. She swung round and found herself face to face with Billy Landis.

'Oh, it's you. You shouldn't have got off here. I told you the *next* stop.'

'You *can't* miss it.' He laughed down into her eyes. 'I couldn't let you go like that, Glory. I said something back there that annoyed you, didn't I?'

She shook her head. 'No. It was just that I didn't want to miss my stop. Look, there isn't another bus for an hour. You'll get into trouble.'

But getting back late didn't seem to worry him. 'Why don't you like the dances, Glory?'

She sighed. 'I didn't say that. I just . . . don't go out much.'

'Well, you should. You're a swell-looking girl, real pretty.' He looked at her anxiously. 'It is okay to say that to a British girl, isn't it?'

She laughed, 'Yes, it's okay.'

He looked relieved. 'Only we all got issued with the little book, see. Seems there's a whole lotta words we use that you British folks get upset at.' He looked around. 'Say, is there some place around here we can get a drink – a coffee or something?'

'Only the Dog and Doublet.'

His eyebrows shot up. 'The *what*?'

'The pub.'

'Oh, I get it – a *bar*. Great.' He took her arm. 'Lead me to it. If you, er, want to, that is.'

In the village pub there was a log fire burning in the open hearth, taking the chill off the evening and scenting the air with the fragrance of woodsmoke. It was too early for most of the locals, but one or two men were leaning against the bar talking to the landlord over their pints of ale. When Gloria came in with Billy they stopped talking to stare at the pretty girl and the good-looking young American airman. Gloria felt awkward but Billy seemed oblivious to their obvious hostility.

'Hi there, guys,' he said cheerily. 'C'n I have one of those, please?' He pointed to the pints of ale on the bar. 'And for my friend . . .' He raised an eyebrow at Gloria. 'What's it to be, Glory?'

'Just a lemonade, please.'

Billy smiled at the two locals. 'Will you guys have another of those on me?' he invited.

The men looked at each other, then smiled sheepishly, accepting his offer and mumbling grudging thanks. As they carried their drinks to the far end of the room, Gloria said: 'You shouldn't do that, you know.'

'Do what?' Billy took an experimental sip of his ale.

'Buy their friendship. Country people can be so rude to strangers. They're not like that in London.'

'I'm sure glad to hear it. We're only here to help win the war, but to hear some folks, you'd think we were the enemy. Getting through to some of these people is like trying to nail Jell-o to the ceiling.'

Gloria laughed, saving up the expression to tell Jane later. 'I know. You should let them get on with it. It's only stubborn British pride. We don't like having to admit that we need help. You should hear my pa. But they'll come round eventually.'

He shook his head. 'We've been told – it's your country. So you get to have the last word no matter what. No getting into fights and arguments.' He peered into his pint mug. 'Say, this stuff wouldn't be too bad if it wasn't so darned *warm*.' He took another thoughtful pull at it. 'Even so, guess I could get to like it in time. Now – tell me all about yourself, Glory.'

'It's *Gloria*. And there isn't much to tell. I work at the aircraft factory and live at the hostel.'

'And you don't go out much. I already got that. What do you like to do, then?'

'I like to see my daughter when I can. She's evacuated to Houlton, about six miles away. Some Saturdays I take her into Northampton to the pictures. That's where I've been today.'

'I see.' He was trying to look at her left hand. 'So you're married?'

'No.' Gloria took a drink of her lemonade. That should cool any interest he had in her. It usually did. But when she looked up at him again he was still smiling.

'Wanna tell me about it?'

He deserved ten out of ten for persistence anyway. 'You wouldn't be interested,' she told him.

'I might. Try me.'

Somewhat taken aback by his directness, Gloria said: 'Well, it's the same old story. I met a bloke, fell for him and believed him when he said he loved me. Then, when it was too late, I discovered he was already married.'

'Gee, that's tough. But you kept the baby. How old is she?'

'Do you always ask so many questions?'

He shook his head. 'No, but then I'm not always this interested.'

'She's twelve years old – almost thirteen, and her name is Shirley.'

He smiled. 'That's a swell name for a little girl. Is she as pretty as you, Glory?'

She opened her mouth to correct him again, then gave up. 'I think I've got some photographs somewhere.' She opened her bag and produced the wallet of photos she always carried with her. There were some taken during Leonie's Christmas concert in 1939 and some more recent ones of Shirley in her new school uniform. 'That's her,' she said, pointing. 'That one there. She was in a concert, the first Christmas she was here. She was supposed to be Ginger Rogers and her friend there was Fred Astaire. Shirley loves to sing and dance. Everyone says she's a dead ringer for Shirley Temple.'

She handed him another snap. 'This one was taken when she started her new school. She won a scholarship to the high school.'

He looked puzzled. 'She needed a scholarship for that?'

'Oh yes. It's special you see. Only the best get in,' Gloria told him proudly.

He was smiling. 'She's a real little honey. I'd sure like to meet her.'

'Yes – well . . .' Gloria put away the photographs and looked at the clock over the bar. 'Look, we'd better go. You don't want to miss the next bus. There isn't another one till half-past ten.'

Billy downed the remainder of his ale. 'You c'n say that again. I'm gonna have to sneak in as it is. Lucky the guy on guard duty tonight is a buddy of mine.'

At the bus stop he held out his hand. 'It's been great meeting you, Glory. Will you come to the next Saturday dance? Aw, *please* say you will. I'd sure like to see you again.' He looked at her with those big brown eyes, appealing as a hopeful puppy in a pet-shop window.

The bus was coming; its dipped headlights could be seen rounding the bend in the road. In another minute he would be gone. 'All right,' she said impulsively. 'All right. I'll be there.'

'You *will*?' The eyes lit up in genuine delight. 'Say, that's great. I'll look forward to that.'

She watched as he leaped effortlessly onto the bus and waved to her from the platform. As she walked down the lane in the dusky, loam-scented evening, she reflected that she had told him almost everything about herself, yet she still knew nothing about him – except that he must surely be nine or ten years younger than her. Why on earth had she said she'd go to the dance next Saturday? She pictured Billy's laughing brown eyes; his annoying way of calling her 'Glory' and the disarming way he had of looking at her with that frankly admiring smile. And she discovered to her surprise that it was because she genuinely wanted to see him again.

★ ★ ★

Leonie sat in the drawing room of the Mayfair flat sorting through the pile of mail the caretaker of the flats had just handed her. Early that morning she had arrived back from a particularly exhausting overseas tour only to find, to her extreme annoyance, that the repairs to the latest bomb damage were still incomplete. There were still patches on the wall where the plaster had fallen off and the bedroom window was still boarded up. The caretaker of the block had apologised, explaining that bomb damage everywhere in London was being repaired in the same arbitrary fashion. It seemed they were only obliged to make the property what the Ministry of Works referred to as 'habitable' and, after all, it was the third lot of damage the flat had suffered since the bombing began. To Leonie's eye the flat wasn't in the least habitable and she had already decided not to stay in it for one minute longer than she had to. Roughing it in tents and huts on tour for the past weeks had made her long for peace and a little luxury. It didn't look as though she was going to get it here. She had already telephoned Molly Jarvis, telling her to expect her at Houlton the following day.

Molly's reaction had been one of delight. 'Oh, Madam, I *am* glad to hear that,' she said. 'Imogen will be so pleased to see you. It seems such a long time since –'

'I'm coming up for a *rest*,' Leonie interrupted sharply. 'I'm exhausted, Nanny. I can't tell you how rough it's been. I'm mentally and physically worn out.'

'Of course. You must be. I shan't let the children tire you,' Molly said. 'They're at school all day now anyway. They both love it at the high school.'

'Really? Well, I'm sure I'll hear all about it when I get there,' Leonie said. 'If I can contact Mr Darrent I might be able to persuade him to join me for a couple of days. We haven't seen each other for months.'

'Oh, that *would* be nice, Madam. I'll get the room ready, shall I?'

'Yes, I've no idea when Tony will be there, of course, but you can expect me some time tomorrow afternoon.'

As she spoke she'd been idly leafing through the pile of envelopes she had collected from the hall, which had been forwarded from the BBC. There used to be a secretary to sort them out for her and deal with the fan mail, but they were short-staffed now and it was down to the individual performers to attend to their own fan mail. It all looked perfectly straightforward; fan letters, requests for photographs, the usual requests for dates and even the odd proposal of marriage. They could go straight into the waste-paper basket. Then she came to the one with the Birmingham postmark and stopped, a feeling of dismay and annoyance bringing a sharp expletive to her lips.

'Shit! He's still writing, blast him.' She saw to her annoyance that he didn't even bother to mark the letter 'Private' any more. Tearing the envelope open, she scanned the smudgy scrawl that was her brother's handwriting.

Dear Eileen,
    Thank you for sending the cheque. Not that it went very far. I'm surprised that you can be so mean when you're earning such pots of money, singing for the troops and broadcasting on the wireless – loved by all, no doubt. If only they knew. Or maybe you think we're not worth any more. Is that it, our Eileen? I meant what I said about writing to that magazine. On second thoughts, maybe I should come down to London. I'm sure your posh friends would like to meet your brother and hear about *my* memories of my little sister. The money what you sent would just about pay for the train fare. If you can find it in that kind heart of yours to spare something to help Mum and Dad, send it to me at the bank as usual. Hoping this finds you as it leaves me,
        your loving brother,
        Norman.

A chill went through Leonie's blood as she sat staring down at the sheet of flimsy paper. The amount of money she had sent in response to his regular demands mounted up to quite a substantial sum now, yet still he wasn't satisfied. How much longer could he go on demanding

181

money in return for his silence? She should never have sent him anything in the first place. She should have ignored his first letter. If he'd gone to the magazine with his story she could have denied all knowledge of him, branded him an eccentric crank, trying to gain attention for himself. She chewed her thumbnail. What about her parents, though? If it were to get around that she had refused to help her aged mother and father, it wouldn't do much for her public image. Norman was threatening to come to London now. Of all the bloody cheek! Yet she daren't call his bluff. He could do her a lot of damage if he wanted to, a hell of a lot. She hadn't come this far only to let that whining little rat ruin it all for her. Suppose she went up to Birmingham and saw Mum and Dad for herself? She could smooth things over and make sure that they thought well of her – she could give them a couple of hundred in person. That should put a stop to Norman's little game. She looked at her watch. She could go now – this afternoon, she decided impulsively; stay at a hotel overnight and then go straight on to Houlton tomorrow as planned.

At Euston she was lucky; there was a train waiting and she was quickly on her way, travelling first class in her most inconspicuous grey suit, wearing a headscarf and a pair of dark glasses. Eager fans were the last thing she wanted at that moment. At New Street she tipped a porter to get her a taxi, but when she gave the driver the address he shook his head.

'Nothing left of Block Street now, missus.'

She frowned. 'Nothing at all? I knew it had been bombed . . .'

'More like flattened,' he said with a grim little laugh. 'Old property, you see. The bit what didn't burn fell down in a cloud of dust.' He peered at her. 'You ain't been up for some time then?'

'No. Tell me, the butcher's shop – Smith's – did that go too?'

'Told you. Nothing left – flat as a pancake.'

'Nevertheless, I'd still like to go there.'

He shrugged and started the engine. 'Up to you, missus. You'm payin'.'

When the taxi pulled up at what had once been the end of the street in which she had been born, Leonie saw that the driver hadn't exaggerated. There was nothing to see but a deserted bomb scar. The rubble had been cleared away long ago and tufts of grass were pushing up between the cracks in the rough ground. She was looking at a patch of wasteland. It was as though the street with its houses and shops had never been there. She paid the taxi and stood looking round her uncertainly. Maybe there was still someone nearby who knew what had really happened to the inhabitants.

Two streets away she found a small sub-post-office and shop that she remembered from her childhood days. She went in and enquired where there was a list of casualties that she could study. The elderly post mistress peered at her sympathetically through the grille.

'Was it someone from round here you were looking for, dear?'

'Yes. The Smith family from Block Street.'

The woman nodded. 'Ah, yes. Well, you can't be a relative or you'd have been notified. Mr and Mrs Smith were killed in the direct hit. The first week of the raids, it was. November 1940. A terrible night, that was. No one round here will ever forget it.' She frowned. 'Wait a bit, though. Now, if I remember rightly, their son was lucky. He was in the Rose and Crown – the pub at the end of this street. They all took cover soon's the bombs started to fall.' She shook her head. 'Came out next morning only to find his home and his poor mum and dad gone, poor feller.'

Leonie thanked the woman and walked out of the shop, fury seething inside her like a near erupting volcano. So her old home had been gone and her parents dead for two and a half years? No wonder Norman had asked to have the money paid straight in the bank. How dare he threaten to expose her? She'd write straight back to him, telling him she'd go to the police if he dared to ask for any more money.

At the end of what had been Block Street she paused. It was hard to believe that she had been born and grown up there. The space that had once held some thirty or so dwellings looked so small, not much bigger than the kitchen garden at Longueville Hall. She tried to feel sad about her parents, but she could feel nothing. She was barely able to remember what they looked like. Part of her was profoundly glad that all this was gone. Now no one could ever point to the mean little street where she had first seen the light of day and say it was where she belonged. Now she could truly belong to herself – to Leonie Swann, the new self that she had created. Now that the past had been erased for ever, she could settle into her new identity and look forward to a bright new future – once she had dealt with Norman.

She had no idea where he lived and she had no intention of finding out. The only address he had given was that of his bank, the reason for which was now painfully obvious. All her cheques had been paid into his account there. She fumed as she thought of the mounting balance in his account and the glee with which he would watch its accumulation, laughing at the power he held over her.

Checking into a hotel, she unpacked her overnight case and sat down to write him a letter, then she rang for a porter and asked him to take it round to the bank where she had sent the cheques. Wait till he read that, she told herself with satisfaction as she closed the door. That's that, she told herself with satisfaction as she closed the door. That would shut his grasping, whining little mouth for him once and for all.

Too shaken by her discovery, Leonie did not go straight to Houlton as planned, but back to the Mayfair flat, where she spent the night thinking. Norman could have contacted her when their parents were killed, but he hadn't done so. Clearly he had planned all this even then. He had been waiting, watching her climb to fame, until he felt that the time had come to strike. His greed and deviousness sickened her. Fame and success could be a lonely business, she reflected. She had letters by the sackful, declaring the undying love and admiration of unseen fans – people she would never set eyes on. But success made more enemies than friends among those closer to home. It generated envy, spite and resentment. Even Tony had turned against her, or so she sometimes thought. They hardly saw each other nowadays and when they did there was no light of love in his eyes anymore, not even the husbandly pride he had once shown when they were in company.

Next morning she shopped for presents; a silk scarf for Nanny, tobacco for Jim, gold cufflinks for Tony, embroidered handkerchiefs for Imogen and a record of Judy Garland singing 'How About You?' for Shirley. There had never been a time when she needed allies more than she did now.

That evening when she and Tony were alone she poured him a large whisky and sat beside him on the settee. Drawing her bare feet up under her, she linked her arm cosily through his, trying not to notice his slight withdrawal at her touch.

'It's so wonderful to be with you again, darling. You are glad to see me, aren't you?'

'Of course I am. That goes without saying.'

'Nevertheless, it would be nice to hear.' She paused. 'You haven't asked me why I wasn't here when you arrived yesterday.'

He sipped his drink. 'I suppose I'm used to you never doing what you say you'll do.'

She frowned. 'That's not fair. Actually I went up to Birmingham.'

'*Birmingham*? Whatever for?'

She was gratified to see that she had his full attention at last. 'I went to see my parents. I've never forgotten what you said about finding out whether they were all right.'

'It took you long enough.' He looked at her enquiringly. 'Well, are they – all right, I mean?

'No.' Leonie swallowed hard, turning her head away slightly. 'Block Street received a direct hit. They were both killed outright.'

There was a pause, then he said: 'It must have been a shock.'

'It was, rather.' She turned to him, his eyes brimming with the tears she found so easy to induce. 'It made me feel suddenly that I have no one.'

He slipped an arm round her shoulders. Her tears never failed to touch him. 'Don't be silly, darling. You have us – Imogen and me. You have your own family.'

'I know, darling.' She sniffed hard and fumbled for a handkerchief. 'But we've all grown so far apart since the war began. Besides, losing one's parents is like breaking a link in the chain.'

'But you hadn't been in touch with them for years.'

She took a deep, tremulous breath and peered up at him from under moist and sooty lashes. 'I never mentioned it to you, but I'd been sending them money. Now I wish I'd gone to see them. Knowing that I neglected them makes it so much worse. I'll never get the chance to put things right now.' She looked up at him and said with a little break in her voice: 'I feel so . . . lost and alone, Tony – so *sad*.'

He drew her close. 'I'm sorry, Leonie. I wish there was something I could do.' He looked down at her as she dabbed the tears from her cheeks. 'What about your brother – Norman, wasn't it?'

'He's gone too.' The lie tripped so easily from her lips. 'So you see, darling, I only have you now; you and darling Imogen, of course. If I lost you I don't know what I'd do.' She touched his cheek with her fingertips, her eyes wary. 'Is there anyone else in your life at the moment – anyone special, I mean?'

Tony shifted her weight from his shoulder. Since Christmas he had formed a relationship with the continuity girl from the unit. She was attractive, she clearly adored him and they had their shared interest in work in common. Sexually, too, they were more than compatible. It was an extremely satisfying relationship. He and Leonie had always been open about these things and he saw no reason why he should deny the affair.

'There is a girl, yes,' he said lightly.

She stiffened. 'I see. I thought as much. Who is she?'

'I don't think there's any reason why you should know. She isn't any kind of threat.'

She got up and walked across the room, pausing to take a cigarette from the box on the mantelpiece and light it. 'I'll never divorce you, you know.'

He looked up at her in surprise. 'No one is asking you to. There's no question of that. Look, Leonie, after Imogen was born you made it clear that you were no longer interested in me physically. I'm a normal man, you know. You surely didn't imagine I was going to become some kind of eunuch.'

'Of course not. And I've never made any secret of the fact that I couldn't risk another pregnancy. You always knew that was the only reason. But things are different now. Contraception is so much safer.' She turned to look at him. 'I've turned a blind eye to your affairs in the past, Tony. But now I *need* you. I need your help and support, your . . .'

'Love?' He almost spat the word at her. 'Please, Leonie, spare me that. You haven't the vaguest idea what it means to love another person, so don't pretend that you have.'

She ground out her cigarette furiously and rounded on him. 'You owe me a little respect and consideration at least, I think.'

He laughed bitterly. 'Owe you? *Owe* you? If it hadn't been for me you'd have stayed where you were – sitting at the cash desk in your father's butcher's shop. I've even given up the career I planned for myself to put you where you are. No, Leonie. I owe *you* precisely nothing.'

Leonie's face turned bright red. 'You recognised my talent, I'll give you that much, but you didn't hesitate to cash in on it, did you? If it hadn't been for me you'd have had none of this.' She threw her arms wide to encompass the lavishly furnished room. 'It was my talent that made you what you are today. Do you think anyone would have employed a washed-up old ham like you if you hadn't been married to me?' She stood over him, a sneer distorting her beautiful mouth. 'I'll tell you something, shall I? Peter only let you do that stupid Shakespeare because he didn't want to lose *me*.' She threw back her head and laughed derisively. 'Henry the sodding Fifth! If you could only have *seen* yourself in those *tights*. The laugh of London. Better than the Crazy Gang. No, darling *Mr Leonie Swann*, that's your only claim to fame. Yesterday's hero.' She laughed harshly, her temper as hot as fire. 'And I'll tell you another thing. I don't believe there's a girl, Tony. That's all a sham. You can't get it up any more, can you? Who'd have you any more? Even the army wouldn't take you with your flat feet and your flabby belly.'

His face white and pinched with anger, he sprang up from the settee and came towards her. The look of cold fury on his face sent a stab of fear through her and she stepped back, raising an arm protectively.

'Don't you dare touch me.'

He stopped in his tracks to stare at her with something approaching loathing. 'I wouldn't touch you with a ten-foot barge pole, Leonie,' he said, his voice low with tightly reined control. 'I hope I never have to touch you again. I wish you could hear yourself. I wish your devoted fans could hear their dream girl at this moment, screeching like some old fishwife. I'm afraid your background is showing, *Eileen*.' He walked to the door, then turned to look at her. 'I'll be leaving first thing in the morning. Good night.'

When he'd gone Leonie stood staring at the door for a long minute, waiting for her pounding heartbeat to quieten. The air still twanged with the vibration of his anger. How could it all have gone so wrong? she asked herself. She had set out to cajole him into a reconciliation. She had really meant to make it work and she had started off all right. It was his mention of that bloody girl that had sent it all spinning out of control. He must have known it would; he must have been baiting her all along – just waiting for an opportunity to start a row. She stamped her foot in frustration. How could she have let her temper get the better of her like that? She had gone too far this time. He'd never forgive those terrible emasculating things she'd said to him. Hell and damnation! She threw herself down on the settee, beside herself with fury. What had she done to deserve so much hate? She – Leonie, the woman every serviceman in England was in love with. If only they knew how alone and unloved – how despised she really was.

Molly Jarvis closed the kitchen door behind her quietly and looked across to where Jim was listening to the nine o'clock news and moving the flags on his war map. He had two pinned up on the wall. One of Europe, the other of England, where he kept track of air raids. As well as London, Coventry, Birmingham and Bristol, this year had seen the relentless bombing of the ancient cities of York, Bath and Exeter. It seemed that Hitler had turned his attention on England's historical and cultural heritage now. Sometimes he was horribly afraid there'd be nothing of the old England left by the time Hitler had finished with it. He'd been a lot happier since America had come into the war. With the help of the US Air Force maybe they could begin to strike back in earnest. It was heartening that at last things were beginning to look more hopeful. He looked up as his wife came in, her brow creased with anxiety.

'Hello. Something up, love?'

Molly sighed. 'It's them.' She jerked a thumb ceiling-wards. 'They're at it again. I really thought they might behave themselves this time, if only for Imogen's sake. If you ask me, they won't be together much longer at this rate.'

'Oh surely not? They've always quarrelled. I expect they'll have made it up by morning.' Jim smiled.

'Not this time.' Molly shook her head. 'He went off to bed in a blazing temper and I heard him say he'd be gone first thing in the morning.' She sank wearily into her chair by the range. 'I don't know, I'm sure. That poor child!

189

She'd been looking forward so much to having both her parents here for a few days. Such plans she'd made. Now he's off again. You'd think with the war and everything that people could try and be nice to each other, wouldn't you?'

Chapter Nine

Gloria stood uncertainly by the bar in the corner of the vast hall decked with flowers and coloured flags. The Stars and Stripes and the Union Jack were draped side by side over the dais at the far end where a band made up of American servicemen was playing. It was the kind of band Gloria had only ever heard in films before. Loud brass and melodious woodwind blended to perfection, filling the air with music that made her toes itch to dance in spite of her nervousness.

Jane nudged her. 'Stop looking so scared. You look smashing in the outfit. I wish I had your flair for fashion, Gloria.'

Gloria was wearing a made-over dress she had stayed up late the previous evening to finish. She looked down at the scarlet chiffon sleeves she had stitched into her three-year-old black dress and fingered the newly lowered neckline. 'You don't think it looks – well, too much, do you?'

Jane shook her head vigorously. 'No. Honestly, Glor, it's really nice and that red suits you a treat. You knock the other girls here into a cocked hat.' She looked towards the bar. 'Come on, let's go and get ourselves a drink. It'll give us something to do.'

But Gloria hung back. 'I don't know. I feel funny. I've never been to a place like this before.'

'Everyone's the same,' Jane said, pointing to the throng of giggling girls around the bar. 'Come on. Who's going to notice two more of us among that lot?'

But Gloria's eyes were anxiously raking the hall for Billy. There were so many people here – girls of all shapes and sizes and of course American servicemen, awesomely handsome in their exquisitely pressed uniforms, their hair slicked down and their tanned faces smoothly shaved. More men than Gloria had ever seen before collected together in one place, and every one looking like a film star – or so it seemed to her. Yet in all that throng Sergeant Billy Landis was nowhere to be seen.

The trip out to the base in the crowded lorry had been uncomfortable. Squashed in among so many chattering girls, Californian Poppy and Soir de Paris mingling sickeningly with female sweat. Gloria had felt her stomach churning with nausea. She'd been grateful when the lorry finally entered the gates of the base and they all tumbled out. Another minute and she was sure she would have disgraced herself and thrown up. Now they were here in this alien atmosphere of loud gaiety, surrounded by men from another country who seemed to Gloria to be looking them over as though they were so many pieces of meat in a street market. All she really wanted at that moment was to be back at the hostel listening to the wireless and doing her sewing.

'Well, I'm going to have a gin and orange,' Jane said, taking the initiative. 'I'll get you one too, shall I?'

Before Gloria could reply she had gone, elbowing her way through the dense crowd at the bar. Left alone, Gloria felt vulnerable. Standing back against the wall she tried to look as inconspicuous as possible as she watched the dancers on the crowded floor. Some couples were jitterbugging – something that was strictly barred in most English dance halls. These Americans seemed to excel at it, throwing their partners around with effortless dexterity. Flashes of thigh and lace-edged petticoat could be seen and sometimes even a glimpse of French knickers. Gloria bit her lip and swallowed hard, wondering what Ma would say if she could see them. Suppose one of them asked her to dance – and then expected her to do that? She'd die of fright.

'Hi there, Glory. You came, then.'

She turned to see Billy standing at her side. He looked so nice in his uniform, his black wavy hair brushed back over his ears. She felt a surge of relief. 'Billy. I thought you weren't here.'

He shook his head. 'I said I'd be here, didn't I? I've been looking for you. Guess I shouldv'e told you some place we could meet up.'

'It's all right.' She glanced around for Jane, who was nowhere in sight.

'I've been looking forward to seeing you again,' Billy went on. 'I was afraid that maybe you wouldn't come.' He took her arm and added almost shyly: 'You look swell, honey. What'll I get you to drink?'

'Oh, it's all right. My friend is getting me one.'

He looked slightly taken aback. 'Friend?'

'Yes, Jane. I didn't want to come on my own – just in case . . .'

'In case I stood you up?' He smiled and gave her arm a little squeeze. 'Gee, Glory, I wouldn't do a thing like that.' He bent close. 'I'm sure glad to hear it's a girlfriend, though. You had me worried there for a second.'

When Jane appeared with the two glasses, Gloria introduced her to Billy, after which he led them across the room to where he had a table earmarked. As they sipped their drinks, Jane glanced at Gloria.

'I'm not going to play gooseberry,' she whispered, leaning across. 'When I've finished this I'll make myself scarce.'

The band started up again and a tall blond airman materialised out of nowhere and asked Jane to dance. Billy took Gloria's glass from her and put it on the table.

'Dance?'

Dancing to the Air Force band, held firmly in Billy's arms, was the experience of a lifetime to Gloria. The music was uplifting and infectious. It gave her the heady feeling that she was taking part in a film. Billy was a good dancer; it was easy to follow him and their steps seemed to match perfectly. They danced the quickstep and slow foxtrot to some of Gloria's favourite romantic tunes; 'That Lovely Weekend' and 'A Nightingale Sang in Berkeley Square'. A little later, when the band got into its stride with the Glenn Miller number 'In the Mood', Billy persuaded her to try some jitterbugging, though, to her relief, he didn't attempt anything embarrassingly acrobatic. Halfway through the evening they stopped for supper and Gloria's eyes opened in disbelief when she saw the buffet laid out for them in an adjoining room. There was everything from ham, chicken and whole fresh salmon to ice cream and mountains of fresh fruit. There was real butter, golden and glistening on the crusty bread, and slices of real lemon and orange floating in the big bowl of punch in the centre of the table. It was the kind of food she hadn't seen, let alone tasted, since before the war. At last she could see for herself that it was all true what the other girls had said.

Billy made sure she had a generous helping of everything and they carried their heaped plates back to the table.

'You know all about me, but you didn't tell me anything about yourself, Billy,' Gloria told him when at last she had eaten her fill of the delicious food.

'Hey.' He looked up with a disarming grin. 'I guess that's true. I was more interested in you the first time we met. Well, I come from a place called Boulder, in Colorado. It's a beautiful part of America, very scenic. I guess you'll have heard of the Rockies?'

Gloria's eyes opened wide. 'Oh, yes. I've seen them – on the pictures.'

Billy smiled proudly. 'Boulder is a kind of health resort and folks come for miles just to take the mountain air. My dad owns the local garage and gas station. When I left college I worked with him for a while. I was going to engineering school, but then I enlisted instead.' He smiled at her. 'My folks were pretty upset at that, but I always wanted to fly and it seemed like a good chance.'

'And do you – fly, I mean?'

The smile left his face. 'I guess that's one dream that won't come true, Glory. I didn't make it through the training course. I turned out to be better at navigation so that's what I'm stuck with. Not that it isn't an important job,' he added quickly. He took a long pull at his glass of beer. 'I was disappointed first off, but I've gotten to like the job now.'

'Have you got any brothers or sisters?' Gloria asked.

'Two sisters. One older'n me. She's married. And one who's still in high school.'

'I wish I had sisters,' Gloria said wistfully. 'But I've got Shirley, of course.'

'I guess you must miss her.' Billy looked at her, his head on one side.

'Yes, but I do see her now and again. It must be harder for you, being so far away.'

He sighed. 'You know, I never thought I'd miss my folks as much as I do. Trouble is, no one knows when we'll get to go home again.'

'Tell you what,' Gloria said impulsively. 'You must come home to London with me some time. And to Houlton to meet my Shirl. You can borrow my family if you like.'

'I *can*? No kidding? That'd be real dandy, Glory.' He looked up as the band struck up again. 'If you've finished your supper we could dance again. I don't want to waste a second of this evening, Glory. I'm having the greatest time.'

At last the evening drew to a close and the last waltz was played. In the romantically dimmed lights Gloria floated round the floor in Billy's arms feeling as though her feet hardly touched the ground. His hair smelled so nice, spicy and clean, and his cheek was smooth and soft against hers. When he turned his face to smile into her eyes, brushing his lips softly against hers, it felt just right somehow, almost as though it was meant to happen. As they neared the doorway he whispered: 'Whad'ya say we sneak out now, before the rush starts? I'll walk you to the gate.'

Together they slipped out and Billy waited while Gloria got her coat from the cloakroom. Taking her hand, he walked out with her into the spring-scented evening.

'I'd like you to know that tonight has been real special for me, Glory,' he said as they stopped in the shallow of a wall. 'Wanna know a secret? This is the first time *I've* been to one of those Saturday dances, too. Some o' the other gals, they scare the pants off me. They're so – well, I guess they're only out for what they can get. You're not like that.'

'I should hope not,' Gloria said indignantly. 'They're the ones who get us all a bad name.'

He shook his head. 'Not that I blame them. You folks have had a real tough time, putting up with the bombing, the shortages and all. And a lot of those guys are no angels, I c'n tell you. They're out for what *they* can get too – if you know what I mean.'

Gloria nodded. 'Oh, I do.'

'But you and me – we're two of a kind, Glory. I could tell that right off.' He slipped an arm around her waist and drew her closer. 'I guess you know I brought you out here to kiss you good night. You're not gonna get mad at me, are you?'

'Well . . . I . . .' But Billy wasn't going to wait for an answer. Drawing her close he kissed her, gently at first, then deeper and more searchingly, gently probing her lips apart with his tongue. Gloria had never liked this kind of kissing before but she found to her surprise that with Billy she was stirred into an instinctive response. Although she couldn't have said in what way, Billy was different from all the other men she had met. Everything about him spoke of sincerity. Somehow she knew that he wasn't just trying to impress. He meant what he said.

She allowed her arms to creep around his neck and her head to fall back, relaxing in his arms and enjoying his kisses, but when his fingers began to unfasten the buttons of her coat she stiffened and drew back. He stopped at once and looked anxiously into her eyes.

'I'm sorry, baby.'

Gloria felt her throat tighten. 'No, *I'm* sorry, Billy. It isn't that I don't like – don't trust you. It's . . .'

196

'I know. You don't have to explain.' He drew her gently to him and kissed her. 'We'll play it by ear, honey. I know you got hurt before. I understand.'

And somehow Gloria knew that he did. She put her arms around his waist and laid her head against his chest. 'Not many men are so understanding,' she whispered. 'Once most of them know I've got a kid they think I'm fair game. They only want me for –' He stopped the words with a finger against her lips.

'Hush. Don't say things like that, honey. Look, I told you; back home I got two sisters and a mom. I hate the way some guys talk. It makes me want to throw up sometimes, just listening to them. I want you to know that I'm not like that.'

'I know you're not, Billy. I wouldn't be here now if I didn't know that.' She looked at him. 'But, look, I think you should know something. I'm older – a lot older than you. I'm twenty-nine.'

He smiled. 'So what?'

'So – how old are you, Billy?'

He nuzzled her neck and gave her earlobe a playful little bite. 'Hey, didn't your mom ever tell you, never ask a gentleman his age?' He chuckled, then grew serious. 'This is wartime, Glory. Years don't mean a thing in wartime, 'cos none of us knows how few we might have left. It's what we *feel* and what we can give each other – that's what's important.'

The increasing babble of assembled voices down by the gate told them it was time for the transport taking the girls back to Boothley to depart. Billy and Gloria walked across the compound hand in hand and he helped her up into the crowded lorry.

'Say, you will come again next week, won't you?' he called.

She bit her lip, suddenly remembering. 'Oh – I can't next week. I promised to go to London to see Ma and Pa.'

'I'll call you,' he shouted. 'At that hostel place where you hang out. I'll call you Wednesday night – okay?'

'Yes, all right – okay.' The gates opened and the lorry revved up and moved away. Gloria waved until she couldn't see him any more. Jane edged up to her in the semi-darkness.

'Well, did you have a good time after all?'

Gloria smiled dreamily. 'Oh, yes. Did you?'

Jane smiled. 'Smashing. I met this chap – I mean *guy*.' She giggled. 'Sounds funny, doesn't it? His name is Chuck. That's Charlie in our language. He's fun and ever so handsome.' She nudged Gloria. 'Here – what about that supper, then? I think I'll come again. Will you?'

'Yes,' Gloria said dreamily. *What we feel and what we can give each other, that's what's important.* Billy's words echoed inside her head. 'Yes, I think I'll be coming again,' she replied, but she didn't add that it wasn't the buffet supper she looked forward to.

'I suppose you think you're going to get the leading part in the play now?'

Linda Freeman, her hands on her bony hips, challenged Shirley as they changed for gym in the cloakroom. 'Just because you were in that soppy film you think you're Vivien Leigh or someone. Well, I can tell you, you've got another think coming. You weren't all that good, Shirley Rayner. In fact some people are saying you were rotten in it.'

Ever since word had gone round the school that Shirley Rayner was the girl who played the leading part in *Jenny and Joan*, she'd had to put up with every kind of teasing, from good-natured ragging to the spiteful baiting that Linda Freeman never seemed to tire of. Linda was a year older and had achieved some acclaim the previous year when she had played the part of Viola in the school's production of *Twelfth Night*. The thought of Shirley, a first-year girl, posing a serious threat to her prospect of pulling off another success was more than she could bear.

Shirley hitched up her navy-blue gym knickers and gave Linda a look of pure scorn. 'Tony Darrent said I was brilliant,' she said. 'And *he* should know better than a bunch of silly girls like you.' She sniffed disdainfully. 'If you want to act in the school play, you're welcome to it,' she added, with a disdainful toss of her auburn curls.

Linda changed tactics. 'Oh, I see, it's not good enough for *you* now you're a film star, is it?' She stood fixing her rival with a steely glint in her green eyes. 'So when is Tony Darrent going to make you his leading lady then, eh?' She laughed shortly. 'Some chance, I *don't* think.'

'Might be sooner than you think,' Shirley said rashly, her chin jutting. 'Then you'll laugh the other side of your silly face, Linda Freeman.'

'I see. So you wouldn't be in the school play if they paid you, I s'pose?'

'I'd be in it if I was asked,' Shirley said nonchalantly. 'Even if you are only a bunch of amateurs.'

'*Amateurs*, are we? Just wait till Miss Halgarth hears *that*.'

'Are you coming, Shirley?' Imogen, who had been listening, intervened quietly. 'Miss Green will be cross if we're late.'

Linda turned on her heel and flounced off, while Shirley pulled a face at her retreating back. 'Stuck-up cow,' she said, reverting to her native cockney. 'Thinks she's the bee's knees just because she was in last year's tatty old play.' She turned to her friend. 'Know what she said? She said that some people are saying I was rotten in *Jenny and Joan*. Dirty little liar.'

Imogen shrugged. 'Well, Daddy always says you can't please everyone,' she said blandly.

Shirley stared at her indignantly. 'What do you mean? I *was* good, wasn't I?' She looked into her friend's face, her confidence slipping a little.

'Of course you were. Everyone said so. But it doesn't do to brag about it. Nothing's worth having people hate you. I learned that.'

'*Who* hates me?' Shirley said, stopping dead in her tracks.

'Well, Linda for a start. And you only make it worse, arguing with her like that.'

'It's just jealousy,' Shirley protested. 'I can't help that, can I?'

'Perhaps not. It's the way you are with them, though,' Imogen pointed out. 'If you just laughed it off they'd soon get fed up and stop. They don't tease me.'

'You didn't have the leading part,' Shirley snapped.

'*See*? That's exactly what I mean.' Imogen touched Shirley's arm. 'Look, I was just like that once. Remember what a rotten time I gave you when you first came to Houlton? It was all because I thought I was better than anyone else. And it was *you* who taught me how silly I was to cut myself off from everyone.'

Shirley was silent. She felt suddenly deflated. She had to stand up for herself. She had always done that, it was her nature. But surely she wasn't behaving in the unbearable way that Imogen had – *was* she?

'Remember how the other kids at the village school used to rag me?' Imogen reminded her. 'And how you stuck up for me and made them let me join in at playtime? I was ashamed then, Shirl, because I knew I didn't deserve it. They'd have hated me for ever if it hadn't been for you. That's why I'm telling you this now.'

Shirley's throat tightened. 'I know. I don't really care what loopy Linda says. I don't want to be in the silly play anyway.'

Imogen peered into her friend's downcast face. 'You know you do, really. Come on, cheer up, misery. Miss Green'll skin us both alive if we don't get a move on.'

The school play was to be *A Midsummer-Night's Dream* and the auditions were to be held on the following Friday afternoon after school. The play was to be put on at the end of the summer term, performed in the open in the school grounds. Later that evening after tea, as Shirley was going upstairs, Imogen called out to her from her father's study.

'Hey, Shirl! Come and look at this.'

Shirley went into the oak-panelled room and saw that Imogen was reading a thick leather-bound book she had taken from one of the bookshelves.

'We're not supposed to touch things in here,' she said. 'What's that book?'

'It's Shakespeare,' Imogen said. 'I thought I'd have a look at the play they're going to do at school.' She looked up at Shirley, her eyes shining. 'There are lots of good parts in it. Let's take it upstairs and read it. Daddy won't mind. There might be a part you'd fancy auditioning for on Friday.'

Shirley pulled a face. 'Shakespeare's stuffy, isn't it?'

'No, not a bit. Daddy used to read it to me sometimes, when I was home for the holidays before the war. There are lots of funny bits in this one. They put it on at my old school,' she said. 'I was too young to be in it that time, but I enjoyed it because there are fairies in it.' She closed the book and looked at Shirley, excitement glinting in her eyes. 'What do you say we have a go at the auditions, Shirl? I can just see you as Puck.'

Her enthusiasm was infectious and Shirley nodded. 'Okay, I will if you will. It might be a laugh. What'll you try for, Imo?'

Imogen smiled ruefully. 'I'd like to play Titania, the fairy queen, if only I wasn't so ugly.'

Shirley stared at her indignantly. 'You're *not* ugly. Whatever makes you say that?'

Imogen tugged at one her thick brown plaits. 'Mummy thinks I am. I've heard her say so lots of times.'

'Well, *I* don't. With your specs off and your hair loose you look smashing.' She grasped her friend's hand. 'Come on, let's see.'

Upstairs in Imogen's bedroom Shirley unplaited her friend's hair and brushed it loose till it hung in shining waves over her shoulders, then she carefully removed the ugly wire-framed glasses and stood back to study her friend thoughtfully. 'Can you see to read without them?'

Imogen picked up the book and held it in front of her, blinking a little as she stared at the words. 'Not as well as I can with them, but it's not too bad.'

'You've got really nice eyes,' Shirley said, studying her. 'No one can see them properly behind those specs. Tell you what – do you think you could learn some of the words for when we do the audition? Then you needn't wear them.'

Imogen brightened. 'That's a good idea.'

With Shirley's help Imogen worked hard and by Friday she was word-perfect in Titania's wakening scene. Miss Halgarth, the English mistress, was impressed by the work the child had put into memorising her lines, and even more impressed at the improvement in her looks without the ugly spectacles. It was the first time she had seen her without her glasses and with her hair loose. With make-up and lighting she could look quite striking as Titania, she had just the right kind of elfin appeal. And after all, she reminded herself, the child was the daughter of a well-known actor and actress. If Imogen was in the play it was possible that the Darrents might even grace the opening night with their presence. If the word were to be discreetly passed round that Tony Darrent and Leonie Swann were to be there, it would be a big draw. Weighing up all the pros and cons, Miss Halgarth decided to give the part to Imogen. Linda Freeman got the part of Puck – Shirley, to everyone's surprise and her chagrin, was given the part of Bottom the weaver.

'Lots of hard work from now on, girls,' Miss Halgarth said from the platform, clapping her hands to silence the babble of excited voices. 'It's a very ambitious project and I want this to be our best performance yet. It may mean coming into school when you'd rather be out playing so I hope you're all quite sure you want to be in it.'

Imogen felt for Shirley's hand and squeezed it. 'I'm sure,' she whispered. 'Are you?'

Shirley pulled a face. 'I don't know. I never thought I'd be playing someone called *Bottom*. Apart from anything else, he's a feller.'

'It was because you read the part so well in the scene with me,' Imogen told her. 'It means we'll be acting together.'

'But I'll have to wear a donkey's head,' Shirley protested.

'Not all the time.' Imogen laughed. 'Oh, come on, Shirl! It's going to be such fun.'

Shirley grinned in spite of herself. 'Oh, well, there are some funny bits in it. It'll be a laugh, I s'pose.'

★ ★ ★

'A *Yank*, did you say?' Ma turned from the gas stove to stare incredulously at Gloria. 'I never thought a daughter of mine'd stoop to that kind of behaviour.'

'What kind of behaviour, Ma? Billy's a nice bloke. I haven't done anything wrong.'

Ma snorted in disbelief. 'That's as may be,' she said, returning to the dried-egg Welsh rarebit she was making for tea. 'It's not what people'll think when they sees you with 'im, though. I've seen the way these gels flaunt themselves with the Yanks. Short skirts an' made up like dog's dinners – brazen as you please. Need their arses tannin' if you asks me. If I was their mothers I'd do it for 'em.' She heaved a sigh. 'There's only one way for it all to end. Only after one thing, them Yanks. They'll be laughin' on the other side o' their painted faces when they finds themselves in the club.'

'Billy is a nice feller from a good hard-working family,' Gloria told her mother patiently. 'I'd've brought him home with me to meet you and Pa this weekend, only he couldn't get a pass. So I thought I might bring him when Shirl and me come at Easter.'

Ma sniffed. 'Well, I dunno, I'm sure. We'll 'ave to see about that. I'm not sure as your pa'll 'ave a Yank in the house after some of the tales we've been hearin'.'

Gloria said nothing. They both knew perfectly well that Pa would do exactly as Ma said in the end. He always did. 'Well, will you ask him?' she said at last. 'I know you'll both like Billy. He's ever so homesick and I – well, I said I'd sort of share you with him.'

'*Share us*?' Ma's eyebrows shot up. 'What a funny thing to say – without so much as a by-your-leave, too.' She looked at her daughter, her hands on her hips. 'I dunno about you, our Gloria. First it's a feller what's married, then that there Tony Darrent you had such a pash on. Now it's some Yank. Why can't you find yourself a feller what's *normal*?'

'Billy *is* normal. He's just like anyone else, you'll see. His dad owns a garage and he's got a mum and two sisters. He's not like some of those you've heard tales about, Ma, honest. If he was I wouldn't go out with him.'

Ma sniffed loudly. 'I'm not so sure about that. And how long've you known this walkin' miracle, may I ask?'

'A few weeks.' Gloria felt that the slight exaggeration was justified. She felt she'd known Billy for years, even though they'd only spoken twice and been together on that one evening.

He'd telephoned as he promised the previous Wednesday evening and, when she'd tentatively suggested that he might accompany her to London at the weekend, the disappointment in his voice had been plain to hear.

'Aw, Glory – I'd love to have gone with you, but there'll be no passes this weekend.'

A tiny stab of fear pierced Gloria's heart. 'Does that mean you're flying?'

'Can't talk about that, baby. You know the score.'

'Sorry. I shouldn't have asked.'

'But if you were to ask me again some time . . .'

'How about Whitsun?' Gloria asked. 'I'm hoping to take Shirl with me then. We could all go.'

'Hey, that'd be just dandy. C'n I let you know nearer the time?'

'Of course.'

'Being with you was just great last Saturday, honey,' he said quietly.

'I enjoyed it too.' She had lowered her voice and glanced around the crowded corridor to see if anyone was listening.

'I can't wait to see you again. How about the Saturday after next? Think you c'n make it to the dance?'

'I'll try.'

'Gee, honey, I sure hope you can. I miss you.'

'I . . . miss you too.'

'Don't sit there moonin'. Get a cloth and dry up some o' them saucepans.'

Jerked rudely out of her reverie. Gloria jumped up from the chair and began to help her mother, who glanced speculatively at her.

'I 'ope you ain't fallen for this Yank.'

'What? Oh, no. Nothing as soppy as that.'

204

'I should 'ope not. Don't want you slopin' orf to America. What would young Shirl make o' that?'

Gloria smiled. 'Shirl's growing up quick, Ma. Wait till you see how tall she is.'

Ma put the toast in the oven to keep warm and looked at Gloria. 'I been meanin' to 'ave a talk with you about Shirl,' she said. 'Pa's not the man he was, you know. The war and the ARP's taken it out of 'im somethin' shockin'. In another eighteen months or so Shirl'll be leavin' school. It's quieter 'ere now, so how'd you feel about her comin' 'ome to giv me an 'and in the shop so's 'e can take things easy?'

Gloria stared at her mother, horrified. 'Shirl won't be leaving school for *years* yet, Ma. She won a scholarship to the high school, remember?'

'But that don't mean she can't leave at fourteen.'

'No – but she *isn't*. I want her to go on and get all the education she can. She can stay at that school till she's seventeen, take her school certificate and matriculation – maybe go on to college. University, even.'

Ma stared at Gloria. '*University*? What's the good o' that to a kid like Shirl? Pretty girl like 'er'll be wantin' to get married before she's twenty. What good'll all that book learnin' be to 'er then?'

'But at least I want her to have the choice, Ma. I want her to have the chances I never had. She's got the opportunity now and she's bright. She can do it.'

But Ma was shaking her head, lips pursed. 'All mothers want the best for their kids,' she said. 'But you've got to cut your coat accordin' to your cloth.' She sniffed. 'Anyway, in the end it's what *they* thinks is best as counts. You're livin' proof of that, our Glor.'

'But that's what I mean, Ma. I don't want her making the same mistakes as I did.'

'You don't want 'er gettin' ideas above 'er station either, do you?' Ma went on. '*That* only ends in tears.'

'Shirley's clever, though. She can make something of herself if –'

'If you ask me, livin' with them Darrents has turned 'er 'ead.' Ma opened a drawer and took out a handful of cutlery. 'All this actin' in films and livin' the kind of life she ain't never been brought up to.' Her words were punctuated by the angry clatter of knives and forks as she flung them round the table. 'It's doin' the girl no favours, you mark my words.'

'But Ma . . .'

'*No*,' Ma turned to face her, red-faced. 'You let 'er leave school soon's she can an' come 'ome. Pa and me'll see 'er right. An' when we retires there'll be a nice little business 'ere for both o' you. Your Pa an' me've worked 'ard for this business all our lives. It may not be much but it'll give you an' Shirl more security than all your book learnin'. You see if it don't.'

Gloria was about to tell her mother of the money she was saving for after the war and the new opportunity-filled life that awaited them, but one look at her mother's face told her that there was no point in complicating the issue further. She sighed. 'Eighteen months is a long time, Ma. Let's just wait and see, shall we?' She looked up hopefully. 'And what about this Whitsun? Can I bring Billy home with me – if he can get a pass, that is?'

Ma shrugged her shoulders impatiently as she applied herself to dishing up the meal. 'Oh, all right then, if you must. But 'e'll 'ave to take us as 'e finds us. You c'n tell 'im there's no standin' on ceremony in Angel Row, Yanks or no Yanks.'

Although it was her parents' reaction to Billy that Gloria worried about, it turned out to be Shirley who caused her the most anxiety. Shirley had met Billy for the first time several weeks earlier when Gloria brought him to Houlton for a visit. From the moment they met she had made no effort to hide her resentment. He had arrived with gifts for everyone. Chocolates for Gloria, canned fruit and ham for Molly and cigarettes for Jim. When he offered the two girls candy bars and chewing gum, Imogen accepted delightedly, but Shirley shook her head.

'No, thank you. I'm not allowed to take sweets from strangers.'

Gloria stared at her in horror. 'Shirl! Don't be so rude. Billy's not a stranger, he's a friend.'

But Billy only laughed. 'I'm sure we'll get along just fine when we've had a chance to get to know each other. I'll just leave the candy here on the table for now,' he said tactfully.

When they were alone, Gloria took Shirley to task about her bad behaviour. 'What did you want to be rude to Billy like that for? I didn't know where to look.'

Shirley pouted. 'I thought it was going to be just you and me this weekend. And now you say he's coming home with us at Whitsun.' She pulled a face. 'Why do we have to have *him* tagging along?'

Angered, Gloria lashed out: 'Because I want him to come, that's why. And you can always stop here if you don't like it. You don't *have* to come with us. Half the time you've got no time for Ma and Pa any more anyway.'

Shirley was stung. Gloria never used to speak to her like that before she met this Yank. She was different since he had come along; always talking about the dances she'd been to and showing off the nylon stockings and perfume this Billy person kept giving her. Shirley knew all about the Yanks. The older girls at school often gathered in little knots in the cloakroom talking quietly and giggling together. When the younger girls tried to listen they shooed them away, but Shirley knew what they were talking about. Some of them had American boyfriends and they liked to compare notes and discuss what had happened when they went out with them. Catching their half-smothered snatches of conversation made her feel funny inside – a strange feeling she didn't understand, halfway between resentment and disapproval, with a good sprinkling of envy mixed in, though she refused to acknowledge that bit. Twelve was a rotten age, she decided. She wasn't a child any more. She understood a good deal more than the grown-ups thought she did. And yet she wasn't properly grown-up either. Now Gloria – her own mother – had one of these exotic creatures to show off and Shirley was determined that she wasn't going to be won over with packets of chocolate and chewing gum. Just because they had so much of everything they thought they could *make* everyone like them. Well, she wasn't going to be a pushover like all the rest. Even if Nanny and Jim fell over themselves to be nice to him, *she* wasn't going to, so there.

Billy had a weekend pass at Whitsun and the three of them travelled up to London together on Friday morning. To Shirley, who hadn't been home for some time, Angel Row looked down at heel and very much the worse for wear. There were glaring gaps in the street where some of the houses, damaged beyond repair, had been demolished. Some of the bomb sites were littered with piles of rubble, and the houses that still stood were shored up and looked frail and precarious. But though battle-scarred, the Rayners' greengrocery and fruiterer's shop was open for business as usual. The sign above the shop was faded and the woodwork was blistered and sadly in need of a coat of paint. But the produce in the window looked as fresh and appetising as ever, thanks to Pa's early-morning visits 'up the market' in Covent Garden. He never bought anything but the best and if there were any oranges or lemons about it was always Rayner's who had them in first.

In spite of her initial disapproval, Ma had been on her knees scrubbing for days and she had the place shining like a new pin for Billy's visit. Shirley and Gloria were to have their old room and Billy was to sleep on the put-you-up in the parlour. When Billy unloaded his bulging grip onto the kitchen table, Ma's eyes were round with disbelief.

'Now then, young feller, I'm not sure I c'n accept all this stuff,' she said warily. She picked up a tin of yellow cling peaches and stared at the label. 'Blimey, I ain't seen these for years; corned beef nor ham neither.'

Billy smiled. 'You're more than welcome to them, ma'am. Us GIs can't accept hospitality without taking along our share. Specially when we know how short of stuff you are.'

Ma bridled proudly. 'We manage all right. You don't want to bother yourself about us.' Her features softened as her eyes fell on the peaches again. 'Still – if you're sure.

It'd be a pity to waste it when you've brought it all this way.'

Shirley stood by the door. So far no one had even noticed her. As usual everyone was making a fuss of Billy. She pushed rudely past him. 'Did you see my film, Ma? Did you think I was good?'

'I'm not sure that I did, miss,' Ma said, looking down her nose. 'What was they thinkin' about, lettin' you be seen in them scruffy clothes at the beginning? I sat there ashamed. I don't mind tellin' you. When you went from 'ere in '39 you was as smart as paint and pretty's a picture.'

'It was only a film, Ma,' Gloria put in. 'And she was smart at the end of it in her school uniform.'

'Mmm – 'andsome is as 'andsome does,' Ma replied. 'We'll 'ave to see what goin' to a posh school and actin' in a film's done to your manners, won't we, my gel?'

Billy chuckled and gave Shirley a playful nudge. She glowered up at him crossly, her face scarlet. How could Ma embarrass her like that in front of *him*? Her resentment of him deepened to out-and-out dislike.

It was the next day that Ma started throwing out hints about leaving school and coming home to help in the shop. Shirley was horrified. Later, when she was alone with Gloria in the room they shared, she asked her about it.

'She won't really make me, will she, Glor?' she asked anxiously. 'You know I want to be on the stage when I leave. Tony says I'm a natural actress.'

'You don't want to take too much notice of what Tony Darrent says,' Gloria warned. 'He means well, I'm sure, but when he gets carried away with his filming he doesn't think. He's probably forgotten all about it by now.'

'Even if he has, *I* haven't,' Shirley said. 'As soon as I'm fourteen I'm going to leave school and get a job on the stage somewhere.'

'Oh no, you're not, my girl. You're going to stay on and take your school certificate. You've got a chance I never had and I'm going to make good and sure you take it. If you're not coming home to help Ma, then you're going on with your education and that's flat.'

209

Shocked, Shirley stared at her mother. Never in her life before had Gloria laid down the law to her like this. Here she was, held fast between two options, neither of which appealed to her one little bit. None of it would have happened, she was quite convinced, if it hadn't been for that Billy.

That evening Billy took Gloria Up West to Rainbow Corner, the American Forces Club he had been telling her about just off Leicester Square. Once again Shirley was to be left out. She was too young, she was told. Instead she had to be content to watch Gloria getting all dressed up. She took hours over her hair, pinning it up high in front to fall in curls to her shoulders at the back. It was the latest fashion and Shirley watched enviously, wishing she could do hers like that too.

'Where are we going tomorrow, Glor?' she asked wistfully. 'We haven't done anything together yet.'

Gloria turned from the mirror, her teeth catching her lower lip as she gazed remorsefully at her daughter. She and Shirl had done nothing but fall out this weekend. If only she'd try and make herself more pleasant to Billy. Heaven knows he tried hard enough to win her round.

'I know. I'm sorry, love. I'll try and bring you back something nice tonight. Billy says they have lovely doughnuts at the club. Like some of those?'

'No thanks.' Shirley shook her head, picking at a loose thread in the bedspread. 'I just want us to be together,' she said. 'Like we used to be.'

Gloria crossed the room and enveloped her in a perfumed hug. 'We will, love, I promise. What do you say we all go up to Hampstead Heath tomorrow? It won't be like it used to be before the war, but it'd still be nice. And Billy's never been there.'

'All right.' Billy, Billy – why was it always what Billy'd like?

Shirley sat in the kitchen with her grandparents downstairs after Gloria and Billy had gone. They listened to *In Town Tonight* on the wireless and later *With Love from Leonie* was on. Pa looked at her.

'She's got a good voice, I'll give 'er that,' he said, relighting his pipe. 'Not a patch on good old Marie Lloyd, o' course, but then no one ever will be, if you ask me.' He puffed till the pipe was well alight. 'Nice to you, is she – this Leonie?'

'She's all right,' Shirley said moodily. 'We don't see much of her, though. I like Tony best. He says I'm a natural actress. That's why I want to go on the stage.'

Ma and Pa exchanged meaningful looks. The sooner the child could be got away from influence like that, the better, Ma's eyes said.

After her favourite Saturday-night programme, *Music Hall*, was over, Shirley said good night to her grandparents and went upstairs. She didn't go straight to bed but amused herself by trying on some of Gloria's clothes and experimenting with her make-up. Then, climbing on a chair, she reached the top of the wardrobe and took down a selection of the magazines Gloria had collected over the years: *Picturegoer* and *Film Review* as well as *Vogue* and other fashion magazines. Shirley never tired of reading about the stars, their private lives and how their careers had started. Getting undressed and slipping into bed, she settled down to read, determined not to let herself fall asleep until Gloria got home.

They came home from Rainbow Corner in a taxi. It was amazing how easily Americans managed to get one. It seemed they only had to snap their fingers and a cab would appear out of nowhere, as if by magic. In the back seat Billy drew her close.

'Enjoy the evening, honey?'

'Oh, yes.' Gloria snuggled up to him in the darkness. Her head was still spinning with the gaiety of the club, the music, the dancing – she was getting quite good at jitter-bugging now – and the lavish food and drink. The club had been filled to bursting with glamorous people.

'I had a lovely time. I'm having a smashing weekend.' She glanced up at him apprehensively. 'I'm sorry about Shirl, though, I don't know what's come over her. She's usually such a good kid.'

Billy smiled. 'Forget it, honey. I guess she's a little bit jealous. After all, she's never had to share you with anyone yet, has she?'

'I suppose not, but still . . .'

'Shhh. Don't give it another thought. I can think of better things to talk about.' Billy's mouth covered hers and for the next few minutes she did indeed forget Shirley – and everything else too.

'Your mom and pop have been really great to me, Glory,' he said, settling her head on his shoulder. 'If it hadn't been for you and your family I'd have been dreadful homesick this weekend – my first Whitsun away from home.'

'I'm glad we've helped.'

'Helped? You've more than just helped, all of you. Even Shirl reminds me of home – fighting with my kid sister.' He looked down at her. 'Glory, I guess you know by now that I've fallen in love with you?' When she was silent he drew his head back to look into her eyes. 'Does that shock you?'

Her eyes glistened in the dimness. 'Shock me? Oh no, Billy. It's just – I don't know what to say.'

'Well, does it make you unhappy?'

'Oh, *no*.'

He cupped her chin and tipped her face up to his. 'Is it too much to hope that you might love me back – just a little bit?'

'Of course I love you, Billy.' She reached up to kiss him. 'It's just that I never thought I'd trust anyone enough to say that again.'

He kissed her. 'I wish I could get to see you more often, Glory,' he said. 'Just the two of us, I mean. We never really get any time alone, do we?'

For a long moment she looked at him. 'There's something I haven't told you, Billy.'

His eyes looked into hers, anxiously. 'Uh-oh. Is it something bad?'

She laughed. 'No. A while ago I bought a little cottage. I'd saved some money and got the chance to buy it cheap.

It's furnished and everything. I had hoped that Shirl and me'd live there together, but I should have thought . . . She's better off where she is at the moment.' She paused, looking at him shyly. 'I was going to ask Jane, my friend, to come and live in it with me, but that wouldn't really work either.' She moistened her suddenly dry lips. 'At – at weekends . . . when you . . . when we were both free, we could . . .'

He pulled her close and she felt his breath warm against her ear as he asked: 'Oh, honey – are you saying what I think you're saying?'

'It's only an idea,' she said. 'Only if you want to.'

'If I *want* to?' He held her away from him to look searchingly at her. 'Wait a minute. Are you sure it's what *you* want?'

She frowned. 'I wouldn't want you to think I was being forward – or cheap.'

'Oh, Glory, you could never be either of those. Don't ever say a thing like that again. I told you, I love you.'

'And I love you, Billy. If I didn't I'd . . .'

'I know, honey. I know.' He looked into her eyes. 'Look, we could get engaged if you like. I could buy you a ring.'

She shook her head. 'No. Let's just keep it to ourselves for now – our secret.'

He smiled. 'Okay, honey, just as you say. But some day, when the war is over, we'll get married, eh?'

'That would be lovely, Billy.'

'And I'll take you back home to Colorado – Shirley too.'

She buried her head against his shoulder. He was so sweet, so good to her. Billy might not be Tony Darrent, but he was here, he loved her and made her feel cherished and cared for. Suddenly everything that had ever worried her – Ma and Pa, Shirl, the cottage, and what was going to happen to them after the war – faded into insignificance. When the war ended she would marry Billy and everything would fall miraculously into place. It all seemed so simple.

It was half-past one when she crept into the little room she shared with Shirley. She undressed as quietly as she could and slipped carefully into bed beside her daughter to lie staring at the ceiling, her head full of dreams. With the blackout curtains drawn back, the room seemed to be lit by a million stars. It was a magic kind of a night – a night she'd remember for the rest of her life.

Suddenly there was a movement beside her.

'Glor, I'm still awake,' Shirley whispered. 'I've been waiting for you.'

Gloria turned to look at her daughter. 'Do you know what the time is? You should be asleep.'

'I've been reading some of your film magazines, Glor, and I've been thinking. There are special schools where you can go to learn about acting. If I stay on at the high school for School Cert like you want, can I go to one of them instead of college?'

Gloria turned over, sleep tugging at her eyelids. 'I suppose we could look into it,' she said. She could afford to be indulgent. After all, by the time Shirl left school they'd probably be getting ready to leave for America.

Chapter Ten

A sunbeam penetrated a chink in the curtains to tease Gloria's closed eyelids. She opened them and turned her head to look at the clock on the bedside table. It was only five o'clock. For a moment she lay savouring the feeling of languor. It was so warm and comfortable here in bed at Rook Cottage. No need to get up for hours yet.

Turning her head on the pillow, she looked at Billy. In repose, with his dark hair tousled and his mouth relaxed and soft, he looked so young. If it weren't for the morning stubble that darkened his jaw, he would look like a little boy. She longed to take him in her arms and hold him there safely till the war was over. Sometimes she felt that he, and so many others like him, had been thrust into manhood before their time.

The past year had been the happiest she had ever known. Ever since last spring she and Billy had spent every free minute here at Rook Cottage. It never seemed to matter to them that they had to light oil lamps and fires through the winter and draw all the water they needed from the well. They were ecstatically happy together. They would light the fire in the range to cook the little treats that Billy brought with him from the base, sharing the chores and the washing-up. It was all such fun – an adventure. They felt like two children playing house.

When Molly first heard about the cottage Gloria had bought, she unearthed some discarded curtains from the attic in Longueville Hall and gave them to her to make over for her new home. She thought it was a pity that

Shirley couldn't share it with her yet, but she agreed that the cottage was a good buy and would be something for them both to look forward to for after the war.

'It wouldn't really be practical for you to try and live there yet,' she told Gloria. 'But there's no reason why you shouldn't start making it nice.' She knew that Gloria spent some weekends there, but no one knew that Billy often joined her. Sometimes Gloria asked herself why she didn't feel guilty about it. But being with Billy, sharing a bed with him and loving him felt like the most natural thing in the world, so what was there to feel guilty about? They were totally committed to one another and as soon as the war ended they would be married. It was no one's business but theirs, she told herself.

The curtains Molly had given her provided several yards of sound, unfaded material. Gloria had made pink brocade curtains and a matching bedspread for the bedroom and a warm pair in wine-red velvet for the parlour. In the winter she and Billy had been so cosy in front of the fire. She would tell Billy tales of her childhood in the East End and he would describe Colorado and his family, planning the life they would share there after the war. Later they would snuggle up together in the big feather bed in the room above. In the warmth and delight of their love and their dreams for the future, the war and all its horrors seemed a million miles away.

Now that spring had come again, they were working on the garden; tidying and planting it for summer. Gloria had never had a garden before and she was planning to have all the old-fashioned flowers – cornflowers and holly-hocks, foxgloves and marigolds – looking forward to the riot of colour and perfume they would create.

The one thing she did feel guilty about was not spending more time with Shirley, but the child hardly seemed to notice her absence. She and Imogen were working on their School Certificate courses now and even though the examination was two years away they always seemed to be up to their ears in homework.

Playing Titania in *A Midsummer-Night's Dream* had finally made up Imogen's mind for her. She was to go to

RADA after school and study drama, hoping for a career as a classical actress. Shirley had taken it for granted that she would go too and this had caused a slight cloud to loom on Gloria's horizon. She hadn't yet mentioned to Shirley her intention of going to America once the war was over to marry Billy. She hadn't mentioned it to her mother either. But she was pretty sure that neither of them would receive the news well.

Billy opened his eyes and looked at her. 'Hi,' he said sleepily.

'Hi.' She slipped her arms around him. 'It's all right, it's early yet, only half-past five. No need to get up.'

'Mmm, good.' He settled himself more comfortably, pulling her close.

'Do you want a cup of coffee or anything?'

'I'd rather have the "or anything".' He laughed softly and began to kiss her.

As always their lovemaking was slow and tender, but no less passionate for that. Billy had known instinctively right from the first time just how to arouse her. Gently caressing her and covering her in tiny kisses, he would wait till he heard her breathing alter and felt the quickening of her heartbeat. He took his time, making sure that she received as much pleasure as she gave him. When he felt her climax approaching he hastened his own so that they reached the height of their passion together. Afterwards he lay holding her quietly till their breathing returned to normal.

'Honey,' he now said. 'Look, I've been putting off telling you, but this might be our last time at Rook Cottage for a while.'

Her eyes opened wide with alarm as she looked at him. 'Why?'

He shook his head. 'There's a buzz on. I can't say more.'

'An exercise?' she asked fearfully. 'Or the real thing?'

He pulled her close and buried her face in his neck. 'Honey, you know better than to ask questions like that.'

'I know, but . . . Oh, Billy, I get so scared sometimes.'

'Don't be. I've told you and now we won't mention it again. We'll make the most of what time we do have.' He sat up and stretched out his arms. 'Hey, it looks like it's gonna be a great day out there. Suppose we get up and make a start on that gardening?'

They ate breakfast together in the kitchen with the back door open so that they could hear the sound of the birds. Billy had taught her how to make the little pancakes that he called 'biscuits' for breakfast and they enjoyed them now with maple syrup he had brought with him from the mess. But as they ate, Gloria's heart was heavy. She couldn't help thinking about what he had said and wondering anxiously if it had anything to do with the 'second front' that everyone was talking about. The rumour was that it would start any day now. But then people had been saying that for months and everyone was weary with waiting. It was wonderful and exciting to think that the war might soon be over and won, but terrible to contemplate the lives that must inevitably be lost in bringing this about. If she lost Billy now . . . She put the thought from her mind and forced herself to smile at him as she rose and began to clear the table.

'Well, shall we put our wellies on and make a start then?'

It was on the morning of 6 June that Jim ran excitedly out to Molly as she hung out her washing in the kitchen garden.

'Molly, Molly! It's happened, love. It's started at last.'

'What's happened?'

'The second front. Our lads have landed in Normandy. We've invaded. It's the beginning of the end, love. We're going in for the kill at last.'

For the rest of the day he hardly moved from the wireless, till Molly got quite tired of moving him every time he was in her way. 'All those poor boys,' she muttered to herself. 'There'll be more broken-hearted wives and mothers tonight.'

When Shirley and Imogen came home from school they

were full of it too. 'Does this mean the war will soon be over, Jim?' Imogen asked.

Shirley was silent. Last month she'd celebrated her fourteenth birthday. Legally she could leave school this summer. Would the end of the war mean that she would have to go back to London before her education was complete? She couldn't help thinking about what Ma had said about her leaving school to help in the shop and the prospect dismayed her more than she could say.

'Of course it'll take time to finish Gerry off,' Jim said, one ear still on the wireless. 'It won't be over yet a while. I reckon it'll take a good twelve-month to clear up the mess old Hitler's made.'

Shirley heaved a sigh of relief.

That weekend Gloria joined them. She looked tired and pale. When the girls were out of the way she told Molly and Jim: 'Billy's gone. The whole unit went a week ago, but they were all confined to base for days before. Heaven only knows where they're headed. I can only guess.'

'We've got a lot to be grateful to those boys for,' Jim said. 'I knew as soon as they came in with us that we'd be all right. All those raids last year – Munich, Bremen, Berlin and the rest. Those Flying Fortresses must've knocked hell out of them; paid them back for what they've done to us. I know it meant a lot of civilians copped it, poor devils, but they never cared about our folks when they blitzed our cities, did they?'

Molly frowned at him and inclined her head towards Gloria. 'Try not to worry, dear,' she said, patting Gloria's shoulder. 'He'll be all right, I'm sure will.' Later she scolded her husband: 'Haven't you got any sense, Jim Jarvis? Going on and *on* about bombing and killing when the girl's worried out her wits about the lad. Anyone with half an eye can see how fond of him she is.'

Early next morning Gloria was surprised to be wakened by Shirley slipping into her bed. She smiled. 'Hello, love.'

Shirley reached for her hand. 'You didn't sleep, did you? I heard you walking about.'

'Did I wake you? I'm sorry, love. I went down to make

myself some cocoa.'

Shirley peered into her eyes. 'It's Billy, isn't it?'

'Yes. I can't help thinking about him, wondering if he's all right.'

'You love him, don't you?'

Gloria blinked hard at the tears that threatened. 'Yes. Yes, I do.'

Shirley nodded. 'It's all right, Glor. I understand. I'm not a kid any more. I haven't been very nice to Billy and I'm sorry now. When he comes back . . .'

'We're going to be married, Shirl,' Gloria said. 'And after it's all over we're going back to America to live. You too, of course.'

'To *America*?' Shirley stared at her. 'But what about RADA?'

'I expect there are drama schools there too.'

Shirley's heart sank. Going to America was the last possibility she'd considered. 'What about Ma and Pa? Will they be coming too?'

Gloria shook her head, smiling a little. 'I can't imagine them wanting to, can you?'

'Not really.' She almost said that she didn't want to go either, but she stopped herself just in time. Gloria was worried about Billy. Shirley wasn't a child any more. She had begun to learn that one must sometimes put other people's needs before one's own, so she kept silent. After all, in Jim's opinion the war was going to last for quite some time yet.

'They haven't seen much of us over the last five years, have they?' Gloria was saying. 'It's not as if we've been together a lot. I don't think they'll mind all that much.'

'No.' Privately Shirley knew that they would mind. She was pretty sure that Gloria knew it too, but this wasn't the time to express such doubts. She thought about her grandmother's disapproval of her going on the stage. If she went to live in America with Gloria and Billy, at least she wouldn't be pressured into leaving school to go and work in the shop in Angel Row.

★ ★ ★

Leonie and her producer, Tim Manson, were having a serious discussion in his office on the top floor of Broadcasting House. He had sent for her after receiving a directive from the board of governors.

'They don't feel that sentimentalism is the thing any more,' he told her.

Leonie stared at him. 'Why ever not, for God's sake? What do they want me to sing, "Land of Hope and Glory"?'

Tim winced. He'd known she wouldn't agree with the board's decision. He wasn't sure that he did either. 'It's just that the War Office seems to think it might have a softening effect on the men; make them lose the will to win.'

Leonie snorted derisively. 'I have it on *very* good authority that both the Navy and the Air Force think my songs send the men off in good heart. You've seen some of the letters I've had, Tim. The boys request those songs over and over again: "Silver Wings in the Moonlight", "A Nightingale Sang . . ."'

'I know, sweetie. It's just the bods at the War Office. They think your love songs are bad for the Army's morale.'

'I've never heard such utter rubbish in my life,' Leonie said. 'So what do they suggest? Am I to stop broadcasting?'

Tim smiled wryly. 'I don't think even the War Office would dare to take *With Love from Leonie* off the air. There'd be a riot.'

'What, then?'

'Well, how about including some of the more rousing numbers in our next recording session? There are some quite good ones, you know. Jolly and forward-looking. "I'm Going to Get Lit Up When the Lights Go On in London", for instance.'

Leonie grimaced. 'I'll think about it,' she said reluctantly. 'Maybe I'll go along to the publisher's and see what's new.' She stood up. 'But I'm not promising anything, mind. And I'm not going to sing anything that isn't

221

me. It wouldn't be popular and it wouldn't do my image any good.'

'Of course not, darling. It's for you to decide in the end.' Tim stood up and went with her to the door. 'Are you doing anything for lunch?'

She adjusted her silver fox furs and turned to look at him. 'I'm meeting Tony, as a matter of fact.'

Tim tried hard not to show his surprise. It was rumoured that the Darrents were separating. They hadn't been seen together for months and all the gossips had it that there was an irreconcilable rift between them. 'Oh, he's in town then?'

'Well, I could hardly have lunch with him if he wasn't, could I?'

Leonie's razor-sharp tone made him wonder if she was nervous about the coming meeting. 'Well, have a nice time, then. And do give him my best wishes, won't you? I enjoyed his last film so much.'

'I'll tell him.'

Downstairs Leonie got the doorman to call her a cab. There was just time to go back to the flat and change. When Tony had telephoned asking her to meet him she'd been surprised. Ever since their cataclysmic row they had avoided each other. Their respective work made it difficult for them to meet anyway, but each of them had been careful to ascertain that the other would not be there when they arranged to visit Imogen at Houlton. After his unexpected telephone call it had crossed her mind that he might be about to ask her for a divorce and she had already made up her mind not to give him one – especially not if he intended to remarry. Quite apart from anything else, the publicity would be disastrous for her.

At the flat she changed into her most glamorous dress and a saucy little hat. Then she took them off and replaced them with a classic suit in a rose-pink linen set off by a screen-printed silk scarf. Her hair was freshly shampooed and set and she touched up her make-up with fresh lipstick and mascara. She'd show him that she could look blooming with or without him. She looked at her watch.

There was just time to call a cab and get to the club in comfortable time for their appointment.

She was just picking up her bag and gloves when the doorbell rang. Biting her lip with annoyance, she went to answer it. It was probably the caretaker with a parcel or a message. But when she opened the door her jaw dropped in shocked disbelief. Outside in the corridor stood her brother, Norman.

His sparse hair was plastered down with Brylcreem and he had grown a moth-eaten moustache since she last saw him almost eighteen years ago. He smiled, displaying crooked and nicotine-stained teeth. 'Hello, Eileen.'

'What do you want?' Leonie's heart was thudding with apprehension. It was almost a year since she had written the letter to Norman telling him she was on to his deception and warning him not to contact her again. Since then she had heard nothing and had quite thought that she'd dealt satisfactorily with the matter.

'Aren't you going to ask me in, our Eileen, after I've come all this way to see you?' Norman's whining nasal voice with its thick Birmingham accent grated on her raw nerves like a steel file. She was aware of the lift doors opening and the voice of her next-door neighbour speaking to a companion as she got out. Any second now they would come round the corner and run slap into Norman. Holding the door open, she said quickly: 'You'd better come in.'

In the hall Norman smiled at her again. 'Well now, isn't this nice?'

'Why are you here and what do you want?' Leonie snapped. 'I'm going out and I haven't got long, so you'd better make it quick.'

To her intense annoyance he ambled into the drawing room, looking around him with interest as he went. 'Nice place you've got here, Eileen. Must have cost you a bob or two, all this fancy stuff.'

'That's none of your business. Look, I told you; I'm going out.'

With maddening nonchalance Norman settled himself in an armchair, took out a tin in which he carried home-

223

rolled cigarettes, and lit one up before looking at her. 'Oh, *dear*. Is that the way to treat your long-lost brother? I'll have you know it cost me thirty-five bob to come down to London to see you.'

Leonie wrinkled her nose at the acrid odour of the cheap tobacco. 'I don't remember asking you to come, actually,' she told him acidly.

'Oh, don't you – *actually*?' Norman mimicked her voice. 'Maybe not, but I'm here now so p'raps you'd better hear what I've got to say.' He picked a shred of tobacco from his lip and flicked it across the room.

'Then get on and say it.' Leonie looked pointedly at her watch. 'Come to the point, Norman. My husband is picking me up any second now. I don't think he's going to be very pleased to find you here.'

'Your husband, eh? I'd like to meet him. Maybe I'll save what I've got to say till he gets here. Shall we have a drink while we're waiting?' He eyed the cocktail cabinet, licking his lips.

Leonie fumed. 'No, we will not have a drink. Say what you've got to say at once or I'll have you thrown out.'

Norman's smile vanished and his pale eyes narrowed to a pair of spiteful slits. 'Don't kid yourself that you can scare me, Eileen, 'cos you can't. I've got you just where I want you. And I 'appen to know there's no husband coming. There was a cab downstairs waiting for you but I told him he could go, so you needn't worry.'

Leonie gasped. 'How *dare* you?' She bit her lip. What was she to do now? Short of going off and leaving him in the flat she was at a loss to know and she knew that he was well aware of the fact. 'I warn you – if you don't go at once I'll call the caretaker and have you removed,' she said.

He chuckled at her modified threat, 'Oh, I don't think you will. Think of the stir that'd cause. I wouldn't go without making a lot of noise and fuss. What would your posh neighbours say?' He recrossed his legs and flicked the ash from his roll-up onto the carpet. 'Okay, I'll tell you what I come for, Eileen. It's quite simple, I've run short of cash and I want some more. You can spare it so why not?'

Leonie's temper flared. 'Of all the bloody cheek! Look, you'll get no more out of me,' she said. 'I told you in the letter I wrote. I know that Mum and Dad died in the bombing. What you're doing is blackmail – demanding money with menaces. It's against the law, or didn't you know?'

'Okay, go to the police.' He leaped suddenly to his feet with a speed that had her stepping backwards in alarm. 'Put it this way: either I get the cash from you or from one of the papers. I don't give a toss either way. They'd pay generously to have the story of how you neglected your mum and dad after you made your name on the stage. The readers'd be all agog to read about the lies you told about your aristocratic family – about how your real mum and dad died in poverty without you caring a bugger about them.'

'Your word against mine. Who do you think would listen to a nobody like you?'

'Ah, but I've got photos.' He grinned up at her. 'A lovely one of you taken at Googe Street Elementary School, along with all the other Block Street kids.' He licked his lips, savouring the look on her face. 'Then of course there's the little matter of your police record.'

She stared at him. 'Police record? What are you talking about?'

'Surely you haven't forgotten the time you got caught for shoplifting in Woolworth's?'

'But – but I was only fourteen then. It was only a lipstick. Dad never used to give me any pocket money.'

'It was lipstick the time you got caught. There were all the other times when you got away with it. Rings and brooches, bars of chocolate. A common little thief – that's what Mum called you when she found out. Said she'd never be able to hold her head up in the street again.' He thrust his face close to hers and smiled evilly. 'Wouldn't go down too well with the fans, would it?'

She turned away in revulsion. 'You'd never prove any of this.'

He smiled triumphantly. 'Oh, but that's where you're wrong, Eileen. Our dad was a very methodical man, you see. He had a tin box with everything in it. Along with the gold watch Grandad left him and deeds of the shop, there was their marriage certificate, our birth certificates, the old photos I told you about – everything. It's all there – even the newspaper cuttings about your appearance in the juvenile court.'

'I don't believe you. The house was bombed – a direct hit.'

'The box was made of steel. It survived and I've got it put away somewhere safe. You pay up, Eileen, and you can have it lock, stock and barrel. If not, it goes to the paper that offers the most.'

'All right. What do you want?'

He paused, taking a last drag of his evil-smelling roll-up before flicking it into the fireplace. 'Five thousand'd see me set up for life. I could buy a little business. Yes, five'd do me nicely.'

'*Five thousand pounds?* You're mad.'

'No, *you'd* be mad to turn me down, Eileen. I give you my word. Pay up this time and it's the last you'll see of me – refuse and I go to the papers.'

Leonie's head was spinning. 'Look, I can't decide just like that. Anyway I don't keep that kind of sum in the flat. I told you, I've got to go out now. I'll . . . I'll have to think about it and let you know what I decide. Please – will you go now?'

He stared at her suspiciously. 'How long's all this thinking going to take? I warn you, I ain't hanging about for ever.'

She shook her head. 'Oh, I don't know. Give me till tomorrow.'

'I've got no money for London hotels.' He looked around him. 'I'll have to doss down here.'

She shuddered. '*No.*' Opening her bag, she drew out a five-pound note and thrust it at him. 'Here, this ought to be enough to get yourself a decent place.'

He pocketed the money. 'Okay. I'll see you tomorrow then – about this time. And you better come up with the right answers if you don't want to make front-page news by the end of the week.'

She let him out and stood with her back against the door. At least she'd got rid of him – for the time being. She waited until she was sure he'd be clear of the building, then went downstairs to call a cab. Tony would already have been waiting for fifteen minutes. She prayed he wouldn't have grown tired of hanging round and left. This time she really needed him.

Tony was waiting for her in the bar when she arrived. He looked handsome in a light-grey suit, his fair hair slightly longer than usual and gleaming with health and cleanliness. He sat on a bar stool chatting to the barman, a dry martini in front of him. When he turned and saw her, her heart skipped a beat as his face lit up in the familiar smile she hadn't seen for so long.

'Leonie.' He got off his stool and came to meet her, hands outstretched. 'Lovely to see you. It's been ages.'

'Yes. It's good to see you too. Get me a drink please, darling, a stiff one. I've had quite a morning.' She chose a table well away from the bar and Tony joined her there with the drinks. He took out his cigarette case and offered it to her; she took one gratefully, and lit it at the flame of Tony's lighter, drawing the smoke deep into her lungs and blowing it out slowly.

'Aah, that's better.'

He watched her as he put away case and lighter. 'Is something wrong?'

She made herself smile, shaking her head. 'Later. Tell me first what prompted this invitation.'

He looked surprised. 'Is it so surprising that I should ask my wife to have lunch with me on one of the rare occasions when we're both in town at the same time?'

Leonie sipped her drink. 'Let's face it, darling,' she said in an undertone. 'We haven't exactly been what you'd call *close* over the past couple of years, have we?'

'I know. And neither of us is going to pretend that there aren't faults on both sides,' Tony said. 'Maybe it's time we buried the hatchet, if only for Imogen's sake.' He smiled. 'Which brings me to one of the reasons I wanted to see you today. I had lunch with Peter and my old friend

Daniel Sherwood yesterday. Daniel's been on the examination board at RADA for the past couple of years. I was telling him about Imogen and how much she longs to study there, and he invited all of us to RADA's end-of-term production. It's on Tuesday and I thought it would be rather nice if we all went together.'

'You want me to put on a show – play happy families?'

Tony frowned at her acid-tongued remark. 'It would mean an awful lot to Imogen. Surely you wouldn't spoil things for her just because of our quarrel? Surely it's time we forgot about all that?'

For Imogen's sake. Nothing changes, does it? Leonie was about to make this bitter observation when she remembered Norman and her pressing problem. She tapped the ash delicately from the end of her cigarette and glanced up at him through her lashes. 'Of course I want to forget our past differences, darling. I'll be honest with you. I rather suspected that you'd brought me here today to ask me for a divorce.'

He laughed. 'Good heavens, no.'

'Your . . . little friend – she's gone, then?'

He lifted his shoulders. 'I can hardly remember her. So, what do you say about the play? I thought we might take Shirley along. I understand she's set on going to RADA too. I'm sure she'd enjoy it.'

'That's a good idea. I could go to Houlton and bring them both back. We could all stay at the flat.' She glanced at him. 'Where are you staying, by the way?'

'Peter put me up at Richmond. I'm only here on a flying visit. I had to come and see him about casting a film. I've been offered a job by the Rank Organisation. I'm hoping to direct a story about the RAF, set at the outbreak of war; fiction this time. We should begin filming in the autumn if everything goes to plan. It's rather exciting.'

He saw that she seemed rather preoccupied and paused. 'But that's another story. Tell me why you've had a bad morning.'

'Oh, Tim called me in. Something about the powers that be at the War Office objecting to sentimental songs.'

He laughed. 'You're joking.'

'I'm not. They seem to think that sentimental songs will turn the men into a bunch of fairies and make them lose the will to fight.'

'I'm sure you can talk them out of that,' Tony said. 'Surely that wasn't all?'

'No.' Leonie ground out her cigarette. 'I'm in trouble, Tony.'

'What kind of trouble?'

'You remember I told you that my parents had been killed in the Birmingham bombing – my brother too?'

'Yes.'

'Well, it appears that Norman is still alive.'

'That's good news.'

'Hardly. He's blackmailing me.'

Tony's eyebrows shot up. 'Blackmailing you? But why – and how?'

'That article in *Home and Beauty* – the one in which I . . . romanced a little about my background. He's threatening to spill the beans. He'll say I neglected my parents and didn't even know they'd been killed till two years later and – oh, God knows what else besides.'

Tony frowned. 'But you were sending them money, so how can he say you were neglecting them?'

Leonie bit her lip. She'd forgotten she'd told Tony that. 'All the time I was sending it, *he* was taking it,' she said quickly. 'I didn't know they were dead and he never told me.'

'But what made you think *he* was dead?'

She swallowed hard. It was getting complicated. 'B-because . . . I didn't hear from him again. I – just assumed. Then he suddenly appeared at the flat this morning, making all these demands and threats.'

Tony snorted. 'Despicable little rat. Let him do his worst, I'd say. It's his word against yours.'

'I can't afford to do that, Tony. He convinced me that he could make it stick. And you know what the papers are when it comes to a juicy bit of gossip. Think what they could make of it. In the eyes of the public I stand for caring and family ties. I'd be finished by the time Norman had done his worst.'

'So what do you intend to do?'

She gave him her wide-eyed appealing look. 'I was rather hoping you'd tell me.'

'Well, you can't give him any money. That would be putting your head in a noose. He'd be back for more.'

'He promises that if I pay up he'll stay away.'

He gave her a rueful smile. 'And you believe him? A man like that? It's what they always say.'

'I can't let him go to the papers.'

'I'd call his bluff,' Tony said. 'Why should anyone believe him, after all? Can he actually prove he's your brother?'

'Yes. It seems he has all the evidence he needs in a tin box my father kept. It survived the bombing. That's what he had for sale.'

'Have you seen it?'

'No.'

Tony shrugged. 'I doubt if it exists. Call his bluff, Leonie. At least stall him for a while and see what happens. He'll probably lose his nerve. His sort are always the same – all huff and puff and very little substance. The worst thing you can do is let him see you're worried.'

Leonie was far from convinced but she didn't press the matter further. They lunched and talked about their respective careers. Before parting they finalised the arrangements to attend the RADA play together, Leonie deciding to go to Houlton the following day to collect the girls. She would leave on an early train and kill two birds with one stone. When Norman arrived for her decision, she'd be gone. She'd leave a note for him with the caretaker, saying she'd been unavoidably called away and would get in touch as soon as she could. Maybe he would lose his nerve. But she doubted it.

When Leonie arrived at Longueville Hall she was somewhat dismayed to find Gloria there. It seemed that

Shirley's mother was taking a week's holiday and, because Shirley was at school, had decided to spend it at Houlton.

Sensing her disapproval, Molly said, 'I hope you don't mind Gloria staying here, Madam. She does bring her own rations and she's a great help in the house and the kitchen.'

'Of course I don't mind, Nanny. It's just that I have an invitation for Shirley. I was going to take both girls to London for a couple of days, but now I suppose Shirley will have to miss the treat.'

'Oh, I see.' Molly watched helplessly as Leonie searched the wardrobe in her bedroom with mounting irritation, pulling out dresses and throwing them onto the bed. 'Can I help?' she offered.

'I was looking for the black Hartnell dress I had made last year,' Leonie said. 'The one with the matching jacket. I've only worn it once and I thought I might wear it to this show we're going to. They'll expect a bit of glamour. Ah, here it is.' Finding the dress, she drew it out of the wardrobe and spread it over the dressing-table stool. 'I'll try it on later, just in case I've put on weight.' She lit a cigarette and stood looking round her. 'You know, this room is beginning to look shabby, Nanny. If only re-decorating weren't so difficult.' Putting her cigarette down on an ashtray, she fingered the bed hangings. 'What do you think – do they need replacing?'

'You'd never get material like that nowadays, Madam,' Molly remarked, 'and wallpaper is unobtainable. I was only saying to Jim just the other day, that carpet in the drawing room –' She stopped, sniffing the air suspiciously. 'Something's burning.'

Leonie glanced round and gave a shriek. 'Oh, my God, it's my cigarette. It's fallen off the ashtray onto the dress.' She snatched up the dress and began to brush the ash from it. The dress itself was unmarked, but there was a hole burned right through the jacket. 'Oh, *hell!* It's ruined,' she wailed.

'Is anyone hurt? I heard someone scream.' Gloria put her head hesitantly round the half-open door.

'It's Madam's dress,' Molly told her. 'A cigarette fell onto it.'

'Oh, dear. Perhaps there's something I can do.'

Leonie shook her head impatiently. 'There's nothing anyone can do about a burn like that.' She thrust a finger through the hole and Gloria saw that it was right in the front. The watered silk material had burned quickly and irreparably.

She took the dress from Leonie and held it up. It had a beautifully cut flared skirt and a tiny backless bodice with shoestring straps. 'The frock itself is all right,' she said.

'But I couldn't wear it without the jacket,' Leonie said crossly. 'The two go together. It's an *ensemble*. It's a Hartnell – specially made for me. I'd set my heart on wearing it tomorrow. Oh, *damn!* Everything seems to be going wrong lately.'

Gloria and Molly exchanged glances as Leonie's eyes filled with angry tears. In Molly's opinion her work and the rift with Mr Tony were making her nervous and overwrought. She had seen her like this before.

'Madam was wanting to take the girls to London for two days,' she said awkwardly, by way of explanation. 'Seems there's something on at the Royal Academy of Dramatic Art.'

'But it's out of the question now that *you're* here, Gloria,' Leonie said bluntly. 'Obviously you'll be wanting Shirley to spend her time with you.'

All three women knew that Shirley would give her eye teeth to go to London. 'I wouldn't dream of standing in the way of a chance like that for Shirl, Miss Swann,' Gloria said quietly.

Leonie looked at her and felt a little ashamed. She really was behaving rather badly. The business with Norman had shredded her nerves and the accident to her dress on top of everything else seemed like the last straw. 'That's very generous of you, Gloria,' she said. 'I know Imogen wouldn't want to go without her.' She smiled. 'Shirley really has brought Imogen out, you know. She's quite a different girl nowadays.'

232

Gloria smiled. 'She's growing up, that's all.'

'While we're waiting for them to come home from school, why don't we go down to the drawing room and have tea together?' Leonie invited.

'Thank you,' Gloria held up the dress. 'What shall I do with this?'

Leonie waved her hand dismissively. 'Oh, just throw it down with the others. It's useless now. I'll send them all off to Mrs Churchill's Aid to Russia Fund or something.'

'Isn't there anything else you can wear?'

'I was counting on wearing that. Everything else I'd left here is hopelessly out of fashion now and I've no wretched coupons left to get something new.'

Gloria said nothing. Looking at the pile of expensive dresses heaped on the bed, she thought wistfully of what she could do with them. Some of her own clothes dated back to the beginning of the war and had been made over to keep up with current fashion again and again. What must it feel like to have a dress by the famous Hartnell specially made for you? But then with Leonie's wealth she supposed it was the kind of thing one would take for granted.

In the drawing room Leonie sank into the settee and gave a sigh. 'Be an angel and bring us some tea, Nanny.'

'I made a Madeira cake this morning,' Molly said. 'Made with real eggs from the farm – none of your nasty dried stuff. Would you like some of that too?'

'It sounds like sheer heaven.' Leonie looked at Gloria who was standing by the baby grand piano, fingering the Chinese silk shawl that was draped over it. 'Do come and sit down, Gloria.'

'I was looking at this,' Gloria glanced at her. 'It's beautiful material – pure silk.'

Leonie was lighting a cigarette from the silver box on the coffee table. 'Yes, I suppose it is. The colours are rather nice too.'

Gloria was looking at her, wondering if she dared voice the idea that was going through her mind. 'I wonder, would you miss it here on the piano?'

233

Leonie frowned as she inhaled the smoke from her cigarette. 'Why? Do you want it?'

'Oh, no – at least, not for me. It's just that I saw this article in a fashion magazine the other day; a little jacket designed by Steibel and made from Chinese silk. It had a nipped in waist and a cut-away front . . .' She described the style with her hands. 'It would set off your Hartnell dress beautifully and I'm almost sure there's enough material here.' She drew the shawl from the piano and let its silken richness slide sensuously through her hands. 'If you can spare the shawl – and you'd trust me enough to try . . .'

Leonie was on her feet, taking the shawl from Gloria and draping it across her shoulder as she looked into the gilt-framed mirror over the fireplace. The reds and golds of the rich pattern complemented her dark colouring dramatically. Her eyes lit up with pleasure. 'Oh – yes, I do believe you're right. It would look quite sensational. And no one else would have anything like it, would they?' She stopped, looking doubtfully at Gloria. 'But surely there isn't time? We'd have to leave here tomorrow mid-morning at the latest.'

'If I got to work straight away I'm sure I could have it finished in time.'

That evening Gloria measured, cut, pinned and fitted, pausing only to eat her dinner. She talked to Shirley as she worked, but the girl, excited about the coming trip, soon disappeared upstairs with Imogen to choose what they would wear. By the time Gloria tumbled into bed late that night, the little Chinese silk jacket lay over the arm of the chair in her room, basted and ready for machining. The following morning she was up at dawn, working away on Molly's old hand-operated sewing machine in the kitchen, and by the time Leonie came down to breakfast the jacket was ready for her to try on.

'Oh, Gloria, you're a *genius*.' Leonie turned this way and that in front of the mirror. 'I can't thank you enough for this. You really must let me pay you.'

Gloria shook her head. 'Oh, no. I enjoyed doing it. I love a challenge like that and the material was lovely to work with.'

'But I must give you something.' Leonie looked at her thoughtfully. 'I know: you must come to London with us,' she said. 'I'm not sure whether there'll be a seat for you at the play, but if not you could still do some shopping in the West End and stay with us at the flat. Oh, do say you'll come.'

Gloria nodded happily. 'I'd love to. Thank you.'

They travelled up on the mid-morning train and arrived in London early in the afternoon. The girls were excited at the thought of going to RADA and seeing the place where they both hoped to study. Leonie had telephoned their headmistress the previous day and arranged for them to have two days off.

As a special treat, Leonie took them all to lunch at the Savoy. In the River Room she told them that during the Blitz part of this very room had been used as a dormitory and that as well as underground shelters there had been a miniature hospital in the building for first aid.

'Thank God that's all over now,' she said to Gloria. 'Your parents must be relieved now that the second front has started. There's no likelihood of any more bombing now. They'll all be too occupied over on that side.'

'Are your parents still living?' Gloria asked.

Leonie hesitated. 'I'm afraid not.' She dabbed her lips with a napkin. 'They both died some time ago.' Suddenly her eyes lighted on a short, stocky man walking across the restaurant towards them and her cheeks flushed rosily. '*OH*! It's Noël Coward,' she whispered.

To her great delight he paused by the table, looking hard at her. 'Leonie, my dear. It's so long since we last met, though of course I'm a great fan of your delectable radio programme. How are you?'

'I'm very well, thank you, Noël. And you?'

'Positively blooming.' He took her hand and kissed it. 'You're looking even lovelier than I remember you. And I haven't forgotten that play I promised to write for you.'

'I'm looking forward so much to working with you.' She looked round the table. 'May I introduce my daughter, Imogen? And this is her friend, Shirley and her mother, Gloria Rayner.'

He gave them a brief nod, then returned his attention to Leonie. 'Tell that husband of yours he should be arrested for allowing you out of his sight looking so ravishing,' he told her with an impish smile. 'Do give me a ring some time and we'll have lunch.'

He moved away with a wave of his hand and Leonie gazed after him, her eyes shining. If it hadn't been for the war she'd have enjoyed a very different kind of popularity by now, she told herself wistfully. But then she couldn't really grumble. Her name was a household word, after all. She'd certainly take Noël up on that offer of lunch, though. Once the war was over there'd be no more need for her kind of request programme. Besides, she longed to embark on a more glamorous career in the theatre the moment the opportunity presented itself.

Tony had arranged to collect the girls from the flat after lunch and take them to RADA to be introduced to his friend Daniel Sherwood and given a guided tour. Leonie had taken both girls to the hairdresser's and they were still out when he walked into the drawing room. Finding Gloria there caused his eyes to widen.

'Gloria! What a surprise!'

She was dismayed at the sudden quickening of her heartbeat. 'I was staying at Houlton for a few days, so Leonie invited me along too,' she explained.

'I see.' He frowned. 'I'm afraid I only have four tickets for the show.'

'That's all right. I thought I might go over to Whitechapel this evening and visit my mother and father. Surprise them.'

He smiled. 'Ah, yes. Well, it's good to see you.'

'Yes. It's been a long time. I dare say we've both been busy.'

'You're still working at the aircraft factory?'

'Yes. I've seen all of your films. They were very good.'

'Thanks.'

'It's good of you to take Shirl along with you to this RADA play.'

'Not at all. I know she's planning to go there when she leaves school.'

'It's what she's planning, but it may not be possible. You see, I'm planning to marry and go to America when the war is over.'

His face broke into a smile. 'You've met someone and fallen in love? An American soldier?'

'Airman.'

'That explains the radiant look. It's wonderful, Gloria. I'm so glad for you. You deserve to be happy.'

Just for a split second Gloria knew a pang of disappointment. He so obviously meant what he said. He *was* happy. There wasn't even the smallest glimmer of regret in his voice. If he never saw her again, it clearly wouldn't concern him one bit. The knowledge hurt.

He sat down on the chair opposite. 'Tell me about him. I hope he's worthy of you.'

But to her relief Leonie and the girls returned before she had a chance to embark on a description of Billy's finer qualities.

When Tony, Imogen and Shirley had gone, Leonie looked at her. 'Now, I don't want any arguments. I've made you an appointment at André's. You're to have the full works – hairdo, manicure, facial and make-up. It's all paid for and it's my treat.'

'Oh, but I couldn't . . .'

Leonie laughed. 'Oh yes, you could.' She took a card from her bag and gave it to Gloria. 'Here you are. I've booked you with Monique. She's the best, I always insist on her. You'll feel and look like a new woman, I promise. Off you go now. It's in Park Lane – only five minutes' walk.'

When Gloria came out of the smart Mayfair beauty salon she felt like a princess. She had never been inside one of those places before and it was quite the nicest present

237

Leonie could have given her. Her blonde hair was piled high in a glamorous pompadour and her skin felt smooth and tingling after its massage. She glanced surreptitiously in every shop window she passed and enjoyed a little thrill of pleasure at the reflection that looked back at her.

Entering the building, she went up in the lift. To her surprise she found the door to the flat ajar and as she went inside she heard voices coming from the drawing room. Meaning to go quietly to her room so as not to intrude, she crept past the half-open door, but she stopped dead in her tracks as Leonie suddenly burst out loudly:

'I'll give you two thousand, Norman. Take it or leave it. It's all you're going to get. I'm not a millionairess in spite of what you think. And you're going to have to give me the box and all its contents for that.'

'What do you take me for?' Leonie's unseen companion chuckled in a way that sent cold shivers down Gloria's spine. 'Give me the two thousand if you like, but make no mistake, I'll be back for the rest. You can have the photos for that. Bring the cash to the address I gave you tonight. I'll hang on to the rest of the stuff – the birth certificate and the cuttings about your shoplifting. You can pay for them when you've had time to sweat a bit more – *if* I don't get fed up with waiting in the meantime.'

'I've a damned good mind to give you nothing.'

'Suit yourself. I told you before, it's no skin off my nose. I'll get the money one way or the other. Either you pay up or I sell the lot to the papers. I tell them that the beautiful Leonie Swann is my sister – who used to be a snot-nosed little kid from a butcher's shop in Birmingham, pinching stuff out of Woolworth's to try and make herself look like someone she wasn't. I'll tell them how this Darling of the Nation dropped her hard-working mum and dad when she made her pile, and made up a pack of lies about who she was and where she came from.' He chuckled sadistically, obviously enjoying himself. 'Why don't you admit it, our Eileen? I've got you right where you bloody well deserve to be, you tight-fisted bitch. I'm gonna squeeze you till you beg for mercy. By the time I'm done you'll be glad to pay me *ten* thousand quid, let alone five – just to be shot of me.'

'*Get out!*' Leonie screamed. 'Get out of my flat, you slimy blackmailing little toad!'

'Oh dear, oh *dear*,' the man mocked. 'I ask you – is that a nice way to speak to your brother?'

There was a crash as some heavy object was thrown across the room. Gloria slipped inside her room and closed the door. From behind it she heard the man's hastily retreating footsteps and the loud slam of the front door. After a pause she heard Leonie gasp and then begin sobbing as though her heart would break.

Chapter Eleven

For a moment Gloria stood listening to the harsh sobs coming from the other side of her door. Her mind went back to that day when Tony told her that Leonie Swann came from a background so similar to her own that they might have been sisters. Perhaps Leonie deserved the things her brother had said to her, but blackmail – demanding all that money in such a vile, cowardly way – she certainly did not deserve. For a moment Gloria stood listening to the sobs, then she made up her mind. She couldn't just stand here doing nothing. Suddenly Leonie was no longer the dazzling star, admired by millions, she was just another woman – a woman exactly like her. And at this moment she needed help. Opening her door, she stepped into the hall.

Leonie stood with her back to the door, one hand to her mouth in an attempt to stifle the sobs that racked her body; tears were streaming down her face.

Gloria took a step towards her. 'I didn't mean to eavesdrop but I heard him. I'm sorry, but I heard what your – your brother said.' As Leonie began to sob afresh, she held out her arms. 'Oh, please don't cry like that.'

Leonie almost threw herself into Gloria's arms, holding on to her as though she were a lifeline. 'Oh, God, what shall I do, Gloria? He'll finish my career. He'll blacken my name . . . *ruin* me.'

'It's no disgrace to come from an ordinary family,' Gloria said quietly. 'You've worked hard to get where you are. You're a success. Why don't you just let the papers have the story yourself? You could make it sound as though that other story was a mistake. You could make it sound like something to be proud of, which it is.'

Leonie shook her head. 'It's too late for that. Besides, there's all the rest – the things I can't be proud of.' She swallowed painfully. 'Shoplifting is hardly something to crow about.'

'There must be something you can do,' Gloria said. 'No one should have the power to hold you to ransom like that, specially for something that happened so long ago.' She led the trembling Leonie gently towards the drawing room. 'Come and sit down. I'll make you a nice cup of tea.'

In the room she saw the mess of broken china on the carpet. Leonie had thrown a large vase at Norman and it had shattered against the wall into hundreds of pieces. 'I'll get this cleared up before the others come back and see it,' she said.

By the time the room had been tidied and the tea made, Leonie had calmed a little. Sipping her tea, she told Gloria about her unhappy childhood and her ambition to be an actress, the way she and Tony had met and the blossoming of her career.

'I was only a child when I took those things,' she said. 'It was just a silly juvenile madness – a few cheap trifles. I'd almost forgotten about it. It's as though it happened in another life. And it isn't as though I didn't learn my lesson. I had my punishment when I was put on probation for shoplifting.' She put her cup down on its saucer, her hand trembling. 'But if it were all to come out now, think what the papers would make of it.'

'But people love you,' Gloria said. 'Surely your fans would be loyal?'

Leonie shook her head. 'No. They expect you to be perfect, you see. To them we're different beings – idols, up on a pedestal, above all normal human failings. Then there are the others – the people within our circle. You make many enemies in this business,' Leonie told her. 'There's a lot of petty jealousy and spite. The higher you

241

climb, the more they want to see you tumble, in spite of calling themselves your friends. But what worries me the most is that there's a lot of this that Tony doesn't know. And I'd do anything to stop him finding out.'

'I see.' Gloria looked at her. It was worse than she had imagined. 'So you're going to pay?'

'I don't have any alternative.' Leonie took a crumpled scrap of paper from her pocket and spread it out on her knee. 'He says I'm to take the cash to this address tonight. It's some lodging house in King's Cross. I'll have to go to the bank now. And when Tony gets back I'll have to tell him I can't go to the play with them. You can go in my place.'

'Won't he wonder what's wrong, though?'

Leonie drew a deep shuddering breath. 'I'll make up some story. I've no choice. I have to do it.' She grasped Gloria's arm. 'Will you promise me you won't say anything to anyone – especially Tony – *ever*?'

'Of course I won't.'

Leonie's shoulders slumped suddenly. 'I've been a bitch in my time,' she muttered. 'I've done and said some awful things. I've been cruel to Tony – and to Imogen.' She raised her eyes to look at Gloria. 'To you, too. That time I came to the factory where you work, I pretended not to know you. It was a despicable thing to do. I'm sorry.'

'It doesn't matter.'

'But it does, I deserve all I'm getting. I –'

'Look,' Gloria stopped her words, a hand on her arm. 'I've had an idea. *I'll* take the money. You go to the play with Tony and the girls as though nothing has happened and I'll take the money to this address and get the box for you. I'm supposed to be going to Whitechapel, but Ma and Pa aren't expecting me so no one need be any the wiser.'

Naked relief shone in Leonie's eyes. 'Oh, Gloria! But I couldn't let you do it.'

'Yes, you could. It's the obvious answer. You go now and get the cash. I'll do the errand for you, then you can destroy all the evidence and forget all about it.'

'But he – Norman will be expecting me. He'll suspect something.'

'Not when I give him the money. That's all he wants, isn't it?'

Leonie made a quick telephone call to her bank manager to make sure she'd be allowed to withdraw that much money in cash without notice, then she put on her coat and left. Half an hour later she returned and gave Gloria a fat brown envelope containing the money – more money than Gloria had ever seen in her entire life.

Gloria got off the bus and looked again at the address on the piece of paper; 128 Markham Street. Finally she found it, a run-down street at the back of the station. Grubby children played in the gutter and an old man with a brown wrinkled face was selling newspapers on the corner outside the public house, calling out his incomprehensible sales cry in a plaintive whine. Gloria tucked her handbag with its precious contents more securely under her arm and began to walk hesitantly down the street of four-storey Victorian houses, looking carefully at the numbers. She was grateful that it was still daylight. She would not have fancied walking here in the blackout.

Number 128 was obviously a lodging house. A rank odour floated up the area step from the overflowing dustbins at the bottom and the paint on the front door was chipped and faded to an indeterminate grey. Her knock was answered by a fat woman who stood wiping her hands on a greasy overall, one eyebrow raised enquiringly. In answer to Gloria's request for Mr Smith she jerked her head towards the stairs. 'First floor back. Number three,' she said abruptly and retreated once more into the dark recess beyond the staircase.

Her heart beating unevenly, Gloria went up the uncarpeted stairs, wrinkling her nose at the assorted stale cooking odours that pervaded the place. She found the door with a 3 painted on it and knocked. It was opened almost immediately by a short man with thinning mousy

243

hair and a straggly moustache. The look of eager anticipation he wore was quickly replaced by one of irritation.

'Wha' d' y' want?' he asked.

Gloria recognised the voice at once. Its accent had been strange to her and she would have recognised it again anywhere as the one she had heard earlier at the Darrents' flat. But the notion that this man was Leonie Swann's brother would otherwise have been unbelievable. 'Leonie sent me,' she said. 'I've brought – what you asked for and I'm to collect what you have for her.'

His expression changed again. Greed made his pale eyes glint in the dim light of the landing as he held the door open. 'Oh. You'd better come in, then.'

'There's no need,' Gloria said, eager to get away. 'Just give me the goods and I'll go.'

The man's eyes narrowed suspiciously. Sticking his head out of the door, he glanced up and down the landing, then grabbed her sleeve. 'Come in. Don't want the whole house listening, do we?'

The room was furnished with the bare essentials. Gloria vaguely took in a sagging bed covered by a faded folkweave bedspread, a table and one chair. The floor was covered in cracked linoleum and a pair of stained brown curtains hung at the window. She looked apprehensively at Norman.

'Where's the box?'

'Not so fast.' He peered at her. 'Where's Eileen? Why didn't she come herself and who are you?'

'She had an appointment. She couldn't get out of it so I offered to do the errand for her.'

'You still haven't told me who you are.'

'There's no reason why I should. It doesn't matter who I am.'

'Oh yes, it does. For all I know you could be . . .'

'The *police*?' She saw him wince. 'Well, I'm not. I'm just a friend, so hand it over and I'll go.'

Norman Smith licked his lips, clearly relieved. 'You've got the cash, you say?'

'Yes.'

'All of it?'

'All of it.'

'Let's see then.'

Warily and keeping a firm hold of her handbag, Gloria showed him the envelope. Loosening the flap, she allowed him to see the bundle of notes inside. 'It's all there. You'll have to take my word for it. I'm not handing it over till I get the box.'

Norman went across to the bed and bent down, drawing out a battered cardboard suitcase. Opening it, he lifted out a dented steel box with a stout clasp. Then, glancing warily at her, he placed himself between her and the door.

'This is it. Now give me the –' The rest of his words were drowned by an earsplitting crash somewhere quite close. The building gave a violent shudder and the door flew open, almost propelling Norman into her arms. Soot cascaded down the chimney and splinters of glass from the shattered window flew in all directions. Gloria turned away, shielding her face and head with her arms, but a long shard of glass sliced into Norman's scalp. He let out a piercing yell as blood began to stream down his forehead and into his eyes.

'Oh, God! Oh, Christ, I'm bleeding.' Dropping the box with a clatter, he clutched his gashed head.

The landing outside was already jammed with the tenants of the other rooms. There was a babble of raised voices as they jostled each other in a mad scramble for the rickety staircase. Someone shouted: 'It's started again – the bloody Blitz is back.' Outside in the street a woman's hysterical screaming could be heard; somewhere a baby was crying and a man's voice boomed stridently, ordering everyone to take cover.

Gloria staggered backwards, falling onto the bed as Norman pushed past her to elbow his way to the door joining the mass of people heading for the shelters. As Gloria watched him disappear, the wound in his head was still bleeding profusely.

For a moment she stood in the sooty and glass-strewn room, rooted to the floor with dazed shock. Then it was as though some force outside her own control took over, galvanising her into action. Scooping up the steel box from the floor, she hastily wrapped it in a scarf she found hanging behind the door and ran down the staircase of the now empty house. The street below was deserted and suddenly uncannily silent. Papers scattered from the abandoned news stand on the corner fluttered silently among the drifts of broken glass. She half ran, half stumbled along the pavement, not stopping till she got to the corner, when a low roaring overhead made her stop and look up.

A plane, the like of which she had never seen before, was passing overhead. It had flames coming out of the tail and as she watched the engine stopped abruptly and the flames went out. Staring at it in fascination, Gloria saw the plane glide heavily onwards, swaying perilously from side to side. For one horrific moment it seemed to be heading straight for her. As she watched, mesmerised, it dipped, then seemed to straighten up and sailed on over her head to take a sudden dive behind the houses of the next street. There was a deafening crash and a rising plume of smoke; then came the force of the blast, which lifted Gloria off her feet and threw her against the wall, knocking all the breath from her body.

When she got to her feet she was smothered in dust and shaking violently. What in God's name was it? Were the Germans sending pilots on suicide missions now? Hastily dusting herself off and making sure she still had the metal box, she hurried on as fast as she could. As she ran she thought about the Darrents and Shirley, praying that they were safe. She thought about Billy – her sweet, dearest Billy, God only knew where, fighting to free them from horrors like this. But her most immediate and urgent thought was to put as much distance as she could between herself and Norman Smith in the shortest time possible. The strange crashing aeroplane, sinister and frightening as it was, had done Leonie Swann the biggest favour of all time – just as long as Gloria could get herself back to Mayfair without getting herself killed.

She got as far as the Underground station on foot, taking cover in doorways three times on the way. The pattern was always the same. The strange-sounding aircraft would roar overhead, its engine would splutter and then cut out; it would glide unsteadily in eerie silence for several minutes, then plunge abruptly into its deadly, devastating dive.

Down in the Underground rumours were rife. The planes were piloted by prisoners of war drugged into compliance, or by men with terminal illnesses snatched from their hospital beds. The most bizarre rumour was that they had no pilots at all. No one could swallow that one. Clutching her priceless prize, Gloria waited anxiously for things to quieten. At last the trains began to run again and she boarded the first one she could, changing at Baker Street for Green Park. She was on her way, her mission accomplished. It was only as she sat there in the train on the last leg of her journey that she remembered the bulging envelope still in her handbag. A smile of delight spread over her grime-smudged face. She had done even better than she thought: she'd got the money *and* the box.

To her relief Mayfair seemed relatively untouched by the evening's bombing. Letting herself into the flat, she looked ruefully at herself in the mirror, remembering the pleasure she had taken in her appearance just a few short hours ago after the beauty treatment. Now the carefully groomed hair hung about her face in sooty strands, and dirt streaked what had been a perfectly made-up face. Never mind, she told herself, it was in a good cause. She was just thankful to be still in one piece. She changed out of her dust-covered clothes, had a bath and washed the dirt – and the expensive style – from her hair.

When Shirley, Imogen and the Darrents arrived home safely at half-past ten, Gloria felt a surge of relief. The girls ran to her in the drawing room, full of enthusiasm for the play they had seen and telling her how it had been interrupted halfway through for the air raid. To them it had only added to the excitement. Tony looked at her white face curiously and asked if she was all right.

'You're looking rather shaky, Gloria,' he said. 'Where were you when the raid started?'

'I was . . . on my way home,' she said, half truthfully.

'To Whitechapel? Did you get there?'

She shook her head. 'No. I came back here as soon as I could.' Out of the corner of her eye she could see Leonie looking at her anxiously. As soon as she could, Gloria excused herself and went to her room. After a few minutes there was a tap on the door and Leonie slipped inside, turning the key in the lock.

'Thank God you're all right. I've been sick with worry,' she said. 'Everyone was saying that the King's Cross area was badly hit.' She looked at Gloria. 'I take it you didn't see him.'

'Yes, I did.' Gloria opened her wardrobe where she had stowed the box. 'I think this is what you want, isn't it?'

'Oh – oh, you got it. Thank God!' Almost weak with relief, Leonie wrenched the box open and searched anxiously through the contents, making sure that everything was there.

'The raid started soon after I got there,' Gloria told her. 'Your brother was cut by flying glass. He made a dash for the shelter along with everyone else in the building. He was very frightened, so much that he forgot all about me – he even forgot this.' She opened her bag and took out the envelope.

Leonie stared disbelievingly at the package, then at her, her eyes round with astonishment. 'The *money*? You've saved the money too?' She threw her arms round Gloria and hugged her hard. 'You risked your life for this.'

Gloria shook her head. 'No, I didn't. You wouldn't have got me into a shelter along with a man like him. No, to tell the truth I was almost home before I remembered the money was still in my bag.'

'Nevertheless, I'll be in your debt for a very long time. If ever I can help you in any way, just let me know,' Leonie said, 'Anything you need – any time, Gloria. Just ask.'

* * *

Gloria and Shirley managed a brief visit to Whitechapel the next morning before their return to Houlton. They found Ma in a belligerent mood.

'I thought we'd done with bombs,' she complained. 'Now it seems that 'itler's gone and thought up something else to chuck at us. I 'ope 'e rots in 'ell when the Allies catches up with 'im.'

'Well, I'm just glad you're both safe and well,' Gloria told her. 'Why don't you and Pa come and live in my cottage till it's over and done with? Can't be all that long now, can it?'

Ma looked scandalised. 'Leave 'ere now? Never. We've stuck it out this long and we'll see it through to the end.'

Gloria looked appealingly at her father. 'What do you say, Pa?'

He shook his head, sucking hard on his pipe. 'Ma's right. Besides, they're going to need experienced ARP wardens again if these new attacks keep on.'

Ma looked at Shirley. At fourteen she was as tall as her mother. Her red-gold hair fell in curls to her shoulders and she was wearing a smart new dress that Gloria had made her. 'Well, miss?' Ma pursed her lips. 'Quite the young lady now, ain't you? Leavin' school this term?'

'No, she isn't, Ma. I told you,' Gloria said. 'She's staying on. Anyway, if Mr Butler gets his way, seems like they'll all be staying on till they're sixteen.'

Ma pursed her lips. 'Not in *my* lifetime, I 'ope. Not for gels leastways.'

'But I won't be able to stay on if the war ends and we go away, will I, Glor?' Shirley looked at her mother. Surely Gloria was going to tell Ma and Pa about marrying Billy. Wasn't that what they'd come for?

Ma looked from one to the other, her eyes narrowing as she asked: 'What does she mean – go away? What's goin' on? Come on then – out with it.'

Gloria licked her lips, wishing Shirley had kept quiet about it. 'It's just that I . . . might be going to America when the war is over,' she said. 'Billy has asked me to marry him.'

Ma's jaw dropped as she stared in stunned silence at her daughter. '*Marry* him?' she said at last. 'But 'e's only a kid. He must be at least ten years younger than you.'

Gloria coloured. 'Of course he isn't – not that much anyway. He's old enough to fight, isn't he? You make me sound like Methuselah, Ma.'

Ma's mouth tightened into a tense line. 'So you're goin' off to America with 'im, are you? That's the last we'll see of either of you, I s'pose.'

'I expect we'll come back for holidays,' Shirley put in.

'Holidays? Do you realise how far away it is? It ain't Margate you're goin' to, you know. It's the other side of the bleedin' *world*.'

Gloria sighed. She'd known there'd be a fuss. She looked at her father in mute appeal. Taking his pipe out of his mouth, he said mildly:

'It's your life, love. You must do what makes you happy.'

'Oh, that's right,' Ma said bitterly. 'You just tell 'er to go off. Tell 'er not to give a thought for the ma and pa what've stood by 'er through thick and thin.'

'Please, don't let's fall out over it.' Gloria kissed Pa, then turned to her mother, but Ma had already turned away to walk into the shop. As they left she was serving a customer. She didn't say goodbye or even look up.

Shirley looked at her mother as they walked together down Angel Row. 'Sorry, Glor. I shouldn't have said anything about America, should I?'

Gloria shrugged. 'She had to know some time. She's got to learn that she can't live our lives for us for ever.'

'Do you think the war'll be over soon?' Shirley was thinking of RADA and all the exciting things she'd seen and heard the previous day. She couldn't bear the thought that she might never get the chance to go there.

'I don't know,' Gloria said wearily. 'What with this new spate of bombing and everything, who can say? Sometimes I think it'll never end.'

Shirley bit down hard on the relief that made her want to smile.

★ ★ ★

London soon learned that the new robotic flying bomb was officially called the V-1, but it wasn't long before it was irreverently rechristened the 'doodlebug'. The V-1s rained down relentlessly on London till September, when a newer, more sinister flying bomb joined the onslaught. The V-2, more like a giant rocket than a plane, fell indiscriminately and without the V-1s warning, exterminating everything in its path. London was once again in the grip of bombardment; just when everyone had been buoyed up with the euphoria over the second front. Mothers and children once again left London for the comparative safety of the countryside, once more crowding into villages and market towns.

With Billy gone, Gloria no longer felt peace at Rook Cottage, so rather than allow it to stand empty she let it to a young woman from Woolwich whose husband was in the Navy. She and her two small boys were grateful to find a place they could have to themselves in the quiet and safety of the country, while Gloria spent more of her weekends with Shirley at Houlton.

Letters came from Billy. They were few and far between, short and scrappy with little or no information, but Gloria was glad to get them just the same. As days came and went with news of bitter fighting, she worried constantly about him. She worried about Ma and Pa too. If only she could get them out of London. Ma had always been difficult and uncompromising, but there had always been a strong bond between them for all that, and Gloria hated the unhealed rift that had opened between them. At Christmas Leonie suggested that she invite them to Longueville Hall, which she did, but Ma wrote back in her careful, spidery handwriting, declining the offer in frigidly polite tones.

It was a beautiful Christmas, bitterly cold but bright and sunny. A hard frost laid a veneer of silver on the lawns and decorated the trees with diamond spangles. Imogen and Shirley were in the village pantomime and Gloria took Jane with her to see them. They laughed till they cried at the wartime jokes and slapstick comedy, and

Gloria was so proud of her beautiful daughter playing principal girl to Imogen's handsome principal boy.

At Longueville Hall they played charades and enjoyed the sumptuous dinner that Molly managed to provide in spite of shortages and rationing. From his depleted wine cellar Tony still managed to produce bottles of Mosel and claret to drink with it and Jim had carefully stored away apples and pears from the orchard.

In spite of the new spate of V-2 bombing everyone felt that the end of the war was at last in sight. Weary Londoners looked upon it as Hitler's last-ditch attempt and no one seriously thought he had a chance of winning now. It was just a case of sitting it out and waiting. Life gradually became easier in many small ways. That winter the blackout had been relaxed to a 'dim-out'. After all, the latest 'bombers' had no pilots to see. To Jim's secret regret, the Home Guard had been disbanded. He had risen to the rank of sergeant and had come to enjoy his evenings drilling the men, the monthly church parades and his nights on watch at various sites around the village.

Over the holiday Tony and Leonie managed to put on a convincing performance, each playing the role of loving spouse. Leonie had remained silent about Norman's failed blackmail attempt. She allowed Tony to believe that she had taken his advice – and that Norman had caved in when she had called his bluff. Tony had been busy with rehearsals for the film he was to make, the shooting of which had been delayed until the New Year. To Leonie's dismay he showed no inclination to share a bedroom with her at Longueville Hall, but slept in his dressing room, fuelling anew her simmering feelings of resentment.

On New Year's Eve they gave a party. Most of the village was invited. Jim cut down a ten-foot fir tree from the grounds, which Imogen and Shirley trimmed with the glass baubles and decorations purchased before the war and carefully preserved and used every year since. With her usual resourcefulness and ingenuity, Molly provided a tasty buffet complete with mince pies and punch, and the hall was cleared for dancing to gramophone records. It was halfway through the evening that Gloria found herself dancing with Tony.

'You're looking especially lovely tonight, Gloria,' he said as he smiled down at her.

Gloria blushed with pleasure. It was a long time since she'd been close to Tony like this. She had never forgotten the summer of 1941 when they had shared a short holiday here at Houlton – the way he'd kissed her and the things they'd talked about. She hadn't forgotten either, the way she had ruined it all by throwing herself at him, or his polite but humiliating refusal. The memory still made her curl inwardly with shame. All she hoped was that *he* had forgotten – as he surely must have done, with the exciting life that he led.

'What are you thinking about?' he asked, lifting her chin with his forefinger. 'Whatever it is, it's making you blush delightfully.'

'It's nothing,' she said. 'It's a bit warm in here.'

He swung her round and pulled her arm through his. 'Let's got into the conservatory,' he said. 'It'll be cooler there and I'll get you a glass of lemonade.' He laughed. 'You see, I haven't forgotten your favourite tipple. There isn't much that I forget, if the truth is known.'

In the conservatory they sat side by side in the basket chairs. Gloria sipped her lemonade and wondered exactly what he meant about forgetting.

'Now tell me all about this American of yours,' Tony invited as he lit a cigarette.

'There isn't much to tell. He's overseas at the moment. He went last June at the time of the Normandy landing.'

'You must miss him.'

'Yes, I do.'

'And when he comes back?'

'We'll be married – I suppose.'

'You don't sound very sure.'

Gloria shifted restlessly in her chair. Ever since Ma's disapproving reaction, she had been doing some serious thinking. 'Sometimes knowing Billy seems a bit like a dream,' she said.

He smiled. 'War's like that. We live life in a series of cameos.'

'My mother wasn't too happy when I told her I was going to marry Billy.'

'It's your life, not your mother's.'

'I know, but she did have a point. There's something else, you see.'

'Which is?'

'Well, he's younger than me.' She glanced at him. 'Quite a bit younger.'

'Do you think it bothers him?'

'It's not that so much.' She bit her lip. 'I wonder sometimes if I wasn't kind of – well, a substitute for his mother.'

Tony laughed. 'I very much doubt that.'

But she shook her head, her eyes troubled. 'Would it be fair, though? Has he thought about it enough? And what about when he arrives home with me – me *and* Shirl – what will his family think? Will I be what they want for him?'

'Surely it's what you and Billy want that's important.'

Gloria shook her head. 'I don't know. There's Shirl, too. She's got her heart set on going to RADA with Imogen. I know she doesn't really want to leave England.'

'You could always leave her here with us.' When she didn't reply he asked quietly: 'Do you love him, Gloria?' He took her chin in his hand and made her look at him. 'Well – do you?' His eyes searched hers.

'Yes, but . . .'

'But *what*? There should be no buts if you love him, Gloria. You must know that.'

'It's just that I wonder if it's the right *kind* of love.'

'How many kinds are there?'

She shrugged, lowering her eyes from his.

'Only one kind that I know of, between a man and a woman,' he said quietly.

The conversation was getting too involved for her liking. How could she tell him that the memory of his kiss – a kiss that meant less than nothing to him – would always

254

stand in the way of any new love that might come her way? Billy was sweet and good and yes, of course she loved him. Who wouldn't? But he was so young – he had his whole life before him. He deserved better than second-hand; second-best. He was worthy of someone who could give him her heart, whole and untouched. She looked at Tony, making herself smile.

'Can we dance again? Listen, someone has put on "Where or When?" It's my favourite.'

He nodded and reached for her hand. 'You're a very sweet person, Gloria,' he said softly. 'A very special person. You once saved – well, if not my life, then certainly my sanity. I'll always be grateful to you for that. Please don't spoil your life. Listen to your heart and do what will make you happy. You owe yourself that.'

They went back to the party and danced in silence. The words of the hauntingly romantic song seemed to hold a message for her as they circled the makeshift dance floor. What she had felt then, she still felt as powerfully as ever, but Tony inhabited another world, and he was married to a woman who had become her friend – a woman with whom she shared a secret. Tony could never in a thousand lifetimes belong to her. She repeated his words inside her head. *You saved my sanity. I'll always be grateful to you for that.* His gratitude was better than nothing, she supposed. And that night – the night when he heard that Claire had died – it had been to her that he turned. The suffering she had shared with him that night would always belong to them; it was a memory no one else could share. At least she could cherish that.

As the clock struck midnight they all raised their glasses and wished each other a happy New Year. Everyone linked arms and Leonie led them in singing 'Auld Lang Syne'. Then Tony proposed a toast, the first of the newly begun year.

'Here's to 1945. The last year of the war,' he said, holding his glass aloft. 'The beginning of the end.'

Glasses were raised and everyone drank, reiterating his toast: 'The beginning of the end.'

★ ★ ★

'I think it went rather well, don't you?' Leonie was taking off her make-up at the dressing table.

'Yes. I'm sure everyone enjoyed themselves.'

She looked up at him through the mirror. 'I was glad to see you being so nice to Gloria tonight.'

'Is there any reason why I shouldn't be nice to her?'

'None at all. Every reason that you should.'

He looked at her. 'You've changed. There was a time when you were as patronising as hell to her. Now you treat her almost like a human being.'

Leonie swung round on the dressing-table stool. 'That's unfair. Gloria's been a good friend to me. I've a lot to be grateful to her for.'

He turned to look at her, one eyebrow raised in surprise. 'Grateful – you? Oh, for the silk jacket she made for you out of the shawl?'

She hesitated, wanting to confide in him, to have him on her side again. Since the business with Norman she had felt a desperate need of warmth and reassurance. 'More than that,' she said. 'I've got to know Gloria a great deal better over the past few months and it has been good for me. She's like the personification of all the people out there who listen to my programme.'

Tony's lip curled slightly. Now she sounded more like the old Leonie. 'You mean she's that strange phenomenon, the woman in the street?' he said cynically. 'A member of your adoring public.'

She ignored the jibe. 'No. Tony. She's a woman, Full stop. A warm, kindly, generous woman. I discovered that when – when she did me a great favour.'

'Did you a favour?' He paused in the act of removing the studs from his dress shirt. 'What favour?'

Getting up, she went to him. 'Tony, there's something I didn't tell you. You remember I told you last summer that Norman was trying to blackmail me – threatening to go to the papers.'

'Yes.'

'Well, I didn't tell you that he came back. I tried calling his bluff, but I could see that it wasn't going to work. I'd no choice but to pay.'

He stared at her. 'You actually gave him money? You fool, Leonie! Why didn't you tell me?'

'There wasn't time and anyway I . . . didn't want to involve you. The thing is that Gloria was there. She overheard everything he said. She was such a help and support, Tony. She promised to keep all of it secret, but not only that, she offered to take the money to him and get the evidence for me.'

He was frowning. 'Wait a minute, when was all this?'

'At the flat, last June. On the day we took the girls to the RADA play.'

'The night of the first V-1 raid?'

'That's right.'

'She offered to take that risk – for you?'

'No one knew there was going to be a raid.'

'You're not telling me that you actually let her do it?'

'She *insisted*, Tony. And really I had no choice. You were due back with the girls any minute. We were going to the play and –'

'How much did you pay him?'

She licked her dry lips. She had expected him to sympathise with her dilemma. It wasn't going as she'd hoped. 'Five thousand.' As his eyes widened in shocked surprise, she hurried on: 'He promised that he wouldn't ask for any more. I *had* to pay it. Listen, I'd seen Noël at the Savoy only that lunchtime. It reminded me how important it is for me to plan for my future career now that the war is almost over. So when Norman threatened to ruin things for me, I had to agree to pay. But I couldn't get the money, go all the way to King's Cross with it and be back before we were due to leave for the play.'

'So you let that girl go across London with all that money on her, to do your dirty work for you while you got dressed up and went to the theatre?'

'It wasn't *like* that. I didn't ask her, Tony. She could see the hopeless tangle I was in and she offered to help. But listen, you haven't heard the best part. They were just doing the exchange when the raid started. Norman panicked and ran off to the shelter. Gloria came back with the evidence – *and* the money. Wasn't she wonderful?'

Tony was shaking his head. 'I saw her later that night, after the raid. She looked like death. She couldn't stop trembling. Now I know why. You let her risk her life just so that you could hang on to that stupid myth about your family background. Christ, Leonie, I knew you were self-centred but this borders on megalomania.' He looked at her. 'And make no mistake, he'll be back for that money. He'll be biding his time but he'll certainly be back. Blackmailers never let go. You realise that, don't you?'

'But don't you see? He can't. I've got the evidence now. He can't hold anything else over my head.'

'What evidence? Where is it?'

'I burned it.'

'Burned what? What was there?'

'My birth certificate, some photographs. All in a tin box thing.'

'What interest could rubbish like that possibly be to a newspaper?' He grasped her by the shoulders. 'I can't believe that you let Gloria risk her life for something so trivial. Sometimes you make me sick, Leonie. You and that vastly inflated ego of yours. I believe you'd sell your own grandmother if you thought it'd get your photograph on the front page of some magazine.' He pushed her from him in a gesture of disgust. 'This just proves to me how selfish and shallow you are.'

'Tony, *no*. Listen.' She ran to stop him leaving the room. 'There's more – other things I haven't told you.'

He sighed wearily. 'No more now, Leonie. I'm tired. I want to go to bed.'

She held tightly to his arm, biting her lip. She was losing his sympathy. Should she tell him the rest – lay her soul bare for him? Should she take the gamble? 'There was something else, Tony. Something serious that I never told you about.'

He looked at her sceptically. In this mood he could never quite tell when she was acting and when she was on the level. 'What? Come on, then, are you going to tell me or aren't you?'

She swallowed hard. 'When I was in my teens, I . . . stole some things from a shop. Damn silly things, rubbish really. But I was caught and charged – put on probation. It was only a childish prank, but because of it I have a police record. That's what Norman was going to tell the papers. He had proof, too. Can you imagine what it would look like?'

He groaned. 'Why on earth didn't you tell me this before?' He looked at her, suddenly seeing her through new eyes. Was this the woman he had sacrificed his career as a classical actor for? A shallow, egotistical, jumped-up nobody who'd step on any face to get where she wanted to be? She had never loved him anyway – simply used him just as she'd used Gloria and everyone else she had ever come into contact with. Suddenly he felt he hated her – hated and pitied her both at the same time.

He stood up. 'So you got away with it? You sent Gloria to do your grubby little deal for you and she pulled your chestnuts out of the fire – *literally*, as it happens. Well, all I hope is that you get what you want. God only knows you've put enough necks on the line for it.' At the door he turned. 'I'll be leaving tomorrow – or rather today. We start filming again next week and there's a lot to do. I don't know when I'll see you again. Good night, Leonie.'

'Found yourself another slut, have you?' she screamed at him. 'I hope you don't fool yourself that they chase you for your sex appeal. Can't you see that they're just cheap little gold-diggers, on the make – out for what they can get?'

He paused in the doorway to look pityingly at her. 'Well, you'd know all about that, wouldn't you, Leonie? I've been married to the queen of all gold-diggers for the last sixteen years, and I'm sick to the back teeth of you. It's warmth and sincerity that I have to look elsewhere for.'

'*Swine!*' She snatched off one of her feathered mules and hurled it after him, but it hit the closed door and fell harmlessly to the floor. Throwing herself across the bed, she pushed her fist into her mouth in anguish. 'Go to hell then,' she spluttered, beside herself with tears of rage. 'Bloody well go to *hell*! I hate you, Tony bloody Darrent. *I hate you*. I hope you burn in hell.'

★ ★ ★

That spring term Shirley and Imogen worked extra hard at school. Because of overcrowding in the school, a handful of particularly bright students had been chosen to take the School Certificate one year early and both girls were among that number. Shirley was especially pleased. If she had to go to America, she could leave with her education complete. A cloud hung over the prospect of her leaving. She and Imogen had become as close as sisters and they could not imagine being apart.

The hardness of winter gentled into spring. Gloria was a regular weekend visitor now that Billy was no longer with them. Shirley worried about her mother. She was quiet and withdrawn much of the time. Unlike the old Gloria, who had always been eager and ready for a trip to the pictures to see her favourite stars, she spent a lot of time in the kitchen, chatting to Molly, or walking by herself, her face closed and preoccupied. Shirley wondered sometimes whether she was as keen on going to America as she made out to be. She had asked her once, but Gloria flared up at her.

'*Want* to go? Of course I want to go. Why? Are you trying to throw a spanner in the works now, like Ma?'

Shirley had stared at her, taken aback by the fiery reaction to her innocent question. 'I only asked, Glor. You seem so quiet sometimes; so far away, that's all.'

Gloria had stared at her for a moment, then bitten her lip, her face crumpling. 'I'm sorry, love,' she'd said tearfully. 'I didn't mean to snap at you. It's just the worry.'

'Billy'l be all right, Glor,' Shirley said, stroking her mother's hair. 'I know he will. The war's nearly over now.'

Gloria was silent. She longed to tell Shirley she wasn't going to marry Billy – wasn't going to America – but she couldn't. Not until she had told Billy himself. And the prospect of telling him was eating away at her heart, making her sick with anguish. How could she hurt him? How could she bear the hurt herself? Because she knew that sending him away would tear her heart out. 'Of

260

course he will,' she muttered, squeezing Shirley's hand. 'Take no notice of me, love.'

Jim still sat by the wireless at every news bulletin. He got especially excited at the news that Allied troops had crossed the Rhine.

'We're nearly there now, love,' he told Molly. 'Won't be long now before we're hanging out the flags.'

Aware of the rift between Gloria and Ma, Shirley wrote to her grandparents every week. It was hard to know what to write about. Ma had made it clear that she didn't approve of too much schooling and she had no interest in the country. Neither did she approve of Shirley's theatrical ambitions or the lifestyle she led here at Houlton. But somehow, in spite of it all, Shirley managed to fill a couple of pages with assorted titbits of news. In return Ma wrote back. The doodlebugs and buzzbombs seemed to have stopped now. There wasn't too much damage around Angel Row, thank goodness. The shop had taken a bit more battering, but London County Council had promised to put it right as soon as they could. The business was still doing well and Pa still made his early morning trips 'up the market'. It was nice to think that Gloria and Shirley would soon be home to help out. She and Pa weren't as young as they used to be. There was news about the neighbours, of marriages and deaths and births. In fact, Ma's letters contained much more news than Shirley's. Sometimes when she was reading them she wondered how she had ever lived in Angel Row. Before the war seemed so long ago – another life, which she only barely remembered. It was a whole world away. And going back to live in it again, as Ma seemed to expect, was totally inconceivable. But she and Gloria would be going to America, so there was no chance of that anyway.

In late March, Peter Jason sent for Leonie. The anticipation of peace filled the London air with a special kind of excitement, as fresh and fragrant as the scent of the daffodils in the flower-sellers' baskets.

Peter had moved back into London now, renting a temporary office in Old Bond Street. Leonie climbed the two flights of narrow stairs, complaining bitterly to Peter when she was shown into his office.

'Really, darling, I'd have thought you'd try to get a place with a lift. After all, you have some very successful clients on your books now.'

Peter smiled. 'All in good time, Leonie. We'll have to take this rehabilitation business one step at a time.'

'So . . .' Leonie settled herself in a chair and smoothed her skirt. 'What have you got for me?'

'A play. I think you're going to like it.'

'By Noël?' Her eyes lit up. 'I knew he'd keep his promise to me. Did I tell you I saw him at the –'

'It's not by Noël,' Peter interrupted. 'This is by a new young playwright called Paul Winspear. He was invalided out of the army after being wounded at El Alamein and he's been writing ever since. I think he's going to make quite a name for himself.'

Leonie was clearly disappointed. 'I'm not sure that I want to commit myself at the moment,' she said. 'Noël did promise and I don't want to find myself too tied up to accept, do I?'

Peter shook his head. 'I wouldn't turn this down if I were you. When you read the script you'll see what I mean. And there's a whisper that a film might soon be made of one of Noël's most popular plays. I'm keeping you in line for a leading part in that – if you're interested, that is.'

'Interested? Of *course* I'm interested. So what is this new play about?'

Peter pushed a bound manuscript across the desk towards her. 'It's called *Joy in the Morning*.'

'And do I play Joy?'

Peter frowned at her. 'It's a serious play, Leonie. A drama about a couple struggling to readjust to normal life after the trauma of war.'

Leonie looked at him. 'No music? No songs?'

Peter sighed. 'Your voice won't last for ever, you know. This is a chance to get into the legitimate theatre.'

Leonie was leafing impatiently through the scripts. 'I know, but isn't this all a bit depressing? There's a character here who actually comes home blind.'

'I know – and you play his wife. It's a very strong part, Leonie. She's a selfish, pleasure-loving woman who finds a new strength through her husband's disablement.'

But Leonie was shaking her head. 'What will my fans think, Peter? They'll come expecting me to be the Leonie Swann who was in *Sunshine Sally* and *Prince of Hearts*; the girl who sang their favourite songs for them and encouraged them all through the war. Now that it's almost over –'

'When the war is over, the struggle will begin for many of us here at home,' Peter pointed out. 'That's the message of the play. Read it, Leonie. Reserve your judgement till you've read it.'

Leonie was doubtful, but she took the manuscript back to the flat, poured herself a stiff drink and curled up in a corner of the settee to read. It was past midnight when she finally laid the script down, having read it through twice. In a state of suppressed excitement she undressed and took a bath. She had never been so impressed by anything in her entire life. The couple in the play were just like herself and Tony. She wanted more than anything else in the world to play the part and she knew with a profound certainty deep inside her that she could make a success of it. Peter had been right: it was *her* part. She had always tried to be close to her fans and in this play she would have the opportunity to show them that she was really *like* them – could weep and suffer and love, just as they did. It would give her a chance to show Tony that he'd been wrong about her, too. She wasn't shallow. In playing this part she would have the chance to reveal the true depths of her character; the warmth and sincerity he had accused her of lacking. She would make him eat his words if it was the last thing she ever did.

When she was comfortably settled in bed, she lifted the telephone and dialled Peter's number. After several rings he answered sleepily.

'Jason here.'

'Peter. I've just finished reading the script of *Joy in the Morning*.'

He gave an audible groan. 'Christ, Leonie, is that all? It's the middle of the night. Tomorrow morning would have been quite soon enough to tell me that.'

She laughed. 'Don't be such an old grouch, darling. It's not that late. I had to ring because I knew you'd want to know that I absolutely *adore* it. I can't wait to play the part and I'm longing to meet the man who wrote it.'

'Then you'd better come along to the office on Friday,' he said. 'He's coming in to see me at eleven o'clock. You can meet him then. And now, Leonie, do you mind very much if I get some hard-earned sleep?'

She put down the telephone, switched off the bedside light and slid down under the bedclothes. Every inch of her tingled with a feeling of excitement that was almost sexual. She had the strongest feeling that she had reached an important turning point, both in her career and her life.

Chapter Twelve

When it came, the news took them all in different ways. Gloria heard at her bench at the factory. A great cheer went up when the announcement was made, and Jane grasped her round the waist and began to whirl her round.

'It's over,' she sang excitedly. 'It's actually *over*. Can you believe it?'

But Gloria felt numb. They had all been waiting for so long that now it had finally come, the news left her oddly unmoved. Her immediate thoughts were of how changed life would be now that they were at peace. To begin with, she would be out of a job. Ma and Pa would expect her to go home, while Shirley would have to stop on at Houlton at least until after her exams. Then there was Billy. She hadn't had a letter from him now for almost ten weeks. It wasn't unusual or surprising, considering all that had been happening. Many of the girls with husbands or boyfriends serving abroad didn't hear for weeks. Now she found herself dreading the immediate prospects of having to tell him of her decision not to marry him.

At Longueville Hall, Jim received the news with quiet satisfaction.

'Well, old England's done it again, love,' he told Molly, looking up from his seat next to the wireless set with moist eyes. 'The Hun has surrendered at last. Surely they'll know now that they can't keep us British down, no matter what the odds. There'll be a lot of changes now. You mark my words.'

'Changes – how?' Molly asked, stopping only momentarily from doing the ironing. 'I can't see how it'll affect us.'

Jim shook his head. 'I reckon we'll be having a change of government for a start. Winston's all right for wartime but when the lads come home they'll be looking for a better world.'

'Well, why shouldn't we get it with Winnie?'

'Why? Because he's against most of the reforms. Beveridge wants this new health plan of his passed, and the sooner the better if you ask me. Better medical attention for everyone, not just those that can afford it. Then there's Butler's education act to be put into practice – properly, not just half-measures.' He shook his head. 'No, things've got to become better now than they were before the war, otherwise they'll likely have a revolution on their hands.'

Molly sniffed disapprovingly. Men! They were never happy unless they were stirring things up. 'I'd have thought people'd be only too happy to let things be as they were before the war,' she said. 'You'd think they'd be glad to be done with fighting.'

'Ah, but now we've got to fight for ourselves,' Jim told her. 'For a better way of life for ordinary folk. No more poverty. Decent housing. I reckon as a nation we've earned that much at least. And if it's to be had with a fresh government, then that's what folks'll vote for.'

'Well, I think it's downright ungrateful,' Molly said, outraged. 'After all Mr Churchill has done for us, are we going to cast him aside like – like an old sock or something?'

Jim smiled. 'I dare say he won't be too sorry to sit back and put his feet up for a change,' he said. 'He's no chicken, after all. The war must've taken it out of him even more than the rest of us – all that responsibility. No, give the younger men a chance, that's what I say. Let Winston retire gracefully and take a well-earned rest.'

At the high school the girls were allowed out early after the headmistress had assembled the school to make the announcement. As they came out into the May sunshine, they saw that the Union Jack had been run up the flagpole to flutter triumphantly in the fresh spring breeze.

'I suppose you and Gloria will be off to America soon now then,' Imogen said glumly as they waited for the bus.

'I don't know.' Shirley looked doubtful. 'Glor doesn't exactly seem excited about going. If I mention it she snaps my head off. Sometimes I wonder if she's gone off the idea.'

'I asked Daddy if you could stay with us,' Imogen said. 'He said it would be up to you and Gloria – that I wasn't to try to influence you either way.'

'You never told me.'

Imogen smiled. 'Just think, if you stayed we could be going to RADA in the autumn, you and I.' She clutched Shirley's arm and squeezed it tightly. 'Oh, Shirl, you won't go to America, will you? You know you don't want to.'

Shirley lifted her shoulders helplessly, torn both ways. 'I don't know, Imo. I'll just have to wait and see what happens.'

'I bet there'll be some fun in town this evening,' Imogen said, cheering up. 'What do you say we take the bus into town later and see what's happening?'

Leonie was at the theatre where a rehearsal of *Joy in the Morning* was in progress. The stage manager called her during a break to say that there was a telephone call for her. She took it in the prop room, which was nearest to the stage.

'Leonie Swann speaking.'

'Leonie, it's Tony. You've heard the news?'

'News?'

'Germany has surrendered. It's all over.'

'Oh, that? Yes, I heard.'

'I thought we might go up to Houlton this evening, celebrate with Imogen, Shirley and the Jarvises. I'm free from now. I could come and pick you up from the theatre.'

'Oh. Well, of course that would have been lovely, but I'm afraid I can't.'

'Why not? Your first night is weeks away yet.'

'There are some snags with the script. Paul is going to have to do some rewriting and Gerald wants me to be here to discuss it with them both.'

'But not tonight, surely? It isn't every day we win the war.'

'You go,' Leonie said. 'Somehow I don't feel much like celebrating anyway, not when I think of all the lives that have been lost – all the heartbreak.'

Tony was silent at the other end of the line. He was frankly taken aback. Leonie – concerning herself with other people's broken hearts? It sounded most unlikely. 'Even so, it would be nice if you could make it,' he said.

'Tell them I love them all very much and I'll get up to see them as soon as I possibly can. Have a lovely time, all of you. I'll have to go now. Gerald will be anxious to get on again. Goodbye, darling. Oh, and I suppose I should wish you a Happy Peace or something.'

'Thank you, Leonie. The same to you,' he said dryly.

Leonie replaced the receiver. From where she stood she could just see Paul Winspear as he stood talking to the director, Gerald Bates, on the side of the stage, and her heart gave the lurch that was becoming so familiar to her. The moment they had met for the first time in Peter's office that Friday morning six weeks ago, something amazing had happened. For Leonie it was like a sudden flash of lightning, a charge of electricity passing between them, taking her totally by surprise with its shocking intensity. In the intervening weeks during the preliminary read-through, discussions and early rehearsals, Paul had never once given her the slightest hint that he reciprocated the powerful attraction she felt, but an almost primeval instinct told her without a shadow of a doubt that it was as powerful for him as it was for her. It was just a question of breaking down his iron reserve – the deeply rooted discipline that had made him such a good soldier – to get to the simmering passion that she sensed lay beneath his calm veneer.

Taking a deep breath, she began to walk towards the two men. Seeing her approach, Gerald turned.

'Ah, Leonie. I've just been saying, we'll call it a day now, as it's something of a special occasion. I dare say the crowds are going to thicken as the afternoon wears on, and some of the cast will be wanting to get home before it gets impossible. I've called the next rehearsal for ten thirty tomorrow morning. Is that all right with you?'

'Fine.' As he walked away to tell the rest of the cast, she looked at Paul. 'It'll take you hours to get out to Teddington. Come back to my flat. You can work in peace there.'

Paul looked older than his thirty-five years. He was a tall man with thick dark hair and the gaunt, almost haunted look of a man who has seen war at its worst. His face was craggy, his eyes the dark, lustrous brown of mahogany, but there was a certain vulnerability about his mouth that made Leonie's bones ache with the urge to kiss him.

'I can only work effectively when I'm alone,' he was saying. 'And as I have a lot of work to do on Act II before tomorrow, I think I'd better try to get home.'

'Oh, but I'll be going down to Houlton,' she lied. 'I'll take you to the flat and get you something to eat before I leave, then it's all yours till tomorrow.'

He smiled, the long, slow smile that turned her knees to water. 'Thank you, Leonie. That's very thoughtful. I must admit it would be a marvellous help.'

Even as they made their way down Shaftesbury Avenue and across Piccadilly, people were beginning to gather, laughing and jostling each other good-naturedly. It was obvious that there was little chance of getting a taxi. Everyone seemed to have stopped work for the day, eager to get out on the streets and celebrate. By the time they had walked as far as Mayfair, they were both breathless. As Leonie unlocked the door and let them into the flat, she turned to him with a smile.

'Well, at least we made it without being stampeded in the rush. I'll make some tea. What would you like to eat?'

He shook his head. 'Don't bother about me if you want to get off. It won't be easy getting to the station. I'm quite capable of looking after my own needs if you'll just show me where everything is.'

Leonie knew that Paul's wife had left him soon after he came out of the army, though she didn't know any details about the split. He had been on his own now for some time and she guessed that he didn't bother too much about cooking himself proper meals when he became engrossed in his writing. Never before in her life could she remember feeling the urge to take care of a man – not till now. But there was something about the way Paul's hair curled into the nape of his neck for want of cutting, and the slightly frayed shirt cuffs, that brought out a maternal instinct she had never known she possessed.

'It won't take me any time at all to rustle you up a quick meal,' she said. 'Eggs and bacon with a few chips perhaps? Men usually like that.'

He rewarded her with the slow smile. 'That sounds very nice. But what about your train. You'll never get a taxi and if those crowds get any thicker . . .'

'I'll manage. Don't worry. Now, I'll show you where everything is.' She showed him the bathroom and where he might sleep, then to the room that Tony used as a study, where she suggested he might work. After that she disappeared into the kitchen to don an apron. Twenty minutes later she called him to a neatly laid table.

'I thought you wouldn't mind eating in the kitchen.'

'Not at all. It looks delicious. Aren't you joining me?'

She shook her head. 'No. I'd better go and see if I can get a taxi now. Enjoy your meal – and the peace and quiet. See you tomorrow morning.'

At a small restaurant on the corner of Maddox Street Leonie ordered chicken salad and a glass of white wine. She followed it with a pot of coffee, over which she lingered for the next half-hour, smoking and listening to the increasing volume of the singing and babble outside in the street. It was eight o'clock when she paid her bill and left.

Outside, Regent Street was now completely filled with people, dancing, singing, letting off fireworks and generally enjoying themselves. Struggling against the tide, which seemed to be making its way down to Piccadilly, she pushed her way back to the flat and made her way up in the lift. Letting herself in quietly, she heard the sound of the typewriter tapping in the study and smiled to herself. In the bedroom she changed into a black skirt and a clinging cream silk blouse and went back into the kitchen to make coffee.

Gloria arrived at Houlton at half-past five. Getting off the bus outside the post office, she set off on the walk up to Longueville Hall, but she hadn't gone more than half a mile when she heard the hooting of a car horn behind her and turned to see Tony pulling up in the smart blue Humber Snipe he had recently acquired. Reaching across, he released the passenger door for her.

'Gloria! Good to see you. Jump in.'

She settled herself gratefully in the deep leather seat beside him. 'Thanks a lot. I wasn't looking forward to the walk.'

'Wonderful news, eh?' He turned to smile at her. 'We had the same thought – to spend this memorable day with our daughters?'

She nodded. 'Yes, though somehow I can't get very excited at the moment. Perhaps it hasn't sunk in yet.'

'Funny, Leonie said much the same thing. I rang her as soon as the news came through. I thought she might join me here to celebrate with Imogen, but she's too tied up with rehearsals to come.'

'That's a pity.'

'Never mind. At least you're here. What do you say we take both girls into town this evening to mingle with the crowds and see the lights go on?'

'If you like. I dare say it's what they'd like.' She wondered if perhaps she might catch the mood herself if she went into town and mingled with the crowd; whether it might help her snap out of the gloom that seemed to have descended on her. So preoccupied had she been that she had even forgotten to bring the new blouse she'd made for Shirley.

'It's a historic occasion, after all,' Tony was saying. 'Something to tell their grandchildren about.' He looked at her. 'You don't have to get back tonight, do you?'

'I'm afraid so, though I did ask Jane, my friend, to cover for me if the buses stopped running and I didn't make it. It's probably anybody's guess what will happen tonight.'

'That's all right. No need to worry. I can run you back.'

'Thank you, Tony.'

He glanced at her pale, drawn face. 'I suppose this means that the time of decision has arrived for you,' he said quietly.

'Not really,' she told him wearily. 'I've already decided, that's the trouble.'

But although he waited she did not offer to tell him more and he did not press her.

That evening Tony, Gloria and both girls packed into the car and drove into town to join in the festivities. Molly and Jim were invited too, but they preferred to stay at home and listen to the celebrations in comfort on the wireless. At ten o'clock they drove back to Houlton and, after the girls had been packed off to bed and they had drunk the cocoa Molly insisted on making them, Tony and Gloria set off for Boothley. As they drove, Gloria was silent.

'You're very quiet, Gloria. Is anything wrong?' Tony asked.

'Nothing that time won't put right,' She turned to him. 'Tony, would you do something for me?'

'Of course, anything.'

'It's just – I made a blouse for Shirley and forgot to bring it with me this morning. If I go and get it, will you take it back for her?'

'Of course.'

As they drew up ouutside the hostel she looked at him hesitantly. 'I'd ask you to come in, but . . .'

He laughed. 'It's all right. I'll wait here.'

'You're wise to.' She smiled wryly. 'You'd probably get mobbed. Some of those girls – especially this evening if they've been celebrating.' She jumped out of the car and went into the building. Hurrying along the corridor to her room, she pushed the door open. Jane was standing by the window. She swung round, startled, as Gloria came in.

'Gloria. I wasn't expecting you back tonight . . .' Her voice trailed off, she looked flustered and her eyes seemed unable to meet Gloria's. 'As a matter of fact I was just thinking about ringing you at Houlton. I . . . didn't quite know what to do.'

'Why? What's happened?'

Jane picked up a folded sheet of paper from the dressing table. 'This came this morning. I didn't get it till we came back from the shift. You'd left by then. It's from Chuck . . .' She paused, seeing from Gloria's face that she'd already guessed that the letter held bad news. 'I think you'd better sit down, love.'

Gloria shook her head. 'Just tell me. Get on with it.'

Jane swallowed. 'It's Billy, Gloria. I'm so sorry, love, but he was badly wounded at the Rhine crossing. He died of his wounds a few days later.'

Gloria sat down suddenly on the chair by her bed. The colour had drained from her face, leaving it deathly pale. 'The Rhine crossing? But that was weeks – *months* ago.'

'I know. Chuck's letter's dated April the tenth. All the mail has been delayed. He knew that you and Billy were sort of engaged but that there was nothing formal so you wouldn't be informed through the usual channels. He . . . felt you should be told.' Jane took a tentative step towards her friend. She was disturbed by the way she had taken the news. Apart from her deathly pallor, it was almost as though she hadn't taken it in. 'Gloria, are you all right, love? Is there anything I can do?'

Gloria shook herself as though trying to rouse herself from a deep sleep. 'No. No, I'm all right.' Getting up, she opened the dressing-table drawer and took out the blouse she had made for Shirley. Very slowly and meticulously she wrapped it in a sheet of tissue paper, then turned to her friend. 'I'm going back to Houlton,' she said calmly. 'I only came back for Shirley's blouse. I'll see you tomorrow, Jane. Good night.'

Jane stared at her, open-mouthed. 'Going back? But how will you get there?'

'Tony – Mr Darrent is waiting for me in the car. If I'm not back tomorrow, tell them . . . something – anything you like. Will you?'

'Of course I will, but . . .' Jane watched helplessly as Gloria hurried out of the room.

Climbing back into the car, Gloria said: 'If you don't mind, Tony, I'd like you to drop me at Rook Cottage. It's on the edge of the village. It's not out of your way. I've decided to stay the night there.'

She pushed the parcel containing the blouse into the glove compartment. 'Give that to Shirl, will you? Tell her I hope she likes it.'

As he drove, Tony could feel the tension emanating from her. He knew that something had happened to upset her, but she didn't volunteer to tell him what was wrong and he didn't know how to ask her. As he drew up outside the little thatched cottage he said: 'I've never seen this cottage of yours. You wouldn't care to invite me in for a nightcap, would you?'

She paused. 'You can come in if you like,' she said. 'But there's nothing much to see and I haven't got anything to offer you in the way of drink.'

'That doesn't matter.' Tony was already getting out of the car. He waited, standing in the porch, while she unlocked the door, then followed her into the little parlour. Taking out a match, she lit the oil lamp and drew the curtains. It was when she turned her face towards him and he saw her expression that his fears were confirmed. He took a step towards her. 'Gloria – something's wrong, isn't it?'

She stiffened and crossed her arms over her breast, hugging herself defensively. 'Billy's dead,' she said flatly. 'Isn't it stupid? I was worried sick about telling him I couldn't marry him and all the time I needn't have been, because . . . because he was dead.'

'When did it happen?'

'It was at the Rhine crossing – weeks ago. All this time I've been eating my heart out for – for *nothing*.' Her shoulders began to shake. Her face crumpled and she seemed almost to disintegrate before his eyes. Tears welled up in her eyes and streamed down her cheeks.

Profoundly moved, Tony stepped forward and put his arms round her rigid body.

'Oh, Gloria. Oh, my dear, I'm sorry – so sorry.' He held her while she sobbed, great racking sobs that sounded as though they would tear her slender body apart. They tore at him too. He felt helpless, able to do nothing but hold her and mutter the useless phrases that had become vacuous from overuse during the past six tear-drenched years.

At last he felt some of the tension go out of her as she sagged against him. He held her away from him, fumbling in his pocket for his own handkerchief and dabbing at her cheeks. 'Let me get you something – a cup of tea. I don't suppose you've got any brandy?'

'No.' She shook her head. 'I – don't want – anything.'

'Let me help you upstairs them. You should try to get some rest. I'll go to the pub and see what I can get.'

He helped her, protesting, up the narrow stairs and into the front bedroom with its big brass bed. She lay down, but when her head touched the pillow she caught the faint scent of the hair cream Billy had used and began to tremble uncontrollably.

'Don't – go,' she stammered between clenched teeth. 'I – don't want to be alone – please.'

He sat down on the bed and took her hand.

'All these past weeks – all I could think of was how to send him away,' she said. 'And all the time he was lying there badly wounded – needing someone he loved to help him. And now he's dead and it's too late. He was so young, Tony. Too young for me. But he gave me more love than I've ever had in my whole life. And all I could think of was how to tell him something I knew would hurt him. How can I live with that? How can I ever forgive myself?'

'But you *didn't* hurt him,' Tony said, stroking her hair. 'It didn't happen. He loved you and I'm sure you gave him so much back.' He looked around the room. 'Did you bring him here?'

She nodded. 'We were so happy here. I can still feel him here, Tony. Still see him. I can even *smell* him.'

'I know. I know.'

She looked up at him, remembering. 'Yes. You *do* know, don't you? I'd almost forgotten. Tony, do you still think of her – Claire? Does it still hurt? Does it ever get better?'

He squeezed her hand. 'Yes. It does get better, I promise you. After a while the hurt begins to soften at the edges. It stops cutting you and only probes gently at the memories. You'll want to keep those memories, won't you?'

'Oh, yes.'

'We can't – wouldn't ever want to forget, not really forget. The trick is to let time wash the memories clean of sadness.' He smiled at her. 'Will you be all right now while I go to the pub to get you something to help you to sleep?'

She held on tightly to his hand. 'Don't leave me – not yet.'

She was still shivering and he pulled the eiderdown up round her; then, after a moment's hesitation, lay down beside her and held her close. 'Do you remember the time you did this for me?' he whispered. 'You were so wonderful to me that night. You'll never know what you did for me. Do you know, if it hadn't been for you I think I might have been tempted to end it.'

'*Don't.*' She shook her head at him. 'Don't talk of dying, Tony. I don't want to think of death any more.' She shuddered and reached out for him. 'Tony . . .'

'Yes, darling?'

'Will you stay with me till morning, please?'

'Of course I will.' He held her close, her tears wetting his face, trying to warm and strengthen her with his own body; held her till he felt the tension slowly ebb out of her; till her breathing deepened and he knew that she slept, emotionally exhausted. It was then that the memory of Claire came back to him as vividly as the day he last saw her; the day they said goodbye. Closing his eyes he saw again her fair hair, lifted by the sea breeze; her beautiful expressive eyes, full of love and sadness; her arm lifted in farewell. And from under his closed eyelids the hot tears crept to scald his cheeks and mingle with Gloria's as the sky outside began to lighten.

'When Gerald first told me that Leonie Swann was to play the part of Janet Freer in my play, I must admit that I had reservations.' Paul sat in the drawing room sipping the coffee Leonie had made.

She smiled at him. 'Is that a polite way of telling me you were appalled?'

'I wouldn't put it as strongly as that.' He smiled. 'A little fearful, shall we say? I couldn't see a woman who was a popular singer and musical-comedy star playing a serious dramatic role like Janet Freer.'

'I see. So what is your verdict now that we've started rehearsals?'

'I wouldn't be telling you any of this if I wasn't one hundred percent delighted with the way you're inter-preting the role,' he told her. 'In fact I wouldn't even be here in your flat.'

'I think what you're saying is that you'd have moved heaven and earth to have had me kicked out if I hadn't come up to scratch.'

'I'm afraid I might have.'

'You might just have had a problem there.' Leonie lit a cigarette, taking her time and blowing the smoke out languidly. 'After all, as you've just said, I am a star – and you are . . .'

'An unknown? A raw newcomer?' He smiled. 'That is something I intend to remedy as soon as I can,' he told her. 'Which is why I would never have tolerated an actress who was wrong for the part. I'd rather have sacrificed the play.'

Leonie put on a mock-horrified expression. 'Good heavens! We must all thank our lucky stars that I wasn't too dreadful then, mustn't we?'

He looked at her thoughtfully over the rim of his cup, deciding to ignore the sarcasm in her voice. 'I'm so sorry you didn't manage to get your train, but it's been a bonus to have had this opportunity to talk,' he said. 'I expect you'd like me to leave now.'

'Not at all. If you've finished the reworking of Act II why don't you try it out on me? Or are you completely satisfied with what you've done?'

He smiled wryly. 'Oh, dear. Did I sound as overconfident as that?'

'Not in the least. We all need to be sure of what we're doing. I admire a man who can recognise his own talent and knows his own worth. And I happen to think you're a very talented writer, Paul.'

A smile lifted the corners of his mouth. 'In that case I shall fetch the script and read it to you.'

They read the reworked act together and Leonie agreed that the adjustments he had made were just what was needed to strengthen the dialogue.

'It makes the relationship between Janet and her husband, Ivor, much more poignant. They are two people who have outgrown one another,' she said. 'Who in normal circumstances would have parted, but Ivor's war injuries – his blindness holds them together. Somehow they each have to come to terms with the fact that he is now totally dependent on her and she is obliged to overcome her inherent selfishness.'

'That's right.' Paul leaned forward, his eyes alight. 'And it's only when their roles have reversed and she realises that *she* is the dependent one that their relationship becomes whole again.'

'It's a wonderful play, Paul.' She paused. 'Forgive me for asking, but was it written from your own experiences?'

'I suppose it was – in a way. But we all have to draw on our own experience to a certain extent, don't we?' He looked at her with his direct dark gaze. 'And you? You

278

play the part with such perception that I confess I've wondered . . .'

'The same thing?' She laughed. 'My marriage to Tony and our reasons for staying together are very complex. Other couples marry for love. You could say that we married for a property. My talent. That was what Tony saw and wanted when we met. He developed it, nurtured it and benefited from it in many ways. But now he despises it because he believes that it deprived him of his own career.'

Paul frowned. 'That sounds very cynical. There must have been love too, surely?'

Leonie drew hard on her cigarette, then stubbed it out firmly. 'No. We were both dazzled. And when you're young that is often enough. Success is a great aphrodisiac.'

He smiled gently. 'You talk as though you're old. You can't be more than – what – thirty?'

Leonie smiled enigmatically. If that was what he thought, then let him. 'I'm only just beginning to realise that I've never known real love,' she said softly. 'I've never missed it – till now.'

There was a pause, then he stood up. 'I must go.' He looked at his watch. 'I wonder if the trains are running normally.'

'I doubt it.' Leonie stood to face him, her eyes holding his.

'Teddington is a very long way to walk. Why don't you stay here?'

He took a step closer. 'I think you know why, Leonie.'

Her heart was hammering so hard in her breast that it was difficult to breathe. She said: 'Stay, Paul. Why not? It's what you want, isn't it? It's what we've both wanted since that first day in Peter's office.' She stepped closer and lifted her hand to trail her fingers down his cheek. 'I'm right, aren't I?'

He stood perfectly still. 'Of course you're right. But I don't make love to other men's wives in their own homes.'

'Home?' She let her head drop back and chuckled softly. 'This hasn't been Tony's home for a very long time.

When he isn't away on location or with one of his women, he stays at a hotel.'

'He's unfaithful to you?'

'To me – *and* to all the others. Amoral would be a better word for what Tony is.'

With one long, sensitive hand he cupped her chin. 'Are you very unhappy, my darling?'

'No. It isn't a case of getting my own back, Paul. It's not a game I'm playing. Until now I've never felt there was anything missing from my life. I've been content to put all my emotional energy into my work. I've never wanted another man; never felt – what I'm feeling now – for anyone.' She lifted her arms and let them creep around his neck, her fingers lacing into his hair, raising her face to his.

For a brief moment he looked deep into her eyes, then his arms closed round her, crushing her close, and his mouth was on hers, kissing her hungrily. Leonie was shaken by the sudden violence of his kiss and the desperation of his hands on her body. She felt her own smouldering desire burst into flame, raging through her like a forest fire. Murmuring helplessly, her lips never leaving his, she pulled off his jacket and began to unbutton his shirt, thrilling to the sensation of his hands on her skin as he slipped the blouse from her shoulders and unhooked the lacy bra beneath.

His lovemaking possessed her totally. For the first time in her life she was not in control – nor had she any desire to be. He overpowered her gloriously both in mind and body; stripping her of all pretensions, charging her emotions, stirring every nerve and sensation till she cried out with the force of a climax that was exquisitely painful and brilliant and terrible. Then, ignoring her pleas for him to stop, he went on and made it happen all over again.

Gloria wakened with the singing of the first birds. At once the realisation of Billy's death hit her like a hammer blow. She turned her head and saw that Tony still slept. She raised herself on one elbow to look at him. He had stayed.

280

He could easily have crept away once she was asleep, but he'd stayed. Gratitude filled her heart, making the tears prick at her eyes. She touched his cheek, finding it rough with morning stubble, and her heart twisted to see that he no longer appeared as he had when she had first seen him in those early films. He was beginning to look his age, though for her the streaks of grey in his hair and the tiny lines at eyes and mouth only made him even more attractive. Had he been very unhappy all these years with Leonie? she wondered. How many women had there been since Claire died? A good many, she guessed. But none who had captured his heart as Claire once had. As she watched, he opened one eye, then both, gazing up at her bemusedly, temporarily disoriented by his surroundings. He blinked and roused himself.

'Gloria. What time is it?'

'Half-past five.'

'How are you feeling?'

'I'm all right. I'll be fine.'

He sat up and ran a hand over his jaw. 'My God! How do I go anywhere looking like this?'

'Don't worry. I've got a razor and things. I kept them here for Billy. He had an electric shaver, you see, and there's no electricity here. I'll go down and get some water.' She made to get out of bed but he took her arm.

'Not yet. Plenty of time.' He smiled at her. She looked frail and innocent, almost waiflike with her hair tumbled and skin devoid of make-up.

'I'll never be able to thank you enough, Tony,' she said.

'For what?'

'For last night.'

He shook his head. 'I'm so glad I was there.' He drew her down into the crook of his arm and she lay for a moment with her head on his shoulder. She turned her face up towards him and it seemed the most natural thing in the world to kiss her. A brushing of lips deepened into a full-blown kiss, both of them aroused by the emotion of the previous night's happenings and the need that each of them felt. Tony looked into her eyes.

'This is the second time we've slept together all night with all our clothes on,' he said. 'Who would ever believe it?' He slipped one hand into the neckline of her crumpled dress to stroke the warm, soft skin of her shoulder. 'Once, a long time ago, you made me the sweetest, most generous offer,' he whispered. 'And I've regretted ever since that I didn't accept.'

'Why didn't you?' she whispered.

'Because I knew it would have meant so much to you. It would have been taking an unfair advantage,' he said. 'Perhaps that sounds conceited and pretentious, but it's true.'

'Because you knew I'd have given myself to you sincerely – while to you it would have meant nothing. Is that what you mean?'

He winced. 'You make it sound so cold and heartless. Believe me, Gloria, it wasn't. It was because I like and respected you too much that I resisted.' He smiled wryly. 'It's not something I'm noted for, I'm sorry to say.'

She was quiet, occupied with her own thoughts. If he had made love to her that night, things might have been so different. Who could tell where it might have got them by now?'

He smiled. 'If you were to make the same offer now I'd be afraid you were only offering out of gratitude.'

'And you'd be wrong. I think I've grown up a bit since then,' she said thoughtfully. 'And I dare say a great many people have turned to each other during the war years out of sheer need of warmth and comfort.' She raised her eyes to his and he saw the raw, irresistible need in them.

'We've always had a special relationship, you and I, haven't we, Gloria?' he said as he drew her closer. 'A deep understanding that very few men and women share.' His lips took hers gently at first, but her eager response aroused him quickly to passion.

Their lovemaking was brief and fiery and sweet and when it was over Gloria felt at peace. Lying quietly in his arms, she wondered what he would say if she were to tell him that her love for him was the reason she hadn't been able to marry Billy. She guessed that he would be appalled, even embarrassed, so she kept quiet. Instead she looked up at him and smiled, stroking his cheek.

'You'd better get up now and have that shave. The Jarvises will be wondering where you've got to.'

'Will you be all right, darling?'

'I'll be fine.'

He kissed her forehead. 'When will I see you again?'

She shook her head. 'Who can say? We both know this was just the once, Tony. It was like I said, for warmth and comfort. Don't let's pretend it was anything else. We'll see each other from time to time, I expect. But you belong to a different world from me. We'd never have met if it hadn't been for the war and now that it's over we'll be going our separate ways.'

'I don't want us to lose touch,' he said.

'But we *will*, dear.' She kissed him softly. 'Don't spoil it. Don't make promises you'll regret. Get up now, Tony. I'll get you some water for shaving. It's time to go, time to say goodbye.'

He began to protest, then looked into her eyes and stopped. He knew that she meant it. And he knew that, sadly, she was probably right.

It was two weeks later that the letter came. Gloria was working out the last week of her notice at the factory and she came off the early shift to find the blue air letter waiting for her in the rack. Puzzled, she turned it over. She couldn't think of anyone who would be writing to her from overseas. The address of the sender was printed in capitals on the back; Mr and Mrs H. Landis, Bluebird Garage, Boulder, Colorado, USA. Billy's parents? With mounting curiosity Gloria tore the air letter open, unfolded it and began to read.

My dear Gloria,

We have never met but my family and I feel we know you from all we have heard of you through Billy's letters. You will know by now that we lost our dear boy

283

just a short time before the end of the war. As you can imagine we have all been totally devastated by his loss. Billy was always such a joy to his father and me, right from the day he was born. We know, dear, that you meant a very great deal to him and he would have wanted us to get in touch with you. We would dearly love to meet you and if you will allow it, we will send the fare for you to come over and visit with us – just as soon as you can. Do *please* try to come, my dear. It would mean so much to be able to talk with the dear girl who shared Billy's last days and who obviously made him very happy. Let me know if you will accept our heartfelt invitation and we will cable the fare to you right away.

For now, God bless. Our love to you,
Louise and Hal Landis.

Gloria read the letter through twice more before the contents completely registered. Billy's parents wanted her to go to America to stay with them, to talk about the relationship she had shared with their son. How could she do that when she had been planning to let him down? It was out of the question. She pushed the letter into her pocket and walked around with it for the whole of the next day, refusing even to think about how she would reply.

It wasn't long before Jane sensed that Gloria had something on her mind. They were having their evening meal together the following day when Jane said suddenly:

'What's worrying you, Gloria? You've been miles away ever since yesterday. I keep speaking to you and you don't even hear me. Is it anything to do with that air letter you had yesterday?'

Without a word Gloria took the crumpled letter out of her pocket and passed it across the table to her friend. Jane read it slowly and carefully.

'You'll go, of course,' she said when she had finished.

Gloria shook her head. 'How could I let them send me all that money when I wasn't gong to marry Billy? If he'd lived I'd have sent him home unhappy. I'm not what they think, Jane. I don't think I could face them.'

284

'You made Billy happy and, as his mother says here in the letter, you were the one he spent his last days with. I think you should go for their sakes, Gloria. You need never tell them about your decision, need you?'

'But what will they think when they see I'm so much older?'

Jane laughed. 'Anyone'd think you were ninety instead of thirty-two. You've always looked younger than you are, Gloria. You don't *look* that much older than Billy. Anyway, I don't think age has anything to do with it.'

But Gloria was still unconvinced. 'I'd be a terrible disappointment to them.'

'Why do you always put yourself down so?' Jane grasped her arm. 'You could never be a disappointment to anyone, Gloria. You're a kind, sensitive, compassionate person. Look at it this way, since Billy was killed you've been feeling bad, thinking you let him down by not wanting to marry him. Well, this is one way you can make up for that. Go and see his folks. Share your memories with them. Tell them what a smashing boy he was and how much you thought of him. You'll feel better for it and so will they. Do it, Gloria. You'll always regret it if you don't.'

'You really think Billy would have wanted me to go?'

'I know damned well he would. And so do you.'

Gloria flew out of Northolt Airport bound for the USA on the day that Shirley and Imogen sat their School Certificate examination. Two weeks later Pa Rayner collapsed at the supper table and was taken to hospital suffering from a severe stroke. Soon after that, Gloria began to suspect that she was pregnant. Little did any of them realise just how much the events that followed in the days and weeks to come would alter the course of all their lives. Nothing was ever to be quite the same again.

Chapter Thirteen

Shirley dragged another sack of potatoes through from the store room to the shop. It was half-past three on the afternoon of Christmas Eve and quiet after the rush, but there still might be a last-minute panic, so best be prepared.

Christmas this year would be a miserable affair. Since Shirley had been back at the shop in Angel Row, Ma had been too busy nursing Pa to bother with much else and Shirley had been working far too hard in the shop to think about making many preparations for the festive season.

Since Pa's return from hospital, the daily routine had had to be altered drastically to allow for the constant care he needed. The shop was now the responsibility of Shirley, helped by Dave Green, a young man with a gammy leg who had been badly wounded in the North African campaign. Dave was glad of the work. He'd been on the dole since his discharge from the Army. Every morning at the crack of dawn he took the horse and cart to Covent Garden to do the buying and on his return saw to all the heavy work. The shop itself was left to Shirley.

Standing behind the counter in the lull between customers, she looked down at her hands. They were chapped and sore, rough and ingrained with the soil from the potatoes and root vegetables. The fingernails she had taken such a pride in were broken and rimmed with dirt. But her fingernails were the least of her worries. The chief cause for her concern and resentment was her mother. When Pa was taken ill, Gloria had been notified by cable.

But Ma had followed it up immediately by an air-mail letter, telling her not to come home precipitately. Pa was in good hands in hospital and there was nothing she could do. After the Landis family had sent all that money, it was only right that she should stay out her time with them, she wrote. She would get Shirley home to help her. So, on the day that Shirley and Imogen left school for the last time, Shirley had packed all her things and come home to Whitechapel.

She hadn't minded at first. It was an emergency after all, and it was only meant to have been temporary. Gloria should be back from America in plenty of time for Shirley to take the entrance exam and go to RADA in the autumn as planned. But Gloria hadn't come home. She had written once or twice from Colorado, saying that she was having a good time and that Billy's family had made her very welcome. But after her leaving Colorado there had been a long lapse in correspondence. Eventually she wrote to say that she had met some English people in the USA who had offered her a temporary job as a house-keeper in Yorkshire, which she had accepted. She would only be away for about a year and she was sure that Ma and Shirley would understand.

Ma had certainly not understood. She was vociferous in her anger and resentment.

'Why 'ave folks turned so selfish since the war ended?' she demanded. 'First it was the election – they ditched Mr Churchill after all 'e done for us. Now it's people. There's no *carin'* no more. It's a case of I'm all right, Jack, bugger you. Even me own flesh an' blood.' She went about her work tight-lipped with disapproval of Gloria's behaviour. Although she didn't really mean to, she took out her pent-up anger on Shirley simply because the girl was there. Inside she felt hurt and let down by the daughter she had loved and stood by. Gloria had known for some time that her father was desperately ill, yet she had never tried to come home and see him, even after her return to England. It was true that Pa was now out of danger and at home, but his stroke had robbed him of his speech and his left side was completely paralysed. It would have meant a lot to him to see his only daughter. Although she would not admit it, Ma felt suddenly old and lonely and afraid.

Shirley couldn't believe it was happening. It was like a bad dream. Gloria had always had such high hopes for her. She had worked so hard and sacrificed so much when Shirley was little to send her to dancing classes and make sure she always had nice things to wear. And she'd been so proud when Shirley had won a scholarship to the high school. She had never stopped saying how determined she was that Shirley would have a better start in life than she'd had, and Shirley had always believed her. Yet Gloria had gone off to this new job without a thought for the sorrow and hardship, the heartbreak of Shirley's missed opportunity. It was unbelievable.

To make matters worse, Shirley heard, just two days before the atom bomb was dropped on Hiroshima and Japan surrendered, that she had passed her School Certificate with credits in five subjects. She had pushed the letter into her pocket without even bothering to tell Ma, who had no use for such things anyway, especially not at this time. A fat lot of good it was going to be to her now, she told herself bitterly.

In September Imogen had written to say she had passed her entrance exam for RADA and would be starting there shortly. Shirley was consumed with envy and bitterness at the thought of her friend doing all the things they had planned to do together. It was so unfair. She had sat down that very night and written to Gloria, pleading her disappointment and begging her to come home. In her letter she described how hard life was at the shop, how much she missed Imogen and the Jarvises and of course Gloria herself, begging her to try to come home at least for Christmas. But all she had received in return was a brief letter from Gloria saying that she was truly sorry that Shirley had to be disappointed but that it could not be helped. She would make it up to her as soon as she possibly could. She ended the letter with a vague promise to come home soon, but saying that she would be needed there for Christmas. What could make these people she was working for more important to her than the family that needed her so desperately? Shirley asked herself again and again. How could she be so uncaring and selfish? Shirley wondered whether perhaps her mother had met another man. But if that were the case, why didn't she say so?

Imogen came to see her unexpectedly one busy afternoon in late November. She looked radiantly happy, attractively dressed in the latest fashion, a Jaeger dirndl skirt in striking red-and-black-checked wool with a smartly cut black jacket to match. Shirley, who was wearing an old cardigan and soil-caked mittens to keep her hands from freezing, greeted her with a scowl.

'Come to gloat, have you?' She glanced through the window to where a little sports car stood at the kerb, surrounded by children, all gazing curiously at its gleaming red bodywork. 'Who's that you've got with you?'

'It's Charles Morgan,' Imogen said. 'His father's Sir James Morgan, the High Court judge. Charles is almost eighteen. He's in his second year at RADA but he'll be leaving soon to do his National Service. He's really nice, Shirley. Do come and say hello to him.'

'Like this?' Shirley held out her dirty hands. 'I suppose it's Lord Snooty's idea of a bit of a lark, is it – *slumming*? Can't you see I'm up to my neck in it? Another time do you think you could let me know when you're thinking of dropping in for tea and cakes?'

Imogen was clearly stung by Shirley's tirade. When she had left, apologising and going away with a sad, hurt look in her eyes, Shirley had felt close to tears. Why had she been so beastly to her best friend? It wasn't Imogen's fault that she was in this impossibly awful situation. It was all Gloria's fault. After Shirley had closed the shop, she had gone up to her room and written a letter to Imogen, apologising for her churlish behaviour and trying to explain the reasons for it. A few days later she received a reply. Imogen said she would come round to see her the following Saturday evening when perhaps they could talk.

When she arrived Shirley took her upstairs to the room she and Gloria had once shared.

'I'm sorry it's not very nice,' she said apologetically as she closed the door. 'I'll switch on the electric fire. It'll soon warm up.'

Imogen took both her hands. 'Shirl, what's the matter? You look so tired.' She looked down at the roughened little hands. 'Where is Gloria?' she asked. 'Why is she leaving you to do all this alone? Is she staying on in America for good?'

'No. She's got herself a housekeeping job up in Yorkshire,' Shirley told her. 'It must be a bloody good job; she isn't even coming home for Christmas.'

Imogen frowned. 'That's not like Gloria. Are you sure there's nothing wrong?'

Shirley shrugged. 'What could be wrong? Maybe going to America has made her feel fed up with us all. She sounds happy enough with her new job when she writes. It's just as if she's finished with all of us – doesn't give a damn.' Shirley swallowed hard. 'It doesn't look as if I'll ever get to RADA now.'

'Look, why shouldn't you study in your spare time? I could find out the names of some drama teachers for you if you like, so you wouldn't be too far behind when you do start.'

Shirley gave her a rueful smile. 'You've got no idea, have you? Look, I'm up at six to help Ma and get the shop ready for opening. After we close at six in the evening there's the copper to light for all the washing. Pa's what they call incontinent, which means he wets the bed. He needs several pairs of clean sheets and pyjamas every day. There's the ironing and the housework, not to mention the cooking and washing-up. Ma does as much as she can but she needs to spend so much time with Pa. She can do with all the help I can give her. On top of that there's all the cashing-up and going to the bank – the books, the shopping. There's no such thing as spare time here, Imo.'

'I'm sorry. Oh, poor love!' Imogen glanced at her friend. 'I was going to ask if you could come home with me for Christmas, but I can see there's no chance of that. Maybe things will look up in the New Year. Why don't you apply for the entrance exam so that you can take it and start as soon as Gloria comes back?'

'I'll see,' Shirley said wearily. It was only too clear that Imogen still didn't fully understand her situation. 'I'll have to see what happens, Imo. It wouldn't surprise me if she never came back.'

'I'm sure she will. And soon too.' Imogen looked at her. 'You won't lose touch with me, will you? I'd hate that.' She took Shirley's hands again. 'Oh, Shirley, I can't tell you how much I miss you. RADA's wonderful but it isn't the same without you. We were going to have such a good time there together.'

'I know. I miss you too.' Tears sprang to Shirley's eyes. 'I miss you and Nanny and Jim and the house and school. I miss Houlton and the fresh air and the fields. Oh, Imo, I *hate* it here! It's smelly and dirty. There's no bathroom or indoor lav and the place is falling to bits from all the bomb damage that's never been fixed properly. It's cold and damp. There's no one to talk to or laugh with. Pa's illness is so awful, Imo. He can't eat properly and he can't talk. He just makes noises and he dribbles. I try to love him like before, but it's so hard. It's as though he's gone away and there's this – this *thing* in his place.' She looked at Imogen with brimming eyes. 'I expect you think I'm awful, saying a thing like that about my own granddad.' She turned away, gasping and fumbling in her pocket for a handkerchief. 'I – I thought when the war was over it was going to be so wonderful, but it's not. It feels like hell here sometimes, Imo. Just like *hell*.'

Imogen put her arms around her friend and they wept together. Imogen out of love and pity for her friend; Shirley out of weariness and disillusionment and sheer agonising frustration.

'I'm sure your grandmother appreciates all you've given up for her,' Imogen said quietly. 'I'm sure she's grateful.'

Shirley rubbed her knuckles angrily across her tear-stained cheeks. 'No, she isn't. She just thinks it's my duty,' she said. 'She never did hold with my going on the stage anyway. She didn't even want me to stay on at school. Well, she's got her way now, hasn't she?'

'I'm sure she doesn't think of it like that. She must have been proud of how well you did in the School Cert. You got more credits than I did.'

'She doesn't know about it.' Shirley sniffed hard. 'I didn't bother to tell her. What's the point?'

Christmas Day came and went. Ma spent most of it sitting upstairs with Pa while Shirley sat on her own listening to the wireless in the kitchen behind the shop and trying not to think of the happy time they would all be having at Longueville Hall.

On the afternoon of Boxing Day there was a knock on the back door and she opened it to find Dave Green standing there. He wore a shiny blue serge suit, his unruly brown hair was plastered down with Brylcreem and his worn shoes gleamed with polishing. He drew a brown-paper parcel from behind his back and grinned shyly.

'I thought you might like this, Shirl,' he said. 'And I wondered if you'd like to come out for a walk.'

Inviting him into the kitchen, Shirley unwrapped the parcel to find a box of chocolates inside. She was surprised and touched at the thoughtful gesture. A box this size must have taken up all his sweet coupons for a whole month.

'Thank you, Dave,' she said, giving him her best smile. 'I'm sorry – I haven't got you anything.'

He shrugged. 'That's all right, I didn't expect it.' He looked at the floor and shuffled his feet bashfully. 'Well, er, would you like to come out, then?'

They walked the deserted streets in the thin winter sunshine, gazing into shop windows and making careful, polite small talk. Shirley discovered that Dave was twenty-two and that his family had all been killed in the Blitz. Since his discharge from the Army he had lived alone in a bed-sitting room two streets away, eking out a meagre living on the small wage that Ma paid him.

'What did you do before the war?' Shirley asked him.

'I was apprenticed to a painter and decorator,' he told her. 'No chance of going back to that with this leg of mine. Can't climb up and down ladders no more.'

Shirley was silent. Maybe she'd been selfish, thinking about the chance she had missed. There were other young people far worse off than she, and poor Pa couldn't help being ill. Next year she might get another chance, but for Dave and thousands of others there would be no second chance.

'You're quiet,' Dave said. 'A penny for them.'

She turned to him with a smile. 'I was just wondering if you'd like to come back to our place for tea,' she said. 'The Christmas cake is only a bought one this year, but it's quite nice, and there's home-made trifle. I made it myself. Will you come?'

Dave's grey eyes lit up delightedly and she suddenly saw that he was quite nice-looking. 'Thanks very much, Shirl. I'd love to,' he said.

Shirley's life grew no easier with the New Year. Pa was no better and Ma continued to spend most of her time caring for him. The work seemed even harder and that winter was especially cold and bleak. The icy draughts found every crack in the little house in Angel Row and it didn't matter how much coal she heaped on the fire or how much oil she burned in the paraffin heater – the temperature never seemed to rise more than a couple of degrees. All through January she got up each morning to find the pipes frozen, and standing in the shop serving vegetables and fruit made her hands and feet numb and painful with chilblains.

But the one bright spot in every day was the sight of Dave's smiling face. He always managed to cheer her up, however bad things looked. He was always around to help in any way he could, far above and beyond the duties he was paid for. And he was always ready with a laugh and a joke in spite of the pain Shirley knew his crippled leg caused him when there was frost.

Saturday night became their regular night for going to the pictures and Shirley began to find herself looking forward to it all week. Dave always arrived on time, dressed in his best suit, his face freshly shaved and his shoes polished. He always saved up his sweet coupons so that he could buy her some sweets, liquorice allsorts or sherbet lemons, which he knew were her favourites. They sat in the two-and-nines and both enjoyed exciting thrillers with Humphrey Bogart or romantic dramas with Ingrid Bergman or Margaret Lockwood. Sometimes they chose a musical and Shirley would sing the songs to herself later in her room as she got ready for bed. Her throat would tighten with nostalgia as she remembered the shows that she and Imogen had taken part in during the war and the career she had looked forward to so confidently.

Shirley had wondered at first if Ma would object to her friendship with Dave. After all, she still had four months to go before her sixteenth birthday and Dave was a good six years older. But surprisingly Ma had raised no objection. She liked and trusted Dave and, although she would never have admitted it, she felt a little guilty about the way Shirley had to work. With Pa as he was, this was no place for such a young girl. It wasn't really fair to expect so much of her. But with Gloria away she'd had no option but to enlist Shirley's help and to take her away from the life she knew she had planned. It was bad enough without making the child resent her position too much. Without Shirley's youth and strength she and Pa would be in a mess and she recognised the fact only too well. What she thought of her daughter, she kept strictly to herself, but whenever Gloria's name was mentioned her lips tightened and her back stiffened. After the shame she had brought on them when Shirley was born; after they way they'd stood by her and all they'd done for her since – to go off like that when her father was ill and she was so badly needed. Ma would never forgive her; never as long as she lived.

Shirley and Dave had been going out regularly for two months before he attempted to kiss her. At first he took her hand in the darkness of the two-and-nines. Then his arm ventured along the back of her seat to drop gently around her shoulders. The week after that, as they said goodnight outside the back door of 10 Angel Row, he slipped his arms around her waist and drew her to him.

'Would you let me kiss you good night, Shirl?' he asked shyly.

'All right then, go on.' She raised her face to his, closing her eyes as he pressed his lips gently to hers. She opened her eyes to look at him, surprised that there was no more to it than that. In the pictures they seemed to feel much more – eyes closed and heads thrown back in apparent ecstasy. Perhaps they hadn't done it properly. She put her arms around him and hugged him tightly, raising her lips to his for a second kiss. This time Dave seemed to lose some of his inhibitions. His lips pressed and moved excitingly against hers and his arms tightened round her. When the kiss came to an end he was slightly breathless.

'Oh, Shirl, you're so lovely,' he said, hugging her close and burying his face in her auburn curls.

She waited for whatever would happen next, but he released her and took a step backwards. 'I – I better be off now,' he mumbled. 'It's getting late. Your ma will be getting anxious about you.'

Shirley took a step towards him. 'Why should she? She knows where I am and who I'm with.'

'That's just it,' he said.

'I don't know what you mean.'

'Look, Shirl, I'm a lot older than you. You're just a kid, really – and yet. . . .'

'And yet what?' She put her arms around his waist and laid her head against his chest. 'Don't go yet, Dave. It's nice out here, just you and me.'

'Better not. I'd better go.'

She looked up at him. 'Wasn't it nice, kissing me? Are you saying that I'm too young for you, that you'd rather have an older girl? Is that it?'

'What I'm saying is that you don't know what you do to me, Shirl,' he said, his voice husky. 'I'm not made of stone. Go on, get indoors now, there's a good girl.' He paused and stepped forward to kiss her once again briefly. 'Of course it's nice, kissing you, silly. *Too* nice, if you want to know. As for me wanting an older girl. . . .' He put his lips against her ear and whispered; 'I wouldn't swap you for Rita Hayworth, Betty Grable and all the others rolled into one.'

That night as she lay in bed, Shirley went over and over what Dave had said. She knew of course perfectly well what he had been getting at when he spoke of 'what she did to him' and the thought that she had the power to arouse him excited her. But at the same time it disturbed her too. Dave was nice. She liked him a lot but she didn't love him. She didn't intend to stay here at the little shop in Angel Row for the rest of her life, God forbid. Sometime in the future she would be leaving – going to RADA or finding some other way into a stage career. She was determined to do it, even if it took her a long time. So she didn't want to get too involved. She didn't want to hurt Dave, yet she didn't want to lose him. She turned over, punching her pillow. What should she do? Who could she ask for advice? She couldn't ask Ma, that was for sure. Try as she would, she couldn't imagine Ma ever being in the same situation. If only Gloria were here! But Gloria's letters spoke of her job, the beauty of Yorkshire, the weather – everything except coming home.

Shirley and Imogen met fairly regularly. It was usually on Sunday mornings when they were both free. Their favourite meeting place was a milk bar in Shaftesbury Avenue quite close to the Lyric Theatre, where Leonie was appearing. One Sunday at the beginning of March Imogen took her to see the photographs of *Joy in the Morning* displayed outside. Leonie looked unusually domesticated in various scenes from the play, which Shirley thought looked dramatic and interesting.

'It's doing awfully well,' Imogen told her. 'They say it's set for a really long run. I went to the first night with Daddy. Mummy is frightfully good. It's a very sad story, about a man who comes home from the war blind. She was about to leave him because they weren't happy together, but of course she has to stay when he comes home helpless.'

'It's not a very glamorous part, is it?' Shirley asked, studying the photographs carefully. 'Doesn't she sing any more?'

'She hasn't given it up,' Imogen told her. 'But the critics have given her such wonderful reviews that she may stick with legit acting from now on. Look, that's Paul Winspear, the man who wrote the play.' Imogen pointed to a portrait of a lean man with dark hair that fell forward over his forehead. He wore an open-necked shirt with a cravat at the throat. 'Isn't he handsome? He looks like those pictures of Lord Byron, doesn't he?'

'Yes, a bit. How's your dad?'

'Oh, he's still busy making a film about the war. You'd think people would have had enough of it, wouldn't you?'

'I might just about get to see that when it comes out.' Shirley looked wistfully at the photographs and wished she could see Leonie's play. She felt so far removed from the glamour of the live theatre since she'd moved back to Whitechapel. Everything had changed so. Even the way Imogen spoke sounded different. Since she started at RADA she had developed what to Shirley seemed a slightly affected way of speaking; clipped and precise, her words almost too perfectly enunciated. She used words like *frightfully* and *awfully* a lot too. It irritated Shirley and made her lapse perversely into her native cockney just to annoy. The meetings with Imogen depressed her. The other girl looked so grown-up. Her long-legged, coltish awkwardness had gone and she moved gracefully now. Tall, poised and sophisticated, she looked much older than her fifteen years. She made Shirley feel like a brash little cockney sparrow hopping about, pecking crumbs out of the gutter.

'I'll never get to study acting now,' she said gloomily as they sat over their milk-shake and sandwich lunch. 'I'll never have a real stage career like you.' She shredded the discarded crust from her ham sandwich. 'You know, sometimes when I lie in bed at night I can see it going on and on like this for ever. I'll probably end up marrying Dave. We'll run the shop together and bring up a horde of kids and I'll probably never even *see* the inside of a theatre again.'

Imogen looked at her wistfully. 'You won't believe me when I tell you that I'd quite like that kind of life.'

Shirley shot her a sharp, angry look. 'No, I bloody well wouldn't,' she said bluntly. 'You don't know you're born, Imo. You think it's like something off the pictures, don't you? All walkin' 'and in 'and into the sunset. Well, it ain't.'

'I only meant that having a husband and children would be nice,' Imogen said. 'I know how hard you work, Shirley, but it won't always be like that. Your Dave sounds so nice. Having a husband who loves you, and babies – that would be lovely. Surely it would make up for the rest?'

'No, it *wouldn't*. You don't know what you're talking about. We just don't live in the same world any more, Imo. No use pretending we do, so just put a sock in it, will you?' Shirley glanced up at the clock on the wall. 'Look, I've got to go now. See you again soon, eh?' She got up and walked quickly towards the door, Imogen hurrying after her.

'I'll walk with you to the bus.'

They walked in silence for a while, Imogen afraid to touch on what was obviously a sensitive subject again. At the bus stop she said:

'Look, Shirl, I've got the name of an acting coach. She used to be quite a well-known actress and now she's retired she gives lessons. She coaches for RADA and LAMDA exams. I saw her name in *The Stage*. That's the paper that we –'

'I *know* what *The Stage* is,' Shirley snapped. 'I'm not *that* out of touch.'

Imogen sighed and took a cutting from her handbag. 'Well, anyway, here it is. I cut it out for you. It's not all that far from where you live. If you could just manage one lesson a week it would help.'

'I suppose you think I've let my accent go to pot again.'

Imogen smiled. 'I know you only do it to annoy me. Actually, I love it. It reminds me of when we were kids.' She smiled at Shirley, her eyes twinkling, and Shirley's good nature got the better of her bad mood. She began to chuckle and the two soon found themselves giggling helplessly.

'Do you remember when I used to give you lessons?' Imogen said. 'In return for you teaching me how not to be a stuck-up little prig.'

Shirley nodded. 'Oh, Imo. I *do* miss you,' she said. 'I'm sorry I was so touchy. We'll always be friends, won't we?'

Imogen hugged her as the bus drew up beside them. 'Of course we will, silly. See you soon.' And as Shirley climbed aboard the bus she called out: 'And don't forget those lessons.'

'I won't,' Shirley called, tucking the cutting into her purse.

On Shirley's birthday in May Dave took her Up West for a meal and to the pictures afterwards. They saw *Meet Me in St Louis* with Judy Garland and Shirley came out of the cinema with stars in her eyes. It was such a beautiful, romantic story of growing up and teenage love, and Tom Drake was so handsome, he made her feel all gooey inside. He wasn't all that unlike Dave to look at, she reflected, looking sideways at him as they rode home on top of the bus. She slipped her arm through his and cuddled up to him affectionately.

'Thanks for taking me out tonight, Dave,' she said. 'I've had a lovely time. You shouldn't have spent so much money, though. It must have cost you a fortune.'

'That's all right,' he said shyly. 'I've been saving up. You're worth it.' He gave her arm a squeeze.

They saw the ambulance standing at the kerb in front of the shop as soon as they turned the corner of Angel Row. Shirley began to run, with Dave limping after her as fast as he could go. As they reached the shop, Ma came out wearing her outdoor things. Her face was white and drawn.

'Thank God you're 'ome,' she said. 'It's Pa. He 'ad another stroke an hour ago. They're taking 'im into the London Hospital again.' She clutched at Shirley's arm. 'He's real bad this time, Shirl. I'm afraid 'e won't get over this one, love.'

'Oh, Ma! I'll come with you,' Shirley said. 'Dave'll stay on here till we get back, won't you, Dave?'

They sat by Pa's bed for most of the night watching the still, ashen face, cruelly distorted by the latest stroke. Although Ma held his hand and talked to him constantly, he never regained consciousness. It was four thirty and beginning to get light when a nurse came to check on his condition. Ma had nodded off in the chair next to the bed, but Shirley was awake and alert. She watched the nurse's face as she leaned over Pa and knew from her expression that it was all over.

'I'm sorry, dear,' the nurse said in answer to the question in her eyes. 'It was very peaceful. He must have just slipped away.' She nodded towards Ma. 'Shall I wake her and break it to her or will you?'

'I'll do it,' Shirley said.

Ma took the news philosophically. 'Well, I did all I could for him,' she said wearily, taking a last look at her husband's face and automatically straightening the sheet. 'He was a good 'usband and father and 'e done all 'e could for 'is country. It's just a pity 'e had to go all through the Blitz just for this.'

'Come home and get some sleep now, Ma,' Shirley said, taking her grandmother's arm. 'We won't open the shop tomorrow. Dave'll help me make the funeral arrangements and I'll send Gloria a telegram.'

Ma's tired eyes flashed and her mouth set in the determined line that Shirley knew so well. 'You'll do no such thing, my gel,' she said. 'She couldn't come when 'er father needed her. There's no call for 'er to come running now 'e's gone, sheddin' crocodile tears. It's too late for all that.'

But Shirley did send a telegram first thing the following morning. Ma wasn't thinking straight at the moment, she told herself. She must surely want Gloria to know and to come home for the funeral.

The funeral was arranged for the following Friday, when the shop was closed and the blinds drawn respectfully. Molly and Jim Jarvis sent a sheaf of spring flowers from the garden at Longueville Hall and wrote Ma a sympathetic letter to say how sorry they were for her sad loss. The Darrents sent a beautiful wreath of gold and white roses. Imogen came in person, bearing a posy she'd made herself from pink and white carnations and delicate ferns. Pa's colleagues from the ARP carried his coffin. There being no other family mourners, Dave escorted Ma and Shirley into the church and it was only as they followed the coffin out at the end of the service that Shirley saw Gloria standing at the back. Ma saw her too; Shirley knew she did by the sudden tightening of her hand on Shirley's arm, but she walked straight ahead, refusing to look at her daughter or give her any sign of acknowledgement.

At the graveside Shirley sensed rather than saw Gloria standing on the fringe of the little group of mourners, but once the interment was completed she whispered to Dave to take Ma and Imogen home in the funeral car, telling him she would join them soon. She ran after Gloria, who was already walking briskly away along the path.

'Glor . . .' she gasped breathlessly, catching at her arm. 'Glor – I'm glad you came. You're coming back to Angel Row, aren't you?'

Gloria looked across the churchyard towards Ma. 'Will she want me to?'

'She'll be all right once she sees you,' Shirley said. 'She's just a bit upset that you never came before, but better late than never, eh?'

Tears welled up in Gloria's eyes and she pulled Shirley to her and hugged her hard. 'I'm sorry, Shirl,' she said. 'I let you all down, didn't I?'

'No – 'course you didn't,' Shirley said, a lump in her throat. 'Everything'll be all right now you're home again.'

She peered into her mother's eyes. 'Why didn't you come when Pa was ill, Glor?'

'I couldn't. It wasn't possible. First I was in America and then . . . then there was this job I was offered. It was on the plane on the way home. It was too good an opportunity to turn down, Shirl. I couldn't afford to. I'd have come to see Pa if I could, love.' She turned to look at Shirley. 'You do believe that, don't you?'

'Of course I do. Yorkshire's a long way away, isn't it? And good jobs aren't easy to find these days, are they?'

Gloria swallowed hard and composed herself. 'It must all sound like a lot of feeble excuses, I know. But it isn't. It's a long story and I'll tell you all about it some time.'

'I know. Shall we go then?' Shirley linked her arm through her mother's and began to walk. The churchyard was empty now. Dave had done as she asked and taken Ma home in the funeral car without waiting, but it wasn't very far to walk. She glanced at Gloria and thought how thin she looked, wondering if it was the black coat she wore that drained the colour from her face, making her look so pale and drawn. 'I've missed you so much, Glor,' she said, hugging the arm she held. 'Last winter was terrible. You don't have to go back to Yorkshire tonight, do you?'

'No. I've left there now.'

'Oh, the job's over, then?'

'Yes. It was only temporary.'

'I see. Are you back in London to stay then?'

Gloria shrugged. 'It all depends.' She looked at Shirley. 'I'm sorry about RADA, love, I know how much it meant to you.'

'It's not too late,' Shirley said eagerly. 'I could still take the entrance exam and go in the autumn.'

'I'm afraid there's no money for it now, love.' Gloria was biting her lip hard. 'The trip to America took most of my savings.'

Shirley's face fell. 'I thought Billy's family paid your fare?'

'They did, but there were other expenses. I couldn't let them pay for everything.'

Shirley was shaking her head in bewilderment. 'But what about this job you've had?'

'It was good but it didn't pay anything like what the aircraft factory paid. The fees for a place like RADA are out of my reach, I'm afraid, love.'

Shirley was devastated. When she had seen Gloria standing there at the back of the church she had fondly imagined that all her dreams were about to be revived. For a moment they walked in silence, then she remembered something. Looking hopefully at her mother, she said: 'Glor – there's the cottage. You don't live near enough to use it any more. It's standing there empty. You could sell it and. . . .' She broke off as she saw Gloria shaking her head.

'I've been advised not to sell the cottage,' she said. 'Property prices are going to go up and if I could have the place modernised. . . .'

'Modernised? Where would you get the money from to do *that*?' Shirley asked, her voice sharp with resentment.

'I'll have to save it, and there is some talk of the new Labour government giving grants for places with no bathrooms and so on. All property is at a premium now and will be till they start a rebuilding programme. I'll be looking into that. Once the place is more up to date I'll get a better price for it. It all takes time, though.'

Shirley fell silent. Gloria was oddly different since last they had been together. Being in America and Yorkshire seemed to have changed her in some subtle, indefinable way. It was as though an invisible barrier had come down between them. Gloria was the same – and yet she wasn't. It was like talking to someone who only *looked* like her. But now was hardly the time to probe the mystery. And disappointed though she was, she recognised the fact that it was no time for arguments about money.

Ma had laid on tea and sandwiches for a few friends and neighbours back at Angel Row and when Shirley slipped into the kitchen she found her grandmother busy brewing up the tea, a clean pinny over her black crêpe dress.

'Ma,' she said, slipping an arm round her grandmother's waist. 'Guess who's in the parlour?'

Ma stiffened, her corsets creaking ominously as she straightened her back and turned to stare unblinkingly into Shirley's eyes. 'If you're talkin' about our Gloria you needn't bother,' she said grittily. 'I saw 'er in the church, but I've got nothin' to say to that young woman. Anyway, I thought I told you not to let 'er know.'

'I had to, Ma. She would have come before if she'd been able to get away. You know Glor better than that.'

'I thought I did.' Ma poured boiling water into the big blue enamelled teapot and turned to Shirley. 'I told your mother years ago that this shop was for you and 'er. It's what 'er pa wanted and it's what we both worked for all these years – all through the Blitz an' all – to give the two of you security for the future, so don't tell me she 'ad to go up to Yorkshire to get a job when there was one 'ere for 'er all the time. A home *and* a job. Not just a job either but a nice flourishin' little business.'

'She's back now,' Shirley said. 'Oh, Ma, you will be nice to her now she's here, won't you?'

'Nice to 'er?' Ma turned steely, outraged eyes on her granddaughter. '*Nice* to 'er – when she turned 'er back on 'er own flesh and blood and chucked a lifetime of 'ard work back in our faces? No, my gel. That's somethin' I *won't* forgive in a hurry.' Ma snorted explosively and picked up the tray, sweeping out of the kitchen without another word.

The sandwiches and tea were partaken of in an atmosphere that was fraught with tension. It was clear to everyone that Gloria's presence at the small gathering had cast a cloud on the proceedings and as soon as they decently could the friends and neighbours made their excuses and drifted away. Even Dave could see that the family needed to be alone and left quietly, kissing Ma's cheek and telling Shirley that he would see her in the morning. When only Imogen remained, Shirley rose and motioned to her.

'Imogen and I will do the washing-up now, Ma,' she said. 'Then you and Gloria can have a talk.'

Ma's back stiffened. 'I'm sure there's no need for us to keep Gloria any longer,' she said stubbornly. 'No doubt she'll be wanting' to get orf and catch a train or somethin'.'

'No, Ma. I'd like to talk,' Gloria said. Her face was deathly pale and Shirley saw that her hands were clasped so tightly in her lap that the knuckles showed white. Quietly she collected up the used cups while Imogen took the sandwich plates, and the two of them went out of the room, closing the door behind them.

In the kitchen, as Shirley ran water into the sink and began to stack the crockery, Imogen said:

'What's wrong with Gloria? She looks terrible. Has she been ill?'

Shirley shook her head. 'I don't think so but I don't really know. I haven't had a chance to talk to her yet.'

Imogen picked up a teacloth and began to dry. 'Your grandmother doesn't seem too happy to see her.'

'She can't forgive her for not coming home to see Pa when he was ill. She'll come round, though,' Shirley said, though she wasn't at all sure that Ma would come round.

They were putting the best china away in the dresser cupboard when the sound of raised voices from the parlour made them exchange glances. Imogen said:

'Perhaps I'd better go now, Shirley. It's family business. I'm only in the way.'

But Shirley laid a hand on her arm. 'No. Come in with me. They'll have to stop if you're there.' She took Imogen's hand and drew her unwillingly through into the parlour where Ma and Gloria stood facing each other on opposite sides of the room.

'Gloria's leavin' now,' Ma said, her mouth drawn into a thin, determined line. 'She's 'ad no use for us over the past twelve months and now we've got no use for 'er.' She glared at Gloria. 'I want you to know, my gel, that from now on as far as I'm concerned I ain't got no daughter. What I 'ave got is a good granddaughter. Our Shirl 'as stood by me like a good 'un while you was orf gallivantin'. She's been a better gel to me than you ever was and I want you to know that this business is 'ers now. I'm 'anding everything over to 'er. When I'm gone Rayner's Green-grocery and all Pa and me 'ave worked for all these years will belong to Shirl. After the way you let your pa down, you ain't welcome in this 'ouse no more, Gloria. And that's flat.'

White-faced, Gloria turned without a word, picked up her coat and handbag and prepared to leave. Appalled, Shirley stepped forward and grasped her grandmother's arm. 'Ma! Ma! *Don't*. Don't let Gloria go like this. You're upset. You don't know what you're saying.' She turned to Gloria. 'Don't go. She didn't mean it.'

But Gloria was already at the door. 'Oh yes, she did, Shirley,' she said quietly. 'I know Ma. She's never in her life said something she didn't mean.' She gave Shirley a sad little smile. 'Don't worry, love. You stay. She needs you. I'll be in touch when I've found a job and somewhere to live.'

Through the sleeve of her grandmother's dress, Shirley could feel her trembling. She shot Imogen a pleading look. 'Go after Glor for me, will you?' she whispered. 'Make sure she's all right. I can't leave Ma like this.'

'Of course. I'll be in touch, Shirley. Bye.' Imogen quickly gathered up her things and left. As the street door slammed behind her, Shirley carefully helped a trembling Ma into a chair.

'Why did you want to upset yourself like that, Ma?' she admonished gently. 'Gloria would have come home sooner if she could. You do believe that, don't you?'

'I believes what I sees,' Ma said stubbornly. She looked up at her granddaughter and squeezed her hand. 'Make us another cuppa, there's a good gel.' She drew a deep, shuddering breath. 'Oh, my Gawd, what a day! I don't mind tellin' you, I'm just about done in.'

In the kitchen Shirley filled the kettle and set it to boil on the gas stove. The row with Gloria on top of Pa's illness and death had taken its toll of Ma. In the parlour just now she had looked every day of her sixty-two years. Shirley's heart was heavy as she recalled her grandmother's words to Gloria. *I'm handing everything over to her. Rayner's Greengrocery will belong to Shirley*. She was trapped. She'd never get away now; never get the chance to make that stage career she had dreamed of. Gloria would never come back to Angel Row while Ma was here. That much was certain. And Ma would be totally reliant on her for everything from now on.

'Gloria! Please wait.'

Gloria was walking fast, as though she couldn't get away fast enough. Imogen had to call twice before she heard, but when she realised that the breathless cry was directed at her Gloria hesitated, turned, then stopped to wait for the girl to catch her up.

'I'm sorry you had to witness all that,' she said as Imogen drew level with her. 'I'm afraid my mother is a very hard, unforgiving woman.'

'I'm sure she'll be sorry once the strain has worn off,' Imogen said. 'She's had a very hard time of it these past months, what with your father's illness and everything.' She paused. 'And so has Shirley.'

'D'you think I don't realise that?'

'Have you got time for a cup of tea or something?' Imogen asked. 'There's a café over there.'

They crossed the road and went into the café. Gloria sat down at one of the oilcloth-covered tables while Imogen bought two cups of tea at the counter and brought them across.

'I would have come when Pa was ill, really I would,' Gloria said. 'But it just wasn't possible. After I'd been to visit Billy's family I got this housekeeping job, you see. I lived in and only had one day off a week. There wasn't time to come all the way down to London and back in a day. And when Pa was taken ill this last time there wasn't even time for me to get here.'

'It's been very hard on poor Shirley,' Imogen said. 'She isn't used to working so hard and she was looking forward to RADA so much. It's a lot of talent going to waste, Gloria.'

'I know, *I know*. You don't have to tell me.' To Imogen's dismay two tears slipped down Gloria's cheeks and dripped onto the table. 'I can't afford to send her now, Imogen. I just can't *afford* it. I haven't even got a job now and all my savings have gone. No one knows what it does to me to have to say no to her – to see all her dreams go out of the window. It's all I've ever wanted and planned for her, ever since she was a baby. It's my dream too, Imogen.'

Imogen watched as Gloria fought back the tears, rummaging in her handbag for a handkerchief. She wanted to ask why Gloria hadn't thought of Shirley before she agreed to go to America. And also why she agreed to take on a job in Yorkshire when she already knew her father was ill. But pity for the woman's obvious distress prevented her. She reached across the table to touch Gloria's hand. 'Look, you said you were looking for work. I know you get along well with Mummy. She thinks very highly of your talent for sewing. She's not happy with her present dresser and she's looking for someone to take her place. Would you like me to ask her to bear you in mind for the job?'

Gloria looked up. She badly needed a job but work for Leonie – where she might run into Tony almost every day. . . . 'Oh, well – that would be marvellous, Imogen, but I'm not sure. . . .'

'Mummy would jump at the chance to get someone she knows well and who is as clever with her needle as you are.' Imogen gave Gloria a wry smile. 'I'm not going to pretend it would be all honey. Mummy can be difficult sometimes.' She paused. 'You probably don't know that she and Daddy have unofficially separated.'

Gloria felt her heart miss a beat. 'No, I didn't know. I'm sorry.'

'Yes, so am I. I hardly ever see Daddy nowadays. He's away on location so much of the time. Anyway, as I said, Mummy isn't the easiest person to work for. She'll pay you well, but you'll certainly earn it.' She smiled. 'But you've got a calmness about you which is just what she needs. Shall I tell her you're available and ask her to get in touch? Can she contact you at Angel Row?'

'No.' Gloria bit her lip. 'I'm afraid not. You heard Ma. She chucked me out – no ifs or buts.'

Imogen stared at her. 'You mean you've actually got nowhere to stay?' Gloria shook her head. 'Not even tonight?'

'I've still got Rook Cottage. I was going to get the train and go up to Boothley.'

'But you can't do that. It's too far away if Mummy wants to see you. Look, you'd better come back with me. I've only got a one-bedroom flat in Earls Court, but you're welcome to sleep on the settee in the living room. Will that do?'

'Thank you, if you're sure it wouldn't put you out.'

Imogen looked at her watch. 'If we hurry I might just catch Mummy on the phone before she goes to the theatre, then you can pop along in the morning and see her.'

As they travelled on the Underground, Gloria looked at the self-possessed young women at her side and wondered why she wasn't living with one of her parents. Poor girl! For all the wealth and privilege she'd had she'd been short of love all her life. If their situations had been reversed, Gloria would have been only too delighted to have her daughter with her. She allowed her thoughts to dwell on the Darrents and wondered what could have happened to bring about their separation. Their marriage had never been happy but she'd been under the impression that they stayed together because of their public image. Had the war changed all that? She sighed wistfully, wondering briefly if she should shoulder any of the blame. She'd made such a mess of everything; was she responsible for this too? The way things looked now, her dreams for Shirley would never come true. They would never even know the pleasure of sharing a home again – and she was afraid that Shirley would never forgive her. In the years to come the chasm between them would widen and widen, forcing them further apart. If only there were something she could do about it.

Chapter Fourteen

Gloria sat in the star dressing room at the Lyric and watched as Leonie took off her make-up after the Saturday matinee. Leonie had made the bare little room with its green-painted brick walls as cosy as possible, bringing in her own furniture, carpet and lampshades to give it a homely feel. As she said to Gloria, 'When one spends so much time in a place it's essential to create a warm and relaxed atmosphere.'

Gloria was reminded nostalgically of the time she had gone backstage to see Tony when he had appeared in *Henry V*. It all seemed so long ago now – a lifetime.

'I must say it's the most marvellous stroke of luck, your being free to take this job just when I need someone so desperately,' Leonie was saying. Her voice was slightly distorted as she grimaced into the mirror in order to get the last vestiges of greasepaint off. 'I really need someone who knows me – who can anticipate my needs and not wait to be *told* all the time. The last woman was absolutely clueless. She had one of those voices that grate appallingly when one wants to be quiet just before curtain-up, and she was always putting out the wrong costume and letting things get tatty. When can you start, darling?'

'Well, if you think I'll suit –'

'*Suit?*' Leonie almost screamed the word. 'You'll do more than suit. You're like a gift straight from heaven. There's no one – absolutely *no one* I'd rather have.'

'Well, I suppose I could start fairly soon if you like. Whenever your present dresser has worked out her notice, I suppose.'

'Oh, never mind that.' Leonie waved a dismissive hand. 'I've already paid her off and let her go. Damned glad to see the back of her.'

'I still have one or two things to sort out, including somewhere permanent to live,' Gloria said. 'That could be difficult in London at the moment.'

Leonie glanced around at her. 'Oh? I naturally assumed you'd be living at home with your mother and Shirley.'

'I'm afraid my mother is still angry with me for not managing to visit while my father was ill. She isn't speaking to me at the moment.'

'Oh, dear. I'm sorry to hear that. I was sorry to hear about your father too, of course – and your American friend.' Leonie shook her head. 'You've had a rough time of it lately, haven't you? And families can be sheer hell at times, can't they?' She swung round to face Gloria. 'We both know how *I've* suffered in that particular area.'

'You've had no more problems with your brother, I hope,' Gloria said, lowering her voice.

'No, thank God. And if you don't mind, Gloria, I'd rather we drew a veil over that particular little episode. It's strictly between you and me.'

'Yes, of course.'

'So – you're homeless? Well, we must do something about that, mustn't we? You must come and stay at the flat.'

'Oh, but I couldn't,' Gloria said. 'When you leave here you must want your privacy.'

Leonie screwed the top back onto her jar of Leichner removing cream and began to put on her street make-up. 'Actually it can get rather lonely sometimes, going back to an empty flat.' She glanced at Gloria. 'Tony and I are no longer living together, you know. I'm surprised Imogen didn't tell you. I'm sure it's no secret that our marriage has been on the rocks for some time. The war and the long separations it brought about didn't help.' She etched in her eyebrows with quick, deft strokes. 'Tony has never been short of female company – I'm sure you know all about that.' She cocked a newly defined eyebrow at Gloria through the mirror, making her blush hotly. 'His ex-wife, Gillian Fane, has been over to make a film. They've been seen around together, then since she left he's taken up with some chorus girl or other, or so I hear. His love life is none of my business any more.' She applied her lipstick and smiled. 'Actually, now that we're apart we get along much better than we have for years. Everything has been amicably sorted out. As for me. . . .' She turned to look at Gloria, her eyes shining. 'Strictly between ourselves, Gloria, I'm in love – I truly believe it's the real thing and I *couldn't* be happier.'

Gloria smiled back. 'Oh. I . . . I'm very glad for you.'

'If you're to stay at the flat it's as well that you know the situation. He sometimes stays over, you see. It's Paul Winspear, the man who wrote this play.' She sighed. 'He's so *wonderful*, Gloria. It was love at first sight – so romantic. He has the most adorable, warm, melting brown eyes and the moment they met mine it was just like fate.'

'Oh, then will you – I mean are you and Tony. . . ?'

'Getting divorced?' Leonie shrugged. 'Who knows? It's difficult. Paul is married too, you see. Oh, she left him soon after he came out of the Army, so it wasn't me who broke things up between them. For the moment we're taking things a step at a time.' She looked at Gloria. 'So what do you say? Would you like to be my dresser-cum-confidante? There's no one I'd rather have and I know I can trust you to be discreet.' She laughed suddenly. 'Oh, how *silly* of me! I haven't mentioned money. How would eight pounds a week and rent-free accommodation suit you?'

Gloria gasped. 'That's extremely generous, but I couldn't impose on you at the flat permanently.'

'You wouldn't be *imposing*, darling.' Leonie's dark eyes flashed and there was a slight edge to her voice as she added: 'Naturally I'd expect you to do a little light housework in return for food and lodging. It's quite impossible to get a reliable maid these days. And the place is quite big enough for us not to get in each other's way.'

'I see. Yes, of course.' The implications were only too clear. Gloria cleared her throat. 'In that case, would you mind if I sometimes went away for the weekend? I still have my cottage at Boothley and I'd like to make sure it's in order.'

'Naturally. You'll want to take Shirley there, I suppose.' When Gloria declined to answer and lowered her eyes, Leonie smiled. 'Ah – you're blushing. Am I to take it that you've found a new man friend then?'

'I . . . you could say that.'

'Well, of course your Sundays through till Monday evenings will be your own free time to do with as you please.' Leonie rose and slipped off her wrapper to reveal a pair of black satin and lace camiknickers. 'Hand me the dress from the hanger over there, darling, will you?'

At that moment the door opened and a man walked in. Leonie launched herself into his arms.

'Paul, *darling*! I wasn't expecting you this afternoon.'

'I know. I thought we might have tea together before the evening performance.' He took her chin in one hand and kissed her possessively. It was only as he was raising his head that he noticed Gloria, who had been standing awkwardly, half hidden behind the door, Leonie's dress over her arm. He frowned at Leonie. 'Oh – why didn't you tell me you had a visitor?'

Leonie laughed. 'You didn't really give me a chance, did you, darling? This is Gloria Rayner. She's a very old friend and she's going to be my new dresser. I'm so lucky that she's looking for a job just when I need her. She's a positive *genius* with her needle. You wouldn't believe how talented she is. Gloria, this is Mr Paul Winspear.'

'Pleased to meet you, sir.' Gloria didn't know whether to offer her hand or not, but apart from a dismissive sweep of his dark eyes, Paul made no attempt to acknowledge her. She cleared her throat. 'Well, I'll er . . . be off now,' she said, edging towards the door. Paul's glowering expression made her feel distinctly unwelcome.

'You can move your things into the flat whenever you like,' Gloria said with a wave of her hand. 'I'll tell the caretaker to expect you. He'll let you in. And don't worry about the job. You'll soon slip into the routine. I'll see you soon.'

The last Gloria saw as she closed the door was Paul Winspear enfolding Leonie in an embrace that looked both passionate and demanding. There was something about the man that she had disliked on sight. The eyes that Leonie saw as warm and melting seemed to Gloria dark and enigmatic, and there was something cruel, almost predatory about his mouth that sent a chill through her. But she told herself it was none of her business whom Leonie chose to associate with. She had given her a much needed job and a place to live and that was her most immediate concern.

Number 127 Manderville Road, Stepney, was the last house in a terrace of shabby Regency villas. Once an elegant town house, it had now been converted into four flats, its stucco façade chipped and its paint peeling. The little wrought-iron balconies that embellished the first-floor windows were rusting and perilously rickety and the railings that had once protected the shallow area had been taken at the beginning of the war.

Magda Jayne occupied Flat 1 in the basement, where she also had her studio. Shirley stood looking down the short flight of steps that lead to a red-painted door bearing a sign that said: 'Stage Coach, Actors' Studio.'

Now that she was here she was nervous. It would use up most of her weekly wage to take two lessons a week, which, according to the advertisement in *The Stage*, was the minimum Miss Jayne accepted. Could she persuade her to accept her for one weekly session? Well, she would never know until she asked, she told herself. Straightening her shoulders she walked down the steps and knocked on the door.

The woman who answered her knock must have been about fifty. She was tall and willowy with abundant dark hair streaked with grey, which she wore smoothed back into a loose knot at the nape of her neck. She wore well-cut slacks and an exotically patterned Chinese silk tunic. But it was her eyes that made the greatest impact on Shirley. They were an unusual hazel-green colour and deeply penetrating. Shirley felt as though they could see right through to all the doubt and insecurity she was feeling. As the woman raised an enquiring eyebrow, Shirley cleared her throat nervously.

'Oh, hello. I – I've seen your advert in *The Stage* and I've come to enquire about acting lessons.'

The woman held the door open. 'Please come in.' Her voice had a deep and impressive resonance that told Shirley that she was in the presence of a seasoned actress.

The narrow hallway was dim but the moment Miss Jayne opened a door to her right, glowing colour seemed to leap out at Shirley from every direction. The walls were painted plain white and on them hung a number of modern paintings, some of them abstracts, each a riot of brilliant colours and bizarre patterns. Over the fireplace was an eye-catching life-sized nude with waist-length raven hair that drew Shirley's eyes like a magnet. She thought it extremely beautiful. Against the wall facing the door stood a divan covered in a red-and-white-striped cover. On it were heaped jewel-coloured cushions, their hand-woven covers embroidered with glowing silks and dotted with tiny pieces of mirror and sequins, and above it hung a Persian wall hanging in luscious shades of gold and wine. The floor was of plain polished boards with a fringed oriental rug in the centre. By contrast to all these sensual assaults, a businesslike desk stood in the window recess, one chair behind it, another to one side. Magda Jayne indicated one of these.

'Will you have a seat, Miss . . .?'

'Oh – Rayner,' Shirley said, trying hard not to stare about her at the exotic room. 'Shirley Rayner.'

'What a pretty name. You want to enrol, Shirley?'

'Well, yes, I'd like to.' Shirley decided to come straight to the point. No use wasting the woman's time. 'The trouble is I don't think I can afford two lessons a week.'

Magda smiled. The smile seemed to light her eyes from within. It relaxed and warmed Shirley like sunshine on a cold day. 'Well, before we talk about money, suppose you tell me a little about yourself. To begin with, would you like to tell me what makes you want to take acting lessons?'

Before she knew it, Shirley was pouring out her life story to this woman – this magnetic stranger she had only just met. All the time she was talking, Magda was watching her shrewdly, the perceptive hazel eyes taking in every detail of her speech and mannerisms. When she had finished, Magda said:

'But what do *you* want, Shirley? It seems to me that you've been heavily influenced by those around you: your mother, your friends and now your grandmother. Have you ever really asked yourself what *you* want?'

'I want to be an actress,' Shirley said firmly. 'It's what I've wanted ever since I can remember. Gloria – that's my mother – would never have pushed me into something I didn't want to do. In fact, she's not as keen on it as she used to be. When I got a place at high school I think she had visions of me being a teacher or a doctor or something. But I still want to act more . . . more than anything else in the world.'

Magda looked at the slender, work-roughened hands that twisted nervously at the strap of the cheap little handbag, then up into Shirley's shining blue eyes. 'I charge twelve pounds a term. That is twelve weeks – twenty-four lessons. Could you manage that?'

Shirley bit her lip. 'I'm not sure. I wondered if I could have one lesson a week . . .' She trailed off, watching as Magda opened a drawer and took out a book. Opening it, she passed it across the desk to Shirley.

'Read that for me.'

Shirley saw that it was a poem by Swinburne, one that they had studied in English-literature lessons at school.

'Just read me the first verse,' Magda prompted. 'Don't worry about it. Take your time.'

Shirley took a deep breath and began: 'When the hounds of spring are on winter's traces, The mother of months in meadow and plain . . .' She loved the poem, and the lush, singing phrases soon made her forget her nervousness. Her enjoyment came out in her voice and her eyes as she read, going on without being prompted to the second verse, after which she stopped, suddenly embarrassed that she had read more than was asked of her.

'Thank you.' Magda was smiling. 'How old are you, Shirley?'

'Sixteen.'

'You do realise that your voice is very nasal and that your breathing is all wrong, don't you?'

Shirley blushed. 'Imogen, my friend, tried to teach me to speak properly, but since I came home again I've let it slip.'

'Don't worry. Once you get into the right habits it won't be possible to let it slip, as you put it,' Magda said. 'It will come as second nature.' She pulled a desk diary towards her. 'So, when do you want to begin?'

Shirley caught her breath. 'Well, as I said, I don't know if I can afford . . .'

'Would half-price suit you?' The hazel eyes were in deadly earnest as they looked into hers.

'Two lessons a week for . . .?'

'For six pounds,' Magda said. 'Children are usually half-price, aren't they? And you are scarcely more than a child. Now, what time of day would suit you best?'

It was arranged that Shirley would go to Magda on Mondays and Thursdays after the shop closed at half-past six. From the beginning she had told Ma where she was going. Although she knew her grandmother would not approve, she was determined not to give way.

For her part, Ma said nothing. She knew better than to argue or try to stop Shirley from following her dream, however silly and futile she considered it. She relied heavily on her granddaughter now that she had fallen out with Gloria and she was alone in the world. She was all too aware that the girl could get a job anywhere. If things got too awkward for her, she would probably go off to live with her mother, and where would Ma be then? Obliged to sell the shop and move, that's where. More than likely she'd end up in some home for old people. She had seen such places: old folk shuffling about aimlessly like a lot of zombies, waiting to die. An ice-cold fear clutched at Ma's heart whenever she thought about it. *No*, she didn't want that. If only the girl would drop this stage fad and take a real interest in the business. But common sense told her that if Shirley was prevented from doing what she wanted, she'd fret for it all the more. Let her get it out of her system, she told herself. When she was a bit older she'd come to realise that a good established business was worth more than all the glitter and tinsel.

Shirley adored the lessons with Magda, looking forward to Mondays and Thursdays – counting the days as though she were waiting for a special treat. In the early weeks she learned things she had never imagined she would need to know – about the anatomy of the respiratory system, the mechanics of the chest, lungs and throat and all the muscles employed in voice production. 'You wouldn't dream of operating a machine without first learning how it worked, would you?' Magda said. Shirley learned how to breathe correctly, controlling her ribs and diaphragm, and how to project her voice and enunciate her vowels, ridding herself of the offending nasal tones. Every day she would get up early and do her breathing exercises in front of her open bedroom window. She would gargle to keep her throat healthy and faithfully perform her voice exercises, steadily elongating the vowel sounds, controlling the sound from a thin whisper to a full-throated, rounded, steady flow, trailing off again evenly to a whisper. As she practised she visualised the sound as Magda had suggested – seeing it as a brightly coloured ribbon flowing from her mouth.

Magda was encouraging. She told Shirley that she had a good lung capacity and a strong larynx, no doubt due to singing from an early age. She promised that as soon as they'd ironed out her vowels they could go on to some poetry and maybe a scene from a play. With this end in view, Shirley worked as she had never worked before.

Downstairs in the kitchen Ma would raise her eyes to the ceiling and shrug helplessly. Gloria hadn't known what she was starting when she put all those highfalutin notions into the child's head. Shirley'd be far better off using her spare time to encourage young Dave. It was plain to anyone with half an eye that the poor feller was hopelessly sweet on her. She could do a lot worse than marry a good steady chap like Dave who'd be a good hubby and only too happy to run the shop with her. Having a gammy leg, he wouldn't be likely to stray either. It was an ill wind, Ma told herself with satisfaction. But then again, she'd noticed that things were very different since the war. The men demobilised from the services were still restless, and the women had got it into their heads that they could have the same freedom that men had. Both sexes seemed to feel that there was more to life than settling down to marriage, a home and children. If they were to ask Ma, she would have told them that it would all end in tears. But no one did ask her.

Dave always went to meet Shirley after her drama lessons. They'd walk home through the streets on the warm summer evenings. As the light evenings shortened and winter drew on, they would sometimes stop off at the Prince of Wales, Dave's favourite pub, for a drink on the way. Shirley passed quite easily for eighteen and there was never any question about her right to be there; nevertheless, she never mentioned it to Ma, who would have been annoyed with Dave for taking her there.

Christmas came once more – a happier and more relaxed one this year, though Ma missed Pa badly. In spite of her announcement to Gloria about the shop being Shirley's, the situation at Angel Row remained the same. Shirley still found herself in the position of employee and received what she considered a meagre wage. But whenever she complained about this, Ma threw out heavy hints that she had changed her will and that Shirley was the sole beneficiary of all her worldly goods, including the shop. Everything would be hers in the fullness of time.

* * *

Dave never knew what mood he would find Shirley in after her lessons with Magda Jayne. Sometimes she would be elated and animated, at other times pensive and preoccupied. He never minded; her mood swings were all part of the excitement. To him she was the most mysterious, magical creature in the world and just as long as he could be with her he didn't care.

Saturday was the day he looked forward to most. On Saturday evenings she was all his. After the shop closed they would go Up West, have tea at Lyons Corner house in Leicester Square and then on to the pictures. Dave looked forward all week to holding Shirley's hand in the dim warmth of the cinema, to breathing her fragrance and tasting the sweetness of her lips when he held her close. He knew that she was young and had great plans for the future; plans that clearly did not at the moment include him. But he refused to look too far ahead or think too deeply about that. If he could make her love him enough, perhaps she would forget her dreams of the footlights and stardom.

Once a month on a Sunday Shirley met Imogen. It was from Imogen that she had learned about her mother's employment with Leonie and that she was living at the Mayfair flat. She deeply resented the fact that Gloria had made no attempt to get in touch or to find out if Ma was well and recovering from losing Pa. Gloria's behaviour since the end of the war was something she would never understand or come to terms with.

Now that she was studying drama at last, she had something to tell Imogen when they met. She felt equal to her again. Just as they had in the old days, they could swap notes and dream about the golden future awaiting them both.

'You never ask me about Gloria,' Imogen remarked one Sunday afternoon when they had taken sandwiches to Hyde Park instead of eating at the milk bar. 'She misses you an awful lot, you know. She's always asking about you whenever I see her.'

'She knows where I am; why doesn't she write to me?' Shirley said, her chin lifting stubbornly. 'I've never heard a word from her since Pa's funeral. Sometimes I think she doesn't give a damn about Ma and me any more.'

'Mummy keeps her pretty busy, I'm afraid,' Imogen said.

'What's wrong with Sundays? She has them off, doesn't she? If she doesn't want to come home she could easily meet me somewhere, but she's never even tried to.'

Imogen sighed. 'I wish you and she would make it up,' she said. 'I always used to envy the close relationship you two had. She's always been my idea of a real mother. She told me she had written to you but you didn't reply.'

'She *what*? That's a laugh. I never got any letters.' Shirley sniffed. 'She's just saying that to make herself look in the right.'

'As for Sundays, she goes to Boothley most weekends,' Imogen said.

Shirley frowned. 'Boothley?'

'Yes. To the cottage. I'll bet she'd like you to go with her some time. It would be so nice if you could spend time together. Oh, Shirl, if only you'd meet her halfway! This thing between you – it's gone on far too long. I'm sure she'd be thrilled to hear all about your drama studies.'

Shirley put down her sandwich and looked at her friend. 'Look, Imo. Glor and I used to be really close, as you said. I'd have done anything for her and I know that all she ever wanted was me. But when Billy came along she changed. I understand that. She's still quite young and he was nice. But after she went to America to meet his family she just turned into another person. I can't think why she didn't stop there. She let me down, Imo. All those years of building me up and then she let me down flat. She let Ma down, too – landed us both in it and went away without even trying to help.'

'Your grandmother was pretty definite about not seeing her again,' Imogen reminded her. 'She said some very hurtful things. I was there, remember?'

''Course she did. She was hurt,' Shirley said defensively. 'She'd just lost Pa. Gloria treated both of them badly. You couldn't blame Ma for being angry. Oh, don't let's talk about her now,' she said suddenly. 'We'll be arguing in a minute and she's not worth it.'

'How's Dave?' Imogen asked after a small silence.

'He's okay.'

'He's awfully nice, Shirley. Are you planning to get engaged?'

Shirley stared at her friend. '*Engaged*? At my age? I've got a better future in front of me than that.'

'I only thought . . .'

'Well, *don't* if you can't think of anything better than that,' Shirley snapped. 'Do *you* want to give up everything just to be someone's wife?'

'I might if I fell in love,' Imogen said dreamily.

'Oh, honestly!' Shirley brushed the crumbs from her skirt and stood up. 'Let's go and feed the leftovers to the ducks before I strangle you, Imogen Darrant. You're the most maddening girl I know.'

When they met the following month, Imogen produced a letter from Gloria. She gave it to Shirley as they sat at their usual table in the milk bar.

'Gloria asked me to give you this,' she said. 'She said she wouldn't risk the post again.'

'Oh, thanks.' Shirley pushed the envelope into her pocket and it wasn't until she was undressing for bed later that night that she found it. Sitting on the bed, she tore open the envelope and unfolded the sheet of paper inside.

Dear Shirley,

Imogen tells me you never received any of the other letters I wrote you. I can only guess at what might have happened to them. I hope you're well, love, and that you've managed to find it in your heart to forgive me for the way I let you down. I honestly couldn't help it and one day you'll understand.

Imogen tells me you're having drama lessons and that you're doing really well. I'm sure you'll make that stage career one day, love, and no one will be prouder of you than I will. I have a good job here with Leonie Swann. It's quite exciting working at the theatre. I get a lot of sewing jobs to do but I like that as you know. I can get you a couple of complimentary tickets if you'd like to come and see the show. I'm sure you could come backstage after if I asked Leonie's permission. I know it would interest you. Let me know if you'd like that, love.

At the moment I'm living at the flat in Mayfair. I have a nice room and my pay is quite good, though I have to work quite hard for it. Leonie makes sure she gets her money's worth. But don't tell Imogen I said that, will you?

I miss you more than I can say, Shirl, and I'd love to see you more than anything in the world. If you'd like to fix something up just drop me a line, or you could ring me at the flat in the mornings. I hope Ma is well and that she's quite recovered now from poor Pa's death. I'd like to see her too, but I'm afraid she won't forgive me for a long time yet – perhaps not ever.

Take care of yourself, darling. I love you.

Gloria.

Her throat painfully constricted, Shirley read the letter through twice, tears blurring her vision till the words swam together. Over the past months she had tried hard to convince herself she didn't care about Gloria's apparent rejection, but it was no use, she cared very deeply. She missed her too. She had felt abandoned when Gloria hadn't got in touch. But she had told Imogen that she'd written, and repeated it here in the letter. Why should she say it if it wasn't true?

Ma was out visiting a sick friend down the street and Shirley crept into her bedroom and began to open the drawers of her dressing table. She hated doing it but she had to satisfy herself that Ma hadn't done what she suspected. It was in the bottom one, where she kept what she called her 'papers' in an old chocolate box, that she found them. Everything was there: identity card, ration book, clothing coupons. There was a copy of Pa's will and her own various insurance policies. Right at the bottom lay a bundle of five or six letters, unopened and addressed to Shirley in Gloria's handwriting. Ma obviously couldn't bring herself to destroy them – or to read them either. She had simply tucked them away out of sight and closed her mind to the deceptive act. After a moment's thought, Shirley put them back where she had found them and closed the drawer. Pa's maxim had always been, Least said, soonest mended. And in this case she reckoned he was right.

Gloria soon found herself acting as cook and housekeeper as well as dresser to Leonie. Sometimes she wondered if she couldn't be described as her nanny, too. She was required to comfort and soothe, to boost Leonie's flagging confidence, to flatter and cajole – and, on the evenings when Paul Winspear accompanied Leonie back to the flat, simply to merge into the background and disappear completely. The agreement about her hours, which were supposed to fit in with opening hours at the theatre, had completely gone by the board. They now seemed to extend from dawn till bedtime. The one thing Gloria had managed to remain firm about was her time off on Sunday and Monday when she would take the train to Northampton and then the bus to Boothley Bottom to exchange her hectic weekday job for the comparative peace and quiet of the countryside.

She had been with Leonie almost twelve months before she saw Tony again. It was a Monday morning and she was busy with the housework while Leonie was out seeing Peter Jason, her agent. Leonie hated the housework being done while she was in. She said the vacuum cleaner brought on her migraine, so Gloria found herself doing the work during any odd moments she could snatch. Leonie was always forgetting her key and Gloria was in the habit of leaving the door on the latch for her if she was in.

Unable to make the doorbell heard above the roar of the vacuum cleaner, Tony had let himself into the flat. When he touched her shoulder Gloria gave a cry of alarm and spun round. But her flushed face paled when she saw the man who stood smiling at her elbow.

'*Tony*! Oh, my God, you made me jump.'

'I'm sorry if I startled you, Gloria. I did ring but I couldn't make you hear. The door was on the latch so I just came in. You shouldn't do that, you know. There are some funny people about.'

'So I see.' As she unplugged the cleaner, Tony laughed.

'I suppose I asked for that.' He perched on the arm of the settee. 'It's wonderful to see you again. How are you?'

'I'm fine, thanks. I'm afraid Leonie's out and she won't be back for a while. She's gone to see Mr Jason.'

'Yes, I know. He told me she was going in to the office this morning. I heard from Imogen that you were here so I came early, hoping to catch you.'

'Catch me? For what?'

He laughed. 'Just for a chat. No need to look so suspicious.' He took out his cigarette case and offered it to her. She shook her head. 'I must say I was surprised to hear you were working for Leonie. How are you finding things?'

'I'm very grateful to have a job and a place to live.'

He looked up from lighting his cigarette and gave her a wry smile. 'That's not what I asked you.'

Gloria sighed. 'Look, Tony, this is an awkward situation. If you're hoping to draw me . . .'

He held up his hand. 'Good heavens, Gloria, hasn't Leonie told you that we're on quite amicable terms? I was only asking as a friend, strictly between ourselves. I've been married to Leonie for a long time, remember? I do know what she can be like. I just hope she's not exploiting you.'

Gloria pushed back a strand of hair. 'I don't know what you mean.'

'Come off it. You're supposed to be her dresser and I find you doing the housework. I wouldn't mind betting she has you cooking and rinsing out her smalls too. Strictly off the record, how much does she pay you?'

'Please . . .' Gloria blushed. 'She pays me enough.'

'Well, I hope you're right.' He smiled suddenly. 'So – tell me your news. How did you get on in the States?'

'Very well. The Landis family were very kind to me.'

'You weren't tempted to stay?'

'No. I'm a Londoner born and bred. I got homesick. I was ready to come home when the time came.'

'And since?'

'I worked in Yorkshire for a few months – for some people I met on the plane coming home.' She hesitated, looking at him. 'Then . . . then my father died.'

'Yes, Imogen told me. Shirley's helping out at the shop, I hear, and taking part-time drama lessons.'

'I felt bad about her not going to RADA but it couldn't be helped. My mother and I quarrelled. It's all a bit . . .'

'I understand. So now you're here, working for Leonie. I'm glad we're all still in touch, Gloria. I've missed you. I mean that.' Tony got up and went to the cocktail cabinet. 'For God's sake put that bloody duster down and have a drink.'

Gloria shook her head. 'No, I couldn't. Besides, it's too early.'

Tony looked at his watch and replaced the decanter of whisky in the cabinet. 'Perhaps you're right. How about some coffee then?'

Over the coffee, which they drank sitting at the kitchen table where Gloria felt more comfortable, Tony told her about his ex-wife's visit to England to make a film for the company he worked for.

'It was great to see Gill again. She brought my son, Marcus, with her too. You should have seen him, Gloria. He's twenty now. Such a tall, handsome fellow. He's at Yale, reading history and English literature. He hasn't decided yet on what he wants to do but he's done quite a lot of acting with his college drama group and Gill says he's good.' He sighed. 'It made me feel damned old, I can tell you. He reminded me so much of myself at that age.' He drew hard on his cigarette. 'Seeing him made me feel I'd missed an awful lot, too. He's my son and yet I don't really know the first thing about him. He doesn't even have my name any more. Gill had his name changed to Fane.'

'I'm sorry, Tony. And I know what you mean.' She looked thoughtfully at him. 'I haven't seen as much of Shirley as I'd have liked since the war. We used to be so close once. Life is full of surprises – and regrets,' she added quietly.

He reached across the table to touch her hand. 'We are still friends, aren't we, Gloria?'

'Of course. Why do you ask?'

'You're – I don't know – different. I get the feeling that you're holding me at arm's length.'

'Perhaps I am. We did say goodbye after . . . that last time, didn't we?'

He looked into her eyes for a long moment as though trying to read what was hiding in their depths. 'How are you, Gloria?' he said at length. 'How are you *really*, I mean?'

'I told you. I'm all right.'

'No new man in your life?'

'No. I hear you have someone new, though.'

He frowned. 'Who told you that?'

She blushed. 'Leonie said something about a chorus girl.'

He looked puzzled for a moment, then threw back his head and laughed. 'Trust Leonie. I was seeing Pat Burnette for a while, but she's a rising musical-comedy star, not a chorus girl. As a matter of fact she reminds me a lot of Leonie at that age – ambitious, full of youthful enthusiasm, a bit brash. She was much too young for me, of course. I had a distinct impression that she only went out with me because she thought I might help her career along.' He smiled wryly. 'The story of my life, eh? And just between ourselves, she had the intellect of a fruit fly. I admit it did my ego good, being seen around with a lissom young blonde on my arm, but after a while even that gets tedious.' He chuckled and squeezed Gloria's hand. 'I can't *tell* you how good it is to see you, Gloria. You and I have always had something a bit special, haven't we? You

327

always make me feel so relaxed. Have dinner with me one evening?'

Very gently she withdrew her hand from beneath his. 'I'm always busy at the theatre in the evenings.'

'Not at the weekends, surely?'

'I always go away at the weekends.'

'Lunch, then?'

'I don't think so, Tony.'

He cocked an amused eyebrow at her. 'Are you giving me the brush-off by any chance?'

'Let's face it, it would make life very difficult. Much better leave it.'

He sighed. 'I don't agree, but if you say so. . . .' He stubbed out his cigarette. 'I'm here to talk to Leonie about selling Longueville Hall,' he confided. 'We hardly ever get up to Houlton nowadays. Anyway, it's time we made things official and started divorce proceedings. I think she'll agree.'

'Sell Longueville Hall?' Gloria was shocked. 'What will happen to Jim and Molly Jarvis if the place is sold?'

He frowned. 'That's the one thing that bothers me. We could pension them off, of course. Or maybe they'd like to come and work here, looking after Leonie. It'd take some of the pressure off you – you look positively shredded. Or maybe she and this Winspear character will buy a house together, who knows? Things are all very fluid at the moment.'

'What will you do?' She looked at him.

'I've got a couple more films to make under my present contract. When they're in the can I'm planning to form a Shakespearean company – touring England first, then Canada. It's still at the planning stage, I'm in the process of working out the details with Peter. I've had enough of making films about the war. I'm even tired of flying.' He smiled wryly. 'I rather suspect I might be getting old.'

She smiled back at him. 'You know you don't really believe that.'

'Taking Shakespeare on tour is what I've always wanted, Gloria. I can't wait to get into rehearsal.' His

328

eyes shone at the thought. 'I'm going to play Macbeth and Hamlet, Richard II – all the roles no one else would ever let me play. I might even have a go at Lear.'

'Well, good luck with it.'

'Thanks.' He leaned towards her, touching her hand. 'You're always so good for my ego, Gloria. You and I go back a long way, don't we? If you change your mind about that dinner I'd be more than pleased. I mean that.'

They heard the front door slam and Gloria got up from the table and began to clear the cups into the sink. 'That's Leonie. You'd better go and see her.'

When he had gone she sat down again at the table and tried to examine the whirling vortex of her emotions. It was still there, what she had always felt for Tony. It always would be; she admitted it now. Hearing about his latest affair, however trivial he protested it was, had given her pain. The fact that he cared so little about it somehow made it worse. No one had been able to stir his emotions as deeply as Claire once had and she guessed that no one ever would, least of all she. There was a bond between them, yes, but Tony clearly had no idea how strong it was, or how deep it went with her. And that was the way it must always stay.

She turned towards the sink and began to run hot water onto the used coffee cups. Thank God he would soon be going out of her life permanently. It would be less painful that way.

As Shirley's course of lessons with Magda progressed, a strong relationship developed between them. Magda often made tea for Shirley when she arrived hot and out of breath after a long day in the shop. She was watching a very promising talent develop before her eyes month by month and it buoyed up her spirits and excited her. When they were talking together over the teacups, she soon recognised the trap the girl had fallen into at home and sympathised with her predicament. In her turn she told Shirley of her own disappointment. She had been at the height of a promising career when the war began. Joining

329

ENSA, she had gone abroad with a repertory company. On the voyage back from Egypt, the ship on which they were travelling was torpedoed. Magda lost a lung and several ribs and was adrift in a boat for days. Her injuries meant the end of her stage career.

'I tire too easily,' she told Shirley. 'And my voice gives out after about an hour's work.' She smiled. 'But I can still teach, and students like you, my dear, make all the heartache and disappointment worth while. I see a great future for you if you continue to work hard.'

Shirley meant to work hard. She had begun to memorise speeches from Shakespeare now, and this evening she could hardly wait to perform Juliet's poison speech, which she had worked hard all weekend to perfect.

'"Farewell, God knows when we shall meet again . . .",She lost herself in enacting the scene. Magda watched, seeing herself as a very young girl, aching for the hope and innocent naivety she saw in front of her. When Shirley had finished and seated herself again at the desk, she asked:

'Do you have a boyfriend, Shirley?'

'There is someone, yes.'

'Have you know him long?'

'About a year and a half, I suppose.'

'And do you love him?'

Shirley was taken aback. What was Magda getting at? What did boyfriends have to do with anything? She'd been hoping to hear what she thought of her performance. 'Well – not really,' she said. 'I'm too interested in acting. Too busy to be bothered with stuff like that.'

'You mustn't shut out life, though. Acting is all about living. You mustn't forget that. Your technique is coming along very well,' Magda said. 'But to play the great dramatic roles you need emotional experience. Juliet was deeply in love. To play her you need to know that anguish, to feel the longing and the pain as well as the joy of being loved in return. You haven't really lived until you've been truly in love.' Magda put her hand against her breast and closed her eyes.

Privately Shirley thought it was nonsense. After all, what was acting if not pretending? 'Oh, so if I wanted to play a murderess, would you expect me to go out and kill someone?' she asked dryly.

Magda opened her eyes and stared at Shirley for a moment. 'Don't be facetious, Shirley,' she said sharply. 'Don't belittle the finer emotions. They are the grist to the actor's mill. You're such a pragmatic child. Learn a little softness. Learn how to weep – how to feel your own sorrow. A good actress must be a little selfish in order to live, but she must also sacrifice and suffer in order to give pleasure. In other words, darling, you need to experience life – to *live*.' She looked at Shirley's crestfallen face and leaned forward. 'Don't look so downcast. Living is something we can't escape. It happens to us all. It will come.'

'I suppose so,' Shirley said glumly.

'Listen, dear, there is something I want to talk to you about,' Magda said. 'The London Academy of Music and Dramatic Art hold examinations three times a year. The next date will be in November. I would like to enter your name. If you pass the exam you will be awarded a bronze medal. You could then go on to take a silver and a gold. Are you interested?'

Shirley's eyes shone. 'Oh yes, please. What would I have to do?'

'You would perform two set pieces in full stage make-up, but without costume or props. You would also be required to read a piece from sight. You would be marked on things like stage presence, business, voice production and stage make-up.' She opened a drawer and drew out a leaflet. 'I already have the syllabus, so if you are agreeable I could obtain the scripts and we could begin preparing next week.'

Dave found Shirley quiet as they walked home together that evening. Her mind was full of the bronze-medal exam and the other things Magda had said. She meant to pass that exam, and pass it well.

'Penny for them?' Dave said, bending to look into her eyes. 'You're miles away tonight. Lesson go well, did it?'

'Oh, yes.' Shirley linked her arm through his and hugged it. 'Miss Jayne is entering me for an exam in the autumn. I'll have an awful lot of hard work to do. It's for a bronze medal.' She looked up at him. 'Dave, how would you like to go to the theatre – Up West?'

Dave looked nonplussed. 'I don't know. I've never been to the theatre. What would it cost?'

'Nothing. Gloria – my mum – is dresser to Leonie Swann, the actress. She's in a play at the Lyric. She'd get seats for us if you'd like to go. What do you say?'

Dave looked unsure. 'You want to go, don't you?'

'Oh, I'd love to, Dave.' She gave his arm a squeeze and smiled up at him. 'So will you come with me?'

His heart twisted inside him as he looked down into those wide blue eyes. It was impossible to refuse her anything when she looked at him like that. He drew her into the shadow of a doorway and kissed her. 'Okay then, of course I'll go if it'll make you happy,' he said, hugging her tightly to him.

Shirley snuggled against him. Dave really was nice and being kissed and cuddled by him made her feel all relaxed and safe. Perhaps it *was* love she felt for him, though she couldn't help feeling that there should be something more – something magical and exciting. If only all this emotional experience – this *living* that Magda talked about – could be hurried up a bit.

That night Shirley wrote to her mother. She didn't give away Ma's secret but said the letters must have gone astray. She told Gloria about her drama lessons and the coming exam. She wrote a few snippets of news about the shop, Ma and Dave too. She ended by telling her how much she had missed her and said that she and Dave would love to accept the tickets to see Leonie in *Joy in the Morning*, possibly going backstage afterwards.

When she had finished the letter and sealed it into its envelope she sat on the bed for a long time, her eyes misty and far away. She'd dreaded her third winter at Angel Row; the finger-and-toe-numbing cold in the shop day after day and the draughty little house with all its uncomfortable inconveniences, but now that she had something to look forward to it hardly seemed to matter. Soon she would escape to a wonderful new life, to success and fame and a dream come true. It was all going to happen for her. She could feel it opening like a beautiful flower inside her. All she had to do was to work hard and wait.

Chapter Fifteen

When Tony had come to the flat to discuss divorce with Leonie, it had shaken her. She had never seen him so positive and determined. He clearly meant business. And as far as she knew there was no other serious love in his life. He had even talked of selling Longueville Hall. Not that she minded that; she was tired of the place anyway. It held too many unwelcome memories. Now that the war was over and she had made her name in the legitimate theatre; now that she had met Paul, her life had changed totally. Why cling to a past that was dead? Tony and she had fallen out of love long ago. Attitudes were changing too. It was no longer a ruinous scandal to be divorced, even for people in the public eye. Too many marriages, entered into impulsively during the war, had failed to withstand the changes that peace had brought.

Yet to Leonie divorce still smacked of failure, especially when neither partner wished to remarry. In a way it was burning one's bridges. She'd stalled Tony that morning at the flat, telling him she would think about it and let him know. She had continued to stall him ever since, but to keep him quiet she'd agreed to let him go ahead and put Longueville Hall on the market. Even Imogen hardly ever went there any more. When she wasn't working hard at RADA she was having fun with the young man she had taken up with. The place was simply sitting there eating money. It made sense to let it go.

Tony had mentioned the Jarvises, asking if she could perhaps offer them employment at the flat. She had rejected that idea out of hand, suspecting him of planning to get them to spy for him – report back all that she was doing with a view to divorcing her on grounds of adultery if all else failed. If she allowed that, she would no longer be a free woman in her own home. Tony knew about Paul, of course, but as yet he had no proof that they were sleeping together. If she was going to agree to a divorce it would be on her terms. She would not be forced into it and neither did she wish to see her private life sordidly reported in the gutter press. Her future as a straight actress was still tenuous. If they were going to do it, it must be done quietly and discreetly.

Her relationship with Paul kept her on her toes, the adrenalin flowing. It was exciting in its sheer unpredictability. He was moody – light-hearted and devil-may-care one day, gloomy and irritable the next. Negotiations were taking place on the sale of film rights of *Joy in the Morning* and he was writing a new play with her in mind for the leading part, but so far he had refused to let her read any of it. When he was working he was taciturn to the point of rudeness. He would shut himself away for days at a time, then turn up in the small hours of the morning elated and amorous, sweeping her off her feet, flatteringly eager to make love. Leonie had long since given up trying to understand him but his mercurial personality thrilled and excited her, and she was convinced that his brilliant talent was going to take her to worldwide stardom. Although she would not admit it, she stood in awe of his superior intellect and feared the quick, explosive temper that even surpassed her own.

On the Saturday night that Shirley was due to come backstage, Leonie was at her best. The show had gone well. The audience had been especially receptive and appreciative and she had responded as she always did, with a deeply emotional performance which, instead of draining her, left her almost incandescent.

As she came down from the stage after the last tumultuous curtain call, Gloria was ready with fresh hot coffee, hot water and a change of clothes. When Leonie burst into the dressing room she was breathless, her eyes shining with elation.

'Did you *hear* them, Gloria? I don't think I've ever had such a rapturous audience, even before the war on the night *Sunshine Sally* opened. Five calls, we took, and even then they were still calling for another.' She threw herself into a chair and kicked off her shoes. 'Oh, I *wish* Paul could have been here to hear it. It was for him as much as for me.' She stood up, turning to let Gloria unzip her dress. 'Did I tell you he's gone down to Cornwall to look at locations for the film?'

'Film – of this play?' Gloria asked, helping Leonie on with her wrapper.

'Yes. Isn't it exciting? The cinema is where the real stars are made. One can reach a much wider audience. It's all still very hush-hush so of course we mustn't say too much yet, but it's been confirmed that the Rank Organisation has bought the film rights of *Joy in the Morning* and with luck filming should begin early next year.' She sat down at the dressing table and began creaming off her make-up. 'I wish Paul would let me read the new play. It sounds even better than *Joy*.' She glanced up at the clock. 'Oh – I've just remembered. Shirley was in front this evening, wasn't she? What time do you expect her round?'

Gloria was examining Leonie's costumes for damage and loose buttons before putting them away on hangers. 'I told them to give us half an hour.'

'Oh, good. It'll be so lovely to see darling Shirley again. She and I always got along so well. You have a very talented little daughter, Gloria. I hope you realise it.'

'Oh, I do. And she's not so little any longer.'

'I can't wait to see how she's grown up. It must be almost two years since I saw her last.'

'I believe it is.' Gloria poured hot water into the washbasin and drew the screen around it for Leonie to wash. Continuing to tidy up the dressing room, she listened to Leonie's continuous chatter mingled with splashing from behind the screen. 'It's such a pity she couldn't have gone to RADA with Imogen. Those two were so inseparable – more like sisters than friends. I suppose your mother couldn't find someone else to help her in the wretched shop, could she? Old people can be so selfish?'

'It isn't just Ma,' Gloria said. 'I couldn't afford to send her now.'

Leonie emerged from behind the screen and sat down at the dressing table again. 'I'd have thought you could have managed it. You don't spend your money on anything else, do you?'

You don't give me the time to, Gloria wanted to say. 'I – have the cottage to maintain,' she said instead, turning away.

'*That* place? I don't know why you don't sell it and let Shirley have the benefit of the money.' Leonie applied her lipstick and ran a brush through her hair, then she stood up and held out her arms for the dress Gloria held ready for her. 'Making a talented child like Shirley miss her opportunities for the sake of a run-down greengrocer's shop in the East End is just plain *criminal* if you ask me. You should speak to your mother – put your foot down.'

Gloria bit hard on the retort she wanted to make. Nobody *was* asking Leonie. It was none of her business. It was all very well for her to talk. She hadn't any idea what it was like to be hard up. If she only knew . . .

At that moment there was a hesitant tap on the door and Gloria opened it to find Shirley standing outside, a reluctant Dave hovering in the background. Shirley wore a suit of soft violet wool. She had saved hard for it, keeping an eye on the shop window for weeks and praying that no one else would get there before her. It was cut in the new Dior style they were calling the New Look. The skirt was calf-length and flared and the jacket had a tiny nipped-in waist and flaring peplum which enhanced the gentle curve of her hips. A tiny stand-up collar framed her face. Her hair was brushed into a shining halo of auburn curls and her only make-up was a hint of pink lipstick. Dave stood behind her, looking acutely uncomfortable in his best blue suit. His face shone with recent shaving and his newly cropped hair was severely disciplined with hair cream.

'Come in, both of you.' Gloria held the door wide.

Shirley said: 'Thanks. This is Dave, Gloria.'

'How do you do, Dave.' Gloria held out her hand. 'I hope you enjoyed the show.'

'Oh yes, Mrs – er, Rayner.'

'It was *wonderful*,' Shirley cut in excitedly. 'Leonie was just terrific. She got *ever* so many curtain calls.'

'I'm so glad you liked it.' Leonie appeared, smiling, from behind the door and threw out her arms theatrically to Shirley. '*Darling* – it's been so *long*.' She kissed Shirley on both cheeks and then held her at arm's length to look at her. 'My goodness, how you've grown up! You were always pretty but you're positively *beautiful* now. Come along in and tell me all about those drama lessons you've been taking. What did Gloria say that actress's name is? Is it anyone I know, I wonder?' Her arm around Shirley's waist, she drew her into the room, leaving Dave standing awkwardly by the door. Gloria smiled at him.

'Would you like a cup of coffee? Take no notice of those two. Shirley was evacuated to Leonie's house when she was nine, so they're old friends.'

'Yes, I've heard all about it,' Dave said. He nodded towards the coffee, laid out on a tray. 'A cup of coffee would be very nice, thanks.'

Leonie listened with rapt attention to Shirley's news, giving every appearance of sharing in her excitement as she bubbled over with the news about the bronze-medal exam she was to take in November.

'So you're not too disappointed about RADA then?'

'Not so much now that I'm at Stage Coach,' Shirley told her. 'I still see Imo. And we have so much more to talk about when we meet.'

On the other side of the room Gloria tried her best to entertain a tongue-tied Dave, who was clearly wishing himself a hundred miles away from this alien environment. Talking to him, Gloria discovered that she had been at school with his oldest sister, Ida, sadly killed in the

Blitz. She knew other members of his family too, but she didn't like to engage him in conversation about his family in case it was painful.

They had been talking for about twenty minutes when the door opened and Paul Winspear walked in. Leonie gave a cry of delight and leaped up from her chair.

'*Paul*, darling! You're back. I wasn't expecting you till tomorrow.' She kissed him so extravagantly that Dave flushed with embarrassment and turned his head away. 'Oh, I *wish* you'd been in front tonight. It was quite the best reception we've had since the beginning of the run.' Remembering her guests, she turned. 'Darling, I'd like you to meet Shirley Rayner. She's Gloria's daughter and she grew up with Imogen at Houlton all through the war. She's planning to be an actress. The young man is her friend, er, Geoff.'

'Hello, Geoff.' Paul nodded briefly towards a blushing Dave, who opened his mouth to correct the mistake and then closed it again as Paul turned his attention to Shirley, who had stepped forward, mesmerised by this tall, striking man. Paul was much better-looking in the flesh than in the photographs Imogen had shown her outside the theatre. The camera could not capture the mysterious light in his dark eyes or the sheer dynamism that emanated from him. She held out her hand and smiled up at him shyly.

'I enjoyed your play very much, Mr Winspear.'

Paul took the hand she offered and looked into the violet-blue eyes. 'Why haven't I met this enchanting creature before?' His words were addressed to Leonie but his eyes never left Shirley's face. 'I thought you said she was a child?'

Leonie gave an uncertain little laugh, noticing for the first time the firm curves of Shirley's figure and her long, shapely legs. 'She *is*. What are you now, darling – fifteen?'

'Seventeen,' Shirley corrected.

Paul smiled. 'So you're Gloria's daughter? How extraordinary. Tell me what you liked about the play.' His hand still held hers and Shirley was sharply aware of its pulsing warmth. Her own hand tingled as though she were

339

being charged with a force – a magical energy that made her feel alive and excited. As she began to tell him what she had enjoyed in the play, the words seemed to come so easily that she surprised herself. It was almost like listening to someone else talking. All that Magda had taught her about the appreciation of drama seemed suddenly to gel and take form.

Paul's eyes widened. 'You're very perceptive. Where are you studying – at RADA?'

Shirley shook her head. 'I'm taking private tuition with an actress called Magda Jane. She has a studio in Stepney. It's called Stage Coach. I'm taking the London Academy's bronze-medal exam in November.'

His lips twitched with amusement. 'Well, you certainly seem to have learned a lot. Stepney – is that where you live?'

'No, I live in Whitechapel. I help my grandmother run her shop.'

'Whitechapel, eh? And not a hint of an accent. Ten out of ten to Miss Jayne, whoever she is.'

Shirley withdrew her hand – the heady spark of confidence he had ignited in her suddenly gone. Was he laughing at her? She looked at Leonie. 'I, er, think we'd better go now. Thank you for the tickets and the coffee. We've enjoyed it so much.'

Leonie, who had been watching with mounting fury, switched on her smile again. 'Not at all, angel. You must come and see me again some time.'

Gloria escorted Shirley and Dave through the maze of backstage corridors. 'Maybe we could meet some time, Shirl,' she said as they reached the stage door.

'Our hours clash, though, don't they?' Shirley said. 'There's only Sundays and Imogen says you go to Boothley at weekends.'

'That's right,' Gloria said unhappily.

Shirley looked pointedly at her mother, waiting for her to suggest a weekend together at Rook Cottage. When she didn't, she said shortly: 'Well, obviously your weekends are all booked up. If you get an evening off some time, just drop me a line. Thanks for arranging this evening for us. Good night, Gloria.'

'Good night, love. Please keep in touch, won't you – and give my love to Ma.'

'I will. Come on, Dave.'

Gloria caught Shirley's arm and drew her back to kiss her cheek. 'Take care, darling. God bless.' Shirley held herself stiffly and Gloria felt her aloofness like a barrier between them. She smiled at Dave. 'It was nice to meet you. Good night.'

''Night, Mrs, er, Rayner. And, er, thanks.'

In the dressing room Leonie glared at Paul. 'Did you *have* to look and speak to the child like that? It's very unkind to pretend to be interested in a girl as young and impressionable as Shirley.'

'Unkind? To whom?' He laughed and sank languidly into an armchair. 'And you can take it from me, that was no child, my dear. The delicious Shirley may not be fully aware of it yet, but she's a highly sensuous young person. And very definitely *all* woman.'

Leonie's heart began to beat faster as she felt the anger swell to almost uncontrollable passion in her breast. 'You were practically *undressing* her with your eyes,' she said, her eyes flashing. 'Hanging on to her hand, looking at her as though you were about to *eat* her. Honestly, Paul, it was so obvious. So – so *blatant*. Right under her mother's nose, too.'

He looked up at her, one eyebrow raised cynically. 'Oh, I see, it's Gloria you're worried about, is it?'

'Well, she *is* an employee of mine. Naturally I don't want to see her offended.'

'I'd no idea you were so solicitous.' Paul stood up, his dark eyes dangerously bright. 'In that case we'd better be a little more discreet in future, hadn't we? Perhaps I shouldn't come to the flat quite so often – certainly not to stay the night. We mustn't upset your dresser's high moral standards, must we?'

Leonie looked at him sharply, a prickle of fear stirring in the pit of her stomach. 'You know I didn't mean that.'

341

'Then just what *did* you mean?' His voice was hard. 'I hope you're not the jealous type, Leonie. If there's one thing I can't stand it's a possessive woman.' He stared at her. 'I believe that's one of the most tiresome things I can think of, Leonie; not to say boring. You're not jealous, are you?' He took a step towards her.

'No – no, of course I'm not. I've never been jealous in my life.' Her heart quickened. She hated it when he looked at her like that. She backed away from him till her back was pressing hard against the wall, flinching slightly as his hands descended heavily onto her shoulders. He bent swiftly and kissed her hard, bruising her mouth and biting her lips painfully.

'Good. I've always felt that you and I are kindred spirits, Leonie,' he said softly as he unbuttoned her dress. 'And that means each of us recognising that the other must be free. If I look at another beautiful woman it doesn't mean I want you any the less.' His hand was inside her bra, the long sensuous fingers caressing her breast. 'And you are completely free to do the same.' As he pressed his body against her she felt the familiar churning in her stomach, the weakness that buckled her knees.

'You know – I'll never want – any man but you, Paul,' she whispered.

He bent and swept her up into his arms, but she shook her head wildly.

'No – not here – not now,' she murmured breathlessly. 'Gloria will be back any minute.'

He paused, then let her go abruptly. 'Just as you please,' he said coldly. 'I made a special effort to come back early to be with you this evening, Leonie. I was actually looking forward to seeing you and telling you all about the film locations I've chosen. I thought we might spend the weekend together, but you don't seem to be in the mood for anything but picking a quarrel.'

'Oh no, that's not true. I hate quarrelling with you, Paul. It makes me miserable.' She caught at his hand as he turned away. 'A weekend together would be lovely. Don't be cross, darling. I've missed you so much.'

'You've missed me and yet you can push me away when I want you. That's not exactly the action of a woman burning with desire, is it?'

'I'm not pushing, it's just . . .' Biting her lip, she went to the door and turned the key in the lock. 'There – just in case,' she whispered as she went into his arms.

As Gloria walked down the corridor a few minutes later, she heard smothered sounds coming from the dressing room. Trying the door gently she found that it was locked. Standing outside for a moment or two, she listened to Leonie's muffled cries and knew what was happening. She'd been awakened by the same cries during the small hours sometimes on the nights that Paul stayed over and she knew that they were not born of ecstasy. As Leonie's dresser she could not help seeing the bruises Paul had inflicted on her body. Clearly he was a brutal lover and equally clearly Leonie needed and wanted him – and what he could do for her career – so much that she was prepared to put up with his sadistic tendencies. She sighed and shook her head. Maybe Leonie had taken on more than she could handle this time, she told herself.

All the way home Shirley's head was in the clouds, her mind on the play. She was busy committing to memory every detail of Leonie's dressing room; storing it all up to fantasise over later when she was alone. One day she would be in her place, she told herself. *She* would be on the stage, receiving all that applause and adulation; *she* relaxing and receiving guests afterwards in her luxurious dressing room. When Gloria had opened the stage door for them, a little group of autograph hunters had stepped forward eagerly, hoping for the emergence of one of the stars. They'd fallen back, disappointed, when she and Dave stepped out. But one day they would greet her with hopeful, adoring eyes, she promised herself.

She thought about Paul, too. No man had ever looked at her like that before, or held her hand in that special, meaningful way. He was Leonie's new man, she had gathered that much from Imogen, though she didn't seem entirely happy about the situation. The way he had looked at Shirley made her tingle all over. Did he really love Leonie? Surely a man in love did not look at other women like that? But she was learning fast that you never really knew with men. There were the nice, safe, dull ones, like Dave, who never put a foot wrong; and the dangerous, exciting ones like Paul who broke all the rules and got away with it. Yet with either there was always the possibility of the unexpected.

When they reached Angel Row she relaxed in Dave's arms and tried to enjoy his kisses, but deep in the secret recesses of her mind the image of Paul Winspear still lurked. She found it impossible not to wonder what it would be like to be kissed by him. With a little frisson of excitement, she guessed that his kiss would be like a powerful drug: once taken, she would be hopelessly addicted. Just one date with him would be an experience. It would provide some of that *living* that Magda was always talking about. She smiled wryly to herself, guessing that just one date with Paul would not be enough. It would provide a one-way ticket to heartache, but there was little need for her to worry. The chances of Paul Winspear asking her out were about as remote as her landing the lead in a West End play.

Neither of Imogen's parents had mentioned to her that Longueville Hall was going to be sold. It was only when she decided on the spur of the moment to go to Houlton for a weekend visit that she discovered the fact.

'But why didn't anyone tell me?' she asked Molly. 'Don't I have a say in *anything* any more? First they plan to divorce, now they're selling my home, and all without a single word to me about it.'

Molly smiled. 'I'm sure they meant to,' she said awkwardly. 'I dare say each of them thought the other had said something to you. Anyway, I doubt if it'll sell quickly. People don't want places the size of this nowadays.' Inwardly she ached for the girl. Her childhood had been insecure through her parents' constant quarrelling, and now that she'd left school to study they seemed to think that she was a completely independent adult with a life of her own – that they no longer needed to be responsible for her welfare. Molly knew different. Inside Imogen craved love and security as much as ever, and once Longueville Hall had gone, once she and Jim were no longer here to provide a safe haven for the girl, where would she go? Who would provide the stability she needed so desperately?

'Never mind. You'll always be welcome in our home, dear,' she said soothingly. 'And this place really is a waste of your parents' money nowadays. It's far too big and neither of them ever comes to stay any more.'

'But I love it so. All the memories. We had such fun here during the war, you and Jim and Shirley and me. Where will you and Jim go?'

'Don't you worry about us, my pet. We're not as young as we used to be and we're quite happy to retire. Your daddy has been very generous and we've saved a bit over the years. We've decided to buy a little house in the village. It's all settled. We were lucky to find it, what with the housing shortage and everything.'

Imogen bit her lip as a thought occurred to her. 'Gloria still has her cottage over at Boothley, Nanny. Do you ever run into her?'

Molly shook her head. 'No, dear, why?'

'She comes up most weekends, according to Mummy, but she never brings Shirley. I think she's planning to get a grant, modernise the cottage and sell it.'

'She hasn't been to see us,' Molly said noncommittally.

'Nothing's the same since the war ended,' Imogen said gloomily. 'People don't seem to care about each other as they used to. I thought it would all be so marvellous when it was over, but look at us. We've still got food rationing, coal and petrol shortages; houses and flats are almost impossible to find.' Her face brightened. 'I think I'll bike over and see if Gloria's at home. It's ages since we had a good natter. Maybe she can talk Mummy out of selling. I certainly mean to nag Daddy into changing his mind.'

The Jarvises exchanged glances. They'd heard the many rumours that had circulated about Gloria and the child, cared for at Rook Cottage, but neither of them had the heart to mention it to Imogen. Jim fetched her old bicycle from the stables and dusted it off, giving the chain a spot of oil and checking the brakes before he pronounced it fit to ride. Then they watched, feeling guilty at their inability to help her, as she cycled hopefully off down the drive.

Rook Cottage looked the same as the last time she had seen it. The tiny front garden appeared a little neglected, full of fallen leaves from the tall elms in the churchyard close by, but that wasn't surprising with Gloria only there at weekends. As she walked up the front path, Imogen wondered how she coped with the inconveniences of the place after the luxury of the Mayfair flat where she lived all week. No indoor sanitation and no electricity or water must come as a hardship in this day and age especially in winter. She knocked on the door and waited.

When Gloria opened the door she looked startled to see Imogen standing in the porch. The colour drained from her cheeks and her eyes widened in shocked surprise.

'Imogen! What are you doing here?'

'I'm over for a weekend at Houlton. I thought it would be nice to bike over and see you.'

'Oh.' Gloria peered out into the lane as though she were afraid someone might be watching. 'Well, you'd better come in then, I suppose.'

Imogen shook her head. 'If I've come at an inconvenient time it's all right. I should have let you know, only there wasn't time and you're not on the telephone.'

Gloria bit her lip. 'I'm sorry, Imogen. I didn't mean to sound rude. It's lovely to see you. Was there something you wanted – something special, I mean?'

'Well, yes. I wanted to talk to you about my parents selling Longueville Hall. Did you know about it?'

'I had heard, yes.'

At that moment the gate creaked and Imogen turned to see a young woman wheeling a pushchair up the path. 'Oh, you've got a visitor. I'll go.'

The young woman unstrapped a fair-haired toddler from the pushchair and carried him into the house past Gloria. Imogen stepped sideways to let her pass. 'Well, I'll go . . .'

'No. Come in.' Gloria held the door open. 'Now that you're here, we might as well have that talk.' She turned to the woman with the child. 'Take Michael through and give him his milk, will you, Margaret?'

The little parlour was chilly and Gloria apologised as she indicated a chair. 'Do sit down. I'm sorry if it's a bit cold but we don't light the fire in here till the afternoon.' She looked at Imogen. 'I'd be obliged if you'd keep this visit to yourself, Imogen – as far as your parents are concerned, I mean.'

Imogen nodded uncomfortably. 'Of course. Perhaps I . . . shouldn't have come. If . . .'

'You'll have gathered that Michael is my child,' Gloria went on.

'Look, you don't have to tell me –'

'No. It's time I told someone,' Gloria said. 'I can't keep it to myself for ever.' She looked at Imogen. 'I'm not asking you to keep it a secret. That wouldn't be fair.'

'I won't tell anyone anyway,' Imogen said. 'Why should I?'

But Gloria seemed not to have heard. 'I discovered I was expecting when I was in America,' she said. 'It was a terrible shock. I came home sooner than I should have done because of it. On the plane I got talking to a woman who told me she'd been to America for special treatment at a clinic. She told me it was her last chance of having a baby. She'd been married ten years and tried everything. The American doctors had told her the treatment wouldn't work in her case and she was terribly depressed. I told her that I was pregnant but couldn't keep the child.' She looked at Imogen. 'You'll have guessed the rest.'

'She offered to adopt the baby?'

'Yes. It seemed like a wonderful stroke of luck, meeting her. They were obviously well off and they'd have done anything to get a child of their own. You can imagine how relieved I was. Well, she and her husband lived in Yorkshire and by the time we landed in England it was arranged that I would go straight there and live with them until the baby was born.'

'So what happened?' Imogen asked.

Gloria paused. 'It was a difficult birth – six weeks premature. Then, when he was born, Michael almost died. He had to stay in the hospital and while he was there they did tests. They found that he had something wrong with his heart.'

'Oh, Gloria, how awful! I'm so sorry.'

'The adoption fell through, of course. The Hensons wanted a perfect child and who could blame them? I couldn't abandon my little son when he was sick and needed me. I'd loved him from the moment he was born, anyway. So . . .'

'You brought him back here?'

'I was lucky. I met Margaret in hospital. Her husband was killed right at the end of the war and she'd lost the baby she was expecting, too. She's got no family of her own and she badly needed a fresh start and someone to love. I offered her a home and a job looking after Michael here.' She looked around her. 'It's not much of a home, but we keep it as warm and cosy as we can and I've put in for a grant to make it better – put in proper plumbing and everything.'

'And what about Michael – is he getting better? Can he be cured?'

'There's an operation for his problem now, thank God. And he can have it under this new National Health Scheme,' Gloria explained. 'It's to widen a valve in his heart that isn't working properly. He's not too bad now while he's so little. He was late walking and he's small for his age. But when he gets more active the problems will start. He mustn't exert himself or get overtired, you see. He needs constant attention.'

Imogen was silent. At the back of her mind something was nagging. 'But surely,' she began, 'surely if Billy's family had known you were carrying their grand-child . . .' She stopped. Billy had left the US Air Force base at Boothley almost a year before the end of the war. Michael couldn't possibly be his child. She smiled apologetically at Gloria. 'I'm sorry.'

Gloria nodded. 'Now you see why I didn't want to tell anyone,' she said. 'As you know, I never married Shirley's father. Ma would have gone mad if she'd known I'd made the same mistake again. She was so good to me. How could I land her with the same problem again, especially with Pa so ill?'

'Shirley really misses you. You used to be so close. She'd understand if she only knew. Couldn't you tell her?' Imogen asked.

Gloria shook her head. 'I can't, not yet anyway. She'd be bound to tell Ma.' She smiled wryly. 'I can imagine some of the things Ma says about me. Shirl wouldn't be able to stop herself from blurting it out. I know her. I can't provide Shirl with a home under the circumstances. In our separate ways we both rely on Ma. Better to leave things as they are, at least for the time being.'

Imogen was silent, remembering the harsh, uncom-promising things old Mrs Rayner had said to her daughter on the day of her husband's funeral, imagining how deeply they must have hurt. 'So you let them go on thinking the worst of you? Let them believe that you're selfishly thinking only of yourself, when all the time . . . ?' Imogen shook her head. 'Gloria, maybe I shouldn't ask but – couldn't the baby's father . . . ?'

'That's out of the question,' Gloria said firmly. 'He must never know.'

Imogen was silenced by Gloria's firm tone. Clearly, for reasons best known to herself, she was determined not to pursue that course. She considered for a moment, then her face brightened. 'Why don't you tell Mummy? I'm sure she'd help. She'd give you a rise in wages for a start. I know she seems thoughtless sometimes but –'

'*No.*' The word was so positive that it stopped Imogen in mid-sentence. 'This is *my* problem, Imogen. It's nobody's fault but mine. I got myself into it and it's up to me and no one else to sort it out. I don't need help, advice or handouts from anyone.'

'I'm sorry. I wasn't trying to interfere. I shan't tell anyone, Gloria,' Imogen said, chastened by Gloria's firm determination.

'As I said, I'm not swearing you to secrecy. I'm not ashamed of having Michael, and eventually everyone will know. But as things are, it's better this way for the time being.' She smiled. 'Thanks for trying to help just the same, love. I appreciate your concern.' She moved to a chair and sat down, an indication that the subject was closed. 'Now – you came here to talk to me about the sale of Longueville Hall.'

Imogen shrugged. 'My problem seems trivial compared to yours. I just thought you might try to persuade Mummy not to sell. I love the place so much. It's the only real home I've ever had. Shirley and I were so happy there. I hate the thought of it belonging to someone else.'

Gloria nodded thoughtfully. 'Change always is painful.' She looked around her at the simple little room. 'This place is full of memories for me. I bought it so I could have Shirl to live with me. If she hadn't been so happy with you at Longueville Hall my life would have taken a completely different turn.' She pulled her thoughts back to the present and Imogen's problem. 'What will Molly and Jim do when the house is sold?'

'They seem to be quite looking forward to their retirement. They've even found a little house for sale in the village.'

Gloria smiled. 'See? You won't have to stop coming to Houlton just because your parents don't own a house here. If I know Molly she'll always keep a bed ready for you.'

Imogen nodded. 'Sometimes Molly and Jim feel more like family than Mummy and Daddy,' she said wistfully. 'Before I go, can I see Michael?'

Gloria looked pleased. 'Would you really like to? Wait there a minute and I'll fetch him.'

She left the room to reappear a moment later carrying the little boy. Imogen thought him the prettiest baby she had ever seen. He was a lot like Shirley, with the same wide blue eyes and softly curling red-gold hair. She reached out her arms to him.

'Hello, Michael. Are you going to let me hold you?'

He regarded her for a moment, then smiled and held out his arms. She took him from Gloria and he put his arms around her neck and pressed his little face against hers.

Gloria smiled. 'He likes you. He's quite shy usually. He doesn't see many people.'

Imogen was enchanted. 'Oh, Gloria, he's a darling. I'd like to take him home with me.'

'You'd soon bring him back.' Gloria laughed. 'He's not so enchanting when he wakes up at three in the morning.'

'I wouldn't mind. I've always wanted babies.' Imogen hugged the little boy. 'Can you talk yet, Michael?' She looked into the baby's face. 'Can you say Imo-gen?'

Michael watched her mouth, concentrating on its movements, but he didn't attempt the name for himself.

'He's a proper little parrot. I bet he'll say it as soon as you've gone.' Gloria took the child back. 'Come and see me again when you're in Houlton, won't you, Imogen? It was good to see you – and talk.'

'Yes, it was,' Imogen said. 'But I wish you'd talk to Shirley. I know she'd love her little brother. It seems so sad that she doesn't even know about him.'

'Believe me, it's better this way for the time being,' Gloria said.

'Molly was wondering why you hadn't been over to visit her and Jim,' Imogen said. 'What shall I tell her?'

'Tell her I'm busy keeping the cottage aired. I only have Sundays off from work. There really isn't time for visiting. All that's the truth, as you know.' She smiled ruefully. 'Believe me, Imogen. There's nothing I'd like better than to see Molly, and I will eventually. One day soon I'll make it all up to everyone. I just have to get Michael sorted out first. You do understand, love, don't you?'

Imogen understood but she felt uneasy that she was the only member of their circle to have stumbled on Gloria's secret. Her main concern was Shirley. They had never had secrets between them before and now she found herself unwittingly in possession of this intimate piece of family knowledge that Shirley had far more right to know about than she.

Shirley put the finishing touches to her make-up and closed the box with its sticks of Leichner greasepaint. Over the past weeks she'd been collecting them one by one. Numbers five and nine, white number twenty for highlighting, carmine for her cheeks, lake and brown liners and the little pots of blue and green eye shadows. Powder and cotton wool, orange sticks and a big pot of removing cream completed the kit, all stowed away in an old cigar box of Pa's she had found. Now she was ready and she sat nervously awaiting her turn in the back room of the church hall where the exams were being held, taking deep measured breaths just as Magda had taught her to control the thudding of her heart. She had come here on the bus, alone. It was a Friday afternoon and Dave was standing in for her at the shop. Ma hadn't said much, but her tight-lipped expression made it more than adequately clear what she thought of the whole thing.

The door opened and the previous student lurched in, leaning against the wall and blowing out her cheeks in exaggerated relief at getting the ordeal over.

'What was it like?' Shirley asked.

The girl pulled a face. 'Terrible. I forgot my lines and had to be prompted twice. Then I rubbed my eye and smudged all my make-up.' She peered at herself in the mirror. 'God almighty! Just look at me. I look like something the cat dragged in.'

'But did you pass?'

The girl gave her a rueful glance. 'What do you think? Anyway, I don't know what *you're* getting worked up about. You look smashing and I bet you're ten times better than me anyway. Look at the pathetic marks I got.' She held out her card, but before Shirley had had time to look at it properly a woman opened the door and called her name.

'Shirley Rayner. Will you come this way, please?'

The stage had been fitted with proper stage lighting and Shirley looked out, shielding her eyes from the glare of the footlights to where the examiner sat at a table halfway down the hall.

'You may begin.' The voice reached her clearly and she hurried to her position, took a deep breath to steady her voice and began the first piece.

Once she had begun she lost herself in the acting, enjoying herself thoroughly and quite forgetting that she was being examined. At the conclusion of the second piece she read the passage from a script the examiner handed to her. It presented no difficulties to her and she read it smoothly and with as much expression as she could. When she had finished there was a pause as the examiner continued to write. Shirley held her breath. After a moment he said, without looking up at her:

'Thank you. Will you come down here, please?'

He was still writing when she reached him. She waited, then he put down his pen and looked up at her with a smile.

'Well, Miss Rayner, you have given me a very nice performance. You have a good presence, and your acting has both spirit and sincerity.' He handed her the card. 'You can read my remarks at your leisure, but I can tell you now that I have passed you with honours and I hope I'll be here to give you an equally good silver medal next year.'

In a euphoric haze Shirley thanked him and walked from the hall. She felt oddly unreal, as though she floated, her feet hardly touching the ground. She was on her way. Someone who *counted* had actually said she was good. It had to be the happiest moment of her life.

In the dressing room the other girl waited. Her face was now cleaned of the smudged make-up and she had her coat on, ready to leave. She looked inquiringly at Shirley.

'Well?'

'I . . . I passed – with honours.'

'*There*. What did I tell you?' the girl said without a hint of envy. 'I knew you would, just looking at you. I've never been any good at this, perhaps they'll let me stop trying now. But you – you're a born actress if ever I saw one.'

Outside the dull, cold November day seemed to melt into spring. Shirley danced rather than walked along the pavement. She felt that everyone was looking at her – as though she were taking the star part in a film. Surely nothing could ever make her feel so happy?

Suddenly she was aware of a car horn hooting persistently behind her and she turned to see Imogen, hanging out of the window of a red sports car.

'Hey, Shirley! Hang on. We've come to pick you up.' Imogen laughed up into her face. 'No need to ask you how it went. Your expression is enough.' She jumped out of the car and hugged Shirley warmly. 'You passed?'

'Yes. With honours.'

Suddenly they were clinging to each other, half laughing, half crying. 'That's *wonderful*,' Imogen said. 'Congratulations, darling. I knew you'd do it. Look, Charles is home on leave and he's offered to take us both out to a nightclub to celebrate. How about that – are you on?'

Shirley's spirits rose. It would be wonderful to celebrate her success. Ma had seemed far more interested in Princess Elizabeth's wedding during the past few weeks than in her exam, in spite of her suspicious grumblings about where all the clothing coupons were coming from for the sumptuous dresses. 'I'd love to, Imo,' she said hesitantly, 'but I've nothing to wear.'

'That's all right,' Imogen said. 'We'll all go back to the flat and you can borrow something of mine.' She tugged impatiently at Shirley's arm. 'Oh, come *on*, Shirl! You can't just go tamely home after passing your bronze. It's a once-in-a-lifetime thing.'

Shirley thought of Ma's lugubrious expression as she had left this afternoon, leaving her to cope with the Saturday afternoon rush at the shop. She was sure to put a damper on her news if she went straight home now. 'Okay, why not?' she said rebelliously. Suddenly her heart quickened, excited at the prospect of an evening's extravagant fun.

At Imogen's flat Shirley chose a swirling cocktail dress of black lace over taffeta. It was quite severely cut, with a boat-shaped neckline; a large pink rose tucked into the waistline was its only decoration.

'You look fantastic in black,' Imogen said, leading her out into the living room where Charles waited patiently with a gin and tonic in his hand. 'Doesn't she, Charlie?'

Charles nodded appreciatively. 'An absolute knock-out.' He looked at his watch. 'Shall we go now? I've booked a table at the Café Romano for eight-thirty. I can't think what you girls do that takes so long.'

Shirley had never been anywhere like the Café Romano. Its plush decor, the soft, warm lighting and glittering chandeliers combined to heighten her glow of achievement and happiness. She ate things she had never tasted before at dinner. Never in a million years would she ever have imagined that she would enjoy snails. Then there was asparagus with its distinctive flavour, delicious breast of wild duck en croûte followed by a wickedly rich chocolate pudding that was redolent of brandy. They drank champagne, Charles and Imogen toasting Shirley loudly so that the other diners turned to look at the pretty auburn-haired girl in black, with indulgent smiles at the uninhibited gaiety of the group of young people.

The band was good. It had played all through dinner in a discreet, unobtrusive way, but now it struck up with more vigour, tempting the replete diners to take to the dance floor. Charles asked Imogen to dance and she glanced at Shirley.

'Do you mind? Will you be all right?'

Shirley laughed. 'Of course, silly. I'm perfectly happy just sitting here watching everyone.'

She watched, fascinated, as couples gradually filled the small floor, swaying gently to the music in the limited space. She had never seen so many handsome men and beautiful women gathered together before, or such high fashion, brilliant colours and luxurious, shimmering fabrics. Gloria would have been bewitched by it all. The music was infectious and Shirley's feet itched to dance too, but she knew she would have to wait her turn to dance with their shared escort. Suddenly she felt a hand on her shoulder and heard a voice say:

'Dance with me?' She looked up to see Paul Winspear's dark eyes smiling down at her.

Her heart did a somersault in her breast as she heard herself reply: 'Oh, thank you, I'd like to.'

His eyes swept over her with undisguised admiration as she rose from the table and went with him to the floor. When he put his arm around her waist she felt a thrill like an electric current course through her veins and it was all she could do not to shiver with delight.

'I've never seen you here before, Shirley.' When she didn't reply he looked down at her. 'It *is* Shirley, isn't it?'

'Yes, it's Shirley. I haven't been here before. My friends brought me this evening. It's a celebration.'

'Oh? Birthday?'

'No. I passed my bronze-medal exam this afternoon.'

'Well, congratulations.' He pulled her a little closer. 'No wonder you're looking so radiant. So what's next?'

'A silver medal, then a gold. Maybe then I'll be able to audition for a job somewhere.'

'I'm quite sure the world will be your oyster. Producers will beat a path to your door.'

She glanced up at him. 'I think you're laughing at me.'

'Oh, no. Believe me, I'm not laughing.' He held her eyes with his for a long moment and she was acutely aware of his long hard fingers on her waist and the hand that held hers in the same pulsating grip she had experienced the first time they met.

'Shall I tell you something, Shirley?' They were right in the centre of the floor now, their bodies pressed close and almost at a standstill among the crowded dancers. Mesmerised, Shirley shook her head. 'Ever since that evening when we were introduced in Leonie's dressing room I haven't been able to get you out of my mind,' he said quietly.

'But – but that was ages ago.' Shirley's heart was beating fast.

'I know. You can't imagine how much I've wanted to see you again. And now suddenly here you are. It's as though I'd conjured you up, just by wishing. Do you know what I'd like to do? I'd like to whisk you away from here – have you all to myself. Will you come?'

'I can't. I . . . . I'm with friends.'

'I know. I saw. But not an escort, I think.'

'No, but just the same . . .'

'Where is the young man you were with at the theatre?'

Shirley shook her head. 'I don't know. He's just a friend. He works for my grandmother.'

'So you're a free agent, Shirley? Footloose and fancy-free, as they say. No suitors jealously guarding your honour?'

'No.' She laughed. 'I don't want any. I've got ambitions. There are too many other things I want to do before I settle down to all that.'

He bent to brush his lips across her cheek. 'I can see that we're two of a kind, Shirley.' His breath tickled her ear tantalisingly. 'So if I can't tempt you away tonight, when can I see you again?'

Her heart was pounding so hard she felt sure he must feel it. 'Oh, I don't know. I mean . . . what – what about Leonie?'

'Leonie?' He smiled down at her bemusedly. 'What about her?'

'Well, aren't you and she . . . ?'

'Leonie and I are like you, footloose and fancyfree. We have an understanding. We each live our own lives. I write plays and she acts in them. But even that could change if either of us finds something we like better – either personally or professionally.'

'Oh.'

The music came to an end and Paul gave her a little squeeze. Slipping his hand into his inside pocket he produced a card and pressed it into her hand. 'My address and number. Give me a ring if you'd like to have dinner some time,' he said, smiling into her eyes. 'I'll be waiting for your call, Shirley. I have a strong feeling it's no accident that we met like this tonight. I don't believe we should try to cheat fate, do you?'

When she returned to the table Imogen was looking anxiously at her. 'Do you know who that was you were dancing with?'

'Yes. Paul Winspear. I met him at the theatre when I went to see Leonie in his play.'

Imogen leaned closer, lowering her voice. 'Be careful of him, Shirley. I've never liked him and I've an idea Gloria shares my feeling about him.'

But Shirley was in no mood to listen to warnings or criticisms. She was almost eighteen; old enough to take care of her own life. She and Paul had a very special rapport. She sensed it and she was sure that he did too. She was certain that he was destined to play an important role in her life. And she could hardly wait for the curtain to rise on it.

When Charles's sports car roared to a stop outside 10 Angel Row it was one-thirty. Shirley crept round to the back yard and let herself in quietly. Taking off her shoes, she crept through the kitchen into the hall and began to climb the stairs in the dark. She was halfway up when the light was suddenly switched on, temporarily blinding her.

'What the 'ell bleedin' time d'you call this, my gel?' Ma stood at the top of the stairs, fearsome in steel curlers and voluminous flannel nightgown. 'Start this kinda caper an' you'll find yourself up the stick like your mother did. I won't 'ave it. D'you 'ear me? *I won't bloody well 'ave it.*'

Shirley stood blinking up at her grandmother, the pleasure of her success and her beautiful evening suddenly crushed. Angry resentment at Ma's thoughtless cruelty flared up inside her.

'Why do you have to spoil everything?' she shouted indignantly. 'I've had enough of slaving behind a counter for you. I'm sick and tired of this dump; being treated like a kid and working for next to nothing. As soon as I can I'm getting another job and leaving here.'

Ma's shoulders slumped and the fire went out of her eyes. 'Yes, my gel,' she said. 'You might *'ave* to do that – and sooner than you think, too.'

Chapter Sixteen

Leonie pulled her fur coat more closely around herself, shivering in the teeth of the icy Atlantic wind coming off the sea. Cornwall in spring was supposed to be balmy and picturesque but she found the rugged coastline gloomy and depressing and as for the weather, they might as well have been at the North Pole.

All week they'd waited here on the cliffs at the edge of the moorland for the rain to stop so that they could shoot the suicide-attempt scene that had been written into the screenplay. The leading man had caught a cold and the director's temper had gone from tetchy to downright explosive. If they didn't get the weather they wanted soon, they would be severely behind schedule.

Filming was a bitter disappointment to Leonie. As a stage actress she found it impossible to get used to shooting scenes out of sequence. It went against everything she had ever learned about leading up to the climax of a role. The hotel was draughty and inconvenient; she hated the interminable waiting about and found the hasty *al fresco* lunches provided by a dubious firm of caterers totally unpalatable. But worst of all was her disappointment over Paul's absence. She had naturally assumed that he'd come on location with them and it had only been on the night before they left London for St Ives that he had told her he wasn't coming.

Although he had been asked to write the screenplay of *Joy in the Morning*, he had declined. He was working on something new and was quite happy to pass the work on to an experienced screenwriter. Privately Leonie thought the man had ruined it and she blamed Paul. Once he had been paid the enormous sum he had received for the film rights, he seemed to have lost interest in the project. But when she angrily accused him of this he had lost his temper. They had parted on bad terms and she'd been uneasy and preoccupied ever since filming had begun, a fact which had hampered her performance. It had hardly endeared her to the director either, who made no secret of the fact that he thought her a whining, uncooperative bitch.

A sudden fresh surge of rain lashed icily into her face as the shower increased to a torrent. She swore ferociously under her breath and glared at the lowering grey sky as she hurried for the shelter of the car once more. Sitting behind the rainwashed windscreen, she loosened her coat and lit a cigarette. She felt distinctly sorry for herself. Everyone seemed to have deserted her. After Paul had left in a temper the night before she left London, she'd been so lonely and desperate that she had even rung Tony, but he was about to leave on location work too, shooting the last film of his contract somewhere up in Yorkshire.

Even Gloria had not accompanied her on location. She had made it clear that she did not want to go so far away. Apparently there was some kind of family crisis and she said she would rather take her holiday while Leonie was away. Being without her had made Leonie realise for the first time just what a treasure Gloria was; always at hand with hot drinks, aspirin or a warm coat; impervious even to her blackest moods; seeming to anticipate every need without being told. The dresser provided by the film company wasn't in the same league; a plain, sullen woman with bad breath who couldn't even make a cup of coffee without spilling half of it in the saucer and who wouldn't have recognised a needle if she'd been impaled on one.

Leonie's thoughts returned as always to Paul, wondering what he was doing while she was away. Was work his only reason for not wanting to come with her? She was plagued constantly by jealousy and suspicion. Did he have someone else? Was he perhaps even at this moment with another woman? Someone younger? When they were out together she often caught him looking at other women, most of them in their early twenties or even younger. It hurt unbearably, but she knew better than to reproach him.

She adjusted the car's rear-view mirror so that she could see herself in it. God, she looked awful! Damn this godforsaken hole. The relentless sea winds were drying her skin and turning her hair into a salt-caked haystack. And now, to add to the horrors, she could see fine but unmistakable lines forming around her eyes and mouth. Depression set in, settling like a chunk of lead in her chest as she reminded herself that she had recently turned thirty-eight. Another two years and she would hit forty. What then? Downhill all the way. She shuddered, pushing the thought away. Paul thought she was five years younger, the same age as him, but at this rate he would soon guess that she had deceived him.

Thinking about it, she was fairly sure that he would marry her if she made it clear that this was what she wanted. After all, they were a good team professionally. Their work was complementary, and they had been together for three years now. That must count for something. His own divorce had gone through some time ago. Hers would have, too, if only she hadn't foolishly clung to her dead marriage. She made up her mind there and then: the moment she got back to London she would contact Tony and tell him to go ahead with the divorce. There would be no need for grounds now that they had been apart for so long. Even the public had grown used to not seeing them together. And then – she smiled to herself, savouring the thought of their reconciliation – then she would tell Paul she wanted them to be married and watch his face light up. She'd make it clear that it needn't tie them down, of course. They would still both be free. Paul's freedom meant a lot to him and she respected that. But if they were married he'd be hers no matter what.

Other women would know it. He'd probably appreciate that. It would stop anything too heavy developing. On second thoughts she wouldn't wait to get back to London, she'd telephone Tony in Yorkshire tonight.

A tapping on the car window startled her out of her reverie. It was Deborah, the director's assistant.

'Rain's stopped, Miss Swann. We're ready to shoot the scene now if you are.'

Leonie dragged herself stiffly out of the car. What a bloody bore. All she really wanted was a hot bath, a good meal and bed. The sooner she got this film over with, the sooner she could go home and get on with her life. All she hoped was that the notices would make it all worth while.

When Ma showed Shirley the official-looking letter she'd had from the council, she'd been stunned to see that it had been written the previous November, almost four months ago.

'Why didn't you tell me about this before?' she asked.

Ma shook her head. 'Never mind that, just read it,' she said, slumping into a chair at the kitchen table.

Shirley read through the letter, then went back to the beginning and read it again to make sure she understood. There was no mistake. In a way it was the answer to all the wishes she'd made when she first came home to Whitechapel. But on reflection she saw that it could have disastrous side effects too. She looked across the table at her grandmother's stricken face.

'Didn't you answer it?' she asked.

Ma shook her head. 'I thought they'd change their minds. I thought there'd be an outcry – tryin' to take folks' 'omes off 'em like that. But I 'ad some bloke round from the council last week about it. 'E said it'd 'appen whether I said yes or not. Tried to tell me it'd all be for the best.'

'He could be right, Ma,' Shirley said gently, sorry for the friction that had developed between them since her outburst on the night of her exam. 'The street was badly damaged in the Blitz. Half the buildings have gone anyway. It'll never be the same as it was before the war. And

363

a nice new flat in the block they're planning to build – just think, no more draughts, a proper bathroom and constant hot water . . .'

'But this is my *'ome*,' Ma wailed. 'Your grandad brought me 'ere when we was first married nearly forty years ago. This is where we worked together all our married life, brought up Gloria an' you; stuck it out all through the Blitz. We was 'ere after the worst of the docklands raids when the King and Queen come round theirselves to see the damage. Mr Churchill 'imself shook Pa's 'and when 'e come down the ARP post that day. You an' Glor was both born in that room up there.' She looked up at the ceiling and Shirley saw with dismay the tears that filled her eyes. She'd never seen Ma cry before, not even when Pa died. 'This place ain't just bricks and mortar, it's my life, Shirl,' Ma said dejectedly. 'Pa an' me 'ad a good life 'ere. We never asked for much. A drink and a sing-song down the pub on a Saturday night an' a seat at the Hackney Empire now and again as a special treat.' She fumbled in her apron pocket for a hanky. 'If they pull it all down they might as well knock me on the 'ead too, 'cause I'll be finished.'

'Oh, Ma, don't take on like that.' Her throat tight, Shirley rose to put her arms round her grandmother's shaking form. 'I'm sorry for all the nasty things I said. You know I didn't mean them.'

Ma dabbed roughly at her eyes, annoyed with herself for displaying weakness. ''Course I know that. Listen, will you do somethin' for me, gel?'

''Course I will. Anything.'

'Get our Glor to come round. I want to see 'er. Will you do it for me?'

'Oh, Ma.' Shirley smiled through her tears. 'Of *course* I'll get her. I'll ring her right away.'

'Tell 'er I ain't on the warpath no more,' Ma added. 'All the fight's gorn outa me since this letter come.'

When Gloria heard Shirley's voice on the telephone she was surprised and pleased. But when she heard that her mother wanted to see her, she was apprehensive.

'What's it about, Shirl?' she asked cautiously. 'She's not ill, is she?'

'No. She's had this letter. They're going to pull the street down. For redevelopment, it says in the letter. They're offering her compensation – what they call "compulsory purchase" – and they'll be rehousing her temporarily till they've built this new block they're planning in the place of Angel Row. She'll get a brand new council flat then.'

'It sounds very fair,' Gloria said.

'Not to Ma, it doesn't. She's really upset, Glor. That's why she wants to see you. You will come, won't you?'

'Look, if you're really sure she wants me I'll come and stay for a few days,' Gloria said. 'I've got some holiday due. Leonie's going away on location with the film company. I want to spend some of it at Boothley, but I'll come home first. All right?'

'Oh, thanks, Glor. Ma wants you all right. I've never seen her so down.' She paused, then added: 'I'll look forward to seeing you too. I . . . I've missed you.' She was about to ring off when Gloria said:

'I heard how well you did with your exam. Imogen told me. I was so proud of you, love.'

'Oh, thanks. I meant to ring you and tell you.'

'I wish you had.'

'I'm sorry. I've been so busy what with the shop and my lessons. I take my silver in the summer.'

'I'll hear all about it when I come, eh? I'll be with you the day after tomorrow, love, if that's all right.'

As Shirley walked back from the telephone box she felt relieved. The responsibility of Ma's predicament weighed heavily on her young shoulders. Surely the time had come to let bygones by bygones? But apart from practical matters, it would be nice just to be with Gloria again. It was so long since they had enjoyed the relationship that had always been special to them. Although in a way she enjoyed the secrecy of her meetings with Paul, she felt uneasy, too. Deception was not part of her nature. She longed to unburden herself to someone she could trust.

She had waited for five weeks before giving in to the temptation of telephoning Paul. Ever since the night they had met at Romano's, the card he had given her had lain at the bottom of her handbag. Every time she caught sight of it she felt a little thrill of excitement at the prospect of what might happen should she pick up a telephone and dial that number, but every time she made up her mind to do it, her nerve failed her.

She and Dave had continued to share their free time, though Dave had been peeved that she had gone off with Imogen and Charles on the night of the exam without even coming to tell him the result. She had argued with all the indignation of one who knows herself to be in the wrong, irritated by his assumption that he should have been the first to hear her news.

'You don't own me, Dave Green,' she had shouted, then been instantly ashamed at the hurt in his eyes.

It had taken a lot of courage to ring Paul. Perhaps by now he would even have forgotten who she was. She pictured his cool response, his handsome brow furrowed as he racked his brain to fit a face to her name. If that happened all her illusions would be shattered along with her confidence. She wasn't sure that she could take it.

She finally rang him one wet Monday evening on her way back from the post office. Her knees trembled as she stood in the phone box, her finger shakily poised over button 'A' as she waited for him to answer the ringing tone.

He had not forgotten her. His response to her hesitant opening was enthusiastic and encouraging: 'Shirley! How wonderful to hear you! I've waited so long for you to ring. I quite thought you'd forgotten me. How are you, darling?'

Her relief was almost overwhelming and his use of the word *darling* had her cheeks glowing with pleasure. 'I'm fine. How are you?'

'Working hard – longing for a delicious diversion like you. When am I going to see you?'

'Oh, I don't know.'

'Tomorrow evening? Dinner?'

It hadn't been easy. Not only did she have to explain to Ma where she was going, there was Dave too. In the end she used Magda. She was taking an extra lesson, she told them – because of the coming exam. She was surprised how easy it was. They believed her implicitly.

It was with mingled feelings of guilt and triumph that she set off to meet Paul that first time. He had arranged to meet her at a hotel in Marble Arch, but she had lost her way slightly and was late. When she arrived hot and breathless in the hotel foyer, she found to her dismay that he was nowhere to be seen. She sat for a while in the reception hall, but the young man at the desk kept looking suspiciously at her. Perhaps he thought she was a lady of the streets, touting for business. Finally she went across to the desk and asked for Paul by name. Immediately the man smiled.

'Ah, you must be Miss Rayner. Mr Winspear asked me to give you a message. I would have passed it on before if only you'd asked, miss. You're to meet him in the bar.' He pointed. 'Just through those doors over there.'

He came to meet her with outstretched hands, waving away her apologies and confused explanations. They had dinner and talked – about Paul's work, a new play which he was having some problems with; about Shirley's classes. Paul complimented her on her appearance and on her voice, which he said was maturing. He could detect a great improvement in its depth and timbre since the last time they'd met. After dinner they sat in the hotel lounge and Paul held her hand as they talked some more. He was so easy to talk to, so sympathetic. He understood her dreams and ambitions as no one else ever had. At ten-thirty he took her all the way home in a taxi. In the back of the cab in the dark he had drawn her into his arms and kissed her. Never in her life had anything made her feel so wonderful. She felt like a glass of sparkling champagne, a Catherine wheel on firework night, a skylark soaring high above the clouds. Lying in bed later that night she relived every minute of their date, savouring the feel of his lips on hers, his powerful arms around her, the masculine scent of his expensive clothes. As they parted he had clung to her hand and said:

'Ring me again soon – promise?'

'I will,' she'd replied breathlessly. Where would they go next time? she wondered. What would he say and do? She couldn't wait to find out.

She had to wait a week, though. She couldn't push her luck. One extra lesson a week was all she could expect Ma and Dave to swallow.

The next time, Paul took her back to his flat after dinner. It was a nice flat, small but comfortable, furnished in a rather austere, masculine style with leather armchairs and muted colour schemes. He gave her brandy to drink, which made her feel pleasantly drowsy. Then, after they had talked a while he stood up and held out his hands to her, calmly announcing that he was taking her to bed. She laughed, not taking him seriously at first, but when he picked her up and carried her into the bedroom she hadn't been laughing. Her heart thudded against her ribs with a mixture of apprehension and anticipation.

She trembled as he slowly undressed her, feeling shy and embarrassed as he examined her body as though it were a priceless piece of porcelain. But her shyness melted in the warmth of her mounting desire as he caressed her sensuously with long, sensitive fingers. Soon every nerve in her body sang. Her heartbeat quickened and her limbs grew languid as they sank together onto the bed. But when he began to kiss her all over she felt her body take on a surprising life of its own, arching towards him convulsively as the torment within her became unbearable.

Having aroused her he undressed swiftly and when he rejoined her and she felt his naked flesh warm next to hers and his hardness against her thigh, she gave herself up willingly and eagerly to his lovemaking. Never in her life had she wanted anything with such feverish intensity.

The pain of his first entering was soon forgotten as their passion mounted. His initial gentleness was overtaken as his need increased and he pulled her this way and that, his face contorted with pleasure as he whispered hoarse instructions, telling her what to do to get the utmost pleasure out of their lovemaking. Urged on by this new-found delight, she became his willing pupil, obeying him until at last she was rewarded by a height of sensation never before imagined. She stiffened, her body arching and her breath suspended in her throat as the soaring waves of ecstasy shuddered through and through her. Then she heard Paul cry out and opened her eyes to see him arch above her, possessed by a powerful, pulsing climax that made his eyes appear opaque and the veins in his neck stand out like rope. Then he released his breath in a sigh and collapsed on top of her, burying his face between her breasts and murmuring her name over and over.

Shirley lay cradling his head, her fingers tangled in his thick hair, savouring the new delicious tingling in her body, relishing this new heady achievement, feeling like a real woman for the first time. Now she knew what Magda meant by *living*.

'I was your first,' Paul whispered as his breathing returned to normal. 'Your first lover. That makes me very proud.' He kissed her. 'It's a tremendous compliment.'

Shirley smiled dreamily. 'I've never wanted to with anyone else,' she said. 'And now I never will.'

Since then they had met three more times. Once a week was all she could manage, but she counted off each day. Never had the weeks seemed so long; never had she longed so much to be with one person, to see, kiss and hold him. Nothing was more important than what she felt for Paul. Even her valued drama lessons took second place. Now she knew what love and living really was.

Gloria arrived the following evening, just after they had closed the shop. Shirley took her through to the kitchen and for a moment she watched as her mother and grand-mother stood staring speechlessly at each other. Then Gloria put down her overnight case and took a step forward, opening her arms wide.

'Ma! Oh, *Ma*, I've missed you so.'

They were clinging to each other, both of them weeping, each of them too full to speak. Shirley turned away and filled the kettle. They'd have a lot to talk about. And if she knew them both, they'd need a large pot of tea to get them through it. She made the tea, put out the cups and left them to it.

When Gloria came up to bed she was able to tell Shirley that Ma seemed resigned to the changes that were inevitable in her life.

'I managed to make her see that she'd soon have to retire anyway,' she said as she undressed. 'She deserves a rest. She should take life easy. The compensation money will be a nice little nest egg and there'll be every convenience at the new flat.'

Shirley moved closer to her mother as she joined her in the bed. 'Good. So she's happier now, then?'

'Yes. She and I are going to the council offices tomorrow to sort everything out.' Gloria turned to look at Shirley. 'All she's worried about now is not having anything to leave to us,' she said. 'I soon put her mind at rest on that one. Told her we just want to see her comfy in her old age.'

'Good. Thanks for coming, Glor. It's been awful without you all this time.'

'I know, love. It wasn't what I wanted, though.'

'But you never came when Pa – I thought you might have asked me to go to Rook Cottage with you. Then even last Christmas you never . . .' Shirley shook her head. 'Oh, never mind. You're here now.' She snuggled up to Gloria. 'Glor, there's something I want to tell you.'

'Me too, Shirl. It's something I should have told you a long time ago, but now seems like a good time.' She paused, summoning up all her courage. 'Shirl, I've got a baby.'

Shirley caught her breath and sat up, staring at her mother. 'You've *what*?'

'I've got a baby. A little boy. He's called Michael and he's two years old.' Gloria put out her hand as Shirley began to speak. 'No, love, hear me out. Don't say anything yet.' She unfolded the story of Michael's birth and his sickness, the failed adoption plans and her hopes for the operation that would allow him to grow up to a normal life. When she had finished Shirley lay down beside her with a sigh.

'Oh, Glor – why didn't you tell me all this? Now I can see why you behaved as you did. So many things are clear now, but why didn't you say? I mean, I can see why you didn't tell Ma – but why not me? He's my brother. He's two years old and I've never even *seen* him.' She looked into Gloria's face. 'Who looks after him when you're working?'

'Margaret, a friend I met in the hospital. She's a widow. She's a good sort, Shirl, and marvellous with little Michael. I applied for a government grant for the cottage when they were first announced. It came through and the builders started a couple of months ago. We're having electricity laid on, and proper plumbing – a bathroom built on behind the kitchen. You wouldn't know the place. Next winter we'll be really snug and cosy. You'll have to come and see when it's finished. Should be soon now.'

'Did you tell Ma tonight – about the baby?'

'No.' Gloria sighed. 'I can't yet. She's got enough to worry about at the moment.'

They were both silent, knowing that telling Ma was the biggest hurdle Gloria had to face. Then Shirley asked the inevitable question: 'Glor, is he Billy's?'

'No. It was after . . . after I heard that Billy'd been killed.'

'I see. Then who . . .?'

'I'm sorry, love, but that part's still secret. It might always have to be. It's not the way it seems either. He – Michael's father is – was very special.'

'And . . . you loved him?'

'Yes. I loved him – long before Billy. I always will.'

'Then why isn't he taking care of you both?'

'Because he doesn't even know about Michael himself.'

'Doesn't *know*? But he might want to help. Surely he should be told?' Shirley was silenced by Gloria's expression.

'It's out of the question, love. Too many lives would be affected by it.'

'He's married, you mean?'

'Just leave it, love. Don't ask me again.'

'All right, I won't.' Shirley switched off the light. 'It's late. We'd better go to sleep now.'

After a moment Gloria said drowsily: 'I'm sorry, love, what was it you were going to tell me?'

Shirley sighed. There had been enough surprises for one day – enough emotional unburdenings. 'Oh, it'll keep,' she said sleepily. 'Tell you tomorrow, eh?'

But long after Gloria was asleep she lay thinking. So Gloria had a baby son – her half-brother. A few months ago she might have been shocked and disappointed, but now that she had met Paul and fallen in love herself, she understood. Poor Gloria! How it must hurt not to be able to be with the man she loved; not to be able to tell him she had given birth to his son. She longed to see little Michael and tried to picture what he would look like. But she dreaded to think what Ma's reaction to this new grand-child would be. Would it cause a new rift between her and Gloria – just when the old one looked like being healed? And then there was the question of her own part in the change in their situation. When the street was demolished and Ma moved, what would become of her? Not only would she lose her home but her job too. And with no wage coming in, how would she be able to afford her drama lessons? Finally there was the problem of Dave. Some time soon she would have to tell him about Paul – just as he was about to lose his job, too. She turned over with a sigh and tried hard to put it all out of her mind for a while and sleep. The future looked full of gaping uncertainties and unwelcome prospects. The one thing she was sure of – shining like a star through her clouded future – was her love for Paul.

* * *

Dave called for her as usual on Saturday evening and they went out, leaving Ma and Gloria to talk. They'd been to see the housing officer the previous day and it had been arranged for Ma to go into a bed-sitting room for six months until the new flat was ready for her. It wasn't ideal but Gloria had assured her that it would only be temporary and that the time would soon pass. So far no one had mentioned Shirley's plans and she hadn't liked to ask what was to become of her. As they walked down Angel Row she told Dave about the redevelopment.

'I know about it,' he told her calmly. 'Luckily the street where I live doesn't come into the plan as yet, so I'll be all right. It won't affect me.'

'But it will in one way. You'll lose your job, Dave,' Shirley said impatiently.

'I've been offered another,' Dave said. 'Quite a good one if it comes off, managing a busy grocer's shop on Hackney Road. The owner's retiring, going to live down in Kent, but he doesn't want to sell the business.'

'I'll not only lose my job but my home too,' Shirley said.

Dave looked at her. 'Won't you still live with your grandmother?'

'Don't see how I can in a bed-sitting room.'

'Oh.' Dave considered for a moment, then his face lit up in a smile. 'Well, the answer's easy. We'll get married.'

Shirley's mouth dropped open in dismay. 'Oh, Dave, don't be silly.'

'Why is it silly?' He stopped walking to look at her. 'It's the obvious solution, Shirl. There's even a little flat over the shop we could have. We'd get married eventually anyway – wouldn't we?'

Shirley shook her head. 'No, we wouldn't. Look, Dave, you know I'm training for a stage career. Besides, didn't it ever occur to you to ask me if *I* wanted to get married?'

He looked crestfallen. 'I love you, Shirl. I just assumed . . .'

'Yes, well, you assumed wrong. I don't want to get married for years yet – perhaps not ever.' Carried away, she almost added: *and certainly not to you*, but stopped herself just in time as she noticed his wounded expression. Taking his arm roughly, she said: 'Oh, come on, let's go and have a drink and talk it over properly. And for heaven's sake take that miserable look off your face.'

It was still early and they found a quiet corner in the pub and settled down with their drinks. Shirley knew that it was now or never but she didn't look forward to hurting Dave even more. He'd been good to her when she needed a friend. She was fond of him, but she couldn't allow him to go on thinking of her as his. She crossed her fingers tightly, hoping she could do this without making life too hard for them both.

'Look, Dave, things are changing. All around us life is starting to look different. We can't stand still. We've no choice but to move with it.'

He looked at her over the rim of his beer mug. 'What are you trying to tell me?'

She took her courage in both hands. There was no other way but to give it to him straight. 'I've met someone else, Dave.'

He looked at her steadily. 'I'd guessed – had my suspicions for a long time, but I didn't want to believe it. All right, who is it?'

'No one you know. No one from round here.'

'Someone well off, I suppose?'

'What do you take me for, Dave? I'm not a gold-digger.'

'Someone who can help you get on then – someone to do with the stage?'

That much she couldn't deny. She shook her head. 'It doesn't matter who he is, Dave. The thing is, I . . . I love him.'

'I see. And he loves you?'

'Of course he does.' For the first time Shirley realised that Paul had never actually said he loved her. But surely actions spoke louder than words, didn't they?

'No doubt he hasn't got a crippled leg like me,' Dave said bitterly, putting his glass down heavily on the table.

'Oh, Dave, don't say things like that. It wouldn't make any difference if I . . .'

He stared at her, his eyes dark with pain, knowing she'd been about to say, *if I loved you*. 'You've let him, haven't you?' he said quietly.

'What do you mean? Let him what?' Shirley felt her cheeks colouring.

'You know what I mean all right. You've slept with him.'

'That's none of your business.'

'All this time you've been going out with both of us. Seeing me at weekends and – and sleeping with him in between.' He swallowed hard. 'Is it him who's been giving you these *extra lessons*?' He laughed bitterly. 'Huh! That's a good one. What kind of lessons, I'd like to know.' He pushed his glass away from him, spilling some of its contents onto the table as he stood up. 'That's that then. I wouldn't have you now if you went down on your knees to me. I worshipped you, Shirl. Now I find you're nothing more than a little slut. Tell your grandmother I've given in a week's notice, will you?' And with as much dignity as he could manage he hurried towards the door.

Shirley got to her feet and went after him. Outside in the street she tried to take his arm.

'Don't go like that, Dave. I'm sorry. I never meant to hurt you.'

'What did you think it'd do to me, eh? Give me a good laugh?' He shook her hand off, his eyes bright with unshed tears. 'Look, you've had your say, now just leave it, will you? I don't want to talk about it any more so just do me a favour and let me go.'

She stood watching helplessly as he walked down the street, his head high, trying hard not to limp. Her throat ached with remorse and pity. She was fond of Dave. She'd have done anything rather than hurt him, but she couldn't have let him go on thinking she would marry him. She imagined them running the grocer's shop together and living in the flat above, going on year after year until they were old. Ending up like Ma and Pa. She shuddered, suddenly needing the comfort of Paul's arms. Turning, she headed for the Underground station.

When Paul opened the door to her she saw that he was unshaven. He wore an open-necked shirt and slacks and his hair was rumpled. He gave her a smile.

'Darling! What a nice surprise! Come in, you're just what I need. I've been working but it isn't one of my better days.'

The flat was a mess. Paul had been working at his desk in the window and the floor was littered with crumpled sheets of paper. Every flat surface seemed to be covered in used coffee cups and there was a plate bearing the remains of a meal in the middle of the floor.

'Sorry about the pigsty,' Paul said, sweeping aside a pile of books so that she could sit down. 'My daily treasure doesn't come in at weekends and I've been too busy to tidy up.'

'That's all right. Let me.' She began to pick up some of the litter but he took her hands.

'Leave that and come here.' He drew her close and kissed her lingeringly. 'Mmm, you taste so good. But why are you here, darling? Everything's all right, isn't it?'

She shook her head. 'No, not really. At least – nothing that need bother you. I just wanted to see you suddenly, that's all.' She looked up at him. 'Paul, do you think we could go to bed, please?'

He laughed, raising his eyebrows at her in mock surprise. 'Good heavens, Miss Rayner, such abandonment! I'm not sure that I should let you corrupt me like this.' He rubbed his jaw. 'Shall I shave first or can you stand a face like sandpaper?'

She slipped her arms around his waist. 'I love you just as you are; besides, I can't wait that long.'

The bedroom was as chaotic as the rest of the flat but she didn't care. She undressed hurriedly and fell unheedingly into the unmade bed to make love to Paul with an urgency generated by her bruised emotions, letting her heightened senses erase the memory of the painful scene with Dave. Later, as they lay blissfully satiated in each other's arms, she said:

'I told Dave this evening that I couldn't marry him; that there was someone else.'

Paul shifted his position slightly to look down at her. 'That might not have been a good move.'

She frowned. 'Why not? I couldn't let him go on thinking I was his girl.'

He sat up and took a cigarette from the box on the bedside table. 'None of us can afford to make enemies, though, can we?'

'Dave will never be an enemy,' she said. 'But I couldn't string him along like that. It wouldn't have been fair.'

He lit the cigarette thoughtfully and looked down at her. 'You didn't tell him about me, did you?'

'Not by name, no.'

'Thank God for that.' He exhaled a cloud of smoke. 'I don't want irate, rejected suitors coming round here, making sordid scenes on the doorstep.'

Shirley felt a pang of disappointment. 'I thought you'd be pleased that I'd given him up for you,' she said.

His eyes narrowed as he looked at her through the cloud of smoke. 'Let's get one thing quite clear, darling. You don't have to give up anything or anybody for me. We're both completely free to live our own lives and to see anyone we wish to. Neither of us is committed in any way. We're good friends, okay? We amuse each other and –'

'*Amuse?*' The colour draining from her face, Shirley sprang up from the bed. 'Is that all it is to you – an amusement? You make me sound like . . . like a toy – some cheap thing you buy from Woolworth's and throw away when you're tired of it. I'm not here for your *amusement.*' Grabbing up her clothes, she strode towards the bathroom, but Paul got there first and threw his arm across the doorway, barring the way. His mouth was curved and his eyes gleamed with amusement as he looked down at her.

'Do you know that your eyes flash like ice when you're angry? Your cockney accent comes back too.' He struck a pose and mimicked her voice: 'Sam cheap fing yer buy from Woolwurf's.' He threw back his head and laughed. 'Just like one of those stallholders from the Portobello Road.'

Almost blind with wounded pride and fury, Shirley raised her hand and slapped him hard across the cheek, the wiry black stubble stinging her palm. Paul caught her arm and twisted it swiftly behind her back, making her cry out in pain.

'Little spitfire. You like to play rough games, don't you?' he said, his face close to hers. 'I've always suspected it.' Kicking the clothes she had dropped out of the way he forced her down onto the floor. 'Let's see if we can make you say you're sorry for that lapse of control, you little cat,' he breathed into her ear.

'Paul – no, *don't*!' She struggled, suddenly afraid of the glint of sadistic excitement she saw in his eyes, but he pinned her body to the floor with his own weight. His mouth closed on hers, crushing her lips mercilessly against her teeth, shutting off her breath until she thought she would suffocate. Striking out frantically at him, she pulled free and scrambled to her feet. Gathering up her scattered clothes, she ran into the bathroom, slammed and locked the door. Leaning against it, her legs trembling, she allowed the tears of hurt and humiliation to stream down her cheeks. How could he love her one minute and treat her like that the next?

He was in the kitchen making coffee when she came out. He wore his dressing gown and turned to smile calmly at her as though nothing had happened. 'Ah, there you are, darling. Coffee?'

'No, thank you. I'm going home.'

He turned to her, reaching out to touch her face. Seeing her flinch, he frowned and said: 'Ah. I went too far. It was your fault, though. You shouldn't have hit me. I misread you – I thought you wanted . . .' He smiled down at her. 'Some women like a little horseplay. Forgive me?'

She looked at her feet. 'You . . . you scared me. You hurt.' She fingered her bruised mouth.

'Darling, I'm sorry.' He pulled her close. 'Sometimes I forget that you're just a baby.'

'No, I'm not.'

'You're thinking that your nice Dave wouldn't have done that to you, I expect.'

'I'm not.'

He tipped up her chin to look into her eyes. 'Oh, dear, do you hate me now?'

Slowly she shook her head and he smiled.

'Good. Kiss me then.'

After a moment's hesitation she raised her lips to his and he kissed her with surprising tenderness. 'There. All better now?'

'You said . . . you said that we could both see anyone we wanted to. That hurt because I don't want anyone else, Paul.'

'Nor I, darling – for the moment. But you're very young. I wouldn't dream of trying to tie you down. It wouldn't be fair. I'm your first lover and that's always special, but believe me, I won't be your last.' When she looked unconvinced, he added: 'Don't you see that the greatest gift I can give you is freedom?'

'I – I suppose so.'

'I've got a surprise for you,' he whispered. 'What would you say to a part in the play I'm working on? It's perfect for you. I wrote it with you in mind. Would you like to read it?'

'Oh, Paul, I'd *love* to.' Her eyes sparkled up at him, the incident in the bedroom almost forgotten. 'Oh, but I've got to go now. Can I take the script home with me? Can I come back tomorrow and –' A sudden ring at the doorbell silenced her and she looked up at him. 'Who's that?'

He smiled. 'Not having my crystal ball handy, I'll have to wait till I've opened the door.'

'Don't go.'

'I must. It might be important.'

She held out her hand. 'Oh, but . . .' Before she could stop him he had walked out into the hallway and opened the door. Standing behind the kitchen door, Shirley was horrified to hear Leonie's voice say:

'Darling – surprise, *surprise*! Filming is all over. Isn't it bliss? I couldn't bear another second down there in that dead and alive hole. I just had to drive straight back to London – and you.'

There was a pause during which Shirley could hear the sound of enthusiastic kissing. In the silence she could hear her own heart thumping away in her chest. The voice went on: 'You must have known I was coming – waiting for me hopefully in your dressing gown.' She giggled. 'Oh, darling, I've missed you so *much*. I thought the wretched film would never be done with. I've got such plans for us both. Just wait till you hear.' Shirley held her breath as she went on: 'I drove all the way up from Cornwall without stopping once and I'm simply *dying* of thirst. That coffee smells marvellous. I'll just help myself, shall I?'

Shirley looked around her frantically but there was no escape. The kitchen door was thrown open and the next moment she found herself looking straight into Leonie's surprised eyes. Her dark hair hung loose about her shoulders and her unfastened fur coat revealed a clinging cream silk dress. At the sight of Shirley the smile vanished from her face and her jaw dropped.

'Shirley?' She turned to stare challengingly at Paul, who stood behind her looking unconcerned. 'What's *she* doing here?'

'I came to read Paul's play,' Shirley said quickly. 'There's a part in it for me.'

Leonie stared at her for a moment, then flung her head back and hooted with derisive laughter. 'Oh, my *God*. Don't tell me you fell for that old chestnut.'

'I don't know what you mean.'

'It's the oldest trick in the book, darling. *You?* Take part in a West End production? It's ludicrous, you're just an amateur. He's stringing you along, darling, trying to seduce you. Didn't you see through it?' She took a step towards Shirley, her eyes narrowing as she took in her bruised lips and slightly dishevelled appearance. 'Or maybe you're not as naive as you look. Perhaps he already has and this is your way of blackmailing him.'

With a shocked gasp, Shirley pushed past her into the hall. Paul put out a hand to stop her, but she shook him off and ran out, through the door and down the stairs into the street, not stopping till she was well clear of the building.

Clearly his relationship with Leonie was as strong as ever. Her head spun. This *freedom* he talked about – she didn't understand it. When you loved someone you weren't free anyway – you didn't want to be. All you wanted was that one person and no one else. Tears almost choked her as she hastened her slowed pace to catch a bus just pulling up at a bus stop. This was the worst night of her life. It was like a nightmare. Nothing could ever possibly be as agonising as this. All she could think about was getting home to Gloria, pouring it all out to her and having her mother comfort her as she had in the far-off prewar days of childhood.

When Gloria answered a knock on the street door to find Dave standing on the doorstep, she was surprised.

'Hello, Dave. I thought Shirley was with you.'

'She was, but . . . Can I come in, Mrs Rayner?'

'Of course.' Gloria held the door open for him. 'There's nothing wrong, is there?'

'No.' Dave stood in the narrow hallway, looking unhappily down at his feet. 'I just wanted to talk to you, if you don't mind.' He licked his lips nervously. 'Is your mother about? I mean, if you like we could go to the pub.'

Gloria smiled. 'It's all right, she's in bed. She decided to have an early night.'

'Oh. It's not that I don't want to see her . . .'

Gloria touched his arm reassuringly. 'Don't apologise. I understand. Come through to the kitchen, Dave. The kettle's on.'

Sitting at the kitchen table, his hands round a mug of hot tea, Dave told Gloria about Shirley's confession that she was in love with someone else. 'I don't want you to think I'm running to you with tales,' he added. 'It's just that I'm worried about her. She won't tell me who this bloke is and I've got an awful feeling she might be heading for a packet of trouble. I didn't know what to do with myself after we parted. I bought an evening paper and decided to go on a bit of a pub crawl. I thought I might get drunk. It's what blokes usually do when they've been chucked, isn't it? But drinking just seemed to make me feel worse. So then I thought if I came and talked to you . . .'

'I might talk her out of it?' Gloria shook her head. 'I'm sorry but I've no idea who her new boyfriend is either, Dave. We haven't been very close over the last couple of years. I can't make her change her mind, I'm afraid. I can't promise to do anything, but I will talk to her and try to get to the bottom of it.'

'Thanks, Mrs Rayner. I'd appreciate that. At least I know you won't let her go and do something she might regret.' He stood up. 'I'll go now before Shirl gets back. I wouldn't want her to know I've been here.' He looked at her. 'You won't tell her, will you?'

'No, of course I won't.' She went with him to the door and saw him out, shaking her head as she walked back into the kitchen. He seemed a nice young man. What a pity it was that all the nice people of this world seemed to get the rough end of the stick while the ones who didn't give a damn got off scot-free. Was it this new man in her life that Shirley had tried to tell her about on her first night at home? She wished now that she'd listened. Maybe she could have done or said something to help avoid Dave's misery.

It was only as she was clearing the table that she noticed he'd left his newspaper behind. A copy of the late edition of the London *Evening News* lay on the chair where he'd been sitting. When she picked it up and unfolded it, the black front-page headline screamed up at her:

FILM DIRECTOR BADLY INJURED IN AIR CRASH.

Underneath the story ran:

Tony Darrent, film-director husband of actress and singer Leonie Swann, was badly injured this afternoon when the plane he was piloting back to London after the completion of his latest film crashed over the Yorkshire moors. He was pulled clear of the burning wreckage seconds before it exploded and taken to Leeds Royal Infirmary, where he is being treated for

third-degree burns and other injuries. A hospital statement gives his condition as 'serious but stable'.

Then followed an account of Tony's career that read
ominously like an obituary.

The kitchen swam sickeningly before her eyes and
Gloria clutched the back of a chair for support. 'Tony,'
she murmured. 'Oh, Tony, my love! Oh, dear God, don't
let him die.' Pulling herself together, she looked at the
clock. It was just after eleven. She'd pack her things and
go straight to the station now. Wait, though – which
station? As she ran upstairs and began to throw her
clothes into her overnight bag, she tried to organise her
confused thoughts. Leeds, the paper said. That would be
either St Pancras or King's Cross. She'd find out which
when she got there.

She crept quietly downstairs and scribbled a hasty note
for Shirley, propping it against the cooling teapot on the
table, then she let herself out of the street door. Maybe if
she was lucky she'd catch a cruising taxi in the main road.
There was bound to be a night train. If not, she would sit it
out till the first one left tomorrow morning, because no
matter what anyone said or did, one thing was crystal
clear. She had to go to Tony, to be with him now – as soon
as possible. It could be the only chance she'd ever get to
tell him that she loved him – that she always had and
always, always would.

When Shirley arrived home, Gloria had been gone a little
over half an hour. She found the note, hastily scrawled on
the back of a used envelope: *Sorry, love, called away
urgently. Couldn't wait for you to get home. Don't worry,
I'll write soon. Love, G.*

Shirley dropped the note on the table and sank into a
chair. She had never needed Gloria as badly as she
needed her tonight. But obviously someone else needed
her more. Was it Michael? She hadn't said. He had
priority in her life now and who could grudge a sick child
the loving care of his mother?

A tear slipped silently down Shirley's cheek and she lowered her head onto her arms. Now that Paul had proved himself to be false, she felt there was no one in the world who really cared about her.

Chapter Seventeen

It was midday when Gloria arrived at the hospital. She had missed the last train to Leeds the night before and sat all night in the waiting room, snatching what little sleep she could on one of the hard benches. On enquiring at the hospital reception desk, she was directed up to the surgical ward, but there she was told that Tony was allowed close family visitors only.

'But I've come all the way from London specially,' Gloria said wearily. 'I'm an old friend. I sat up all night, waiting for a train. Please don't tell me I can't see him.'

The nurse looked at her tired face sympathetically. 'His daughter is with him at the moment,' she said. 'If you'll just wait here. What name is it?'

'Just tell her it's Gloria, she'll know. We've been friends for years – please . . .' Gloria watched as the nurse rustled her way back down the corridor and disappeared through a door. Moments later she reappeared and beckoned to Gloria.

'Just five minutes,' she said. 'I'd better warn you, you may be shocked by his appearance, but try not to show it. He's very weak, so please don't excite him in any way.'

As she entered the small side ward, Imogen rose from her chair by the bed. She looked tired and deathly pale.

'Gloria! How good of you to come.' She crossed the room and hugged Gloria briefly. 'I've been here since last night. They telephoned me and Charles drove me up at once. How did you know?'

'The paper. It was in the evening editions.' Gloria was looking past Imogen at the figure in the bed. Tony seemed to be swathed in bandages. 'How is he?' she whispered.

'He's asleep at the moment. His leg was badly crushed and they operated on that last night – inserted steel pins. He's still drowsy from the anaesthetic.' She turned towards Gloria, her face fearful. 'He has dreadful burns to his face and hands, too. The surgeon tells me that they'll do skin grafts later, so it'll be a long job.' She tried to smile. 'But the good news is that his eyes are all right, and his flying helmet saved him from more severe head injuries. We have to thank God for that.'

'Will he . . . will he be disfigured?'

Imogen shrugged. 'God only knows, Gloria. All I really care about is that we still have him.' Her voice broke and Gloria took her hands.

'You look so tired, love. Why don't you go and get some sleep?'

Imogen shook her head. 'I want to be here when he wakes.'

'Does Leonie know?'

'I tried to locate her,' Imogen said. 'I left messages everywhere I could think of. I'll just have to hope that one of them reaches her.'

Gloria nodded. 'The nurse said only five minutes.' She went hesitantly up to the bed and looked down at Tony's still form. She couldn't see much of his face. It was hard to believe that this heavily bandaged person was the vital, talented man she loved. As Imogen said, it was a miracle that he was still alive. They must hang on to that for now – take things a day at a time. She wondered about his future career. When he knew the nature of his injuries he would be devastated. He would need all the help, all the love and support they could give him. She hoped that somehow she would be allowed to give him hers.

The nurse looked in. 'I'm sorry. I'm going to have to ask you to leave now.'

Imogen reached for Gloria's hand. 'Where are you staying?'

Gloria shrugged. 'I haven't even thought yet. I suppose I'd better find somewhere.'

'I'm staying at the Great Northern. I've got a double room. If you don't mind sharing you can come with me.' Imogen rummaged in her handbag for a pencil and paper. 'I'm in number twenty-three. I'll write them a note. Why don't you check in and have a bath and a sleep? Then you can come back and take over from me if you want to.'

Gloria was asleep when Imogen returned to the hotel. She shook Gloria's shoulder gently.

'Gloria, it's me – Imogen.'

Gloria opened her eyes and gazed round at the unfamiliar room as consciousness seeped back. She sat up. 'Imogen. Tony – how is he?'

Imogen smiled. 'He's awake. He's going to be all right, Gloria. He's still under heavy sedation for the pain, but he was able to say a few words to me.'

'Can I see him? Did you tell him I came?'

'I did, and he seemed pleased.' Gloria made to get out of bed but Imogen put out her hand. 'Don't get up. Rest a bit longer. They want Daddy to rest now until this evening. The surgeon will be in to see him this afternoon.' She took off her coat and sat down.

'You look all in, Imogen,' Gloria said. 'Why don't you get some sleep now?'

Imogen shook her head. 'I still haven't located Mummy. I can't think why I haven't heard from her. After all, if you saw it in the papers, surely she must have seen it too.'

'Isn't she filming in Cornwall?'

'Yes, but they were almost finished last week. She could be on her way home.' She got up and went to the telephone. 'I'd better try ringing round again.'

Half a dozen phone calls later, Imogen was still no nearer to locating Leonie. She had tried the Mayfair flat twice on the off chance that Leonie had gone home for the weekend, but the number seemed to be out of order. Little did she know that Leonie was in fact there all the time, heavily asleep after taking the telephone off the hook and swallowing two strong sleeping tablets.

Her row with Paul after Shirley had left had been fiery and spectacular. Finding Shirley at the flat had shaken her badly. Her own dresser's daughter! She couldn't believe that Paul could be so indiscreet, or so lacking in discernment. Finally, vowing never to speak to him again and promising all kinds of retribution, she'd stormed out of his flat and taken a taxi to Mayfair.

When she arrived at the flat the telephone was ringing. Thinking it would be Paul, she snatched up the receiver.

'I don't want to speak to you, you two-timing sod – '

'Leonie, it's me, Max.'

She stopped, biting her lip with annoyance. What the hell did the director of the film mean, calling her at this hour? Couldn't he let her have a weekend in peace? Trying hard to keep the irritation out of her voice, she said breezily: 'Max. Sorry, darling, I thought it was someone else – someone who's been – '

'Look, I've been ringing your number for hours. I'm afraid it's not good news, Leonie,' Max interrupted. 'I've just finished looking at the final rushes of *Joy in the Morning*. It's a sheer bloody disaster.'

'Oh, surely you're wrong, Max,' she said tartly, her temper still smouldering. 'In fact you'd better be. If I've wasted my valuable time on a flop, I warn you, I'm going to be extremely angry.'

'*You're* going to be angry?' Max's voice thundered down the line at her. 'Listen, Leonie, the film drags from beginning to end. It lacks sparkle. It lacks interest, suspense, conflict – everything that makes a film stand out. In fact, for my money it's pure dross. And the reason I'm ringing you is because I attribute all this to *you* and you only. You've been obstructive and downright bloody-minded all along. There's hardly a member of the cast or crew who you haven't upset. If the film flops – and I'm very much afraid that it will – you'll have only yourself to blame.'

'You're just trying to cover your own back, aren't you, Max?' Leonie hissed into the receiver furiously. 'For instance, wasn't the cretin who wrote the screenplay a friend of yours? Couldn't any of it possibly be *his* fault?'

'Everyone knows about your relationship with Paul Winspear, Leonie,' Max said evenly, 'and that you'd have liked him along to pander to your every whim. The screenwriter I chose is an experienced professional. I've worked with him countless times and in my opinion he made a damn good job of it – unlike you. Look, Leonie, a lot of good actors have given their best for this film – banking on it for their future careers. You've let them down with your carelessness and your arrogance. You've let us all down. I want you to know that I shall make it clear to everyone who matters that I will not consider working with you again.'

'You're wrong, Max. The film *will* be a success,' Leonie said stubbornly. 'You're underrating my popularity. People will come to see it on the strength of the play's good notices – they'll come to see *me*.'

He gave a laugh that sounded more like a growl at the other end of the line. 'I sincerely hope they don't, for your sake, Leonie. If they're counting on seeing a good performance from you, they're in for a *big* disappointment.' He rang off abruptly, leaving her trembling with rage.

She slammed the phone down and poured herself a large gin, which she swallowed at a single gulp. What a night! One bloody awful thing after another – and none of it her fault. She had always said that the screenplay made rubbish of Paul's play. And who would have thought that Shirley Rayner, the child she had taken in to save her from the Blitz, and for whom she'd done so much over the years, would turn out to be nothing better than a scheming little tart? Just wait till she saw Gloria again. She'd have something to say to her about her daughter.

Lighting a cigarette and puffing furiously at it, she paced the room, but try as she would she could not rid herself of the vitriolic anger that churned her stomach and made her head pound. Finally, making up her mind, she ground out her cigarette and went to the bathroom. Taking a bottle from the cabinet, she shook out two sleeping tablets. Back in the drawing room, she took the receiver off its rest and laid it on the table, poured herself another generous measure of gin to wash down the tablets and went to bed.

Sitting at the bedside alone, Gloria was able to give way to the emotion she'd had to hide while Imogen was present. Watching over the sleeping Tony, she allowed the tears to flow. His eyes were closed; he'd been asleep ever since she arrived. She longed to touch his face or hold his hand, but it was out of the question. She looked at the heavily bandaged hands that lay outside the covers and wondered just how serious his injuries were and whether the doctors would tell her – a mere acquaintance – the truth if she asked. Then, as she was watching and speculating fearfully about the future, he suddenly opened his eyes.

'Gl-Gloria?' His lips moved with obvious difficulty and she could only just make out the whispered word.

'Darling, I'm here. I came as soon as I knew. Don't worry. Don't try to talk. Everything will be all right.'

His eyelids fluttered. 'You . . . won't go? Won't leave . . . me?'

'No, I'll stay.' She leaned forward. 'I wish I could hold your hand, darling. I wish I could put my arms around you.'

He narrowed his eyes in the semblance of a smile. 'Me . . . too. Soon – eh?'

'Yes. Soon.'

'Gloria, the doctor is here.' Imogen's hand was on her shoulder. 'He wants to examine Daddy. Shall we go and have a cup of coffee while we wait?'

She hadn't heard the girl enter the room and now she turned to see Imogen standing at her side. The ward sister and a doctor were just coming into the room. Gloria stood up, then, with a last look at Tony, followed Imogen out into the corridor.

In the visitors' canteen they faced each other across the table. Gloria took a sip of her coffee and looked at Imogen's thoughtful face.

'You've seen the doctors. Have they said how he is?'

'So far, so good, apparently. But he has a big ordeal to face – a lot of painful treatment before he's well again. Even then they can't guarantee that he won't always be badly scarred. When he's a little better they're going to transfer him to a special burns unit in London.' Imogen hesitated, then said: 'Gloria, I don't know whether you know. Daddy wrote to me last week to tell me that Mummy had been in touch to say she'd agree to a divorce if he still wanted one.' She glanced up at Gloria. 'I don't know what the situation is between them at the moment. Do you know?'

'I think they're still on friendly terms.'

'Did you know he wanted a divorce?'

'He mentioned it, yes. But I thought your mother was set against it.'

'Is it – is it for your sake he's asking?'

'Mine?' Gloria's eyes opened wide. 'No, of course it isn't.'

'How could you bear to work for her when all the time. . . ?' Imogen broke off, shaking her head. 'I'm sorry. I've no right. It's just that . . .' She licked her lips and looked at Gloria. 'Your child – Michael. He's Daddy's, isn't he? I couldn't help overhearing you just now, and seeing the look on your face when you thought you were alone with him. Suddenly it all fell into place. It's been going on for some time, hasn't it?'

Gloria looked at the pain in the girl's eyes and felt herself shrivel up inside. 'Imogen, please don't look at me like that. It isn't the way you think. We . . . he was only unfaithful to your mother with me once. It was when I heard that Billy had been killed. I felt so bad. Your father was kind and caring. It just happened.' She reached blindly for the girl's hand, tears running down her cheeks. 'I've loved him for years, Imogen. I loved him long before I met him – through his films. My bedroom at Angel Row was covered in pictures of him. If it hadn't been for the war we'd never have met, and when we did he was even more wonderful than I could ever have imagined. How could I not love him? Once, a long time ago, I was able to help him through a particularly bad time. It made a sort of bond between us. But I would never have done anything to break up your family. I never wanted to hurt you or to end his marriage.'

'You couldn't have anyway.' Imogen's fingers curled round hers and squeezed tightly. 'He and Mummy hadn't been happy for years. As long as I can remember they've quarrelled. Sometimes when I was at home in the holidays, when I was little before the war, I'd lie in bed and hear them shouting at each other. It used to frighten me. I felt so lonely, guilty too, wondering if it was somehow all my fault – if they'd both go off and leave me. Mummy never wanted me, you know. I suppose she blamed us both for spoiling her life. And I always knew that Daddy had his little flings.' She shook her head. 'Poor Daddy! I asked him once if they only stayed together because of me. He said it was because of their public image – the scandal a divorce would cause. So I knew that at least it wasn't my fault they continued to live together, making each other miserable.'

'And now you say Leonie has agreed to divorce him?' Gloria said. 'She must have decided very recently.'

'I expect she was missing Paul Winspear.' Imogen bit her lip. 'Gloria, there's something I think you should know. I hate telling tales, but did you know that Shirley has been seeing him?'

'Paul Winspear?' Gloria looked up in surprise. 'No I didn't.'

'I warned her,' Imogen said. 'I don't trust Paul. There's something about him – I don't know, a cruel, predatory streak. I couldn't bear to see Shirley hurt.'

Gloria's mind was working fast, remembering the night that Shirley had tried to tell her something, but never got round to it. And now she had broken with Dave and told him there was someone else. It all fitted with what Imogen was telling her. 'But he's years older than her,' she said lamely.

'He's a womaniser,' Imogen said. 'His wife left him. He can't resist a pretty face and the younger and more vulnerable they are, the better. I've seen the way he looks at them. He even tried to make a pass at me once.'

'Oh, God.' Gloria was picturing Shirley coming home the previous night and reading the note she had left. After the break-up with Dave, she'd have been desperate to talk; she would have needed her. And once again Gloria had failed her. But even if she were to go back to London now, there was Michael. He, too, needed her. She'd have to get back to him soon – she couldn't leave everything to Margaret. And now it appeared that Leonie – who paid her salary and provided her with a home – would be back in London any day and needing her too. She felt torn in all directions. To whom did she give priority, her children who needed her or the woman who employed her?

'Does Daddy know?' Imogen was saying. 'About Michael, I mean.'

Gloria sighed and shook her head. 'No. I didn't want to complicate his life any further.'

'Will you tell him now?'

'This hardly seems the time.'

'I don't know; maybe it is. It could be just what he needs to help him over the ordeal to come.'

Gloria looked uncertain. 'I don't know. I'll have to leave tomorrow anyway, Imogen,' she said. 'I can't possibly stay any longer, much as I'd like to. Especially now that your mother has finished filming.'

'Of course. I'll have to go too. But once Daddy's been moved to London it'll make things easier.' She looked at Gloria. 'Will you tell him before you leave?'

'Perhaps. I'm still not sure it's the right thing. Imogen, there's something I'd like to ask you to do for me.'

'Of course, anything.'

'When you get back to town, will you see Shirley for me? Talk to her about Paul Winspear. She'll listen to you. I'm so afraid for her.'

'Of course I will, Gloria. By the way, does she know about Michael?'

'She knows about him, but she's never seen him.'

Imogen nodded. 'As long as I know.'

Gloria made one more visit to Tony before leaving. Sitting beside his bed she talked brightly to him about his war films, all of which she'd seen and enjoyed; about her work with Leonie and the theatre; about Shirley's drama lessons and the redevelopment plans for Angel Row. Everything, in fact, except the one thing Imogen had urged her to tell him. Something at the back of her mind kept telling her this was not the right moment. When that moment came – if it ever did – she would recognise it instinctively.

When it was time to go she leaned over him and touched her lips softly to his in a kiss that was no more than a butterfly's touch.

'Goodbye for now, darling,' she whispered. 'Once you're back in London I'll come as often as I can. I'll be thinking about you all the time. God bless.'

Tony's eyes swam with tears and his lips formed the words: 'I'll miss you.'

At the door she turned to wave, her heart as heavy as lead within her.

Imogen had written Shirley a note, asking to meet her at their usual place on Sunday afternoon. She hadn't received a reply to the note, but she was there early, in the hope that Shirley would come. She'd been waiting for about ten minutes at a table close to the window when she saw her coming in through the milk-bar door. She waved, then watched Shirley threading her way through the tables. She looked older, more sophisticated and yet sad, her eyes hurt and wary. When she reached the table she smiled apologetically.

'Hello, Imo. Sorry I didn't have time to answer your note.'

'It's okay. Don't bother to get a coffee. I've got a pot and two cups.'

Shirley sat down. 'It's awful about Tony, Imo. How is he?'

'Making progress. They'll be transferring him to one of the main London hospitals soon, for skin grafts.'

'Is it bad?'

'Bad enough.' Imogen sighed. 'I imagine it's the end of his acting career. He was taking a Shakespearean company to Canada, you know.'

'I heard that.'

'It's still going ahead. Everything's in place for the tour. It's scheduled to begin next month.' She paused. 'Actually he's asked me to go instead of him.'

Shirley's eyes widened. 'Oh, *Imo*! What a chance.'

'I know. I can't actually take his place, of course. He was to have directed and played some of the major roles. Other people will take over that side. I'll only be going along to represent him, really – as another Darrent. But I'll be playing a few small parts, and it'll be wonderful experience and enormous fun.'

Shirley smiled wistfully. 'I really envy you. What about your boyfriend, Charles?'

'He's going anyway. He applied for a job as an assistant stage manager some weeks ago and got the job. It's the lowest of the low, general dogsbody, but he'll be able to learn a lot. He wants to be a director eventually, you see.' She leaned forward. 'Between the two of us, he's asked me to marry him, Shirley.'

'I guessed he would soon.' Shirley smiled. 'And will you?'

'I'm tempted. He's a lovely person. I do adore him, and you know how much I've always wanted babies.'

'But your career?'

Imogen shrugged. 'I've seen at close quarters what ambition can do to a marriage – and a family. I'll never repeat that, God willing.' She reached out to touch Shirley's hand. 'Shirley, are you still seeing Paul?'

Shirley stiffened and withdrew her hand. 'No.'

'I see. You quarrelled?'

'Not exactly. If you really want to know, your mother came back from Cornwall and found us together at his flat. You can imagine the scene. But even before that it was beginning to go wrong.'

Imogen searched her eyes. 'Darling, I'm sorry for you, of course, but I can't pretend I'm not relieved. I've never liked Paul. You're not hurt, are you?'

'I hate myself, Imo,' Shirley said thickly. 'I should have seen what kind of person he was. I was just so stupid, blinded by love, I suppose – or infatuation. The worst thing is that I hurt Dave, the best friend I've ever had – apart from you. Now he's gone, Gloria's gone, soon Ma and Angel Row will be gone, and now you too. I . . . I feel I'm gradually losing everything and everyone, Imo. It feels as though life is giving up on me.'

'I'm sorry, darling. Something nice will happen for you soon, just you wait and see. I'm sure of it.'

'I wish I was.' Shirley shook her head. 'Do you remember the fun we had at Houlton during the war, Imo?' she said wistfully. 'The concerts we were in; our Fred and Ginger act? We had such plans, didn't we? Life was going to be so marvellous, so full of opportunities for us after the war, when we were grown-up.'

'I know. They were good days, weren't they?'

'Ever since Gloria went off to America things have gone from bad to worse. When she came home last week it was almost like the old days, but then she just took off again – quite suddenly and without any real explanation. She didn't even say where she was going.'

'Oh, I thought you knew. She went up to Yorkshire – to see Daddy in hospital. She shared my room at the hotel for a couple of days and she told me a lot of things while we were there together.'

'Did she tell you about Michael?'

'I knew anyway,' Imogen confessed. 'I found out quite by accident. I was staying with Molly and Jim at Longueville Hall for a weekend and I cycled over to Boothley to see Gloria. It was quite a shock. He's a lovely little boy, Shirley. Have you seen him?'

'No. I want to go to Boothley as soon as I can, though. I can't believe I've got a half-brother I've never set eyes on. Until I've seen him for myself it won't seem real.'

'I wanted Gloria to tell Daddy before she left, but I don't think she did,' Imogen said.

Shirley looked puzzled. 'Why should she tell *him*?'

Imogen bit her lip. She had assumed that Shirley knew who Michael's father was, but by the look on her face she clearly did not.

'Michael's his – Tony's, isn't he?'

Imogen sighed. 'She should have told you. I wish she had.'

'I'm always the last to know things,' Shirley said.

There was an awkward silence between them, then Imogen asked: 'Where will you go when you have to move out of Angel Row?'

'I don't know. I suppose I'll find a bed-sit or something.' She sighed. 'Life's pretty dreary at the moment. If I could only get a job in rep or something I'd be off like a shot, but according to what I've heard all the small theatres in the provinces are closing through lack of business. Everyone's buying television sets and staying at home to stare at them.'

Imogen squeezed her hand. 'Poor Shirl. I'm sure things will soon start looking up for you.'

'I hope you're right.' Shirley smiled ruefully. 'But with my luck I wouldn't bank on it if I were you.'

Leonie stepped out of her taxi outside the hospital. She wore her fur coat and her favourite 'disguise' of headscarf and dark glasses. She paid the driver and walked into the hospital.

'I'm Leonie Swann,' she told the girl on the reception desk. Taking off the glasses, she said, 'Mrs Tony Darrent, in other words. I'd like to see my husband, please.'

The girl looked up, her face pink with surprise at being suddenly face to face with a famous actress. '*Oh*! Miss Swann, I mean Mrs Darrent. Of course, I'll get a porter to take you straight up.'

In the lift the porter, slightly less impressed than the receptionist, eyed Leonie's expensive fur coat and sniffed appreciatively at the waft of French perfume that filled the lift.

''Ad to come far, 'ave you?' he enquired chattily.

Leonie gave him a withering look. 'From London. I've been away filming on location. No one thought to inform me of my husband's accident till yesterday.'

She had finally learned of the plane crash on the day after her return, when she had tried to contact Tony in Yorkshire in order to pour out her troubles to him. Getting no reply at his private telephone number, she had rung the location office number only to be told of the crash.

'Everyone's been going frantic, trying to get hold of you, Miss Swann,' the office girl told her. 'Your daughter, the hospital, and Mr Jason, your agent. Thank goodness you've rung in at last.'

Leonie had poured herself a large brandy and sat down to assimilate the impact of the shock. Tony badly injured – *burned*, they said. How ghastly! And just when she had decided to divorce him. Now everyone would think she was dumping him because of his accident. What rotten timing!

She telephoned the hospital to enquire about him and was relieved to hear that he'd come through surgery well and was improving. At least he wasn't going to die. It would have looked so bad if she hadn't been at his side. Now her first priority had better be to get up to Yorkshire as soon as she could.

She'd awakened to find her temper had cooled and she began to review her situation with Paul. After sleeping on the previous night's row she had decided that he was merely having a little fling with Shirley while she was away. It couldn't possibly be serious. She had behaved like a jealous schoolgirl, losing her temper like that when she should have played the scene with cool detachment. Paul's new play was almost finished and if the film did flop, as Max feared it would, she would need a new vehicle. A good one – and quickly, if her popularity was to be sustained. As for Shirley, maybe Leonie could use her influence to get the girl out of the way.

Another brandy and a pot of coffee later Leonie's thought processes had moved into overdrive. It was an astonishing stroke of irony that this accident of Tony's had placed her in an almost identical situation to that of the character she had played in *Joy in the Morning*. What marvellous publicity it would make for the film once the papers got hold of the angle. It was just possible that what Max had feared would be a hopeless flop might be turned into a success after all. She wondered briefly if Tony would be out of hospital in time for the premiere. If she could be photographed arriving at the cinema on his arm, it would cause an absolute sensation. She could already see the headlines: BRAVE ACTRESS'S TRUE-LIFE TRAGEDY, LEONIE SWANN HIDES HER ANGUISH BEHIND A SMILE . . . She got up from the table and headed for the bathroom. There was no time to be lost. She must start preparing for the role of attentive, loving wife immediately.

When she first saw Tony, the shock was like a kick in the stomach. No one had prepared her for what he would look like. If she had been unexpectedly confronted with the man propped up in the bed, she would not have recognised him as her husband. Her stomach churned unpleasantly and for a moment she thought she was going to be sick. The nurse with her touched her arm.

'Are you all right, Mrs Darrent?'

'Yes – yes, I'm all right.' She forced a smile onto her face. 'Tony, *darling*. I hear you're quite the star patient. You're doing *so* well, I'm told. Moving back to London soon, too. Won't that be nice?' She looked at the bandaged hands lying on the coverlet and was overcome with relief that she had a good excuse not to touch him. The sight of the blistered, blackened facial skin made her want to gag. She swallowed hard and looked at the nurse, who'd been watching her with unnerving closeness. 'Thank you, nurse,' she said brusquely. 'I'd like to be alone with my husband now, please.'

When the nurse had withdrawn, she pulled up a chair and sat down beside the bed. Tony was looking at her in a way that set her teeth on edge. It was impossible to assess what he was thinking with that blank, expressionless look.

'How are you, Leonie?' he managed to say.

'I'm fine. The film is in the can, as they say. It should be released in a couple of months' time. I think the premiere will be at the Leicester Square Theatre.'

He turned his head slightly to look at her. It was typical of Leonie that she had placed herself where he could not see her without painful movement. 'You must be glad you decided to go ahead with the divorce now,' he said.

She caught her breath theatrically and gave him a reproachful look. '*Darling*, how can you be so cruel? Of course I won't divorce you now that you need me so badly. What wife could be so heartless?'

'It shouldn't be too difficult – for you,' Tony said emotionlessly.

'You're bitter. It's understandable. Our marriage has hit some rough patches in the past. We've both been selfish. But you know I've always loved you, darling, no matter what. You surely can't have doubted that. I want you to get well just as quickly as you can and come home to me. I'm going to take care of you. I'll be the perfect nurse. You'll see.'

Something suspiciously like a groan escaped Tony's lips. 'Leonie,' he said. 'I'm sorry but I'd like you to go now, please.'

She hesitated. Was he feeling ill, or was he giving her the cold shoulder? It was impossible to tell. She would have to give him the benefit of the doubt. She stood up. 'All right, darling. But I'll be back. I'm going to give you all the attention you deserve – make up to you for all the years we've lost together.' She forced herself to bend closer. 'I won't kiss you. It would probably hurt, wouldn't it?'

'Yes, it probably would.' As the door closed behind her he groaned again. Christ! What had he done to deserve this? He felt like some poor defenceless animal caught in a trap. Leonie as the devoted wife and nurse was one role she'd never sustain. If only he felt strong enough to tell her that all he wanted was that she should go away and leave him alone.

* * *

Whan Ma heard of Shirley's quarrel with Dave, she was furious.

'What are you thinkin' of, my gel, turnin' down a steady young feller like Dave? You could go a lot further and do worse, y'know.'

'But I don't want to get married just for a job and somewhere to live,' Shirley protested. 'Life has to have more than that to offer.'

Ma sniffed in loud contempt. 'You're still 'ankerin' after the stage, ain't you? Time you woke up to life an' got them stars outa your eyes, my gel. Blokes like Dave don't come along that often you can afford to kick 'em in the teeth. You'll be sorry for what you done. You mark my words.'

Gloria returned to pay them a flying visit, and, seeing that there was animosity between her mother and daughter, she invited Shirley to go with her to Boothley for a visit. She explained to Ma that the girl looked peaky and needed a break. Shirley was torn between a desire to go and guilt about leaving Ma to cope with the shop alone.

'I'll go and have a word with Dave,' Gloria promised. 'I'm sure he'll come and help out for a couple of days. Anyway, the shop'll be closing soon for good. I can't see that it'd make much difference if it closed now.'

Dave agreed to help out and two days later Shirley and Gloria set off for Boothley. Once they were on their way, Shirley told Gloria that she had seen Imogen and heard about her visit to Leeds to see Tony.

'You and he have always been friends, haven't you?' she said, glancing at her mother.

'We've always got along well together, yes,' Gloria said guardedly.

'Imo seemed to think you should have told him about Michael,' Shirley ventured. 'I don't see why she should have thought that would help him.'

But Gloria made some noncommittal reply and turned to look out of the window, refusing to be drawn.

At Boothley, spring was in evidence everywhere. The trees were bursting into leaf and the cottage gardens were full of daffodils. At Rook Cottage a smiling Margaret was ready for them with a meal. Little Michael sat in his highchair with his bib tied on in readiness. When Shirley saw him she fell instantly in love with him and insisted on sitting beside him at tea and taking him up to bed later.

'He's so lovely,' she told Gloria later. 'But I can't believe you kept him from me for so long. I wish you hadn't, Glor. I've missed all his babyhood.'

'I had my reasons,' Gloria said. 'Some day soon maybe you'll understand.'

'He looks so well. I can hardly believe he's ill.'

'Margaret tells me she took him for his check-up at the hospital this week,' Gloria told her. 'They think they might be able to operate within the next six months or so.'

Shirley looked at her. 'When he goes into hospital, will you let his father know?'

Gloria turned away. 'I don't know. I'll see.'

Rook Cottage had improved beyond all recognition. A new bathroom extension had been built on at the back with an extra bedroom above it. The kitchen had been modernised and they now had the benefit of electricity. Margaret had decorated most of the rooms and the whole place shone like a new pin.

'We're going to re-plan the garden this summer, now that the workmen have finished,' Gloria told her. 'We thought we'd make a feature of the old well. Have it thatched, and have a wooden top made so that Michael can't climb up and fall in. We can stand pots of geraniums on it.'

'Do you ever see Nanny and Jim Jarvis?' Shirley asked.

Gloria shook her head. 'I haven't seen them for years. I wish there was time, but there never is. When I come it's usually a flying visit.'

'So they don't know about Michael?'

'Not from me, though they've probably heard about him.'

'Glor – you're not ashamed of him, are you?'

'Of course I'm not. What a silly thing to say,' Gloria was stung into replying. 'It's just that it'd be awkward, trying to explain. I'm not in a position to tell them – or anyone else – what they'd obviously be curious about.'

'I can't see Nanny or Jim asking awkward questions or pointing fingers at you,' Shirley said. 'It's not their style. And I know Nanny would love Michael.'

'That's as maybe,' Gloria said. 'But at the moment I'm not planning to put them to the test.'

Gloria had intended to broach the subject of Paul Winspear with Shirley; to ask her whether Imogen had managed to speak to her about him. But try as she would she could not summon up the courage to bring up the subject. Who was she to preach to Shirley about men? she reasoned. Shirley would probably be quick to point out to her mother that she'd made a big enough mess of her own life. She thought nostalgically of the days long ago before the war and the close relationship they'd all had and she couldn't help wishing they could be as they'd been then – knowing with a deep sadness that they never would.

The two-day visit to Rook Cottage was over all too soon and Shirley reluctantly kissed little Michael goodbye and accompanied Gloria back to London. They parted company at Euston Station, Shirley to Angel Row and Ma; Gloria to Mayfair and Leonie. Over the past few days she had been thinking hard and now she had come to a firm decision. All that remained now was to deliver the news to Leonie.

Leonie was in the blackest of moods. On her brief visit to Yorkshire she had found Tony less than enthusiastic over her plans to nurse him back to health, then on her return to London she had found Paul's response distinctly cool. He had refused to discuss the new play. Things were not going her way, but she was determined that she would make them, come hell or high water.

She greeted Gloria's arrival at the flat with sarcastic surprise. 'So there you are. I've been wondering when you'd do me the honour of coming back to work.'

'My holiday doesn't actually end till Monday,' Gloria reminded her. 'I've come back to give you my notice, Leonie. I'll be leaving in two weeks' time.'

'*Leaving*?' Leonie stared at her, taken aback by this new blow. 'But you can't. I need you. Just look at the state of this flat.' She seemed oblivious to the fact that she'd created most of the mess herself. 'I take it you've heard about poor Tony's dreadful air crash?'

'Yes.'

'I've just been up there to see him. I've decided not to go ahead with the divorce after all; I'll bring him home here and nurse him back to health. I'll be busy soon with a new play, so of course I'll need you here to care for him.'

'*Me*?'

'Of course. *I* can't take on the role of nurse, can I? Not that I'd be any good at it even if I had the time. You should see his face, it's the most *frightful* mess.' She shuddered delicately. 'I've always been squeamish when it comes to things like that. Poor Tony, his days as a heart-throb are decidedly over.' She lit a Turkish cigarette and peered at Gloria through a cloud of perfumed smoke. 'He doesn't want to come. Can you believe that? You'd have thought he'd have been grateful to me under the circumstances, wouldn't you?'

'I don't think he has all that much to be grateful to you for, Leonie,' Gloria said, her heart thudding with anger. 'He made you a star, gave up his own career for you, and you've treated him with contempt for as long as I've known you.'

'How *dare* you? Don't be so bloody impertinent,' Leonie snapped. 'Tony should consider himself lucky. No one else will want him now, that's for sure. He's just being a fool. If he plays his cards right we can capitalise on this accident of his – make it work for us. Being seen together at the premiere of *Joy in the Morning* will give both our careers a tremendous boost.'

Gloria felt sick. She could hardly believe that even Leonie could stoop so low. 'You'd actually use Tony's disfigurement to get publicity?' she said incredulously. 'I can't believe it. Don't you care *anything* for his feelings?'

'Oh, don't be so po-faced.' Leonie tapped off the ash from her cigarette. 'Tony would have been the first to appreciate the opportunity himself a few years ago. Publicity is everything in our business. But he's gone soft in his old age.' She looked at Gloria. 'He's forty-seven now, you know. He's not the handsome, dashing young matinee idol he was before the war. Those days are gone for ever.'

'We're *all* older,' Gloria said.

The remark stung Leonie far more than anything else Gloria could have said. She peered curiously at her pale face, the anxiety of the past few days clearly etched about her mouth and eyes. 'You're in a strangely waspish mood today, aren't you, Gloria? I know you once did me a little favour, but that doesn't give you the right to such familiarity.' She lit a new cigarette from the stub of the last one before crushing it out. 'Anyway, in my opinion you should be more worried about that daughter of yours. I caught her behaving like a little tart with Paul Winspear when I came back from Cornwall. It's patently obvious that they're sleeping together. It's *her* you should be worrying about.'

'I'm quite capable of taking care of my own family. Which is what I intend to do from now on,' Gloria said, her stomach churning sickeningly. 'And I'm sorry but I still intend to leave.'

Leonie opened her mouth to argue, but one look at Gloria's expression told her that she'd be wasting her time. 'Oh, suit yourself then, Gloria,' she said with a wave of her hand. 'You're not indispensable. Dressers are ten a penny, and I can always get an agency nurse in for Tony.'

In the weeks that followed, Shirley attended every audition she saw advertised. They ranged from the chorus of a Drury Lane musical, where she joined a long line of hopeful young girls at the stage door and queued up for hours, to auditions in a Camden Town church hall for a female juvenile lead for a northern repertory company. The producer was an old friend of Magda's and she'd promised to put in a good word for her, but the weeks went by and when Shirley heard nothing she had to admit that she wasn't going to get a job easily, however talented she might be.

Ma made no secret of her relief. 'No good'd come of it,' she said with a sniff. 'Say what you will, it ain't steady work. You get yourself a nice job in a shop, my gel. Do what you know.' She pulled an envelope out of her pocket. 'Look, I got this this mornin'. They've found me a little two-room flat, so you c'n move in with me when we leave 'ere. You won't mind sharin' a bedroom with your old Ma, will you?'

Shirley's heart sank. She thought of Imogen, going off with Charles on the Canadian tour with Tony's newly formed company. It wasn't fair. If it hadn't been for her famous father she'd never have got a job like that straight out of drama school. Imogen wasn't really all that dedicated to the theatre either. It wasn't that Shirley grudged her the chance, of course, but she couldn't deny that she felt envious and a little resentful.

Dave had already moved on to take up his new job. Shirley had hardly seen him since their row and when she ran into him two months after he'd left Whitechapel she was surprised and impressed by his improved appearance. He looked well groomed, almost handsome, with his hair cut in a fashionable, slightly longer style. He wore a new suit too, with a longer jacket and drainpipe trousers that accentuated his slim build. She'd been to Stepney for her drama lesson and was getting off the bus when she saw him walking towards her. At first she wondered whether to look the other way. Being snubbed by Dave was the last thing she needed and she wasn't sure whether he'd want to speak to her or not. But while she was still hesitating he spotted her and smiled.

'Hello, Shirl.'

'Hello, Dave. What are you doing over this way?'

'Just came to pick up one or two things I left with my old landlady,' he told her, falling into step beside her. 'On your way home?'

'Yes.'

'Got time for a drink?' He glanced uncertainly at her. 'Only if you want to, I mean. Don't feel you have to.'

'No – yes, I'd like to.'

In the pub he looked at her. 'You okay, Shirl? You've lost weight.'

She shrugged. 'Ma and I have moved into a two-room flat. There isn't really room for me. We have to share a bed and Ma is so restless. I don't get much sleep. I've been trying to get a job, but no luck so far.'

'That's a shame.' He took a sip of his beer. 'I, er, thought you might be planning to get married.'

She looked away. 'That's all over, Dave. And anyway there were never any wedding plans.'

'I see.' He paused, clearing his throat. 'Look, there's a vacancy at my shop. I know it's not what you're looking for but the money isn't bad.'

She glanced at him with a rueful smile. 'Is there really a job? Or do you mean you'd make one?'

'Oh, nothing like that. I'm still answerable to the owner. No, one of the girls is leaving soon – she's expecting.' Shirley said nothing and he went on quietly: 'I'm not saying I wouldn't make room for you if I could, though, Shirl. My feelings haven't changed. I might as well admit it. I still feel the same about you. Reckon I always will.'

She sighed. 'Oh, Dave. You make me feel awful. I never wanted to hurt you, honestly.'

He looked at her. 'As long as you're not with – with *him* any more, could we see each other now and again? I mean, no strings or anything. What do you say?'

She looked at his hopeful eyes and melted. 'Oh, all right them, why not?'

His eyes lit up. 'That's smashing. You must come and see the shop, Shirl. I've reorganised it all and I've got the flat upstairs. Three rooms, a bathroom and kitchen. I've never had such luxury. And that job's still there if you want it, remember. Think about it and let me know.'

'Okay, Dave. I will.'

Shirley took her silver-medal examination two weeks later and passed, once again with honours. But her triumph was marred by what she read weekly in the theatrical paper, *The Stage*. Television was what the public wanted now. Small provincial theatres were closing down one after another through lack of business and because of it the valuable practical training ground where generations of young actors had traditionally learned their craft was vanishing fast.

Finally, through sheer necessity, Shirley was forced to admit defeat and accept the job Dave had offered. And soon after, much to Ma's delight, they fell into a regular habit of going out together once a week. It was over a drink one Saturday evening in June that Dave passed her a copy of the London *Evening News*.

'Isn't that your friend's mum?' he asked, pointing to a picture on the front page.

Leonie was pictured arriving at a West End cinema for the premiere of *Joy in the Morning*. Dressed in a shimmering black evening gown, she clung to the arm of Max Forsythe, the film's director. Underneath the picture the caption read: 'BEAUTIFUL SAD LEONIE ATTENDS PREMIERE. The brilliant, multi-talented star of *Joy in the Morning* takes time off from her vigil at the bedside of sick husband Tony Darrent to attend the premiere of her strangely prophetic first film.'

'She sounds a really devoted wife,' Dave remarked. 'And they've been together for twenty-two years, so the paper says. Just shows. Some of these show-business marriages work okay, don't they?'

Shirley, who knew better about the Darrents' marriage, said nothing. Dave went on: 'Shirl, now that you've settled down in the job and you and I get along okay again, you wouldn't like to get engaged, would you?'

Shirley bit her lip. 'Oh, Dave . . . I don't know.'

'It makes no sense,' he said, 'you and your gran squashed into that tiny flat, sharing a bedroom, when I've got all that space. We get on all right, don't we? I mean, I know you don't feel as strong for me as I do for you. But I know I could make you happy. What do you think?'

Shirley had an audition in two days' time. It would be the twenty-eighth she'd taken this year. When she started working with Dave she had given up her drama lessons with Magda and decided not to try for any more stage jobs, but deep inside a stage career was still her dream and when she'd seen the audition advertised in *The Stage* last week she'd had a really strong hunch about it. She hadn't mentioned it to Dave. Luckily it would take place on their half-day closing so she wouldn't have to ask him for time off. She'd have just one more try, she promised herself. And if she didn't get the job this time, she'd definitely give up.

'Just give me a few days to think about it,' she told him. 'I'll let you know at the end of next week.'

It was even worse than usual. There was only one vacancy in the company, another rep, this time in the Midlands where live theatre still seemed fairly healthy. Twenty hopeful girls took turns to stand on the stage in the dimly lit theatre and perform their carefully rehearsed audition pieces. But afterwards there wasn't even the hope of waiting for a telephone call or letter. The director made his choice there and then; a tall dark girl who reminded her of Imogen and who had already had two years' experience of repertory work. Once again Shirley came away with her hopes shattered.

At the shop she let herself into the side entrance and climbed the stairs to Dave's flat. He was doing the books at the kitchen table and looked up in surprise when she walked in.

'Shirl? What are you doing here?'

'I just came to tell you that I'll marry you, Dave,' she said. 'If you still want me, that is.'

Instantly he was on his feet, his arms around her, hugging her close. 'Still *want* you? Oh, God, Shirl, if you only knew how much.' He kissed her, holding her so close that she could feel his heart beating against her own. She knew she had made him happy and as she rested her head on his shoulder she tried to feel glad and to share his happiness. There would never be anyone who loved her more, she told herself. He'd make a good husband. She was a lucky girl. But there was a huge lump in her throat and deep inside her heart ached for the dream that would never now come true.

Chapter Eighteen

When Leonie learned that Tony was finally fit enough to leave hospital, it came as a shock. Since Gloria left her she'd had a string of maids, none of them any good. They all wanted endless time off and a wage that was ridiculous. And of course none of them was likely to be the slightest use when it came to caring for an invalid. She'd tried hard to get Gloria to come back, but to no avail. In spite of all Leonie's enticements Gloria had remained adamant. Paul's new play was about to go into rehearsal any week now and she didn't see how she was going to cope with that *and* with having Tony at home. It was all too tiresome for words.

'But I've tried to tell you, Leonie,' Tony explained for the hundredth time when she outlined her difficulties. 'I don't *want* to come back to the flat. It's all arranged. When I leave here I'm going to Houlton – to Longueville Hall.'

'But Longueville Hall is up for sale and Nanny and Jim have left. The place is empty,' Leonie said with studied patience. Since his accident she had developed a ponderous, patronising way of speaking to him as though he were a retarded five-year old and it tried his patience so hard he could have screamed at her.

'Leonie, I've already told you, I've had the place taken off the market and Nanny and Jim are going to move back in with me until I can find another housekeeper. There's absolutely no need for you to worry. I'm not an invalid. And I've absolutely no intention of being a bloody nuisance to anyone.'

'But I wanted you to be in London,' she complained. 'You've already missed the film's premiere. If you're worrying about people seeing you, I'm sure there's no need. They'll soon get used to your appearance just as I have. How do you expect to pick up your career again if you hide yourself away from everyone?'

Tony sighed, his tolerance stretched to its limit. 'I'm not hiding myself away, as you put it. And I think you're talking about *your* career,' he said. 'No, Leonie. You've had all the mileage you're going to get out of my accident, so why don't you just agree to the divorce now and leave me alone?'

Tony's skin grafts had healed well. The surgeon had done all that he could, but in spite of the infinite care he had received, Tony was still scarred. The first time they had allowed him to look into a mirror he had been totally devastated. The face that had looked back at him, with its unnatural-looking shiny pink skin and slightly lopsided expression, seemed to him that of an ugly stranger. But gradually over the months the improvement of his appearance and his acceptance of it met somewhere in the middle and he finally came to terms with the reflection that the mirror offered him each morning. He was getting back the mobility of his facial muscles so that the stiff, expressionless look was softening, and, most important of all, he was learning to smile again.

Talking to the doctor and other patients in the burns unit where he had received his treatment, he had realised how lucky he was to have got off as lightly as he had. The rest of his body functioned perfectly normally. There was no reason why he should not pick up his career as a director again. His hands, though scarred and misshapen, still worked so that he'd be able to drive and attend to his own needs. Leonie's concern, he quickly realised, was more for herself than for him. She had basked in the 'faithful, devoted wife' image and now she was afraid of the adverse publicity a divorce would create.

'I'll make sure it's all done with the minimum of fuss,' he promised. 'I'll do my utmost to keep it out of the papers or at least to make clear that the decision is mine. Let's face it, Leonie, no one knows better than you that our marriage is dead. You and I are the only two people it really matters to. Why not just let it go?'

For all Leonie's protestations that she cared only for his welfare, Tony knew that if he agreed to return to the flat he would regret it deeply. Sometimes he was sure he detected a gleam of triumph in her eyes when she looked at him. The fact that his good looks had gone for ever gave her the edge over him. She would like to have him dependent on her; to be able to trundle him out as living proof of her selfless devotion whenever it suited her. But he was determined that it would never happen. He would not be subjected to that kind of humiliation. He had done enough to boost the career of Leonie Swann. Now he was determined to pick up the threads of his own life and make a fresh start.

'You know, one of the other burns patients said something to me the other day,' he told her. 'Something that hadn't occurred to me before. He said: Everyone's looks go in the end. There's no escaping that. We all change as the years go by. With us it's just happened suddenly instead of gradually. In a way we're lucky because we know where we are. Those who really love us will love us whatever we look like.' He smiled wryly. 'He was right, wasn't he? No surer way of finding out who your true friends are than getting your looks ruined.'

Leonie shuddered. The real irony of his words failed to reach her, but they probed uncomfortably at her chilling dread of passing time, something she was becoming increasingly aware of. 'Oh, Tony – *don't*.'

'So you won't want me around as a living reminder of life's cruel folly, will you?' He smiled his rueful, lopsided smile and she turned away, pulling on her gloves.

'All right, Tony. Joke about it if you must,' she said stiffly. 'If that's the way you want it, go to Houlton. And you can put the divorce plans into motion seeing that you're so determined. I can see now that all my concern for you has been wasted.'

* * *

All through the long and painful months of recovery Gloria had visited Tony whenever she could. When she left her job with Leonie she had gone to live with Margaret and Michael at the cottage in Boothley. It was wonderful to be able to spend more time with Michael and she'd managed to get a job behind the bar of the Dog and Doublet. Ever since Ken Doubleday, the landlord, had lost his wife he'd been short-staffed. She and Margaret helped him in shifts, turn and turn about. During her week of evening shifts, Gloria travelled up to London to spend a day visiting Tony. She put in a flying visit to Ma too and saw Shirley whenever she could. She looked forward very much to seeing Tony and watching him improve, both physically and mentally, week by week. They would walk together in the hospital grounds and she would tell him all her news. He learned of Shirley's failure to get work in the theatre and of her engagement to Dave Green, and of Gloria's worry concerning her mother and what she would do once Shirley had married, leaving her alone.

Imogen wrote twice-weekly letters to her father, describing in detail everything that happened on the Canadian tour. She seemed happy and was obviously learning a lot and enjoying herself. Having little news of his own to tell, Tony would read Imogen's letters to Gloria and together they would look at the photographs she sent.

'You must be terribly disappointed not to be there with them,' she said. 'The Darrent Shakespearean company was your dream, wasn't it?'

He smiled resignedly. 'Some dreams just aren't meant to come true, Gloria. As we get older, that's one of the realities we have to face.' He touched his cheek thoughtfully with one forefinger. 'When something like this happens to you, life takes on a different perspective. I can't grumble. I made a success of my war films and I've done a lot of the things I set out to do. I'm only just beginning to realise how lucky I am.'

'Lucky?' She looked at him.

'Luckier than many. You only have to look around you.' He smiled and took her hand. 'Other dreams take the place of the broken ones. And sometimes they're even better. For instance, if this hadn't happened to me you wouldn't be here with me now. You really meant it when you said goodbye to me, didn't you?' He took both her hands. 'I can't tell you what your visits to me have meant, Gloria. I look forward so much to seeing you and hearing your news.'

'I just wish you were nearer,' she said, 'so that I could see you more often.'

'Me too.' He squeezed her hands. 'Which is why I've made up my mind: when I leave hospital I'm going to Houlton, to Longueville Hall.'

She smiled delightedly. 'Oh, Tony, that's wonderful. I'll be able to visit you every day – if you want me.'

'Of course I want you. I fact . . .' He glanced at her speculatively. 'How would you feel about coming to keep house for me?'

She caught her breath. 'At Longueville Hall? Oh, Tony, I'd love to but I don't think I could.'

He looked crestfallen. 'I thought you'd be pleased. Why not?'

'Well, to begin with, what would Leonie have to say about it?'

'Nothing. I believe that if the truth were known she'd be relieved that someone else was taking on the responsibility. She's agreed to a divorce at last. I'm starting proceedings as soon as I can see a solicitor. Leonie's not a problem.'

'There's another reason,' Gloria said, frowning. 'I'm not exactly free to do as I like, Tony. There's someone else I have to consider.'

'Not Shirley? She has her own life now.'

'No. Not Shirley.'

'Your mother? You feel you should move back to London and live with her?'

'No.'

'Then who?' He was looking at her intently. 'Someone you've met? A man?'

Gloria smiled. 'I suppose you could say that.'

415

He sat back in his chair, letting out his breath slowly. 'Ah – I see. Well, it was bound to happen, wasn't it? You're a very attractive woman, Gloria. You still have your life ahead of you.'

'Tony . . .' She touched his hand. 'Tony, I'm talking about my small son. He's two and a half and his name is Michael.'

He turned to look at her. 'Your *son*? You have a child – two and half years old?' His eyes widened incredulously as they looked into hers. 'Gloria, is he . . . is he. . . ?'

'Yes, Tony.'

For a moment he stared at her, too stunned for words, then he was out of his chair. Pulling her to her feet, he held her close. 'My God, Gloria, why did you never tell me before? Why haven't I *seen* him?'

'At the time it seemed better not to,' she said. 'It would have caused so much trouble for so many people. I was in America when I found out I was pregnant. It was a shock. I decided to have the baby adopted. I intended to come back with it all behind me. But he was born with a heart defect, and anyway, once I'd seen him I couldn't have parted with him.'

'A heart defect?' He held her away from him. 'What is it? Is it serious – can it be cured?'

'Yes. It's a heart valve that isn't functioning as it should. At one time there would have been no cure, but now they can operate.'

'We must get another opinion. We must see that everything is done for him – and as soon as possible. Oh, Gloria, when can I see him? I can't believe it! I have a *son*. It's like being given another chance to make a go of life.' He looked at her. 'As soon as my divorce is through we'll be married. My son must have my name. Michael Darrent.' He said the name experimentally. 'It has a fine ring to it, doesn't it? Do you think he'll grow up to be an actor?'

Gloria laughed. 'He'll be himself, whatever that may be. But I know you'll love him, Tony.'

'Of course I will.' He looked into her eyes. 'I love you too, Gloria. You do believe that, don't you?'

'I believe it,' she said happily.

'Now I've got something to live for again – something to look forward to,' he said.

Gloria held him close, gratitude filling her heart. At last she'd been able to admit to Michael's existence. She'd felt so guilty about keeping him hidden away from all the people who mattered most, especially his father. It was almost as Shirley had once said – as though she were ashamed of him. Now she felt as though a great burden had been lifted from her shoulders. 'Tony,' she said softly. 'You don't have to marry me because of Michael, you know. If you really want it we can have his name changed to yours, but I'd never hold you to anything. That was partly why I've kept it to myself all this time.'

Tony held her away from him to look gravely into her eyes. 'Gloria, listen. I want you to know that I'm asking you to marry me because I love you, not just because of the child. And for the same reason you mustn't feel obliged to agree. If you don't feel you could love me in return, or if you can't face life with me, crocked up like this, I'd understand. I wouldn't blame you.'

She placed her fingers over his lips, her heart full. 'Tony, *Tony*, don't say things like that. Of *course* I love you.' She swallowed hard at the lump in her throat. 'I've always loved you and I always will. To me you're just the same person that you've always been and I can't think of anything I want more than to be married to you.' She stood on tiptoe to kiss him tenderly.

An ironic little smile drifted across his face as he looked down at her. 'It's funny, I used to dread getting old. I was always peering into the mirror, looking for grey hairs and wrinkles, worrying about going bald or putting on weight. Now none of that matters any more.'

'It never mattered – not to me,' she told him. 'And I'm not trying to flatter you when I say that to me you look as good as you've always looked.'

'Bless you.' He kissed her. 'All these months you've been the one person who has come to see me because you really wanted to and not out of a sense of duty. We've always had something special and you've proved to me the value of what we have.'

It was strange, the way good could come out of bad, Gloria reflected. If it hadn't been for the war she and Tony would never even have met. And if it hadn't been for his terrible accident he would never have known he had a son. They might have gone their separate ways for ever.

Leonie considered Paul's new play, *Give Me Yesterday*, even better than *Joy in the Morning*. Her own part was that of the widowed mother of a wayward daughter who was growing up to an awareness of herself as a woman. Both women fell in love with the same man, a feckless young American artist who was totally unable to cope with the situation and who finally destroyed all three. It was a powerful drama that required strong, emotional acting from both the older and the younger woman. At the first read-through it became clear that the actress who had been cast as the daughter was totally unequal to the demands of the part. Afterwards, over a drink at a nearby pub, Paul expressed his fear that a serious mistake had been made in the casting.

'Never mind, darling,' Leonie said. 'I'll ring Peter Jason after lunch. I'm sure he'll have someone on his books who'll fit the part nicely.'

But Paul was shaking his head. 'I still think Shirley could do it.'

Leonie stared at him. 'Shirley? Shirley who?'

'You know perfectly well who I mean. Shirley Rayner.'

She stared at him, trying to conceal her annoyance. 'You can't be serious. The girl has absolutely no experience.'

'She's had training and she has talent, Leonie. She has that spark of vitality that the part needs.'

'Paul, you're a brilliant playwright,' Leonie said placatingly, 'but you have absolutely no idea when it comes to acting. Shirley would never cope with a role like that. She isn't ready for the West End theatre, or any other theatre either if it comes to that. It just isn't in her.'

'I happen to believe it is,' he said stubbornly. 'She's young, but she's eager to learn.'

'Oh, I've already gathered that,' Leonie said sarcastically. 'Anyway, it isn't your job to cast the play. You should leave it to the production team. You'll make yourself unpopular if you try to interfere.' She took in his brooding expression, and, reading the danger signals, reached out to touch his arm. 'Darling, why don't you let me get Peter to send round some girls to audition? I'm sure he has plenty of talented young actresses with experience on his books who'd jump at the chance.'

'Where *is* Shirley these days?' he asked, shrugging off her hand.

She frowned. 'I've no idea. They pulled down the street where the family used to live. I haven't a clue where she is now.'

'You know where her mother is, though. You could find out.'

Leonie swallowed her anger. How dare he ask her to do his errands for him – go looking for his past floozies? If she hadn't been so afraid of his temper she'd have told him where to go in no uncertain terms. But she had to tread carefully with Paul these days. It had taken a lot of ingratiating to get back on his right side. His temper was explosive and unpredictable, especially when he was thwarted. Nowadays it took more than an hour or two in bed to assuage it. Sometimes she wondered if persuading him to move into the Mayfair flat with her was a good idea after all. Living with him was like sharing a cage with a half-tamed tiger at times.

'Give me Gloria's address and I'll get in touch with her myself,' he said.

Leonie looked at him warily. On second thoughts maybe it would be better to handle this herself. Already an idea was beginning to form in her mind. 'Don't worry, I'll fix it, darling. If that's what you really want.'

Later that afternoon she knocked on the door of Magda Jayne's studio in Stepney. When the drama teacher opened the door, she was astonished to find Leonie

Swann standing on her doorstep. Leonie was graciousness itself as she sat drinking tea with Magda in the studio.

'I've heard so much about you from Shirley Rayner that I felt I really must come and pay you a visit,' Leonie said chattily. 'Shirley stayed with me all through the war, you know, at our country house in Northamptonshire. I flatter myself that it was I who first awakened her interest in the theatre.'

'I've heard all about the wartime concerts,' Magda said. 'Shirley is extremely talented. The poor girl has tried so hard to get her foot on the first rung of the ladder, but I'm afraid she hasn't had any success. It's a very tough time for young actors trying to break into the business. I know that if things had been normal in the theatre she'd have been well on the way to a brilliant career by now, but with so many small theatres closing up and down the country it's become almost impossible to get a job.'

'I know. Do you know where she is nowadays?' Leonie asked casually.

'Sadly, no.' Magda spread her hands helplessly. 'She isn't with me any more, I'm sorry to say. She was so disappointed after the last audition that she lost heart and decided to give up trying. She's working in a grocery shop in Hackney now, I believe.'

'What a sad waste! Has she auditioned many times?' Leonie asked.

'A great many. She'd set her heart on the last one. It was with a rep in Birmingham. They were looking for a girl to play juvenile leads.'

'Really? Do you know who the producer was?'

'Gerald Maddox, I believe.'

'Gerald?' Leonie beamed. 'He's a very old friend of mine. We worked together before the war. I'm sure that he'd find a place for darling Shirley if I were to give him a ring.' She stood up. 'Thank you, Magda. It was so nice meeting you. I've been promising myself a visit to you for some time. I try to keep up with what the young hopefuls are doing and help wherever I can. After all, they are the theatre's future, aren't they?' She began to pull on her gloves. 'Goodbye. It's been so nice having this little chat, and if I can put any students your way you can be sure I will.'

All the way home in the taxi Leonie hugged the information to herself. What luck that it should have been Gerald Maddox who last auditioned Shirley. He owed her a favour from the time she'd got him the job of assistant stage manager on *Sunshine Sally* – his first foot on the ladder. She'd be sure to remind him of that. The moment she got back to the flat she put through a call to the Mask Theatre in Birmingham. This way everyone would be happy, she told herself contentedly as she listened to the ringing tone. And Birmingham was such a nice long way from London, too.

'How are you, Ma?' Gloria looked round the cramped little flat that her mother shared with Shirley and wondered how they could tolerate it. Rook Cottage was small but at least they could get out into the fresh country air whenever they wanted to. Here, opening a window only filled the room with air polluted by carbon monoxide from the constant stream of traffic on the busy road below.

'Have you heard yet when you'll be moving into the new flat?' she asked as she took off her coat.

'No. Sometimes I wonder whether I'll live to see it 'appen,' Ma said gloomily. 'When Shirl gets married next month I'll be stuck 'ere with nothin' to do but twiddle me thumbs all day. It won't even be worth cookin' meself a meal with no one to share it with.'

'Surely it won't be that bad?' Gloria said. 'You've still got your friends and your whist drives to go to.'

Ma shook her head. 'It ain't the same as it used to be. Since the war Whitechapel ain't a patch on what it was. Half the old streets've gone, people scattered 'ere there and everywhere – them as weren't killed in the Blitz. The 'eart's gone out of the place. It's the end of the good old life we knew. Them days won't never come again. Sometimes it don't feel like we won the war at all.'

Gloria looked at her mother. She'd never seen her quite this depressed. Since moving from Angel Row she had aged. The loss of the little shop that had been her life for more than forty years had left an irreplaceable void in her life. There was no longer anything to get up for in the mornings, and Gloria could see that when Shirley left Ma would miss her badly. There'd be no one young and lively coming home in the evening; no link with the outside world. If only she could get her to move closer so that she could keep an eye on her.

'Ma, look, now that I'm so far away it isn't convenient for you, living here. I can't come up to visit you as often as I'd like to and Shirley will be too busy to come often when she's married, what with the shop and a husband too. Won't you think again about coming to live in Boothley?' Seeing her mother's features beginning to set in the familiar stubborn lines, she went on hurriedly: 'Listen, I've got something to tell you, Ma. It might come as a shock. I'm getting married.'

Surprise took the place of stubborn discontent on Ma's face. '*You* are?' Her eyes opened wide. 'Who to?'

'To Tony – Tony Darrent.'

Ma's mouth was a startled O. '*"im*?' she barked. 'But 'e's already married – to that there Leonie Swann.'

'They're about to be divorced. He's coming out of hospital soon and going to live at Longueville Hall. I'll be going there to look after him.'

Ma folded her arms and her mouth into uncompromising disapproval. 'I don't 'old with divorce. Never 'ave. You know that.' She eyed Gloria suspiciously. 'You've always been stuck on 'im, 'aven't you? Well if you asks me you're 'eadin' for trouble, bitin' off more than you can chew. D'you think 'e'd marry the likes of you if 'e 'adn't been disfigured in that there accident? Course 'e wouldn't. Can't get no one else to look after 'im, that's what it is. That Leonie won't want 'im no more. That's the only reason 'e's asked you.'

'That's a very unkind thing to say, Ma. And it's not true.'

Ma shook her shoulders. 'Well, time'll tell, gel. That's all I got to say. Thank God young Shirl's seen some sense

422

at last. Marryin' young Dave Green is the best thing she could do. I been prayin' it'd 'appen.'

'Ma, there's more – something else I have to tell you.' Gloria was surprised to discover that her heart was beating faster at the prospect of what she was about to reveal. It was incredible that at thirty-five she still feared her mother's angry disapproval. Clearing her throat, she went on: 'I . . . I've got a little boy, Ma. Michael. He's three and a half. He's Tony's son. Very few people have known about him till now. Not even Tony himself. Margaret Jeffs, a friend I met in Yorkshire has helped me bring him up at Rook Cottage since he was born. He was the reason I couldn't come home when Pa was ill; the reason I stayed away when you needed me. I'm sorry.'

A variety of startled expressions chased themselves across Ma's features. For a moment or two she seemed to have lost her power of speech, then she folded her arms across her bosom and said: 'Well, since the goin's-on in the war nothin' surprises me no more. Always flung yourself at that feller's 'ead. It was bound to 'appen, I s'pose. Still, I'm glad to 'ear 'e's doin' the decent thing. That's somethin', I s'pose.'

Relief surged through Gloria. 'So will you at least pay a visit to Boothley to see Michael, Ma?'

'Dunno. I'll 'ave to think about that. I'm not sayin' I approve of any of it. I don't want you to go thinkin' I do.'

'He'll be going into hospital soon, for a heart operation,' Gloria told her. 'It's something he was born with. But they can operate now.'

This made Ma sit bolt upright in her chair, riveted. 'Why didn't you tell me before? Poor little mite.'

'The doctors say he'll be all right. He's quite a tough little thing.'

'All right – when he's got 'eart trouble? That's it then.' Ma's eyes shone now with the determined glint Gloria hadn't seen in them since she waged her one-woman war with Hitler. 'I reckon you're goin' to need some 'elp, our Glor. What with a feller gettin' over an accident an' an invalid child. I know me duty. I'll not see you strugglin'. I'll come.'

423

'You *will*? Oh, that's marvellous. You can have Rook Cottage, Ma. Margaret, my friend, has been courting Ken Doubleday from the Dog and Doublet for the past year. I think they'd like to get married as soon as they can. That'll leave Rook Cottage empty. Oh, Ma, just wait till you see it. You'll love it now that it's been modernised.'

'Well, that's as maybe.' The light in Ma's eyes belied her stern expression. 'I've never liked the country as you know – all them smells.' She sniffed, wrinkling her nose. 'But I dare say I'll get used to it in time. Most important thing we've got to do is look after that child.'

Shirley and Dave were to marry at the local register office. The date was set for 4 August. It would be the Saturday before the bank holiday so they'd be able to go away for a long weekend. Dave had booked a room at a guesthouse in Southend.

He'd been counting the days, crossing them off the calendar in the kitchen at the flat. He had bought a new suit to wear for the ceremony and he'd been busy for weeks redecorating the flat ready for Shirley to move in with him after the wedding.

Shirley, on the other hand, grew more apprehensive as the day drew nearer. Each week, as she received letters from Imogen, she studied the postmarks: Toronto, Ontario, Quebec. They sounded so far away, so exciting. Imogen wrote of full houses and ecstatic receptions. They were well received everywhere they went, it seemed. She wrote of the small parts she was playing while understudying larger ones, and of all that she was learning, far more than at drama school, she said. She made it all sound so exciting and such fun, relating anecdotes, mentioning the comradeship of the other members of the company and the team spirit they enjoyed. In every letter she mentioned Charles and their growing relationship. The most recent one was full of the news that they planned to marry on their return to England in the spring. She sounded so fulfilled and happy, so in love with Charles and with life. Shirley couldn't help envying this ecstatic happiness that had somehow eluded her.

Am I doing the right thing? she asked herself again and again. Can I really settle down with Dave? Can I really give up the idea of a career in the theatre? Am I being fair to him – to either of us? On the other hand, she did not have Imogen's opportunities, her entrée to all the right people and places. At the very best all she could expect was a small part with a touring company that would last perhaps six weeks before she'd find herself back on the dole, auditioning for jobs again.

Once again everything around her was changing. Ma was about to move to Boothley to live in Rook Cottage. And although she would never admit it, she was delighted at the prospect. An ecstatic Gloria was to marry Tony and move into Longueville Hall with him and little Michael. It seemed there was no place in their plans for her. Dave was all she had. He was kind and safe and he loved her. She was lucky and she really should be grateful. She went Up West alone to buy her wedding dress. She would have liked Gloria's help in choosing it, but, knowing how busy she was, she didn't ask.

To Ma's horror she chose green. 'Couldn't've picked a more unlucky colour,' she exclaimed with a shake of her head. 'I dunno, I'm sure,' she grumbled. 'I always dreamed my girl'd 'ave a white weddin'. Gloria never 'ad one at all, an' now you're gettin' hitched in one o' them registry offices – in *green* of all colours. I tell you, no good'll come of it – even if it do go with your new name.'

That was another thing, Shirley reflected as she hung up the apple green two-piece. Shirley Green sounded so ordinary. Shirley Rayner had always sounded as though she just *might* have become someone special. But Shirley *Green* – never in a million years could she achieve fame with a name like that.

On the evening before the wedding Shirley washed her hair and packed her clothes into two large suitcases, ready to move to Dave's flat. Ma had decided to go to a whist drive with a friend so that she could have the flat to herself. It was a warm evening and she sat at the open window, drying her hair in what breeze there was. Looking down into the street, she saw the telegram boy enter the building and a few minutes later there was a tap on the door. Pulling her dressing gown round her, she went to open it.

'Telegram for Miss Rayner,' the boy said, handing her the small orange envelope. Shirley's heart plummeted. Telegrams meant bad news. Everyone knew that. During the war parents and wives had dreaded the sight of the telegram boy in his blue uniform. But who in the world could be sending a telegram to her? And what would it say?

'Better open it, 'adn't you?' the boy prompted cheekily. 'In case there's a reply.'

With trembling fingers Shirley ripped open the envelope and unfolded the sheet of paper inside. The printed strips read: FURTHER TO RECENT AUDITION, VACANCY FOR JUV. ACTRESS. NOTIFY IMMEDIATELY IF ACCEPTABLE. The sender was GERALD MADDOX. THE MASK PLAYERS. BIRMINGHAM.

The words danced a crazy jig before Shirley's eyes as she read them over and over. Could it be true? Was someone playing a joke on her?

'Well?' The boy was still waiting.

'Oh, er, no reply, thanks.' Shirley closed the door and went to sit at the table. Spreading the telegram out in front of her she read it yet again. How ironic that her chance should come now, when she was unable to take it. Now she would never know if she'd have been a success – a star, even. If only – oh, if *only* she were free to accept the offer! She could have been travelling to Birmingham tomorrow, starting work as a real professional actress instead of marrying Dave and turning into plain Mrs Shirley Green.

Suddenly she made up her mind. Jumping up from the table, she ran to the window and leaned out, calling to the boy who was just leaving the building. 'Hey, boy! Can you come back up here, please? I've got to send a reply after all.'

She scribbled her acceptance on a scrap of paper and paid the boy, then she dressed hurriedly. When she was ready she took Ma's pad of lined notepaper and a packet of cheap envelopes out of the sideboard drawer and sat down at the table. Biting the end of the pencil she searched her mind for the right words. The notes to Ma and Gloria weren't so difficult. It was the one to Dave that was really hard. Poor Dave. He didn't deserve to be jilted and she felt dreadful about it, but she couldn't help herself. This was probably the only chance she'd ever get to do what she had always wanted to do. She *had* to take it. If she didn't, she'd regret it for the rest of her life and probably resent him too. Somehow she must try to find the words to temper the deep wound she was about to inflict with understanding.

At last the three sealed envelopes lay on the table. She stood up and put on her coat, then, picking up the suitcases she'd packed earlier, she walked out of the flat and down the stairs.

Gloria stepped down from the bus and headed for Mason's Stores, reflecting as she had before what a good position it had. With its double windows stacked with pyramids of tins of fruit and packets of custard powder, it stood right in the middle of the little shopping centre close to a bus stop.

Inside there were plenty of customers and as she waited she looked around appreciatively at the improvements Dave had made since he took over as manager. Wearing a spotless white coat, he was serving at the provisions counter, deftly slicing bacon with a shiny new electric machine as he made pleasant conversation with his customer. When he looked up and saw her, he smiled in surprised recognition.

'Mrs Rayner. Good afternoon. What can I get for you?'

'I'd like a word, please, Dave,' she said. 'I know this isn't the best of times but I'm only up from Boothley for the day.'

'It's okay. I was just about to take my lunch break anyway. We can go upstairs to the flat if you like.' He wiped his hands on a clean cloth and called to one of his assistants. 'Mary. I'm taking my break now. Take over here, will you?'

Gloria followed him through a storeroom at the rear of the shop, piled high with cartons and boxes; through a door and up a flight of stairs to the flat. As he closed the door she looked around approvingly. It was bright, the walls freshly distempered and brand-new linoleum on the floor. Dave opened the door to a tiny kitchen.

'Come in. I'll put the kettle on.'

'Don't let me stop you having your meal,' Gloria said.

'It's okay. I only have a sandwich and a cuppa midday. I usually get it ready before I open up in the morning. I cook myself a proper meal after closing.'

'You seem very well organised,' Gloria said, looking round at the smart blue and white paintwork.'

'A case of having to be,' Dave said ruefully.

'Dave, I've been meaning to come and see you for weeks. I expect you know why I'm here.' Gloria looked at him. 'What Shirley did – it was unforgivable. I want you to know that neither Ma nor I knew anything about it before you did.'

Dave shrugged helplessly. 'I won't pretend I wasn't gutted when I got her letter that morning, Mrs Rayner. In fact, that would be putting it mild. Getting chucked on your wedding day's no joke.'

'I know, Dave. And believe me, we were terribly upset too. I tried to get in touch with you that Saturday, but . . .'

He shook his head apologetically. 'I know. I'm sorry. After Mrs Rayner sent Shirl's letter round I just shut myself away up here all over the bank holiday; didn't answer the doorbell or the phone. I couldn't face anyone.'

All the colour had drained from his face and Gloria bit her lip in anguish. She hadn't come here to make him relive the trauma. Perhaps she should have left well alone. For the hundredth time she asked herself how Shirley could have done this to him. 'In a way I blame myself,' she said painfully. 'Ever since she was a baby I've encouraged her to want a stage career.'

Dave poured out two cups of tea and took the cover off a plate of sandwiches, which he passed to Gloria. 'Do sit down and have one, Mrs Rayner. They're the best ham.' He grinned wryly. 'One of the perks of the job, you could say.' 'He took the chair opposite. 'You mustn't blame yourself,' he said. 'Shirley's a born actress. I always knew that. If she'd let that chance go by she'd have regretted it for the rest of her life. I can see that now. She might even have come to hate me if she'd given up everything she wanted to marry me. She's got talent – got what it takes, as they say. And to be fair, I think it hurt her too, doing what she did to me. She's not a selfish girl at heart.'

'I hope she realises how much pain she caused us all,' Gloria said angrily. 'I was upset when I found out what she'd done, but Ma was devastated. It hit her really hard. She thought the world of you, Dave. In her eyes Shirley was a lucky girl and she's convinced that she'll rue the day she let you down.'

'No.' Dave shook his head. 'Like I said, it'd probably never have worked out anyway. I'll go and see the old lady some time and try and explain that to her. I always liked her too. She'll be lonely now that Shirl's left.'

'Not for long. She's coming to live nearer to me,' Gloria told him. 'I'm getting married myself soon and going to live in Northamptonshire.'

'That's good news. I wish you luck,' Dave said.

'Look, Dave, if there's anything I can do.' She bit her lip. People always said that. It had such a hollow ring. 'I mean – look, don't be lonely, will you? I know you've got no family of your own.' She took a scrap of paper from her handbag and scribbled the address of Rook Cottage on it. 'Here, this is where Ma will be living, and I won't be far away. If ever you want to come and see us – stay for a weekend, or longer – you'll be more than welcome.'

Dave took the paper and folded it carefully. 'Thanks a lot, Mrs Rayner. I'll remember.'

'And good luck with the shop. It all looks very nice. I'm sure you'll make a great success of it.'

'Thanks. I'll do my best.'

Outside in the street, as she waited for the bus, Gloria asked herself again whether what had happened was her fault. Since Shirley had jilted Dave she'd asked herself the same question time and time again. She hadn't been a good mother to Shirley; she hadn't had the chance to be a mother to her at all, really. But that was largely the fault of the war and their enforced separation. If Shirley had grown up at 10 Angel Row, Whitechapel, would she be the same young woman she was today? Would *any* of them be the same? Gloria knew that war had changed them all. They were the helpless victims of fate. Her dream for Shirley had been fame and fortune, but everything has its price, and sometimes dreams have a nasty way of rebounding on you in unexpected ways.

Since Shirley's departure, one letter had arrived at Rook Cottage. It bore a Birmingham postmark and it was brief. She begged to be forgiven for walking out and leaving Gloria and Ma to pick up the pieces. She said she had found a nice room and was enjoying her job with the Mask Players. She had signed a three-month contract and was earning eight pounds a week.

A three-month contract. She had given up security and broken the heart of the man who loved her for the chance to be an actress for three months. Gloria only hoped that she wouldn't regret it. She hoped that the pain she had caused wouldn't return to haunt her.

She made several attempts to reply to the letter, but she couldn't find the words to say what she really felt. Half of her blamed herself and sympathised with Shirley's all-consuming obsession for the stage, while the other half could not forget the thin young man with the pale, earnest face who had loved and wanted her so much. For her it brought back a poignant reminder of the unbearable ache rejection and unrequited love brought. She knew from bitter experience that that ache would live in Dave's heart for the rest of his life. In the end she did not reply at all.

A week before Tony was due to leave the hospital, Molly and Jim moved back into Longueville Hall to get everything aired and ready. Gloria had been to see them to make arrangements as soon as she had a date from the hospital. She found Molly there alone and, sitting in the cosy little living room of the Jarvises' cottage over the first fire of the autumn, she told her of the Darrents' impending divorce and of the marriage plans she and Tony were making. Then, taking her courage in both hands, she told Molly about Michael. The older woman received the news without surprise.

'We knew there was a little child.' She reached out to touch Gloria's hand. 'My dear, you can't live in a rural community like this and keep things like that to yourself,' she said. 'You can't stop the rumours spreading either. Local folks have speculated about little Michael ever since you first brought him here as a baby.'

'What are they saying?'

Molly smiled. 'Everything except the truth, as it happens. But gossip isn't important. What *is* important is that the three of you are going to be together at last.'

'Imogen knew before anyone else. She paid me a surprise visit.'

Molly nodded. 'I know. I tried to stop her coming but I couldn't think of an excuse. To the girl's credit, she never breathed a word.'

'She guessed later, after Tony's accident, that he was Michael's father.' Gloria looked at Molly. 'It wasn't me who broke up the marriage, you know.'

'Bless you, love, I know that. Jim and I used to hear the rows.' She raised her eyes to the ceiling. 'Some of the things she used to say to him. She's no lady, you know, for all the glamour. Her lack of breeding used to come out when she lost her temper. We always knew she made him miserable. I always guessed that you and he had a soft spot for each other too. And after all that's happened he deserves some happiness.'

'So you're not shocked?'

Molly smiled. 'Knowing the truth – all the facts, *and* the people concerned – how could I be?'

431

'Ma was, till I told her about Michael's illness. That seemed to alter everything for some reason. I didn't tell you; I'm planning to bring her to live in Rook Cottage.'

Molly smiled. 'What a good idea! You can be sure we'll make her welcome here,' she said. 'I'll get her to join the WI and the Mothers' Union.'

Gloria laughed. 'Well, you can try,' she said. 'Since Princess Elizabeth got married, her main interest is the royal family. She's even made a scrapbook and she cuts out all the pictures she can find of the royal couple and little Prince Charles.' She smiled. 'Between ourselves, I think she identifies with the Queen now that she's a grandmother. She says the royal family don't let you down even if your own does.' Gloria smiled. 'But I'm hoping that Michael will help her settle down here. I'm sure he'll make her feel useful and at home again.'

Tony finally came out of hospital one Friday afternoon towards the end of October. Gloria collected him and they travelled by hired car to Houlton. It was late afternoon when they arrived at Longueville Hall and as they drove up the drive Gloria reached for Tony's hand.

'Welcome home, darling.'

'This really feels like coming home,' he said. 'Now that you're here with me.' He turned to look at her. 'Will Michael be there?'

She nodded. 'Yes. Margaret said she'd bring him so that he was here to meet you.'

'Will he know who I am?'

'I've been telling him for weeks that he's going to meet his daddy.'

Tony's eyes clouded. 'When he sees me, he won't be . . . frightened of me, will he? It's the one thing I've been dreading.'

Gloria pulled his arm through hers and hugged it. 'Of course he won't. A little shy perhaps, but not frightened. Why should he be?'

Tony rubbed his jaw. 'Because of this. I'm no oil painting any more.'

'You are to me,' she whispered. 'As for Michael, he's never seen you before. Children have a way of accepting people at face value.'

He turned to smile at her. 'Face value. What an apt expression.'

Molly had the front door open as the car drew up. She stood there on the threshold with Jim beside her.

'Welcome home, Mr Tony.' She held out her arms as they came up the steps and Tony hugged her warmly.

'It's good to be home, Molly. Thank you both for all you've done.'

Jim carried in the bags and they all went through to the kitchen. Sitting on the floor in front of the Aga, playing with his toy cars, was Michael. Tony stood in the doorway for a moment, looking at him, his eyes apprehensive. He took a step forward.

'Hello, Michael.'

The little boy looked up. 'Hello.' He got to his feet and walked across to where Tony stood and stared up at him for a long moment, his blue eyes assessing. 'Are you my daddy?' he asked, glancing at his mother and then back at Tony.

'Yes, I am. Is that all right?'

Michael studied him for a moment, then he said: 'Do you want to play with my cars?'

'Thank you. I'd love to.'

Gloria watched as Tony got to his knees on the hearthrug and began to play with his son. As he reached out for one of the cars, Michael tentatively touched one of his misshapen fingers.

'You've got a poorly hand,' he said with some concern.

'I did have, but it's all right now,' Tony told him gravely.

'Did the doctor make it better?' Michael asked.

'Yes.'

'Did it hurt?'

'No, not much.'

'The doctor's going to make me better soon too,' Michael told him.

433

'I know, and after that you're going to come and live here with me. Will you like that?'

Michael glanced up at Gloria. 'Can Mummy come too?'

'Of course she can.' Tony looked up with a smile. 'All three of us together. Won't that be fun?'

Gloria swallowed hard and turned to Molly. 'I think I'll go upstairs and unpack for Tony,' she said.

Molly nodded understandingly. 'You do that, love, and I'll put the kettle on,' she said. 'I'm sure you'll all be wanting your teas.'

Ma moved into Rook Cottage a fortnight later. Most of her luggage was sent on ahead and Gloria went up to London to fetch her and one suitcase of essential things. All the way in the train she listened to her mother's complaints, tolerating them because she knew they were the product of her anxiety and apprehension.

'If I don't like it, our Glor, I'm comin' straight back,' Ma said at least a dozen times. 'London might've changed, but at least it's what I *knows*. If it wasn't for you needin' me I'd've stopped where I was, y'know.'

'I know, Ma,' Gloria said. 'And I really appreciate it. But just give it a chance, that's all I ask. See how you get on. No need to stay if you don't like it.'

Ma grunted and stared moodily out of the window. 'All them years of gropin' about in the blackout, an' now, just when they've switched the lights back on, 'ere I am goin' where they ain't never 'eard o' street lights.'

'We're going to get them soon, now that we've got the electricity laid on,' Gloria told her. 'And you must admit you won't miss the noise and the traffic, now will you?'

'Will folks be friendly, though?' Ma muttered, thwarted at having her argument shot down. 'Country folks don't understand us Londoners. I'm warnin' you – I'm not stoppin' where I ain't welcome.'

All through the journey she found fault with everything, but once she arrived at Boothley and met Michael all thoughts of returning to London seemed to fly out of the window. The moment they met, Ma and her grandson

434

formed an instant rapport and within minutes it was as though they had always known each other. As for Rook Cottage, the place surprised and delighted her, though she would have died rather than let anyone see it.

'Mmm, don't seem too bad,' she said grudgingly, looking round her. 'It don't seem to be damp, even if it is in the country.'

'Wait till you see your room, Ma,' Gloria said. 'I've given you mine. I'm moving in with Michael until we move to Longueville Hall. It overlooks the garden. It's not much to look at now, but you wait till spring. You never know, you might even find that you like gardening yourself,' she added optimistically.

Ma soon made the little room with its pink-striped wallpaper and flowered curtains her own personal territory. Pa's photograph took pride of place on the dressing table, but the big studio portrait of Shirley, taken when she was five in her best Shirley Temple frock and ballet shoes, had been banished from sight on the day that Shirley had jilted Dave. Her name hadn't passed Ma's lips since.

When Gloria saw that her mother had set out her brush and comb and hung her clothes in the wardrobe, she heaved a sigh of relief. It was a sure sign that Ma had given the place her seal of approval. She had decided to stay.

Margaret was married quietly to Ken in late December. Gloria and Tony shared their first family Christmas with Michael and Ma at Longueville Hall. Molly and Jim joined them too and it was almost like old times, except for the fact that Imogen and Shirley were missing. Nevertheless, it was still a happy time for them all as they watched Michael's eyes grow round with joy and wonder at the glitter and presents. Then, in the first week of the New Year, Gloria was notified by post that Michael was to have his operation at last.

She and Tony drove up to Great Ormond Street with him on a cold blustery day in late January. Unaware of the coming ordeal he and his parents faced, he chattered happily to them all the way, while Gloria tried to hide the cold fear that clutched her heart. Had fate smiled too kindly on her these past months? Was she about to pay the price of happiness yet again? Tony was beside her now to share the anxiety. But she wasn't sure that even that would be enough to sustain her if she lost Michael now after all they'd both been through.

Chapter Nineteen

Give Me Yesterday had enjoyed good business in the West End. They had played to packed houses ever since opening night, but the theatre was booked for a new production and already the management was faced with the decision either to find a new venue or take the play on tour.

As usual at this stage, Paul had lost interest. He was well into writing a new play and utterly absorbed in his work. Leonie too was becoming bored and restless. The legitimate theatre was all very well but she missed the acclaim that her wartime singing had brought her. Peter Jason had recently received an exciting offer for her to tour Australia. There would be a series of concerts at which she would revive her recorded wartime favourites and a couple of guest appearances on TV shows. She hadn't done any TV before and she was tempted to accept. The only thing that stopped her was Paul. When he was working he neglected himself terribly. Since they'd been together she'd discovered things about herself that she had never suspected before. She actually liked looking after him and organising his disorganised life, soothing him when he was tired and frustrated and making sure he got enough to eat. Ever since they had parted during the filming of *Joy in the Morning*, she had been trying to persuade him that it would be a good idea for them to marry, but Paul simply laughed the idea off, refusing to believe she was serious. She was pretty sure there was no one else and he still insisted that Shirley had meant nothing to him. She was fairly confident that she was the only woman in his life and that he needed her. For the moment, she told herself, that would have to be enough. Part of Paul's attraction was his unpredictability. If she were to go on the extended Australian tour, however, things might well be different. And so Leonie kept the tour offer to herself. It might yet prove to be an effective trump card.

The news that Tony was to marry Gloria and, furthermore, that they had a child had shaken her to the core. How could that common little slut have worked for her, lived in her flat and accepted a salary from her when all the time she'd been sleeping with Tony behind her back for years? They said that the quiet ones were the worst, but really – Gloria of all people! She had always known that Tony had questionable taste, but she could only imagine that he'd been feeling particularly deprived when he'd taken that little guttersnipe to bed. Apparently the child they had spawned had something the matter with it – probably the result of a botched abortion attempt. Well, it was no more than the pair of them deserved. Clearly he would never have considered marrying her if it hadn't been for his accident, she told herself with a bitter little smile. The way he looked now he was lucky that even Gloria was willing to take him on. They were just a couple of panic-stricken people, clutching desperately at their last chance.

But although Leonie was unaware of it, there was trouble brewing. Paul was far from happy or contented with their arrangement and her complacency was about to suffer a severe setback. It was on her birthday, the last day of January, that things came to a head between them. She had instructed Paul to pick her up at the theatre after the show and take her out to dinner. When he was not in her dressing room when she came down after the final curtain, she rang the flat but there was no reply. Thinking that he must be on his way, she changed and waited. By the time an hour had passed with no sign of him and still no reply to the telephone, her temper was simmering dangerously.

She went home in a cab only to find Paul sitting in the study tapping away furiously at the typewriter. A cigarette dangled from the corner of his mouth and the ashtray on the desk overflowed with stubs. He wore his dressing gown and there was twenty-four hours' stubble on his face.

Standing in the doorway, she unleashed her fury. 'So *this* is where you are. Do you realise that I've been sitting waiting for you this past hour? We had a table booked at the Café Royal for ten thirty.'

Unruffled, Paul glanced at his watch. 'God, is that the time? I'll get ready. They won't mind if we're a bit late.'

'A *bit late*? By the time you're ready it'll be after midnight. I've been ringing till I'm blue in the face. Why didn't you answer the phone?'

He shrugged. 'You know what I'm like when I'm working. I didn't even hear it.'

'Well, if you think I'm going out now you can think again.'

'Act III is coming along so well that everything else just went out of my head,' he said coolly. 'So if you really don't want to go out, I'll carry on. After all, we can go tomorrow, can't we?'

'No, we can't,' she snapped. 'I'm sick and tired of taking second place to your work, Paul. I wait on you hand and foot, care for your every need, yet you can't even put yourself out for me on my birthday.'

He sighed. 'I've said I'm sorry. I can't do more. Make up your mind, but don't stand there nagging like a fish-wife. It's tedious and boring.'

His calm, unrepentant attitude infuriated her. Coming into the room, she slammed the door behind her and stood facing him, her eyes flashing. 'Tedious and *boring*, is it? Who the bloody hell do you think you are? I've had about enough of playing mother to you, wiping your nose, bolstering your inflated little ego and telling you a hundred times a day that you're a sodding genius. You don't seem to realise that I have a career too. I wasn't going to tell you, but I've had the offer of an Australian tour. Peter keeps asking me when I'm going to make up my mind. All that's holding me back is *you*.'

His expression hardened. 'Wait a minute, let's get this straight, Leonie; I'm not holding you or anyone else back. You know damned well that ever since my divorce my maxim has been; Travel light, travel free. It was only at your insistence that I moved in here with you. Now, if you've had a good offer, then for Christ's sake take it. I don't want you for ever whining on about all you gave up for me, like some snivelling suburban housewife.'

'I *see*. So that's all the thanks I get, is it?'

'I think it's fair enough. We've been good together a lot of the time. I've written good parts for you. You've played them well. Some of the time it's even worked, our living together. But there comes a time when things get too demanding – claustrophobic. If you want to know, I think the time has come for a break.'

Leonie stared at him, sitting there so calm and so cold, this man she had given so much of herself to – her mind, her body, her compassion – far more than she'd ever given Tony. And now he was tossing her aside with as little thought as he'd give to a page of his writing that hadn't worked. After all the time they'd been together, how could he be so casual about breaking with her? Suspicion stirred in the back of her mind. Was it possible that he had someone else? Had she perhaps been here tonight – under her own roof? Was that why he hadn't been available to answer the phone? 'All right, Paul, who is she?' she demanded. 'Don't tell me there isn't anyone. I know you better than that. You can't do without a woman in your life. When I was away on location you even took up with that child half your age.'

'There's no one. And who's this *child* you're talking about?' He began to laugh, heating her temper to boiling point. 'I must say, this is the first time I've been accused of child molesting.'

'You know bloody well who I'm talking about.' She hissed at him like a feral cat, the hair on the back of her neck prickling as it rose. 'And even after that night when I

440

found the two of you together it wasn't over, was it? You'd have put her in the play – you'd have risked your reputation – everything to have the little tart around. You'd have done it too if she hadn't gone off to the job in Birmingham.'

He spun round, his brows meeting in a fearsome frown. 'Do you think I don't know it was you who engineered that, Leonie? Do you really imagine that I haven't been onto your manipulative, devious little mind right from the first? I knew you'd wangled Shirley that tuppeny-hapenny job in rep to stop her getting the part I wanted her to have.'

Her mouth dropped open. 'You knew – how?'

'Never mind. It doesn't matter now.' He laughed wryly. 'And even if I were second-guessing you've just confirmed it for me, haven't you? Sometimes you're not as clever as you think you are, Leonie.'

She stepped away, biting her tongue for allowing herself to fall into his trap. 'I was only saving you from making a fool of yourself,' she said scathingly. 'You'd been seen together. People were beginning to talk. Someone had to get you out of her clutches.'

'Out of hers and into *yours*, is that what you're saying?' Suddenly his temper got the better of him and he sprang to his feet to grasp her by the shoulders. 'All this is down to sheer, raw jealousy, isn't it? You were jealous of her youth, her looks and her vitality – *and* her talent, of course.' He shook his head. 'Who do you think you're kidding, Leonie? You're as transparent as a pane of glass.' He stared down at her, his eyes like burning coals. 'This birthday you're making such a fuss about, which one is it, eh?' he taunted. 'You'd have me believe it's your thirty-fifth, but it's really your fortieth, isn't it? And you thought you'd fooled me about that, too. I'm surprised you actually wanted to celebrate it.'

The colour drained from her face. 'You *bastard*! You cruel bastard.' She squirmed in his grasp, wincing as his fingers bit deeper into her flesh. 'Let me go, you swine. You're hurting.'

'First tell me how you fixed it. Come on, let's have it, Leonie. It'll be interesting to see if you can be straight for once.'

'I went to see that drama teacher of hers,' she said between clenched teeth. 'Magda Jayne or whatever the woman's ridiculous name is. She told me Shirley had had an audition with Gerald Maddox, but that he hadn't given her a job. Gerald owed me a favour from way back, so I asked him to make her an offer. Is that so dreadful?'

'I see. I made it easy for you, didn't I?' He let her go abruptly. 'You told me she had no talent, that she wasn't ready to appear in any theatre. If you really thought that, why saddle Maddox with a dud actress?'

'So as not to spoil your play, of course,' she said, rubbing her bruised shoulders. 'I did it for you. Because at the time you were too damned stupidly besotted to judge properly.'

'Oh, how *kind* and thoughtful,' he said sarcastically.

'Anyway, I hear that Shirley's still with the Mask Players and doing quite well. I probably did her a favour.'

'Don't kid yourself. She'd have had her name in lights by now with my help and you know it. But you weren't going to risk that, were you, Leonie? You got her a piddling little job in the provinces, one you knew she'd jump at. You put her on the road. Well, now I'm putting *you* on the road.' His voice was as cold and sharp as steel. 'You can go off on your Australian tour – or a tour of hell for all I care. I want you out of my life just as soon as you like.' He got up and slammed the cover onto his typewriter, then he strode out of the room. Crestfallen, she followed him into the bedroom, where he had begun to throw his clothes into a suitcase.

'Paul, wait – don't be so hasty. I was only thinking of you. I meant it for the best, honestly. Sleep on it. We can work something out.'

'I've already worked it out,' he said.

'You won't get far without me,' she flung at him. 'You'll never make it on your own. Who's going to make sure you eat properly and see that you have clean clothes to wear?

Who's going to chase away unwanted visitors so that you can work in peace? You'll soon find out how hard I've worked for you.'

He spun round to look at her and she shrank from the look of sheer dislike in his eyes. 'If you really want to know, Leonie, I'm sick and tired of being treated like a pet poodle and told what to do and having my friends chosen for me. It's *over* – understand? Neither of us is suited to sharing our lives. I need freedom and space, you need to stifle and possess, like – like a bloody boaconstrictor. We're incompatible. It's time you faced it.'

In the hospital waiting room Tony sat holding Gloria's hand. The sister on the surgical ward had begged her to go home and get some rest, assuring her that they would telephone the moment Michael was out of surgery, but she was adamant. She wanted to stay, to be as near as possible. 'He might need me,' she said over and over. 'If he asked for me and I wasn't here, I'd never forgive myself.'

Tony felt helpless. He didn't know what to say to her, and in a way he felt left out. He was anxious, too. Only now did he realise what Gloria had been through during the past four years and how much the child meant to her. Because of the war she had missed much of Shirley's childhood and circumstances had forced her to allow someone else to bring Michael up. She'd missed so much of his precious babyhood. It would be too cruel if he were to be taken from her now. The surgeon had assured them that although a valvotomy was a delicate procedure, it had so far proved effective and successful. Michael was a strong child. He saw no reason for concern, he kept telling her. But in spite of Tony's repeated attempts to comfort her she seemed far away, unreachable as she sat next to him, staring into space. Even the contact of their hands was not enough to bridge the gulf between them.

The hours ticked by. He left her to go to the canteen and brought back a tray of tea and toast for her, which she left untouched. Finally, unable to bear it any longer, he said, 'Gloria, for heaven's sake, let me in. Don't shut me out like this. He's mine, too, remember. It isn't my fault that I haven't known him from birth.'

She turned her head to look at him, almost as though she were noticing him for the first time.

He took both her ice-cold hands in his. 'Gloria, I've only known Michael for a few weeks, it's true, but the bond is there between us. It was there from the very first moment. I love him. I love you too. It's the kind of love I thought would never come to me again. I couldn't bear it if anything happened to take that love away from me now.'

For a moment she stared at him, then her face suddenly crumpled and she was in his arms, sobbing out all the tension she had held in. 'I'm sorry, darling. It's just that I've been on my own so long. Everything I've gone through, I've gone through alone. Putting up a wall of defence has grown to be a habit.'

He held her close. 'It's a habit you can drop from now on.'

'I've been thinking about Shirley such a lot lately,' she confessed. 'I wish now that I'd answered her letter. I should have tried harder to understand what she did. I feel partly to blame – and I miss her so *much*, Tony. But she's gone from me now, perhaps for ever. She's a grown woman with a life of her own. She doesn't need me any more.'

'You have me now,' Tony said quietly. 'And Michael.'

She looked at him. 'I know, darling. I'm so lucky to have you. You'll never know how grateful I am.'

'I want to be a comfort to you – to share it all,' he said, stroking her hair. 'The worrying times, the sadness as well as the happiness. That's how it's going to be from now on, I promise you. Michael will come through, you'll see. He *has* to.'

She found that his cheeks were wet too and she held him close as their tears mingled. He'd been through so much himself, and now he was suffering again for Michael – as much as she was. How could she have been so thoughtless? 'Of course he will,' she whispered.

He held her away from him to look into her eyes. 'The moment he's fully recovered we'll be married,' he said. 'Let's set a date here and now. It'll give us something positive to look forward to and work towards – a goal.'

'All right.' She smiled. 'May? Michael should be fine by then, surely. The first of May. I love the spring.'

He kissed her. 'May Day it is. And I'll –' He stopped as the door opened and Sister came in.

'Mr Harvey-Moreton will see you in my office if you'd like to come this way.'

Gloria gasped and rose shakily to her feet, her heart thudding in her breast. 'Michael – is the operation over? Is he all right?'

'Please don't be worried.' Sister smiled. 'The operation is over and everything went to plan. But Mr Harvey-Moreton would like to tell you all about it himself, so if you'd like to come with me . . .'

It was through Imogen that Shirley heard of her half-brother's successful operation. Apparently she had received the letter on the last leg of the Company's tour of America and had written straight away to Shirley to say how pleased and relieved she was that Michael could begin to live the normal life none of them had dared to hope for.

I was so sorry not to be able to visit him, or to accept your invitation to the wedding on 1 May. It's sure to be a happy occasion and I know that Daddy and Gloria will be happy together. Best of all is that it makes you and me members of the same family. Have you realised, Shirley – we share a little half-brother and Daddy is now your stepfather? Isn't that fun? We've always been close, but now we can actually call ourselves sisters – well, stepsisters anyway. By the way, my other half-brother, Marcus, came to see me the other day. We got along well together but it was strange to think that we'd never set eyes on each other in all these years. You must write and tell me all about the wedding –

every detail, since Charles and I won't be able to attend. . . .

Clearly she had no idea that in spite of the letters she'd written, Shirley hadn't heard of her mother's impending wedding or of Michael's operation either.

Shirley had been with the Mask Players just ten months. Her original contract had been extended at the end of the initial three months. When Gerald Maddox had asked her into his office one morning the previous November after the morning rehearsal, she had been dreadfully afraid she was going to be given notice, but to her relief Gerald had begun by telling her how pleased he was with her work.

'I must admit that I had reservations when Leonie Swann asked me to give you a break,' he said. 'I know her of old and she's a devious woman. I had an idea that there was some ulterior motive behind her insistence that you should be given a chance to prove your ability.'

Shirley stared at him. 'Leonie asked you? I had no idea.'

'But you do know her?'

'Oh, yes. I was evacuated to her country house during the war. I grew up with her daughter Imogen, but I wouldn't have thought . . .' She trailed off, remembering that the night Leonie had walked in on her and Paul, he had mentioned a part for her in his play. She began to see the obvious reason for Leonie's assumed altruism.

'Well, perhaps she's mellowed with age, or perhaps I'm maligning her unfairly,' Gerald said. 'Whatever her motive, she did both of us a favour. You've worked really hard and now I'd like to offer you a twelve-month contract with the company. Bernice Selby is leaving, which means you'll take her place and I'll engage another ASM.' He smiled. 'All those juvenile leads and character parts you've been longing to tackle will fall to you now, and of course it will mean a small salary increase too.' He looked up at her. 'Well, how does that sound to you?'

'It sounds wonderful.' Shirley felt herself flush with pleasure. 'Thank you, Gerald, I'll do my best. I promise I won't let you down.'

'I know you won't and I'm looking forward to seeing you blossom as an actress.' Gerald smiled at her and held out his hand. 'Welcome as a permanent member of the Mask Players, Shirley. And good luck.'

It was the proudest day of her life and Shirley reflected later that if only it hadn't been for the rift with her family she would have been completely happy. However, she knew now, as she always had, that she had done the right thing in not marrying Dave. She had written to him again, apologising for walking out on him but pointing out that it was the best thing she could have done for both of them. He had replied promptly, generously forgiving her and agreeing with her that their marriage would probably never have worked. It was a friendly letter, full of news about the shop and his job. He ended by saying that he would be pleased to see her whenever she was in London and that he wished her the best of luck.

In view of this she could see no good reason for Gloria to stay angry with her. She'd written to her at Rook Cottage several times, but never received any reply. It was so unfair. She could understand Ma's disapproval. She'd never been in favour of her taking up a career in the theatre, but Gloria had steered her towards it from babyhood, so why was she so angry now that she'd achieved her aim? She longed for her mother to see her play a major role – yearned for her approval and pleasure. Once they'd been so close, but now they had grown so far apart that it seemed almost impossible to remember the special relationship they had once shared. She'd even had to find out through Imogen that Tony was Michael's father.

When Gerald Maddox scheduled a run of R. C. Sherriff's all-male play *Journey's End* for the last two weeks in June, the female members of the company knew that they would be getting a week off. It did not take Shirley long to decide what she would do with her holiday. She would go to London and try to get herself an agent. She would see the latest West End plays, too – as many as she could squeeze in – and, if she could summon up enough courage, she would go to Whitechapel and try to make her peace with Ma.

During her ten months in Birmingham she'd had little on which to spend her money. She had saved quite a bit and she booked herself into an inexpensive hotel in Woburn Place for the week. It was close to the Underground and not too far from the heart of things. On the first morning she went to see Peter Jason. He was the only agent she knew personally, having met him a couple of times when he had visited Tony and Leonie at Houlton. She climbed the stairs to his office in Charing Cross Road and asked the receptionist somewhat hesitantly if he would give her a few minutes of his time. The girl went away and, to Shirley's surprise, came back to say that Peter would see her. He stood up and greeted her warmly when she was ushered into his office.

'It's Shirley, isn't it?' He smilingly indicated a chair. 'I'd never have known you, of course. The last time I saw you you were just a little girl.'

Shirley felt at ease with the kindly grey-haired man at once and when he agreed to represent her she could not disguise her delight. 'Thank you very much, Mr Jason. I must admit that I thought it would be quite hard to get an agent to take me on,' she confessed.

Peter smiled at her. 'You're getting a good grounding with the Mask Players,' he said. 'I'm sure I'll be able to get you plenty of work once your contract there expires.' He rang through to the outer office for coffee and sat back in his chair, regarding his delightful new client with interest. 'Tell me, how did you get the job with Gerald Maddox? An audition?'

Shirley smiled. 'Yes, I did an audition for him.' She did not tell him that Leonie had engineered the job offer. After all, she had proved her own worth since.

'I expect you'll be going to see *Give Me Yesterday* while you're in town. It's still playing, though with an almost entirely different cast. Leonie has gone on an extended tour of Australia, but I expect you've heard all about that.'

'No, I hadn't, actually. I'm a bit out of touch since I've been in Birmingham.' She glanced at him. 'Have you seen anything of Tony?'

'Tony Darrent?' He smiled. 'I was at the wedding, of course. He seems to have got over his accident extremely well and he looked very happy with his new bride.' He frowned. 'Wait a minute – aren't you related to her?'

'She's my mother.'

Peter looked surprised and a little embarrassed. 'Oh. But you . . .'

'I wasn't invited to the wedding,' Shirley put in quickly. 'When I took the job with the Mask Players I upset my mother by walking out on the man I was to have married.'

'I see. Well, it happens in the best of families,' he said dismissively. 'I'm sure it will blow over.'

'Is Tony working again yet?'

'Oh, yes. He's doing quite a lot of radio drama now. The Third Programme are planning a classical season and he's been very much involved with that.' The receptionist came in with coffee and as she withdrew Peter said: 'As you're family, so to speak, I'll let you into a little secret; I've offered Tony a partnership with this agency. I think it might be something he'd enjoy. He's still thinking about it as a future possibility but I feel confident that he'll accept eventually.'

Shirley smiled. 'That's wonderful.'

'Completely selfish motives as far as I'm concerned,' Peter said. 'I've only a few more years to go before I retire and I'd like to think there'd be someone like Tony to carry on. He knows most of our clients personally and an agent who is also an actor is a tremendous bonus.'

When they'd finished their coffee Peter noted all Shirley's particulars and enclosed them in a file along with the photograph she'd brought. 'I'll make the trip up to Birmingham to see you work,' he said.

Shirley's eyes sparkled. 'Will you really?' She opened her handbag and eagerly searched for a programme of the

Mask Theatre's forthcoming attractions. 'We're doing *The Corn Is Green* in three weeks' time,' she said, passing it across the desk to him. 'I'm playing Bessie Watty. We start rehearsals next week. I'm really looking forward to that.'

Peter smiled at the refreshing glow of enthusiasm in the youthful face opposite him. 'Then that's when I'll come,' he said, making a note on his desk diary.

Outside in the street Shirley felt as though she walked on air. She had an *agent*. One of the best agents in London, too. Now she was really on her way.

At the shabby apartment house in Whitechapel she was told by a neighbour that Ma had left some months ago.

'Can you give me the address?' Shirley asked. 'Has she moved to the new block? She was promised a flat there.'

The woman shook her head. 'Bless you, no, love. She's gone to live in the country with 'er daughter. Some village in Northamptonshire, or some such place. I'd a nice card from 'er at Christmas. Seems she's got 'er own place – a real thatched cottage. Roses round the door an' all, I shouldn't wonder. All right for some, ain't it?'

So Ma had gone to live at Rook Cottage? All the people she loved were together now. Only she was left out. Hurt sat like a sharp-edged stone in Shirley's chest, depressing her deeply. She went back to the hotel, determined to enjoy the rest of her short holiday in spite of it all.

She went to see Magda, who insisted on making coffee and sitting her down to relate all that she'd been doing. The studio Shirley had once found so exotic now looked shabby and vaguely pathetic. But the welcome was warm and Magda was delighted to hear all her news, especially that she'd been promoted to a permanent place in the company.

'You remind me so much of myself at your age, Shirley,' she said. 'There'll be no war to ruin your career before it gets off the ground, please God. I shall watch your progress with great interest and pride. You won't lose touch with me, will you?'

Shirley kissed her. 'Of course I won't. If it hadn't been for you, none of it would have been possible.'

That afternoon she paid a brief visit to Dave. She had to steel herself for the visit, half afraid that seeing her might upset him. Yet she was loath to go back to Birmingham without trying to put right the wrong she'd done him.

When she walked into the shop the staff eyed her with a mixture of curiosity and resentment. Most of them had been working there when she was, and they returned her greeting with hostile, challenging eyes. But Dave was his old self. When he saw her his eyes lit up in the familiar smile and he lifted the counter flap and called to Mary to take over for him. Upstairs in the flat they were to have shared he made tea for her, asking about her new life and her budding career with genuine interest.

'Now, tell me what you're planning for your week off. I expect you'll be off to Houlton to see your mum and gran.'

She looked at her hands. 'No. There's still bad feeling between us, Dave. They were very angry with me for going off as I did. I've written to Gloria several times but she hasn't replied. Seems she can't forgive me.'

He looked troubled. 'I'm sorry to hear that, Shirl. I'd no idea.' There was an awkward pause, then he pushed a plate of chocolate biscuits towards her. 'Come on, eat up,' he urged her with a smile. 'So, have you been to the theatre?'

'I'm going every night,' she told him, seizing the chance to change the subject.

'And Hampstead Heath? The funfair – are you going there too?'

She shook her head. 'Fairs are no fun by yourself. Besides, there are so many plays I want to see. The rest of my days are going to be full.'

'Oh, but you can't go back without a visit to the fair,' Dave said. 'What are you doing on Saturday?'

'Well . . .'

'You'll be cross-eyed with staring at a stage by then. Come up the Heath with me – just for old times' sake?'

She looked at him with new eyes. He had developed a new assertiveness since he'd been his own boss. Once he'd

451

have been tentative and shy about asking her, especially after what had happened. Now he looked as though he could take her refusal in his stride with no ill feelings. This new attitude took her off guard and she laughed. 'Okay then. Thank you, Dave. I'll look forward to it.'

He smiled. 'Good. So will I. I'll pick you up at your hotel about six. I've got a little car now. It's only second-hand, but it gets me around. We'll have a bite to eat first.' Again it was a positive statement rather than a question.

As he let her out of the rear entrance of the shop, she looked at him and said: 'You've changed, Dave.'

His eyebrows rose in surprise. 'I have? In what way?'

She lifted her shoulders. 'I don't know. You're more grown-up. I think *sophisticated* is the word I'm looking for.'

He laughed. 'Sounds much too grand for me. You've changed too, Shirl.'

'Have I?'

'Oh, yes. You've developed a kind of gloss.' He nodded towards the shop. 'The girls in the shop saw it. Didn't you see the way they looked at you?'

'I thought that was resentment.'

'Envy, more like. One look at you and anyone can see that you're confident – fulfilled. You look as though you know who you are and where you're going.' He smiled a little wistfully. 'I could never have made you look like that.'

She bit her lip. 'Dave . . . I . . .'

He held up his hand. 'No, don't say it. That's all over, no reproaches. Now we're both free to enjoy being friends.' He opened the door for her. 'Enjoy the rest of your holiday, Shirl. See you on Saturday.'

During the months she'd been away, London had lost its tired look. Clearly much hard work had been put into making the city bright and clean again. Many of the bomb sites were still there, but they'd been tidied up and fenced off and new buildings had begun to spring up to take the place of those that had been bombed.

She spent the rest of the week going to the theatre, in some cases twice in one day; queuing for the gallery to

452

make her spending money go as far as possible, she saw all the latest West End productions. Sitting on her hard seat high up in the 'gods', she took notes and learned as much as she could from the performances of all the actors, male and female, old and young alike. On her last evening she treated herself to a ticket for the upper circle at Wyndham's to see Paul Winspear's play *Give Me Yesterday*. She enjoyed it very much, taking special interest in the actress who played the part she imagined that she herself might have played. It was a very good part and, as the play progressed, part of her hated Leonie for doing her out of it. But on deeper reflection, she realised that playing in the West End so early in her career might easily have led her down a blind alley. At the Mask Theatre over the past year she had learned much about the theatre in general. She'd had to turn her hand to many other things as well as understudying and playing walk-ons. She'd made coffee and swept up; she'd helped with stage management and props, sat in the prompt corner with the script, even done a little scenery painting. Once she'd assisted the electrician when his lad was ill with flu. Most important of all, she had learned how very *little* she knew. If she'd gone straight into Paul's play she might never have developed the humility that every true performer needs. She might have grown conceited and cut herself off from much valuable knowledge and experience. Maybe Leonie had inadvertently done her a favour after all.

When the curtain came down on the last act, she hung back in the auditorium after the audience had filed out, drinking in the atmosphere of the theatre with its traditional gilt and plush decor. Maybe one day she would be appearing here herself, she told herself with a little frisson of excitement.

She was just walking out into the corridor when the pass door leading to the backstage area opened. Out of the corner of her eye she saw a tall man in evening dress, and when she heard him call her name she turned.

'By all that's wonderful – *Shirley*.'

She turned to see Paul Winspear coming towards her, a smile on his face. It was too late to escape so she decided

453

to face out the unwelcome confrontation as coolly as she could. 'Hello, Paul.'

'What are you doing here? I hope you're not "resting".' He grasped both her hands.

'No, I'm not resting. As a matter of fact I'm a permanent member of the company now.'

'At the Mask?'

'Yes. I had a week out so I came up to see some shows and to get myself an agent.'

'And were you successful?'

'I certainly was. Peter Jason has taken me on.'

His eyes widened. 'Peter? My word, you won't regret that. He's one of the best.'

She couldn't be sure that he wasn't mocking her – stringing her along. 'He's coming up to see me working in a couple of weeks' time,' she said. 'We're doing *The Corn Is Green*. I'm playing Bessie.' She was suddenly aware that she sounded like a bragging juvenile and felt her cheeks redden embarrassingly. 'Look, I'm sorry, I've got to go now.' She turned but he took her arm.

'Hang on. Don't run off like that.' His eyes swept over her, taking in the slender figure in the stylish black suit with its pencil-slim skirt and nipped-in jacket, the skilful subtlety of her make-up and the new short, crisp hairstyle. He had thought her attractive before but now she was positively beautiful. 'You haven't told me what you thought of the show yet.'

'Oh, I enjoyed it very much, Paul. It's even better than *Joy in the Morning*.'

'I'm glad you thought so. Look, have you got a dinner date?'

She hesitated. 'Well, er, yes,' she lied, peering at her watch. 'I'm sorry. I'll have to run. It was nice seeing you, Paul – bye.'

'Goodbye, Shirley.' He watched her go thoughtfully. 'Or should that be *au revoir*?' he added quietly.

Hampstead Heath was sheer delight. Shirley and Dave dined at a little Greek restaurant first, then drove out to

Hampstead. It took Shirley back to her childhood when she saw the coloured lights twinkling in the trees and felt the infectious excitement of the throng of people making their way towards the funfair. They walked around, looking at everything, and tried their hands at various sideshows. Dave won a giant teddybear at the rifle range and a box of chocolates at dart throwing. They saw a young girl packed in a coffin filled with ice, and ate candyfloss and toffee apples with childish enjoyment. Then there were the rides: the breath-taking Big Dipper, and the Dragon ride. Dave seemed to have endless energy, throwing himself enthusiastically into the spirit of the fairground, till at last Shirley had to beg for a break. He looked at his watch.

'Good heavens, I hadn't realised how the time had flown,' he said. 'You're right. It is time we took a break.'

Although there was a stall nearby, selling coffee and doughnuts, he led her towards a café on the edge of the fairground with umbrella-shaded tables around it. 'This looks just the place,' he said, pulling out a chair for her at one of the tables. 'Sit there and get your breath back while I get the coffee.'

She sat looking round her. The dusk was deepening now, and the brightly coloured lights that were strung everywhere glittered and shone. The funfair was coming into its own special magic time of day. Shirley drank it all in; the brassy music and the lights, the colour, the noise, laughter and screams of delight from the more daring rides. She breathed in the scent of sawdust, toffee and frying onions. Almost *anything* could happen on a night like this, she told herself happily. She was so glad she'd agreed to let Dave bring her. It was the perfect ending to her week's holiday.

Suddenly she looked up to see a strange man standing in front of her. He was smiling. 'Hello, Shirley. It's good to see you.'

'Oh – I'm sorry but . . .' She half rose, apprehensively, then something in his smile froze her blood. It was *Tony*. She hadn't seen him since his accident. She knew he'd been burned badly and had plastic surgery, but she hadn't been prepared for a change like this. The handsome features that had claimed the hearts of millions of film- and theatre-goers were blurred and distorted, altering his expression completely. If he had not spoken to her she would never have recognised him. Quickly she gathered her control. She mustn't let him see how shocked she was. Apart from his scars he looked well and happy, and infinitely pleased to see her. She smiled and held out her hands.

'Tony! What a surprise! How lovely to see you after all this time.'

The hands that grasped hers were scarred and cruelly misshapen, but they were warm and pressed hers with genuine affection. 'How are you?' she asked him. 'And what are you doing here?'

'I'm here with my family,' he said proudly, turning slightly to look behind him.

Shirley followed his gaze to where Gloria stood on the fringe of the tables. She was holding the hand of a small boy who was hopping excitedly from one foot to the other. Shirley let go of Tony's hands and walked slowly across to them, her eyes fixed on the two figures, almost afraid to blink in case they disappeared. 'Gloria,' she said, her throat tight. 'Oh, *Glor*.'

Gloria dropped the child's hand and gathered Shirley into her arms. 'Oh, Shirl, love, it's so good to see you. I've missed you so *much*.' They looked at each other, almost too full for words. Tears shone in Gloria's eyes as she said: 'Just look at you. You look so grown-up and so lovely.'

Shirley laughed shakily. 'And you look happy. You and Tony are married, I heard about it from Imo. And little Michael had his operation.' She bent to hug the be- wildered boy. 'Hello, Michael. Remember me?' She looked at Gloria. 'Is he really all right?'

'He's fine. Just fine, thank God.'

'Oh, Glor – why did you stay so angry with me? Why didn't you answer my letters?'

Gloria frowned. 'Letters? I only got the one – just after you left. I'm sorry, love but I didn't know how to answer it. I hoped you'd write again, but . . .'

'But I *did*. I wrote several more, to Rook Cottage. I tried to –' Shirley broke off, remembering the other time when Gloria had failed to contact her. The same person must be responsible for intercepting the letters. They looked at each other, both arriving at the thought simultaneously. In unison they said: 'Ma.' And both burst out laughing.

They shared a table. Dave brought a tray of coffees and a lemonade for Michael, who was preoccupied with the teddy Dave had won. They toasted each other, laughing and talking, trying confusedly to catch up on all their news at once. Then Shirley said:

'I can't get over the coincidence of meeting you here like this.' She broke off as she saw Gloria and Dave exchange glances. 'Dave – it was you!' She looked at Dave. 'You fixed it all.'

He held up his hands. 'Guilty, I'm afraid. I couldn't let it go on. I knew there had to be some kind of misunderstanding. I telephoned Gloria at Houlton and arranged for us all to meet here this evening.'

'Tony was already up in town, making recordings,' Gloria explained. 'We'd been promising Michael a trip to Hampstead Heath and this seemed a good opportunity. Tony stays at his flat in Earls Court when he's recording. I brought Michael up by train this morning.'

Shirley pulled the little boy onto her lap. 'It's a late night for you. Aren't you tired?'

He shook his head, grinning up at her with wide blue eyes. 'I went to bed this afternoon, so I can stay up all night now.' He treated her to his most winsome of smiles. 'Can I have this teddy, please?'

'Of course you can.' Shirley hugged him. 'If I'd known I was going to see you I'd have brought a present for you anyway.'

'When do you have to go back?' Tony asked. 'Can you come back to Houlton with us for a couple of days?'

Shirley shook her head regretfully. 'I must go back tomorrow. Rehearsals start on Monday. It's my first big part.'

'But you'll come home soon?' Gloria said eagerly. 'Just as soon as you can – please. Tony is away a lot and I get a bit lonely at times. It'd be lovely to have some time together again, just you and me.'

'I'll come. But you'd better prepare Ma,' Shirley warned. 'She might not want to see me.'

'After what she did with those letters she can hardly argue,' Gloria laughed. 'I hardly see her myself nowadays. You wouldn't believe it, but she's become a real countrywoman. She's joined the WI and the Mothers' Union and she's become a keen gardener, too. Rook Cottage has never looked so pretty.'

'I'm glad she's happy,' Shirley said. 'Maybe she'll find it in her heart to forgive me.'

The four said good night at the park entrance. Michael rode on Tony's shoulders, thumb in mouth and heavy-eyed with sleepiness, still clutching his teddy. Shirley stood on tiptoe to kiss him and ruffle the curly hair.

'Night-night, darling. See you soon.'

He gave her a sleepy smile and took his thumb out of his mouth briefly to answer her. 'Night-night.'

There were hugs all round, then they went their separate ways, promising again to get together just as soon as they could.

In the car Shirley looked at Dave. 'Thank you for tonight, Dave. It was a wonderful surprise.'

He grinned. 'It's not often I get the chance to play Santa Claus. I enjoyed every minute.'

'You're a good man, Dave.' After a moment's silence she said: 'Dave – are you happy?'

He turned to look at her briefly. ''Course I am. I've got a good job, better than I ever expected to get. My own home with all mod cons –'

'You know what I mean,' she interrupted.

He smiled. 'If you're asking me if I still carry a torch for you, as they say, the answer's no. I'll always admire you,

458

Shirl. I'll always be here as a friend for you, but as for the past – well, it's the past. As a matter of fact Mary and I are talking about making a go of it. She's a good girl. She likes the business and she's worked hard to help me. I reckon we're well suited to each other.'

'Didn't she mind about tonight?'

He shook his head. 'She trusts me. Besides, she knew I was planning to get you back together with your mum. She's all right, Mary.'

'You love her?'

'You know I've never been one for flowery talk, Shirl, but since you ask, yes, I love her. Best of all, she loves me – in a way that no one ever has before.'

Shirley blinked as tears filled her eyes. 'I'm glad. You deserve it, Dave.'

Looking out at the starlit summer sky she felt suddenly wistful. She had achieved her goal; she had her foot firmly on the first rung of the ladder of success. She was about to embark on her first major role, the chance she had prayed for to show her talent at its best. And tonight she had been reunited with her family. All her dreams were coming true. But seeing the way Gloria looked at Tony, clearly loving him now with all his scars as much as she did when he was acclaimed the most handsome man in the English theatre, and hearing the hidden emotion in Dave's voice when he talked about his Mary stirred an unfulfilled longing deep inside her. 'You haven't really lived until you've been truly in love,' Magda had once said. Shirley had thought she'd discovered love with Paul, but she knew now that what she had thought of as love had been purely physical. Their relationship had been ill-advised and had ended in hurt and betrayal. All she could say of it was that it had been useful experience to her as an actress. The real, true love that other people had was still as elusive to her as a will-o'-the-wisp.

But as she gazed out of the car window at the star-studded, velvet night she thought how wonderful it must be to love and be deeply, unselfishly loved in return. Would she ever know that love? Or must she resign herself to finding fulfilment in her career alone?

Chapter Twenty

Sitting in his seat in the front stalls of the Mask Theatre, Marcus Fane gazed up at the cast of *The Corn Is Green* as they lined up for the final curtain. But his eyes were on one member of the cast alone; the young woman who had played Bessie Watty. Not only had she given a captivating performance, but he thought she was quite the most beautiful girl he had ever seen. As the leading man led her forward to take a final bow, she seemed to smile straight into his eyes. He applauded enthusiastically, glancing at his companion.

'Wasn't she just great? I can't wait to meet her. Do you think you can fix it for me?'

'I should hope so,' his elderly companion replied with a smile. 'After all, I am her agent.'

Shirley took a last bow along with the rest of the cast before the curtain came down. It was Saturday night and the last performance of *The Corn Is Green*. She had enjoyed rapturous receptions every night and had loved the part of Bessie Watty, the brash cockney teenager. As she made her way to the dressing room she shared with Frances Moss, the middle-aged character actress who had played Miss Moffat, Jack Brown, the stage doorkeeper, stopped her in the corridor.

'There's a feller to see you, Miss Rayner,' he said. 'He says he wants to see you on business, but y'know what some of 'em are. Tell you any old yarn to get in.'

'Did he give a name?' Shirley asked.

'Yeah, but you know what my 'earin' is, I didn't catch it properly.' The little man frowned. 'Jacobs, Jansen – summat like that.'

Shirley's heart quickened. All week she'd been expecting Peter Jason to come and see the show, but he hadn't put in an appearance. By Saturday's matinee she had resigned herself to the fact that he hadn't been able to make it. 'Jason,' she said excitedly. 'Was it Jason?'

Jack nodded eagerly. 'Reckon that was it, miss.'

'He's my agent, Jack. Don't keep him standing at the stage door.'

'Sorry, miss. What d'you want me to tell 'im?'

'Ask him to give me ten minutes to change, then I'll meet him in the green room.'

'Right you are, Miss Rayner. Ten minutes it is.' He hurried off and Shirley turned and went into the dressing room.

Her fingers trembled as she took off her make-up and changed into cream slacks and a black corduroy shirt. Frances, watching shrewdly from her side of the room, cocked an enquiring eyebrow.

'Got a date, ducky?'

'My agent was in front,' Shirley said. 'He wants to see me. He promised he'd come up to see the show but I thought he'd forgotten.' She paused to look at herself in the mirror, suddenly besieged by doubts. Suppose it was bad news? Suppose he hadn't liked her performance and wanted to break it to her that he couldn't represent her after all? She turned to look at the older woman. 'Tell you what, Frannie, why don't you join us?'

'You and your *agent*?' Frances laughed. 'You must be joking, lovie. Neither of you will want an old ham like me hanging around mucking things up. He's probably about to make you the offer of a lifetime.' She had changed into her outdoor clothes and was hanging up her costume. Placing the wig she wore for the play carefully on its stand, she gave it a final tweak. 'Well, that lot can go back to Wardrobe. It's goodbye to old Moffat, poor old cow.' She began to put on her coat. 'I'm off,' she said. 'My landlady

461

has invited me to supper. She says she's making steak-and-kidney pie and it's my favourite, so I mustn't be late.' She winked. 'When you get to my age the promise of a plate of steak-and-kidney pie is often the only thing that gets you through a performance by the last show, Saturday night.' She picked up her bags of shopping, done between shows, and bustled out of the room. 'Have a nice weekend, ducky. And break a leg with your agent. See you on Monday morning.' She paused in the doorway. 'It's a ten-o'clock call, Monday. Don't forget.' She said this every Saturday night without fail and Shirley smiled indulgently.

'I won't. Night, Frannie. Enjoy your steak-and-kidney.' High on adrenalin, and with the applause still ringing in her ears, Shirley wondered if she would ever get as blasé about her work as Frances. The older actress was brilliant at character parts like Miss Moffat and seemed to put so much of herself into her performances, yet the moment she was off stage she was herself again – grumbling about her landlady or planning a visit to the laundrette. It was as though she took off the character along with the costume.

Applying a dash of bright lipstick, Shirley picked up her bag and was about to leave the dressing room when there was a tap on the door. She opened it to find Peter Jason standing in the corridor.

'Peter. I was just on my way to meet you in the green room. Didn't Jack give you my message?'

'Yes, he did, but I'm not alone and there's something I wanted to ask you first.' He smiled at her. 'I enjoyed the show very much, Shirley. And I thought you were very good indeed.'

Shirley blushed with pleasure and relief. 'You *did*? I'm so glad. You can't go wrong with a play as well written as that, though, can you?'

Peter shook his head. 'Oh yes, you can,' he said. 'She's a flamboyant, character, the easiest of parts to overplay, but you played it with just the right balance. You never fell into the temptation to burlesque.'

'Thank you, Mr Jason.'

'Peter, please.' He peered round her into the room. 'May I come in, or is someone in there still changing?'

'Oh, no.' She held the door open, blushing at her own thoughtlessness. 'Do please come in. I'm afraid I can't offer you a drink.'

Peter shook his head. 'We'll go up to the green room in a moment. As I said, there's someone waiting to meet you. I just wanted to have a word with you first.'

Shirley swallowed hard. It sounded ominous. Perhaps his compliments had been the sugarcoating for a bitter pill he was about to hand her.

Peter sat down in the chair she pulled out for him. 'I'll come straight to the point. You know Paul Winspear's play *Give Me Yesterday*?'

'Yes, I saw it in London.'

'It has been decided to take the show on a tour of the provinces, but most of the cast have other commitments. How would you like to play the part of Jessica on that tour?'

'Oh!' Shirley stared at him with wide eyes. 'Oh, Mr Jason – er, Peter, I'd love to, but . . .'

'It's all right. I checked. Your contract here will have expired before the first rehearsal date. But anyway, I know Gerald would have released you.'

'When do you want me to come and audition?'

He smiled. 'We can dispense with that. As a matter of fact Winspear himself put your name forward. I believe you and he knew each other slightly.'

'Yes.'

'He tells me he met you through Leonie and that you met again briefly when you went to see the play in London the other week.'

'That's right.' A sudden thought struck Shirley and she looked at him apprehensively. 'How much will Paul have to do with the production?'

'Nothing. He's working on a new play at the moment, and when it goes into rehearsal he'll be very much involved with that.'

'Is it Paul you've got with you?'

Peter laughed. 'Good heavens, no. As a matter of fact it's a very eager young American actor called Marcus Fane, over here to get some stage experience. He's going to take over the role of Jason Hamilton, the young artist in the play, so you'll be working together. That's why I invited him to come up with me. He enjoyed the show enormously. I think I can safely say that he's already a fan of yours and he can't wait to meet you.'

'Oh, that's nice,' Shirley said inadequately. She felt slightly unreal, as though she were dreaming it all. She had waited so long for something like this to happen; prayed and fantasised about it, but now that it had she couldn't seem to react as she should.

Peter stood up. 'Right then, that's settled. I'll draw up a contract for you and make all the necessary arrangements with the management. I'll send everything to you for signing in due course.' He held out his hand. 'Right, shall we go up to the green room and have a celebratory drink? If I know Marc, he'll be getting restless by now.'

Upstairs in the green room Peter led the way across the crowded bar to where a tall, loose-limbed young man sat on one of the stools at the bar. 'Marc, I'd like you to meet Shirley Rayner,' he said. 'Shirley, this is Marcus Fane.'

He wore casual clothes, slacks and a white polo-neck sweater under a cinnamon-brown corduroy jacket. He uncoiled his long length from the bar stool and turned a pair of startlingly blue eyes on Shirley.

'Hi, Shirley.' He held out his hand. 'Great to meet you.' His voice was deep and musical, with an attractive hint of a West Coast accent. 'I enjoyed the show very much.'

For a moment she was taken aback, sure she had met him somewhere before. There was something about those eyes and the way he smiled that struck a familiar chord, but she could not place it. She took the hand he offered.

'Hello, Marcus. How nice to meet you.'

'I thought you were just great tonight,' he said enthusiastically. 'And Peter tells me you might be touring in Paul Winspear's play with me.' He looked at Peter. 'Did you get her to say yes?'

464

'I certainly did.'

The blue eyes blazed their delight.

Shirley smiled and shook her head. 'I still haven't quite taken it in. It's very exciting. I can't wait to begin rehearsing.'

'Me neither – especially now.' His eyes held hers, making no attempt to disguise the admiration in them.

Peter was watching them, a slightly amused expression in his eyes. 'Look, why don't you two grab that corner table over there,' he suggested. 'I'll get the drinks and bring them across.'

As they sat opposite each other, Shirley said: 'You know, it's the strangest thing, but when I first saw you I felt sure I knew you from somewhere.'

Marcus laughed. 'Hey, that's supposed to be my line. Matter of fact, I do happen to be English. I was born here; I still have an English passport. I'm only American by adoption, I guess you could say. My father lives here.'

'Really?'

'It's true. He and my mother were divorced when I was a kid and she had my name changed to hers. I've only actually met him once since then. Mom and I came over about five years ago, soon after the war ended. His name is Tony Darrent and he's an actor too. He was injured in a plane crash a while back. I haven't seen him but . . .' He stopped speaking, puzzled at the smile on her face. 'I guess I talk too much. What is it – did I say something funny?'

'I'm sorry. No. It's Peter. He's laid all this on deliberately. You see, I know your father very well. I was evacuated to his country house when war broke out. I lived there all through the war and grew up with your half-sister, Imogen.'

His eyes widened in amazement. 'Imogen? But that's amazing. I made the trip up to Vancouver specially to meet her when the Darrent Shakespeare Company played there some time back. It was she who suggested I should contact Peter when I came over to England.'

'Did she tell you that your father was married again?'

'Sure, she seemed very pleased about it.'

'But you wouldn't know that it was my mother he married?'

He sat back to stare at her in astonishment. 'Say, what do you *know*?' He grinned at her. 'Peter sure kept all of this up his sleeve.'

At that moment Peter joined them with the drinks. 'No need to ask if you two have been getting to know each other,' he said with a smile.

Shirley looked at him reproachfully. 'You knew about the family link between Marc and me all the time and you never said a word to either of us.'

'I wanted it to be a surprise,' he said. 'But I did have other reasons for not telling either of you. I didn't want you to prejudge each other. And I wanted to be sure you were going to get along together. A twelve-week tour can be absolute hell playing opposite someone you can't stand the sight of.'

'Well, that's one problem you can put out of your mind.' Marc addressed Peter but his eyes were on Shirley. 'Shirley and I are going to get along just fine. You can bank on it.'

'What brought you over here?' Shirley asked. 'Apart from wanting to meet your father again, I mean. Is it hard to find work in the States?'

'It's not too bad. I've done a lot of summer stock since college. It's great experience. The trouble back home is that once people get to know who Mom is I never can tell whether I'm getting a job because I'm good or because of my name. When you've got a well-known parent it's hard to go places on your own merit. Over here no one knows who I am and that's the way I aim to keep it.' He smiled at her. 'But that's enough about me. So your mom and my dad got married?' He shook his head. 'I can't get over it. What does that make us? Stepbrother and sister, I guess.'

'I've been trying to find the time to go to Houlton one weekend. Would you like to go with me? It would be a marvellous surprise for Tony.'

He picked up his glass and took a drink, looking at her doubtfully. 'I'd love that, Shirley, but not yet. I'm here to make it on my own and that's what I mean to do. I've even sworn Peter to secrecy, so I'd be obliged to you if you'd keep all this to yourself.'

'Of course, if that's the way you want it, Marc.' She smiled at him ruefully. 'It does seem a shame, though. I'm sure he'd love to see you.'

'Oh, I'll go and see him, eventually. I've promised myself that.' He paused, twisting his glass in his hands. 'It's always been a big regret of mine that I never got to know my dad.'

'I know what you mean. I never knew my father either,' Shirley told him.

'I never had much family life at all,' Marcus said. 'I wasn't much more than a baby when Mom and I went to the States for her career. I had a whole string of nurse-maids till I went to school. Guess I was kind of a lonely little kid.'

'It was the war that broke up my family,' Shirley told him. 'Before the war there was just Gloria, she's my mother, and my grandparents, but we were close and happy. Then the war split us all up and life was never the same again for any of us.'

He put his hand over hers. 'Guess we've got a lot in common, Shirley.'

She looked up at him. That sudden, dazzling smile reminded her of his father. Her first fleeting impression that they'd met before had been in that smile. His re-semblance to Tony as he'd been all those years ago when she'd first known him was quite uncanny. He had the same clear, expressive blue eyes and the finely sculptured features, cruelly devastated now for Tony since his acci-dent. 'Marc,' she said quietly, 'your father was badly scarred in that plane crash. When you do go to see him you should be prepared for quite a change in his appearance.'

'I guessed that. But he's still my dad, isn't he? The only one I've got.'

On a sudden impulse she turned her hand over and curled her fingers round his, returning their pressure. 'I'm glad we're going to be working together, Marc,' she said simply.

'Me too.' His eyes still holding hers, he said: 'Hey, look. I'm not busy this weekend. Why don't I check into a hotel in town? We could spend some time together. You could show me the town – if you're not doing anything.'

'I'm not doing a thing.'

'I brought the script of the play with me. We could try out some of our scenes together.'

Peter cleared his throat noisily. 'Well, I think I'll be off now. I've got a long drive in front of me and it looks as though I'm going to have to make it on my own.'

Marc looked concerned. 'Hey, Peter, I'm sorry. If you'd rather I came back with you . . .'

Peter laughed. 'No, you stay and get to know each other. I'm not quite so decrepit that I need someone to hold my hand.' He tossed back the last of his drink and stood up. 'Besides, I can see that you two are planning to do a lot of talking and, er, rehearsing.'

As he made his way out of the theatre, he smiled to himself. He had a hunch those two young people were destined for great things together – and not all of them to do with acting.

Insisting that the night was young and that meeting up with a stepsister warranted a celebration, Marc consulting the green room's barman and discovered the name of the city's ritziest night spot. Before Shirley could catch her breath he had telephoned to book a table. She had to beg him to let her go home and change first. They took a taxi to the street where she had her small two-room flat and Marc came up with her and waited while she changed into a dress of indigo taffeta with a romantic swirling skirt and stand-up collar. The rich dark colour accentuated the creaminess of her skin and the golden lights in her hair. When he saw her Marc gave a long, low whistle.

'Wow, you look a knockout, Shirley.' He fingered the neck of his polo-neck sweater, looking slightly doubtful. 'Say, d'you think they'll refuse to let me in, dressed like this? I didn't bring any other clothes. I wasn't really figuring on stopping over.'

Shirley laughed. 'Don't worry. The moment they hear your accent they'll fall over themselves. It's been like that ever since the war.'

'Well, okay, if you say so.' He offered her his arm. 'Let's go on the town.'

Shirley couldn't remember enjoying herself so much. Marcus was such good company and it turned out that they really did have a lot in common, sharing the same ambition and taste in plays. They ate and drank, talked nonstop and danced till two thirty in the morning. Finally Marc hailed a taxi, where she dozed against his shoulder all the way home, feeling relaxed and slightly light-headed.

It was only when they reached her flat that he remembered that he hadn't booked a room. 'Darn it. It went right out of my head. Never mind, I guess I'll find a motel somewhere,' he said with a shrug.

Shirley looked at him. 'Not here, you won't. We don't have motels over here. You can get almost anywhere in England in one day, so there's no need.' She looked at her watch. 'And you won't get a hotel to take you at this time of night – specially without any luggage.' She pushed the door open. 'Nothing for it but to stay here.'

He followed her into the flat. 'Look, Shirley, I hope you don't think I've done this on purpose. I wouldn't want to . . .?'

She turned and looked him gravely in the eye. 'If I really thought for one moment that you had, I'd give you the address of the local Sally Army hostel.' She laughed at his expression. 'I'll find you a pillow and a couple of blankets. The settee is quite comfy.'

Neither of them slept much that night. Shirley lay staring into the darkness, deeply aware of the close proximity of Marcus a few yards away on the other side of the thin partition wall. She was remembering all the things they talked about during the evening, and the way his eyes shone when he talked about the theatre and his fierce determination to make a name for himself on his own account and without help from either parent. She thought of the little dimple that appeared at the corner of his mouth when he smiled, which more than once she had caught herself itching to touch; of the lock of hair that would keep falling across his brow. She thought of the easy, magical way their steps had matched when they danced together and how good his arms felt around her.

Marcus, lying on the settee in the living room, was blessing his luck at meeting such a fantastic girl – not only meeting her but discovering that they were to work together for the coming twelve weeks. When he closed his eyes the bright, vivacious face with its violet-blue eyes and halo of red-gold hair was still there. He could still feel the delicious sensation of her slender body in his arms when they danced. He bit his lip hard and turned over. If his friends back home knew that he was wasting an opportunity like this, they'd never let him forget it. They'd brand him as the biggest idiot under the sun not to take advantage. But he knew that he and Shirley needed to take things a step at a time. What they were about to share was too important, too good to rush. It would happen, there was nothing surer than that. And when it did it was going to be out of this world. It was going to mean something very special for them both.

On Sunday they read through the script of the play together, their heads close over the shared manuscript. Then they went out to lunch at the pub round the corner. Marcus was keen to soak up the atmosphere of one of the traditional English pubs his mother had told him about. After lunch they walked in the park and talked some more before returning to the flat for tea.

'What time does your train go?' Shirley asked.

He shook his head. 'I don't know. I guess there'll be a pretty good service from here to London, though.'

Shirley laughed. 'You don't know British Rail on a Sunday.'

'You mean there aren't any trains?'

She began to put her coat on. 'There are, but you have to take pot luck. They're always repairing the lines or something. I'll come to the station with you.'

He was secretly disappointed to find that there was a fast train due in ten minutes. On the platform they looked at each other. Marcus said: 'When will I see you again, Shirley?'

'When we start rehearsals, I suppose.'

He took both her hands. 'I can't wait that long. I have to see you again before that. Can I come up here again – soon?'

'Of course, if you really want to. But I'm sure there are lots more exciting things for you to see in London.'

Still holding her hands he drew her close. 'Not for me. You're the most exciting thing that ever happened to me, Shirley. But I guess you already figured that out.' His lips found hers. He kissed her lightly, then looked down at her inquiringly. 'So, do I get to come back next weekend?' His eyes searched hers, desperately trying to read a response in them.

Shirley was trembling. His kiss had been light and brief but it had affected her like a glass of champagne on an empty stomach. She gave him a quick hug and said as light-heartedly as she could: 'Of course you do, Marc. I'd love you to come. I'll look forward to it.'

She more than just looked forward to it, counting the days till the following weekend. But her time was too busy to make the time drag. Playing in the current production and rehearsing for the next, she tried hard not to let thoughts of Marcus ruin her concentration. On the contrary, anticipation gave her performance a new edge. There was a new sparkle in her eyes and a lightness in her step. Frances was one of the first to notice it.

'Anyone would think you'd fallen in love,' she said teasingly. 'It wouldn't be anything to do with a certain young American, would it?'

'I haven't the slightest idea who you mean,' Shirley said, turning wide, innocent eyes on the older woman. They laughed together, both knowing that with her usual perception, Frances had hit the nail squarely on the head.

Marcus was sitting right in the centre of the front row when the curtain went up on Saturday evening. The moment Shirley made her entrance at the beginning of Act I she spotted him immediately. Her heart skipped a beat but she didn't allow it to throw her. Later, however, when Frances had tactfully withdrawn, leaving them alone in the dressing room, she admonished him for it.

'When I came on and saw you sitting there I almost forgot my first line,' she said.

He laughed. 'Not you. I wouldn't have done it if I didn't know you're a pro right down to your fingertips.'

It was the nicest compliment he could have paid her and she forgave him at once. Standing on tiptoe she kissed him lightly. 'Well, what are we going to do?'

He looked into her eyes for a long moment. 'I'm better organised this time. I've hired a car, so we can drive out of town. I guess we're going to eat first,' he said. 'Then dance a little, then . . .' He drew her close and kissed her – deeply this time, putting into his kiss all the longing he had endured during the past week. 'I've missed you, Shirley. I thought Saturday would never come.'

'I've missed you too,' she said.

They dined and danced, barely moving on the postage-stamp-sized floor, their arms around each other, cheeks softly touching. The longing they both felt affected them like sweet, heady wine until Marcus whispered:

'I guess it's time to go, Shirley.'

She looked up at him. 'It's such a shame to have to say good night.'

He frowned, affecting mock distress. '*Darn* it, would you believe I went and forgot to book a room again?'

They looked at each other for a moment. 'Well,' he said, nuzzling her ear. 'Do I get the address of the Sally Army hostel or will you take pity on a poor homeless waif?'

Her eyes shone softly in the dimmed lights. 'I suppose I'll just have to take pity on you,' she said.

Neither of them spoke much during the drive back. Together they climbed the stairs to the flat and the moment the door closed behind them they were in each other's arms. In the darkness they clung to each other. To

Shirley it was like being suspended in time and space. Their lips met and met again in hungry, searching kisses that left them both breathless and spoke more vehemently of what they both felt than any words. Then Marc lifted her in his arms and carried her into the bedroom.

Shirley knew right from that very first time that she was in love; this time the deep, true love that Magda had spoken of. This was being alive – this was the *living* that made the very meaning of her being crystal clear. This was what she had been born for. Best of all, it would last for ever – and beyond. At the height of their lovemaking she was aware of calling out his name, of saying 'I love you' over and over. With anyone else it would have been reckless and ill-advised. With Marcus, she knew instinctively that saying what was in her heart was intrinsically right.

Afterwards, as they lay in each other's arms, still dazed with the wonder of what they had experienced, Marc said:

'Do you believe in destiny, Shirley? Do you believe that some people are meant to meet – and love? Drawn together by some irresistible power?'

'I never have, till now,' she said dreamily. 'But when I look back, everything that ever happened to me seems as if it was pointing me in your direction.' She looked at him. 'Do you feel that too? Is that what you mean?'

He drew her close. 'That's exactly what I mean,' he said with a contented sigh. 'Oh, Shirley, now that I've found you I'm never going to let you go. I love you so much. You're so . . . so perfect.'

'No.' She stirred uneasily. 'I'm not perfect, Marc. No one is perfect.' She twisted her head to look at him. 'You don't really know me at all,' she said. 'I've got faults just like everyone else. Maybe when you've had time to get to know me better you'll change your mind.'

'Never,' he said happily. 'Nothing you could do could ever make me feel any different.' He grinned at her. 'What could you possibly have done that's so terrible?'

For a moment she looked into his eyes. Was this the time for confessions – for telling about the selfish things she'd done, her bad points as well as the good? *Of course it isn't*, a small voice in the back of her head told her. A moment like this was too precious, too tenuous to spoil by putting it to the test. It was a new beginning, a rebirth, not to be tarnished by the mistakes of the past. She grinned mischievously. 'Well, there was the bank robbery, of course.'

'Is *that* all?' He laughed and kissed her. 'Oh. well, I think I can live with that.'

Gloria could not remember being so happy. Since Michael's successful operation and her marriage to Tony, life had been so wonderful that sometimes she had to pinch herself when she woke in the mornings, just to make sure she hadn't dreamed the whole thing. But as the summer passed and Tony began to work normally again, two problems arose. First, Tony's radio work took him away from home more and more frequently. Most weeks he stayed at the London flat and came home at weekends. Then, in early September Michael started nursery school and she found herself spending most of the day alone.

Soon after the wedding they had decided that Longueville Hall was far too big for the three of them. Since the war, few women seemed to want domestic work any more and there were far too many rooms for their requirements. The house was sold early in August and they bought Hindley Lodge, a pretty little Georgian villa next to the church.

Gloria had occupied herself happily for weeks, planning the decor and colour schemes, making curtains and other soft furnishings. But once it was all done and Michael had started school she found herself once more with time on her hands. She was used to working, to occupying her days with something more useful than housework, and she felt restless and bored, living only for the weekends when Tony, Michael and she could be together.

Tony was sympathetic and suggested she invited friends to stay. Margaret came to see the new house and stayed the night, but life at the Dog and Doublet in Boothley was busy and with the shortage of staff she couldn't be spared for more than one night. Gloria had hoped that Shirley might visit more, but with her working till late on Saturday evening there wasn't time. She wrote regularly and promised to come for a few days as soon as she could, but all that seemed a long way off.

She invited Jane. They had kept in touch in spite of the fact that they'd hardly seen each other since the wartime days at the aircraft factory. Jane was married now to a civil servant and lived in Gloucestershire. The two of them had a wonderful time, reminiscing and catching up on all their news. But when she went away the days seemed longer than ever. Michael was growing up fast. He had his friends to play with and seemed to need her less and less now that he was fit and well.

Talking things over, she and Tony agreed that to return to London permanently would not be fair to Michael. It was healthy for him here in the country. He was growing into a happy, sturdy little boy, who loved the freedom of the country lanes and fields. It was where he belonged. Then there was Ma. Having persuaded her to move, it would hardly be fair to leave her high and dry. It seemed that, for Gloria, there was nothing for it but to settle to a life of waiting for weekends.

It was when Imogen and Charles came home at last at the end of October that the idea first came into being. They had been quietly married in America towards the end of the company's extended tour and Imogen was already pregnant. But although Tony was disappointed not to have been at his only daughter's wedding, he forgave her when he saw how happy she and Charles obviously were. Imogen was positively radiant over the coming baby. At last she was to start the family she'd always longed for.

'So far we're keeping it to ourselves,' she told Gloria as they unpacked together in the guest room at Hindley Lodge. 'At least, I'm not mentioning it to anyone in the company. I want to go on working as long as I can. The

DSC is to tour this country now. We've got a couple of weeks out and then we're off to Brighton to start the tour. I'm looking forward to it so much and I've never felt so well in my life.' She pulled a face. 'My only problem is my costumes. They're all so tight and if I ask Wardrobe to let them out they'll probably guess.'

'If you can get them to me, I'll do them for you,' Gloria offered.

Imogen's eyes lit up. 'Oh, would you, Gloria? That would be marvellous.'

The following weekend Imogen smuggled the costumes home with her on the pretext that she wanted to have some photographs taken. In Gloria's bedroom she paraded in them.

'See what I mean?' she said, standing sideways in front of the cheval mirror.

Gloria laughed. 'You look as slim as a wand to me, but I dare say you might be feeling a little uncomfortable round the waist. I can easily let them out if there's enough material. Let's have a look.'

But when Gloria turned the costumes inside out she could see that they would allow only the barest half-inch of adjustment.

'They're dreadfully tatty,' she said, sitting back on her heels and fingering the material. 'The hems are frayed and the trimmings are tarnished and split. Most of the seams are beginning to go, too. If I start altering them I'm afraid they'll probably fall apart.'

'I know. We've all complained about it,' Imogen said. 'They were second-hand when we got them – prewar, I shouldn't wonder. But commissioning new ones would cost the earth. We've been told we'll just have to make do. Luckily they don't look too bad under stage lighting.'

Gloria said nothing. An idea was taking shape in her head. It was making her eyes sparkle and Imogen was quick to pick up her excitement.

'Gloria, what is it? Are you thinking what I *think* you're thinking?'

Gloria laughed. 'That sounds Irish, but yes, I believe I am. I could make the company a whole new set of

476

costumes. It'd take a little time, but I'd love to do it. You'd have to bring me photographs of all the ones you've got . . .' She stopped, looking up at Imogen doubtfully. 'Oh – but maybe your producer wouldn't trust me to do it.'

'*Trust* you? After the miracles you worked on the costumes for those wartime concerts? All you had then was some butter muslin and a few bits of tinsel, yet you created sheer magic. And I've still got the photographs to prove it.' She stopped, suddenly remembering something. 'I've also got that little Chinese jacket you made for Mummy. She gave it to me and I still wear it. That proves how clever you are, if anything does.' She threw her arms round her stepmother. 'Oh, Gloria, when I tell our producer this piece of news he'll forgive me anything – even getting pregnant.' She grasped Gloria's hands. 'We could go up to Wardour Street together and get everything you'd need from the theatrical costumiers. You must read all the plays and I'll lend you my collection of historical costume books. And when I have to give up work because of the baby, I could help you with it – do all the boring bits so as to leave you free to design and create. We could work on it together.'

Gloria's eyes shone with anticipation. 'Oh, Imogen, this is just what I've been wanting. It'll be my contribution to the DSC. After all, I'm a member of the Darrent family now.'

'Leave it to me,' Imogen said. 'I'll get it all laid on.' As she was changing back into her own clothes, she said suddenly: 'Talking of families, have you heard anything from Marcus?'

Gloria looked puzzled. 'Marcus?'

'Marcus Fane – Daddy's son by his first marriage.'

'No. Should we have heard from him?'

'He came to see me when the company was in Vancouver,' Imogen told her. 'He said he was coming over to England to get some stage experience. I gave him a letter to take to Peter Jason. I just thought he might have been in touch.'

Gloria shook her head. 'Not as far as I know. Peter is still urging Tony to go into partnership with him. They see each other regularly. I'm sure he'd have mentioned it.'

Imogen shrugged. 'Oh? Well, maybe he thought better of the idea.' She smiled. 'It was the first time I'd met him. I liked him a lot. I think you would too.'

'It's sad for Tony that his son grew up without knowing him.'

'Well, he's made up for it with Michael.' Imogen laughed. 'I've never seen a father and son so besotted with each other. They're inseparable.'

'I know. And it means so much to me, Imogen, after the years when I was struggling to bring him up alone. I'm so very lucky. I have a healthy little son and a husband who adores us. It's just that sometimes I feel a bit guilty about Shirley.'

'You made it up with her, though, didn't you? She wrote and told me all about your meeting at Hampstead Heath and she seemed happy with the Mask Players.'

'Yes, but I don't think she really looks on Tony and me as her family,' Gloria said. 'Sometimes I think she's keeping away so as not to intrude. Yet I don't want her to feel duty-bound to come here.' She sighed. 'Maybe we've drifted too far apart. Sometimes I wonder if it's too late to mend things properly between us. Ma still doesn't mention her name much, but I know that secretly she'd give anything to see her again.'

'Maybe Daddy feels a bit like that about Marcus,' Imogen said thoughtfully. 'Except for him I suppose it *is* too late. They're total strangers. Two grown men with completely separate lives.'

Shirley took her leave of the Mask Players the first week in October. The company gave a party for her. It was an emotional parting. Gerald Maddox made a little speech and presented her with a cream leather vanity case the company had bought her as a parting gift. The only thing that spoiled it for her was that Marcus wasn't there. He had sent a telegram at the last minute to say he couldn't make it, but would meet her at the station the following day.

On the Sunday she travelled to London. They were to begin rehearsals in a week's time. In the meantime she planned to show Marcus her London – all the places the tourists never saw. She was looking forward to it so much. After their break there were to be two weeks of intensive rehearsal before the tour opened in Manchester, but she had been studying her part and already knew her lines almost perfectly.

Marcus was waiting to meet her train. Since their first meeting he had spent every weekend except this last one in Birmingham and they had both looked forward to the time when they would be working together. Marcus had the use of a flat in Smith Square that belonged to an old friend of his mother and it had been arranged that Shirley was to stay there with him until the tour began.

As she got down from the train at Euston Station and walked down the platform, her heart lifted. She saw him at once, standing there at the barrier, tall and handsome in the casual clothes he loved to wear. Now their life and their shared career could really begin. He saw her and lifted his arm in greeting. She waved back and hurried towards him.

In the taxi she chattered eagerly, telling him about the party the previous night and showing him her present, which she carried with her. She was too excited to notice his air of aloof preoccupation.

The flat was comfortable and spacious. Shirley walked from room to room while the taxi driver helped Marc to carry up her luggage. When they were finally alone she held out her arms to him.

'Oh, darling. I can't believe I'm here at last. The last few days have seemed like an eternity. I was so sad you couldn't come to the party.' She stood on tiptoe to kiss him but instead of his arms encircling her, they hung unresponsively at his side. She looked into his eyes, sensing for the first time that there was something wrong. Standing back to look at him, she said: 'What is it? You *are* pleased to see me, aren't you?'

He smiled, but it wasn't the joyous, spontaneous smile she loved. 'Of course I'm pleased to see you. Now, what'll you have to eat? I've got –'

She caught at his arm, stopping him in mid-sentence. 'Marc, what's wrong? Don't tell me it's nothing. Something's upset you, I can see that.'

His eyes clouded and he drew away from her to walk to the window. 'I wasn't going to say anything. I'd made up my mind not to let it make any difference.'

'*What*, Marc?' She went to him, her heart thudding with fear and uncertainty. 'If something's happened I want to know about it – please.'

He turned to look at her, one hand brushing back his hair in the familiar mannerism. 'I met Paul Winspear,' he said quietly. 'Peter took us both to lunch at the Garrick Club and Winspear and I stayed on to talk about the play after Peter went back to the office. I disliked the guy on sight, but I wasn't prepared for what he'd say. He didn't know that you and I had become close. He . . . said things about you; things that made me want to smash his face in. If he hadn't been who he is I believe I would have.'

Her heart sank. 'Oh, Marc.' Taking his hand she led him to the settee and drew him down beside her. 'I don't know what he told you, but I'll tell you the truth and I hope you'll believe me. Paul and I had an affair. I thought I was in love with him. I was pretty naive, I suppose. I knew that he and Leonie Swann had been together for some time and I should have realised that he was just amusing himself while she was away on location. When she came back to London he dropped me like a hot potato. What did he tell you?'

He didn't look at her. 'He told me what a good pupil you were – in bed. That he was your first lover. He described how you couldn't get enough of him.' He turned away from her. 'It made me feel sick, hearing you spoken of like that.'

'Oh, Marc. I should have told you before. How could he?'

'He went on to tell me how you jilted some other guy – walked out on the eve of your wedding. He seemed to think you did it because you couldn't forget him. Is that true too?'

'*No*. At least . . .' She swallowed painfully. How dare Paul talk about her like that – twisting the truth in such a vicious, devious way? But having her own past held up to her like this, especially by Marc, hurt more than Paul's lies and betrayal. It made her sound so hardboiled and self-centred. She touched his arm. 'Yes. It is partly true, but it wasn't the way Paul tells it. I'd known Dave for a long time. He was – *is* a good man. He asked me to marry him at a time when I was vulnerable, when I felt a failure and needed someone badly. Deep down I always knew that it wasn't right. Then the offer from the Mask Players came, right out of the blue, and I had to make the decision.'

'So you walked out on the guy?'

'Yes, I walked out. I got the telegram offering me the job the night before the wedding and I knew that I just couldn't turn it down. It was everything I'd longed for. It was like standing at a crossroads, Marc. And seeing the right way all brightly lit and signed for me.' She looked at his face and was suddenly afraid. 'Dave and I are still good friends. He understands and agrees that what I did was right. We'd have made each other unhappy. He's found someone now who suits him down to the ground. And I've found *you*, Marc. So I did make the right decision, didn't I?' She looked at him beseechingly, but the eyes that looked back at her were dark with doubt.

'If you ever did that to me . . .'

'But I *won't*.'

'I've never fallen for anyone the way I fell for you, Shirley. I've seen so much of this kind of thing all my life. Mom was always dating some new guy and bringing them home. As a kid I was always finding some strange guy in her room and it still hasn't stopped. As soon as I was old enough I moved out. Recently she's been dating younger and younger guys – some of them are even younger than me. How do you think it made me feel, hearing folks make crude jokes about her – hearing my own mom referred to as an ageing nymphomaniac?'

481

She went to him. 'I didn't know. I'm sorry, darling. But I'm not like that. I never could be. Surely you don't believe . . .?'

He turned away. 'How can I be sure of that now?'

'How can any of us be sure of *anything*?' she asked desperately. 'I know I love you, Marc. I believed you loved me too. But if you can doubt me like this, if you can't trust me, then perhaps we should . . . we should stop seeing each other.'

He paced the floor angrily, avoiding her eyes. 'How can we not see each other when we're supposed to be working together?'

'I could find myself somewhere else to live,' she said quietly. 'We don't have to share this flat.' When he didn't reply, she added: 'Are you saying you'd rather I gave up my part in the play?'

'No. There's no need for that.' He shook himself angrily and turned to face her. 'I've already decided to fly back to the States on the first flight available. I'll be letting Peter know first thing in the morning.'

She stared at him, her heart freezing. 'You're going home? But why?'

'I have to. I'm so mixed up over all this, I can't think straight any more. They want guys my age for the army – this war in Korea. Maybe I'd better enlist. At least that way I'd be doing something worth while.'

'Marc – no!' She went to him and grasped his arm, her distress turning to frightened anger. 'Marc, listen. What Paul told you – it happened before I met you. Didn't *you* ever make a mistake? Have you gone through life being perfect? For all I know there are things in *your* life that *I* wouldn't like.'

He stared coldly down at her. 'Well, you can think yourself lucky that you'll never have to go through the trauma of hearing about them as I did.' He turned on his heel and walked out of the room.

Shirley sank onto the settee, her heart numb with disbelief. It was like the worst kind of nightmare. How could Paul have done this to her? How could Marc believe him and not her? It was so unfair. Reaching for the telephone she put through a call to Houlton. Gloria answered:

'Houlton 234.'

'Gloria. It's me – Shirley.'

'Shirley! How lovely to hear you. We heard from Peter that you're going to tour with *Give Me Yesterday*. Are you going to come and see us first?'

'I'd like that,' Shirley said. 'But there are a couple of things I have to do in London first. I'm ringing to ask you a favour. The thing is, I had arranged to stay with . . . with a friend, but it's fallen through. Can I stay at Tony's flat in Earls Court, or is he using it? It'll only be for a couple of days, till I can fix something else.'

'Of course you can. Tony's here with me. He says stay as long as you like. He'll telephone the caretaker and tell him to let you in.'

'Thanks. I'll ring you again tomorrow and let you know when I'm coming up to Houlton. I'm longing to see you all.'

'Do try to come this week, Shirl. Imogen and Charles are here at the moment.'

'I will. I promise.' She said goodbye, then rang for a taxi, collecting her luggage together and waiting with it on the landing. When the taxi came, Marc still had not reappeared.

At Tony's flat she busied herself finding sheets in the airing cupboard and making up the spare bed, then she made herself a strong cup of coffee and sat down to think. Inside her heart was still cold with shock. How could Paul name her for a part in his play one minute and deliberately try to ruin her life the next? In the spare room she lay down on the newly made bed fully clothed and let her frozen heart thaw into tears of despair. How could life be so cruel? Must this hammer blow fall just when everything looked so bright and promising?

She fell into an exhausted sleep after a while. When she awoke the sky outside was dark, but her mind was crystal clear. She knew exactly what she had to do. Sitting up, she reached for the telephone. Paul should not be allowed to get away with this. Maybe losing Marc was her fault. She should have told him about Paul and Dave in the first place. But she had to make Paul see what he had done. She had nothing to lose. She had already decided to give up her part in the play and she'd lost Marc anyway. Nothing could hurt her as badly as that.

The phone rang several times before he answered. 'Hello, Paul Winspear.'

'Paul, it's Shirley Rayner.'

'Shirley, darling. How nice to hear from you. All ready to begin rehearsals?'

She ground her teeth at his mockingly jocular tone. 'Paul, I have to see you.'

'What a delightful prospect! Perhaps we could have dinner one evening next –'

'*Now*, Paul. I'm at Tony's flat. I want you to come round here now. It's important.'

There was a pause, then he said: 'It all sounds rather ominous. As a matter of fact, you only just caught me. I was just going out.'

'I must see you. As soon as possible.'

'May one ask what it's about?'

'I said *now*, Paul.' She slammed down the receiver and sat thinking. Her heart was pounding and her hands and feet were like ice. She must calm herself before he arrived or she wouldn't be able to say what she planned to say effectively. Getting up, she washed her face and applied a careful make-up, then she went into the living room and poured herself a large whisky from Tony's cabinet. By the time the doorbell rang she felt more in control of herself.

When she opened the door he looked at her imperiously. 'I had to cancel an appointment to come round here, Shirley. I hope it really is important.'

'It is,' she said succinctly, turning and walking into the living room. He followed and looked pointedly at the drinks cabinet. She ignored his tacit request and went straight to the point. 'I hear you've been telling some rather unpleasant stories about me.'

'Really? Who can have told you that?'

'I think you know perfectly well who it was, Paul. Marcus Fane and I met some weeks ago. We fell in love and everything was fine – until you started pouring poison into his ears.'

He affected surprise. 'Me?'

'Yes, you. What you told him upset him so much that he's decided to fly back to the States tomorrow. He's even talking of enlisting in the US Army.'

'How very melodramatic,' he sneered. 'It sounds suspiciously like emotional blackmail to me.'

'I think you should know that I'm not prepared to take part in *Give Me Yesterday* without him.'

He stared at her, clearly taken aback. 'You can't back out. You're under contract.'

'I don't care.' She walked towards him. 'If the management wants to sue me, let them. I'll tell them how you slandered my character to another member of the company, making it impossible for me to work.' Her words had clearly shocked him at last and she went on: 'Why did you do it, Paul? You put my name forward for the part. You want your play to be a success, so why sabotage it? You hurt me once for no reason. Wasn't that enough?'

'All this fuss about a couple of innocent man-to-man remarks. How was I to know that you and he had a thing going?' He was blustering now. 'All I said was –'

'I *know* what you said,' she interrupted. 'The damage is done. I'll be going to Houlton tomorrow, taking a long rest with my family. I'll ring Peter and I'll write a letter of explanation to the tour manager.' On trembling legs she walked to the door and opened it. 'Now I'd like you to leave, please.'

Paul hesitated, then he walked purposefully to the door and closed it firmly. 'Listen, Shirley, I'm sorry for what I said. I certainly didn't mean for all this to happen. What I said to young Fane was said jokingly.'

'Well, I'm afraid the joke has misfired, Paul. Marc didn't see the funny side, and neither do I.'

He sighed. 'All right. It was vindictive of me. I admit it.'

'But why, Paul – *why*?'

He turned away and lit a cigarette, drawing deeply on it before he went on: 'Oh, I don't know. There he was, all eager, virile youth, raring to go and lusting after you. Every time your name was mentioned his eyes lit up like a bloody pin table. I could almost hear the bells ringing inside his head.'

'I see. So you had to smash his happiness, like a spoilt child.'

He stubbed out the barely smoked cigarette. 'Yes – *yes*, all right. It was sheer spite. Now are you satisfied?'

'Satisfied? When you've just ruined my life *and* my career? I'll never forgive you, Paul – never.'

He looked again at the drinks cabinet. 'Oh, for God's sake give me a whisky and listen to me for a minute, will you?'

'Why should I?'

'Look, I'm not trying to make excuses for what I did, I'm just saying that it isn't entirely my fault.' He looked at her. 'Well, are you going to do me the courtesy of hearing me out?'

Silently she splashed some whisky into a glass, added soda and handed it to him, then she sat down and looked at him. 'All right, I'm waiting.'

He took a deep gulp and winced as the fiery liquid scalded his throat. 'You know that I was badly wounded in the war,' he began. 'It was a head injury. I lay in hospital for weeks, unconscious. I think they thought that even if I pulled through I'd end up like a vegetable. Eventually I came round, but for months I didn't know who I was – didn't remember a thing. Well, to cut a long story short, I was lucky. In spite of the fact that I still had bits of shrapnel floating about inside my head, too deeply embedded for them to risk removal, I made a full recovery. But the man I had been was gone for ever. When I came home my wife said my personality had completely changed. My temper was unpredictable. It would flare up without warning. A couple of times I actually struck her, which was why she eventually left me.' He looked at her ruefully. 'No doubt you remember my flashes of violence. I do inexplicable things too at times; irrational, cruel things such as speaking to young Fane like that about you.' He paused to light another cigarette, studying her face and trying to assess her reaction over the flame of his lighter. 'Do you think I'm proud of myself, Shirley? The one good thing in all of it is that I can still write. Without that I think I'd just put an end to it all. One of these days one of those pieces of junk will pierce something vital in my brain and that'll be my final curtain anyway.' He drew smoke deep into his lungs and let it out slowly. 'I don't know if you've heard, but Leonie and I split up before she went to Australia. Again, it was my fault. I more or less kicked her out in one of my black moods. The trouble is that now she's gone I miss her like hell. Now that I've lost her too, I realise that we were right for each other. I really believe that we brought out the best in each other, for whatever that's worth.' He looked at her. 'It was feeling bitter about my own damned stupidity that made me want to spoil young Fane's smug satisfaction, I suppose, though I know that can't be of much help to you now.' He stubbed out the cigarette he'd just lit. 'I've made up my mind, Shirley. Once I've got my new play off the stocks I'm flying out to Australia and I'm going to try to get her to take me back. If she wants to be married, then that's what we'll do. I know now that I can't live without her.'

Shirley sank slowly into a chair. 'I hope you'll break it to Peter first that it's you who messed up the tour of *Yesterday*,' she said bleakly. 'Not to mention what you've done to two people's lives.' She choked on the last word. She hadn't known about Paul's war injury and subsequent illness. It explained a lot, of course, and now she couldn't even blame him for what had happened. She was left as always to take all the blame herself. It was a bleak prospect.

'I'm sorry, Shirley,' he said quietly. 'I'm really sorry. If there's anything I can do . . .'

'There isn't.' She turned away so that he wouldn't see the tears only barely held at bay. 'Just go. Just leave me.

487

Maybe it's for the best. After all, if Marc was willing to believe . . .' She heard the door bang shut as Paul made his escape.

On his way down in the lift he drew a long breath and let it out slowly. He'd got out of that very nicely. Thank God for his creative powers and his ability to think on his feet. She'd change her mind about giving up her part in the play once she'd calmed down. Shirley's career was too important to her for her to pass up a good chance when she saw one. After all, she'd thrown one bloke over for it. He smiled to himself. Funny – women were always a soft touch when it came to war wounds, though he'd pushed his luck a bit far this time. Amnesia *and* embedded shrapnel was stretching it a bit. Still, she'd swallowed it all right. A good thing no one had access to his discharge papers. Shooting yourself in the foot while cleaning your rifle wasn't nearly as romantic as amnesia. The bit about wanting Leonie back hadn't been invention, though. He only wished to God it was. Even if she did take him back they'd probably make each other's lives hell, but he hadn't any option. Life without her wasn't life at all any more. He only hoped she felt the same.

Shirley was up early next morning. She hadn't slept and she wanted to get the business of cancelling her contract over as soon as she could, then go to Houlton. Her first visit was to Peter Jason's office. When she told him she was pulling out of the tour, he stared at her incredulously.

'What's wrong?' he asked. 'What's happened to bring about this sudden decision?'

'Marcus and I – things have been said about me. Marcus believed them and we . . .'

'Are you telling me that the two of you have had a row – a lovers' tiff?' Peter sighed and shook his head.

'It's more than that.'

'It damn well better be.' Peter's normally mild face was dark with annoyance. 'If you ask me to get you out of this contract at this stage in the proceedings you'll have to find yourself another agent. And you might not find that easy.

488

I've got a dozen young actresses on my books who'd give their eye teeth for a chance like this. You got this part on the author's recommendation, without even an audition. Let them down at the last minute and the word will spread like wildfire.' He leaned towards her. 'Unreliability, unprofessionalism – they're the worst labels any actor can acquire. You might never be offered a decent job again.'

To his dismay Shirley burst into tears. Fumbling in his pocket for a clean handkerchief, he passed it across the desk to her.

'Oh, come now, there's no need to upset yourself like that,' he said gruffly. Reaching across the desk, he patted her shoulder. 'Come on, dry those tears. I'll ring for some coffee and you can tell me what this is really all about.'

Shirley swallowed hard, deeply embarrassed by her own lack of control. 'You mean you . . . you haven't heard?'

'Heard – from who?'

'From Marcus. He's flying back to America.'

Peter's eyebrows shot up. 'Him too? This is the first I've heard of it. What the hell is going on? Is everyone going mad? When?'

'Today. As soon as he can get a flight, he says.'

She poured out the whole story to him, including the story Paul had told her the previous evening about his war injury. Peter did his best to hide his impatience with Winspear's capriciousness and the folly of young love and forced himself to be as understanding as he could.

When Shirley had finished her story and been calmed by a cup of coffee, he said soothingly: 'Look, I'll tell you what – why don't you go off and spend a couple of days with your mother and Tony? It'll do you the world of good and I know they'll be pleased to see you. I'll be in touch tomorrow or the next day. If Marcus is going home, I don't see why you should turn down your part. This could be an important step in your career, Shirley. Don't throw it away for a mere whim.' He smiled indulgently. 'At this moment you think your heart is broken, I know. But I promise you it isn't. And even if it was, I can assure you that work is the very best therapy.'

Deep inside she knew he was right about work, though she had to make herself ignore the way he made light of her pain. She promised him she would take his advice and rethink her decision, then she dried her eyes and left. It seemed to her once more that she was destined to have either career or love, never both.

She telephoned the time of her train before she left the flat and when she arrived at Castle Station in Northampton Tony was waiting on the platform. He hugged her and took her case.

'I can't tell you how excited everyone is at the prospect of seeing you,' he told her as they drove up Marefair towards the town centre. 'Gloria is dying to show you the new house and all she's done to it and Michael didn't want to go to school this morning in case he missed something. Gloria did tell you that Imogen and Charles are home with us at the moment, didn't she?'

'Yes, she told me. It'll be lovely to see Imo. It seems ages.'

'She's expecting a baby in May.' He turned to smile at her. 'I'm going to be a grandfather. A couple of years ago that would have panicked me. Now I can hardly wait.'

Shirley smiled tremulously. 'Imo's always wanted children. I'm so . . . so happy for . . .' She swallowed, suddenly overcome with emotion.

Tony glanced at her. 'Everything is all right, isn't it?'

'Yes, yes, of course.'

'I was delighted to hear about the tour.'

'Yes. Thanks.' She watched as the familiar streets flew past, the landmarks so dearly familiar to her and so little changed: All Saints' Church, Abington Square, the Racecourse and Kingsley Park. Although she was a Londoner, born and bred, this town was where all her happiest memories were. This was where she had grown up. It felt more like home than London ever had. As the shops and houses gave way to the Northamptonshire countryside, leafless now in its austere winter beauty, her thoughts went back to the warm September day when she had seen Houlton for the first time. How strange and alien it had all seemed then, so green and quiet! How scared she'd been, lying in bed, listening to the strange country sounds; how homesick for her family and the bustle and grime of the city. Her heart was full of the same nostalgic longing now – the feeling of being uprooted and torn apart. But this time it was a deeper emotion, one that would not be so easily soothed and dispelled.

Tony broke into her thoughts: 'Your grandmother is coming to lunch.' He smiled wryly. 'Just thought I'd better warn you.'

Shirley looked at him, her reminiscences momentarily forgotten. 'Ma? Oh, dear. I'd hoped to go and see her tomorrow – on my own.'

Tony laughed. 'Can you imagine her being left out of the reunion? The moment she knew you were coming she invited herself. I think she's secretly dying to see you again.'

'If I know Ma she'll be planning to give me a piece of her mind. I'll be lucky to get away without a thorough telling-off.'

'You might be pleasantly surprised,' Tony said. 'Your grandmother has mellowed since she's moved to Boothley. Believe it or not, she's become a confirmed countrywoman. She's made the garden at Rook Cottage look a perfect picture and she's quite revolutionised the WI ladies.' He laughed. 'She's even joined the church choir.'

Shirley stared at him incredulously. 'Ma? With her voice?' She laughed. 'Pa always used to say it was made for selling coal.'

'I'll say this for her, no one dozes off in the back pews while *she's* singing.'

As they drove through the village, Tony pointed out the sign above the door of the post office. 'See that?' He slowed the car so that she could read it.

Shirley read aloud: 'Postmistress Matilda Jane Marks. *Tilly?* She stayed on, then?'

'She certainly did. One of the youngest postmistresses in the country, so I'm told. The Phippses are so proud of her.' He looked at her. 'Remember the film we made? Your character was modelled on Tilly.'

'I remember.' She smiled. 'The war must have been the luckiest thing that ever happened to poor Tilly. It's a funny world, isn't it?'

He nodded. 'It certainly is.'

At Hindley Lodge Shirley was welcomed warmly. Gloria and Imogen came out into the drive to hug her, while Charles stood somewhat shyly in the background. They went into the house together and Shirley found herself standing in the square, oak-panelled hall with its polished floor and glowing Turkish rugs.

'The house has a lovely warm, welcoming feel,' she said. Then, looking round, she whispered: 'Where's Ma?'

Gloria laughed. 'She's waiting for you in the drawing room. Sitting in state like a duchess, ready to give you an audience.'

'A good wigging, you mean.' Shirley took a deep breath and squared her shoulders. 'Oh, well, I'd better go in and get it over with.'

Gloria led the way to a door on the right of the hall. 'Don't let her manner put you off. She's longing to see you, really,' she said. 'You know Ma. She always has to have her say.'

The drawing room was square and perfectly proportioned, decorated in pastel colours. Softly draped, rose-coloured velvet curtains hung at the windows and the floor was covered by an Indian carpet in soft greens and pinks. In the hearth of the white marble fireplace a basket of flowers filled the room with perfume. Ma sat straight-backed in a chair by the long window that looked out over the garden. She turned as Shirley came in and looked her up and down sternly.

'So – you've condescended to come 'ome at last, 'ave you?' she said. 'An' about time too, you bad girl you.'

Shirley crossed the room to her, surprised to see that Ma looked much smaller than she remembered her. She looked well, but milder and less forbidding in spite of her tone of voice and the disapproving set of her mouth.

'Hello, Ma,' she said. 'I've missed you. I hope you've forgiven me.'

Ma folded her arms across her bosom. 'Not sure as I 'ave, my gel. What about that poor feller you jilted them, eh?'

'Dave's forgiven me,' Shirley said. 'He's marrying a girl who really suits him. I think I probably did him a favour, Ma.'

'That's as may be.' Ma sniffed. 'Be all the same if you 'adn't, though. Fat lot *you* cared, goin' orf like that without so much as a by-yer-leave. Made me ashamed, you did. That a granddaughter of mine should –'

'I *did* care, Ma.' Shirley drew up a stool and sat close to Ma's feet. 'It wasn't an easy decision. And if it makes you feel any better, someone . . . someone very special has just done the very same thing to me.'

Ma looked at her for a long moment, her eyes softening, then she bent forward to take Shirley's face between her hands. 'Someone's 'urt you? Yes, I can see it in your eyes. So you know now. Not that I'd ever wish that for you, love.'

Shirley swallowed. The last thing she wanted was sympathy. She could just about cope with Ma's abrasiveness, but kindness would be the undoing of her. 'I'm all right,' she said, swallowing hard. 'At least I will be now that you and I have made it up.'

Ma bent and kissed her. ''Course we 'ave. You know your old Ma's bark is worse than 'er bite. Life's too bleedin' short to bear grudges. I've missed you somethin' rotten, gel. Many's the time I've 'oped you'd send me a letter, but you never did, you naughty gel.'

'I thought you wouldn't want to hear from me,' Shirley said. 'I did send you my love, though; in the letters I wrote to Glor at Rook Cottage.'

'Oh – yes.' Ma coloured guiltily. 'I did wrong to 'ide them letters. But I did it because I didn't want you getting round Glor. She's as soft as grease – anybody's for a few soft words. That's 'ow she got 'erself into so much trouble. Still, I shouldn't'a done it. I was just too stubborn to admit it at the time.' She looked at Shirley. 'We both done wrong, you 'n' me, but all that's over now, eh?'

Shirley knew this was the closest Ma would ever get to an apology. She smiled and squeezed her hand. 'Of course it is.'

Ma peered at the clock. ''Ere, come on, it's dinnertime and I dunno about you but I'm starvin'.' She got to her feet and took Shirley's arm. 'Y'know, I just *can't* remember to call it lunch. There's a lot of things I have to remember now Glor's gorn up in the world. But I tell them they'll 'ave to take me as they find me or not at all.'

Shirley laughed. 'No one in their right mind would ever want you to change, Ma.'

Lunch was a festive occasion with Jim and Molly Jarvis especially invited as a surprise for Shirley. Afterwards Gloria and Imogen showed her their costume project. A large room at the top of the house had been converted to a sewing room. On a rail under a muslin shroud several finished costumes already hung. Shirley exclaimed at the bright jewel colours and the luscious textures of the satins and velvets, specially made for theatrical work. She admired Gloria's skill in creating dresses that looked as though they had stepped straight out of a bygone age. Her mother seemed so happy and fulfilled here with her husband and child, she reflected, and now this new occupation which Imogen was to share during the later stages of her pregnancy. Later, when she and Imogen were alone together in her room, she implied wistfully that she felt she no longer had a place in the family.

'You're not the only one,' Imogen surprised her by saying. 'I always have felt odd-man-out, I've been away so long now that Mummy has gone to Australia and Daddy has remarried I feel I don't really belong anywhere.' She smiled quickly at Shirley. 'Not that I'm not happy for Daddy. Gloria is the best thing that ever happened to him. He's so relaxed and happy and he's come to terms with his disfigurement more contentedly than I'd ever have dared to hope.'

'But you have Charles now. And soon you'll have your baby too. As for me . . .' Shirley's eyes filled with tears.

Imogen touched her arm. 'Shirl, darling, something's wrong, isn't it? I've known it ever since you arrived. Can't you tell me about it?'

'Oh, why is it that we can't love the right people?' Shirley burst out. 'If only I'd been able to love Dave as he loved me, none of this would have happened.'

'Life is rarely that simple,' Imogen said gently. 'What is it?' Her brow creased into a frown. 'It's not Paul Winspear again, is it?'

'Not in the way you mean.' Shirley hesitated. Marcus had said he didn't want his family to know he was here until he had made a success of his career. But Imogen had been the one who advised him to come. And anyway, by now he was probably on a plane, somewhere over the Atlantic. 'I met Marcus,' she said. 'Your half-brother. Peter introduced us. He was to have taken the part of Jason Hamilton, the young artist in Paul's play.'

Imogen's face broke into a smile. 'So he *did* come over? But that's wonderful news. I liked him a lot. You and he would make a perfect couple. It would be –' She broke off as she saw the distress on Shirley's face. 'What went wrong?'

'Oh, *everything*. We've been seeing each other for weeks. He'd been coming up to Birmingham, spending every weekend with me. It was all going to be so marvellous, being together on tour, working. Then Peter introduced him to Paul Winspear.'

'And . . .?' Imogen took both of Shirley's hands. 'Tell me, darling. Come on, get it off your chest.'

'Paul told him that he and I had had an affair – with salacious details, by the sound of it. He also told him how I walked out on Dave the night before the wedding. He said I did it for love of him.'

'Oh, no.' Imogen frowned. 'The *rat*. And Marc actually listened – and let it ruin things between you?'

'It hit him hard,' Shirley told her. 'It seems that his mother was quite promiscuous. She had a lot of men in her life. Marc had a traumatic childhood. Now he thinks I'm the same kind of woman.'

'Didn't you make him listen to the truth?'

'It wasn't easy. Paul had twisted things so. And the trouble was, I couldn't actually deny any of it. My explanations weren't enough, Imo. He's totally disillusioned with me. He's given up his part in the play and gone back to America.'

Imogen watched with helpless dismay as the tears slipped down Shirley's cheeks. 'Oh, darling. I'm so sorry. If only there were something I could do.'

'There's nothing anyone can do,' Shirley said. 'Except that I want you to promise me you won't tell Tony or Gloria. I promised Marc that I wouldn't tell them he was over here and I don't want him to think I let him down in that too.'

When Michael came home there was a special tea, then they all played together till his bedtime. He insisted that Shirley went to read him a story and proudly showed her the teddy she had given him at Hampstead Heath.

'He guards my bed for me when I'm at school,' he told her, hugging the bear. They had a long talk all about school and his friends after she'd finished reading to him. 'I like having a sister like you,' he said sleepily. 'You won't go away again, will you?'

She smiled. 'I have to, darling. I can only stay for a couple of days. I'm going away on tour soon, you see. But we'll be bringing the play to Northampton in a few weeks' time, so I'll see you then.'

'Oh. That's good.' He was having trouble keeping his eyes open but he sat up suddenly, remembering something. 'Shirley, do you know what Imogen told me?'

'No, darling, what?'

'She says that when her baby is born I'll be its *uncle*. Won't that be good? I'll be the only boy in my class who's an uncle.'

Shirley laughed. What a complex family they'd become, the Darrents and the Rayners. Their lives seemed to become more and more entwined. Briefly she wondered how Michael would get along with his American stepbrother, Marcus. It seemed doubtful that he'd ever get the chance to find out now. And it was probably all her fault.

At last Michael couldn't keep his eyes open any longer and she was able to tuck him in snugly and creep quietly away. Downstairs in the drawing room the rest of the family were watching television. Now that there was a station close enough to Houlton, Tony had bought a set.

'This is the medium to aim for,' he told Shirley as she sat down beside him. 'It won't be long before this takes the place of the cinema.'

Gloria shook her head. 'Surely not? People will always enjoy going to the pictures,' she said, remembering her happy days as an usherette at the Adelphi. 'They'll always want big stars to look up to and copy. I'd hate to think the cinema would ever die.'

Tony nodded. 'I agree with you, of course, but TV is closing the repertory theatres. I'm afraid it's only a matter of time before cinemas go the same way. It's called progress and I'm afraid the period of adjustment is always painful.'

At nine o'clock Ma began to yawn and Tony got ready to drive her home. Shirley went along too and was shown round the new-look Rook Cottage.

'I've got runnin' water *and* a bathroom,' Ma told her proudly. 'The well's still in the back garden, but I don't use it any more.' She snapped a switch and the room was flooded with light. 'There y'are,' she said triumphantly. 'I never thought things in the country could be more modern than London, but everythin' 'ere is better than what I 'ad there – includin' nice clean air to breathe. Can't think why I didn't want to come before.' She smiled wistfully. 'Pa would've loved it 'ere. I often think I was selfish not to move when 'e was alive. 'E always fancied a little place in the country where 'e could grow 'is own vegetables when we retired.'

'But you're not lonely. You've made friends?' Shirley asked.

Ma shrugged. 'Oh, yes. I 'ave now. Some of 'em was a bit stand-offish at first, but I soon let 'em know what's what. Now they knows they can take me or leave me.'

'So they take you?'

'Most of 'em. Them as don't ain't worth botherin' with anyway.' Ma kissed her. 'Take care of yourself, duck. And don't forget to write an' tell me 'ow you are.' She bent forward to whisper in Shirley's ear. 'As for this geezer oo's broke your 'eart – just you forget 'im. Get on with what you've worked 'ard for. It's taken a lot of guts to get where you are, so don't you let nuthin' 'appen to stop you now.'

Shirley hugged her. 'I won't, Ma. Good night and take care of yourself.'

Her short stay came to an end all too soon and it was time for her to leave. Tony was due to go up for a one-day recording session at the BBC so they travelled down to London together. Sitting opposite him in the train, she suddenly realised to her surprise that she had forgotten all about his scarred face. It was because he was so happy, she decided. Since his accident and his marriage to Gloria he was so much more relaxed. He wasn't obsessed with his looks any more. He smiled a lot – that same dazzling, bright-eyed smile that Marc had. It tugged painfully at her heart every time she saw it. Feeling her eyes on him, he looked up from his newspaper.

'All right?'

'Yes, thanks.'

'Are you happy, Shirley?'

The question took her by surprise. 'Happy? Yes, of course.'

'I know this part is a big chance for you, but your mother is afraid you're nervous about it.'

She laughed. 'Nervous? Well, yes, of course I am, but not unhappy.'

'I probably shouldn't tell you, but she's worried that there's something wrong. Is there – in any other area of your life, I mean? I heard what your grandmother said about a broken heart.'

'There has been an . . . emotional upset,' she told him. 'But it's nothing that time won't heal. Ma's advice was the best I've had: to put all my energy into my work and forget what happened. That's what I intend to do.'

Tony smiled sympathetically. 'Well, you know we're here whenever you need us, don't you? You know we're your family and we love you?'

She nodded. 'I do – now.'

Rehearsals for *Give Me Yesterday* were to take place in a church hall in Islington. Shirley had spent the weekend at Tony's flat concentrating on her lines and as she travelled to the first rehearsal she was fairly confident that she was word-perfect. She had rung Peter as soon as she was back in London, to reassure him that all was now well and she had regained her composure. He had reminded her of the schedule and also that John Gerard, the director, was a stickler for punctuality. 'He's a prickly devil,' he said. 'He has a short fuse but a good sense of humour and he's a positive genius for getting the best out of actors. Try and get on his right side. If he likes you and your work you'll find him quite tolerant.'

She arrived at the hall with five minutes to spare and hung up her coat in the cloakroom. Most of the cast had already assembled and stood warming their hands on the radiators or talking to each other. They seemed quite a pleasant, friendly crowd. Shirley introduced herself to an attractive older actress with red hair, whose name, she discovered, was Lesley Fraser. She told Shirley that she was taking the part Leonie had created.

Suddenly the door at the end of the hall flew open to admit a draught of icy air and a stocky man with longish hair. He wore a cracked leather jacket and carried a tattered, bulging briefcase. Lesley muttered: 'That's John Gerard.' Shirley looked at him with slight apprehension. 'He's impatient and impossibly eccentric, but quite brilliant,' Lesley went on. 'I've worked with him before. He certainly knows his stuff.'

Shirley watched as the perceptive, needle-sharp eyes swept the room, taking in the material he was to work with. She could well imagine that he had an explosive temper.

Striding to the stage at the end of the room and dumping his briefcase on a chair, he clapped his hands as though they were a crowd of unruly children.

'All right, everyone. I'm your director, John Gerard, the bloke whose guts you're going to love to hate for the next few weeks,' he said. 'Now I'd just like to ascertain that I have a full cast. I'll tick you off from the cast list so as to put faces to names.' He began to read out the names of the characters, looking up as the actors answered with their own names. When Shirley replied he glanced up at her, his dark, penetrating eyes assessing her shrewdly.

'Ah, yes, Shirley Rayner,' he said enigmatically, ticking her off and leaving her to imagine what he might have heard about her. Had Paul been talking to him too?

She was last from bottom of the list, the last character being Jason Hamilton, the part Marcus was to have played. When he read out the name there was silence. The other members of the cast glanced inquiringly at each other. John Gerard read the name again, his voice a shade louder. He looked up, his dark eyes flashing impatiently.

'Oh, for Christ's sake. Look in the gents, someone. We haven't got all bloody morning to hang about.'

One of the men went off and Shirley, quaking in her shoes, took a step forward. Surely Peter should have let him know, but as it was partly down to her that they were one short she'd better try to offer some kind of explanation.

'Excuse me, Mr Gerard.'

He looked up with an irritated frown. 'The name's John,' he snapped. 'No formalities, for God's sake. This isn't an insurance office.'

'No – sorry.' Shirley cleared her throat. 'I . . . I was just going to say that . . .' She felt a cold draught on her back again and turned to see that someone had just opened the door. He pulled it shut behind him and turned. She stared at him, her heart leaping in her chest as the cry burst from her: *'Marc!'*

John Gerard looked up from his clipboard. 'Yes, you were saying? Marc who?' He broke off to stare in amazement as the girl and the newcomer flew into each other's arms and clasped each other in a passionate embrace.

'I couldn't go. I couldn't leave you,' Marcus whispered. 'I know he must have been lying – I knew it all along, really. I must have been crazy to risk losing you like that. I'm sorry, darling.'

Shirley shook her head and clung to him, her heart too full to speak. She was oblivious to the astonished faces all round her. *Marc was back*. He hadn't left her after all. It was a miracle.

'Oh, bloody *hell*, this is all I need.' Gerard flung his script in the air. 'I know I said no formalities but this is ridiculous. It's going to be one of *those* tours, is it?'

To his astonishment and Shirley's acute but happy embarrassment, the rest of the cast burst out laughing.

March 1950

Imogen ushered her father and Gloria along the corridor of the New Theatre and into the box she had booked for them. 'I got the prompt side for you, Daddy,' she said. 'I know you hate being able to see into the prompt corner.' She was almost eight months pregnant now and had been living at Houlton, helping Gloria with her costume collection, since Christmas. Planning this evening had given her so much pleasure and excitement, though she had let Gloria in on the secret.

'I can't think why you chose Monday night to book for us,' Tony complained. 'You know the first night in a new theatre is always tricky. I'd have preferred to wait till they settled down and got their bearings.'

'I had my reasons,' Imogen said enigmatically, with a wink at Gloria. 'Shirley will join us after the show, which is why I got a box. She can slip in through the pass door. It's just along the corridor from here.'

They settled themselves on the blue upholstered chairs and Tony looked down into the rapidly filling auditorium. It was a large theatre with white and silver decor and seats in royal-blue plush, a theatre normally used for variety or musical shows. Tony shook his head.

'I'm glad to see they're getting a good house for their first night,' he remarked. 'Though I must say that this theatre hasn't really the intimate atmosphere needed for a straight play.' He glanced round. 'Did anyone think to buy a programme?'

Imogen laughed. 'What did your last servant die of?' She handed him the programme and waited, looking at Gloria in anticipation, but to her disappointment he put it to one side with only the briefest of glances.

The orchestra pit filled with musicians who began to play a medley of popular light music. Then the lights dimmed, the music faded and there was a soft swish as the blue and silver curtain rose on Act I. Tony leaned forward with interest, while Gloria felt nervously for Imogen's hand in the darkness.

Shirley was good. Gloria hadn't seen her act professionally till now and she was astonished at how far she had come. Her movements were graceful and easy, her voice strong and musical and she played the part with a wisdom and emotional power far beyond her years. As Gloria watched her daughter there was a lump in her throat. Shirley had made it. She'd done it by herself, in spite of all the obstacles and disappointments she had encountered along the way. She had exceeded all the dreams and hopes she'd had for her. She was a daughter to be proud of.

Act I was almost halfway through when Marcus made his first entrance. Tony, who had been leaning forward, his arms resting on the box's ledge, suddenly sat up straight. For a few minutes he watched, then Gloria saw his hand reach out for the programme. She nudged Imogen, who bit her lip excitedly, holding her breath as she saw her father scan the cast list. Finding the name he was looking for, Tony dropped the programme and leaned forward again, peering intently at the handsome young man playing the part of Jason Hamilton.

Imogen quietly moved from her seat to sit next to her father. 'Now you see why I wanted you to come tonight, Daddy,' she whispered.

He turned to look at her and she saw that his eyes were very bright. 'You *knew*? Why didn't you tell me?' he whispered. 'No one told me he was an actor. I didn't even know he was in this country. Why hasn't he been in touch?'

'He wanted to wait till he'd had a chance to prove himself,' Imogen said. 'He didn't want help or special influence. He wanted to make it by himself.'

'Well, he's done that all right,' Tony said. 'He's good. Damned good.'

The curtain came down on the first act to loud applause and Tony sat back in his seat, looking round incredulously at his wife and daughter. 'You *both* knew about this,' he said as he caught sight of Gloria's face. 'And neither of you breathed a word. Peter must have known, too. Did Shirley know when she came home last November?'

Imogen took his hand. 'That's another surprise, Daddy. Marc and Shirley are engaged. Peter Jason introduced them when the tour was first cast and they fell in love almost at once.'

'Shirley and Marcus? Well, I'll be . . .' Tony beamed with pleasure as the house lights began to dim again and the curtain rose on Act II.

All three watched, enthralled, as the rest of the play unfolded; then it was over and the cast lined up to take the curtain calls. Shirley, aware of the special party in the box, looked up with a smile as they responded to the enthusiastic reception. The curtain fell for the last time and the audience began to file out.

'We're to wait here,' Imogen said excitedly. A moment later the door at the back of the box opened and Shirley stepped in, still in her costume and make-up. She was followed by a bewildered-looking Marcus. Imogen got up to greet him.

'Marc, how nice to see you again. I enjoyed the play so much. I thought your first night here would be a great opportunity for a family reunion, so I arranged one. This is Gloria, Shirley's mother. And I don't think I need to introduce this gentleman.' She stood aside and Marcus and Tony came face to face. For a moment they looked at each other, both lost for words, then Tony said:

'Congratulations – to both of you. You were very good indeed.' He shook his hand. 'But I wish to God someone had told me what to expect this evening. It would have given me time to think what to *say*.' The tension was broken as they all laughed. Marcus stepped forward, holding out his hands to his father.

'Me too. Who ever heard of a speechless actor? All I can think of right now is, it's great to see you again – Dad.'

In the excited conversation that followed, Tony looked at the two vibrant young people. They brought with them into the small space of the box the very essence of all that was close to his heart: the scent of greasepaint, the throbbing pulse of excitement that had epitomised the theatre and the life he had loved ever since he could remember. Just for the briefest of moments he envied them, feeling a deep nostalgic yearning sweep through his veins for all that he had lost. But it was only for a split second. At that moment, as though she read his thoughts, Gloria turned to him and reached for his hand, giving it a reassuring squeeze and smiling the special smile that told him without words how much she loved him. He was lucky. He had survived an appalling accident and been reborn to a new and better life. He had his new career in radio and the promise of a partnership with Peter. He had the love of a loyal wife and a beautiful little son. And if all that wasn't enough, here was Marcus, handsome and talented, treading in his footsteps and looking for his father's approval. He had so much – so very much to be thankful for. He was luckier than he could ever have hoped.

Later that evening the five of them drove back to Houlton together. In the back seat of Tony's Bentley Shirley sat between Imogen and Marcus.

'I can't wait to show you the village where I grew up,' she told Marcus, squeezing his arm. 'I can't wait for you to meet Michael and Ma and Charles. Isn't it great that we actually share the same family? They're all such special, unique people.'

'*We* are, you mean,' Imogen said and laughed. 'We're wonderfully, hopelessly entwined.' She smiled as Marcus slipped an arm around Shirley and drew her close. 'And getting more so by the minute,' she concluded happily, turning to look out of the car window.

Above them a new moon pierced the spring sky and a handful of stars twinkled brightly.

Warner now offers an exciting range of quality titles by both established and new authors. All of the books in this series are available from:
Little, Brown and Company (UK),
P.O. Box 11,
Falmouth,
Cornwall TR10 9EN.

Alternatively you may fax your order to the above address. Fax No. 0326 376423.

Payments can be made as follows: Cheque, postal order (payable to Little, Brown and Company) or by credit cards, Visa/Access. Do not send cash or currency. UK customers: and B.F.P.O.: please send a cheque or postal order (no currency) and allow £1.00 for postage and packing for the first book, plus 50p for the second book, plus 30p for each additional book up to a maximum charge of £3.00 (7 books plus).

Overseas customers including Ireland, please allow £2.00 for postage and packing for the first book, plus £1.00 for the second book, plus 50p for each additional book.

NAME (Block Letters) ....

ADDRESS...

....

☐ I enclose my remittance for _____

☐ I wish to pay by Access/Visa Card

Number ☐☐☐☐☐☐☐☐☐☐☐☐☐☐☐☐

Card Expiry Date ☐☐☐☐